DANGEROUS DESIRES

DEE DAVIS

FOREVER

NEW YORK   BOSTON

This book is a work of fiction. Names, characters, places, and incidents are the product of the author's imagination or are used fictitiously. Any resemblance to actual events, locales, or persons, living or dead, is coincidental.

Copyright © 2010 by Dee Davis Oberwetter
Excerpt from *Desperate Deeds* copyright © 2010 by Dee Davis Oberwetter

Cover design by Diane Luger
Book design by Giorgetta Bell McRee

Forever
Hachette Book Group
237 Park Avenue
New York, NY 10017
Visit our website at www.HachetteBookGroup.com.

Forever is an imprint of Grand Central Publishing.
The Forever name and logo is a trademark of Hachette Book Group, Inc.

Printed in the United States of America

First Printing: July 2010

10 9 8 7 6 5 4 3 2 1

The rain lessened to form a fine mist.

Still shivering, she tried for forward motion, but her legs refused the order, buckling instead, sending her headfirst into brush.

"I've got you," Drake said. He carried her over to the fire, and set her down on a mat made from palm leaves. "We need to get you warm," he said, "and that means getting rid of those sweats for now. They're soaked."

She nodded, and with gentle fingers he peeled them off, then pulled her into his lap, her body cradled against his warmth. She lifted her head, opening her mouth to thank him, but the words stopped in her throat as she met the dark heat of his gaze. And then he was there, his mouth against hers. The kiss deepened and sensations exploded inside her.

Her heart skittered to a stop as a low menacing growl cut through the still night air. Just off to her left, two golden eyes gleamed as a big black cat crouched low, ready to attack...

Also by Dee Davis

Dark Deceptions
Desperate Deeds

For Lexie and Robert.
The lights of my life.

Scíentia Potéstas Est ... Knowledge Is Power.

PROLOGUE

San Mateo Prison, Serrania Del Baudo, Colombia

Madeline Reynard squinted in the bright light. After three days of total darkness, the dappled sunlight hurt her eyes. She flinched as the guard shoved her forward, losing her balance and careening into the exercise yard.

"I've got you," Andrés said, his voice raspy, his English heavily accented as he steadied her. "I've been worried."

"They put me in solitary," Madeline whispered. "I have no idea why."

"Sometimes there is no reason." Andrés shrugged. "The main thing is that you're out now. Are you all right?"

"I'm fine. It's getting easier." This was the third time she'd been relegated to the dank, windowless cell in the far recesses of the prison. "I just try to think of somewhere else and let my mind carry me away." She'd spent a good portion of her childhood locked in a closet only slightly smaller than the solitary cell. Her father had clearly believed the adage "out of sight, out of mind." But the experience was not without value. If Madeline could survive living like that, she could survive anything. Even San Mateo.

A place for political prisoners, the prison lacked creature comforts. In point of fact, it lacked most everything. Which meant that days loomed long, the only bright spot the minutes spent outside under the canopy of trees. The surrounding jungle reminded her of the cypresses back home, their gnarled arms curving downward into gray-green umbrellas of whispering leaves. The bayou had meant safety. And now the Colombian jungle offered the same.

"It's best if you find a way to separate yourself from the reality here," Andrés was saying. He nodded toward the people scattered about the yard. It was nearly empty, this hour relegated to women and the infirm, her friend falling into the latter category. It had been a long time since she'd had a friend. There'd always been too much to hide. Too much to risk. But now—*here*—her past didn't matter.

"Are you sure they didn't hurt you?" Andrés asked, his voice colored with worry.

"I told you I'm fine," she reiterated as they walked slowly across the yard, her muscles protesting the movement even as her mind rejoiced in her newfound freedom. "I'm just a little stiff, that's all."

She'd met Andrés on her second day in the yard. At first, his matted hair and filthy clothes had been off-putting. But after almost a week in this hellhole, she'd been desperate for human contact.

When he'd spoken to her in his halting English, it had felt like a gift, as her Spanish was limited to schoolgirl verbs and useless nouns. Which didn't matter when she was alone in her cell, or being leered at by the guards. It didn't take a vocabulary to interpret their catcalls. But real conversation, without English, was impossible. And it was conversation that kept the mind sharp. She'd come to need Andrés as much as she needed food and water.

Madeline closed her eyes, shutting out the small, barren exercise yard, its occupants wretched in their filth.

"You need to keep moving," her friend said, his hand warm against her back. "It's important to stay strong."

"I know you're right, but sometimes when I think about spending the rest of my life here, it doesn't seem worth it."

"You won't be here forever," he said, his tone soothing. "Someone will come for you."

Madeline laughed, the sound harsh. "I killed a man. There's nothing anyone can do to change that."

"But there were extenuating circumstances." He frowned. "That should count for something."

"Maybe in a fair world." She shrugged, shivering as memories flooded through her. Her sister's screams, her fear cutting through the haze of the drugs. The big man pinning her to the wall of the flophouse in Bogotá, one hand gripping her wrist as he tore at her clothes. Madeline had acted without thinking, the gun in her hand an extension of her anger. She'd told Jenny to run, and then checked the body, cringing as she touched his lifeless skin. Then she'd tried to follow, but it was too late.

The Colombian police had found her. The man was a prominent politician. Jenny was a drug addict. No one believed Madeline's story. Her sister disappeared, and Madeline had wound up here at San Mateo. But if she had it to do over again, she'd do the same. Her mother had made her promise. With her last breath of life.

"Take care of your sister, Maddie. She's not strong like you."

Madeline had only been ten, but she'd promised. And she'd kept her word. She sucked in a breath, pulling her thoughts from the past. Jenny was safe now. She had to believe that. It was the only thing that kept her going.

"Anyway, even if it would make a difference, there's no one to come," Madeline said. "What about you? You told me you have family. Why aren't they trying to help you?"

"They think I'm dead." Andrés shrugged.

"How horrible," she said, shuddering at the thought.

"Believe me, it's better this way." His expression was guarded. "For them. And for me. Sometimes the truth is better left buried."

"I suppose you're right." She nodded as they stopped by the far wall of the yard. "Anyway, we have each other now, right?"

His smile was gentle. "You have been a good friend. But I'm afraid all good things must come to an end."

"Why would you say that?"

"I'm a marked man," Andrés sighed. "My days are numbered."

Madeline dipped her head, tears filling her eyes. She'd heard the shots fired late at night.

"The only reason I was allowed out here with you is that I was so sick. But I am better now, and that means I will be returned to my original cell. I overheard the guards," he said. "I'm being moved back. Which means this is my last time in the yard."

"No. I won't accept that." She shook her head, panic

mixing with dread. "Maybe you can pretend to be sick again. Something, anything that might keep you here— with me. I...I can't make it without you."

"Of course you can," Andrés said. "You're much stronger than you know."

"Señor?" A guard called from the doorway, his machine gun held at the ready. *"Ven conmigo ahora."*

Madeline turned to the guard, then back to Andrés, heart pounding. "What does he want?"

"He wants me to come with him." Andrés shrugged. "It's time."

"No. You can't go. I can't do this on my own." She waved at the yard, and the guards.

"Yes, you can." His smile was gentle, his teeth white against the dark growth of his beard. "You're a survivor. Never forget that."

The guard moved impatiently, his lips curled in a sneer. *"Apurate!"*

"Uno momento," Andrés said, holding up a hand. "Here, I have something for you." He reached into his pocket and produced a grimy card. "Take this. It may be of help to you."

She took the card, the battered face of the Queen of Hearts staring up at her. "I don't understand."

"If you can get this to the American Embassy, they'll help you. No questions asked."

"But it's just a playing card." She shook her head.

"Trust me," Andrés said, closing her fingers around the card. "And keep it safe."

"But if this truly does have some kind of significance, shouldn't you be the one using it?"

"Señor, ahora," the guard called, his eyes narrowing with impatience.

Madeline ignored him, her gaze locked on her friend's. "Andrés, tell me. Why not use it yourself?"

"Because it is too late for me. I have accepted my fate. And it gives me pleasure to think that perhaps I can be of some service to you. No matter what you have done, you don't belong here."

"Neither do you," she whispered, her voice fierce now. "Keep the card."

"It is yours, my friend. I give it freely. Now I must go." He shook his head, waving a hand toward the guard. "Use the card to find your way home, Madeline. And then forget this place ever existed."

"I can't do that," she said. "Because if I did, that would mean forgetting you."

Tears slid down her face, the first she'd shed since landing at San Mateo. She wasn't the type to get sentimental. Andrés was right. She was a survivor. But something about the man had touched her heart. Reached a place she'd thought long dead.

And now they were taking him away.

When he reached the guard, Andrés stopped and turned, lifting a hand to say good-bye. Madeline's heart stuttered to a stop, her breathing labored as she clung to the wall, watching as her friend disappeared into the prison.

She sank to the ground, her back sliding against the rough-hewn stone of the wall, and opened her fingers, the mottled face of the Queen staring up at her. It was just a card. Unless of course she'd somehow fallen down the rabbit hole. A bubble of hysteria washed through her.

San Mateo wasn't Wonderland. And she was no Alice.

She was simply a woman who'd run out of options. Life wasn't fair. It was as simple as that. Angrily, she dried her eyes. There were two kinds of people in this world. The ones who survived. And the ones who did not.

She'd learned that lesson long ago.

CHAPTER 1

Sopron, Hungary—three years later

He'd had the dream again—his brother alive and well and giving him hell. As always, it had seemed so real. And he'd hated to wake. To lose this last connection with Tucker. But there was no denying reality. His brother was dead. Had been for five long years.

Drake Flynn sat up, running a hand through his hair, wondering when the pain would stop. Street light filtered into the hotel room, the resulting shadows shifting with movement on the street. The bedside clock glowed an eerie green. Three-thirty-five. Too early to get up and too late to go back to sleep.

He frowned, wishing that Cassandra was still here. He'd have liked to lose himself in her heat. Forget his losses. Concentrate on the here and now. He couldn't remember when exactly she'd left. Probably hours ago. She wasn't big on cohabitation, which, in the beginning, had suited Drake just fine. But now, he wasn't as certain. They'd been together, off and on, for almost a year, and for the first time since Tucker died, Drake actually felt a stirring of hope.

Which was goddamned ridiculous when he thought about it. He and Cass might both be operatives in the same game, but they played for different teams. And although their objectives coincided for the moment, he'd been around long enough to know that that could change in an instant.

He knew that was why she kept him at arm's length, even agreed with her on some intellectual level. But the ache in his groin wasn't interested in logical arguments. He needed her. It was as simple as that. And although he was loath to admit it, the need might be turning into something more than just physical.

Pushing out of bed, he pulled on a pair of sweats and grabbed the room key from the bedside table. No sense in overthinking the issue, and even less point in denying himself unnecessarily. Their operation was technically over. They'd secured the information they'd been sent to retrieve. It was locked safely in the next room. Later today they'd transport it to a safe house, a neutral facility where both their governments could access and analyze the data they'd acquired.

Score one for the good guys.

Drake grinned, thinking that now might be a good time for a little R&R. And not just here in the hotel. He wasn't big on vacations, but with Cass it just might be worth it. Maybe they'd go to an island somewhere. His mind trotted out an image of Cass in the surf, her sun-warmed skin glowing as he lifted himself over her, the water caressing them as he thrust into her tight, wet heat . . .

Damn. He shook his head. *I have it bad.*

He shoved the key into his pocket and started for the door, but then froze as a sound filtered through his lust-filled reverie. Tensing, every nerve in his body on alert, his mind cleared in an instant. Scooping his gun from the table, he released the safety, his finger on the trigger, and moved from the bedroom into the living room.

He squinted into the shadows, trying to find the source of the noise he'd heard. Something or someone moved in the foyer, the darkened shape of the closet door taking form as his eyes adjusted to the dim light.

He took a step forward, his muscles tightening in anticipation, and then relaxed as he recognized Cass, his arm dropping harmlessly to his side. "Jesus, darlin', you sure know how to scare the hell out of a guy." He grinned, dropping the gun on the bureau. "You must have read my mind. I was just wishing you were here."

"Drake," she whispered as she swung around, her full lips parting in surprise, the street light playing on the gun in her hand. "I was hoping you wouldn't wake up. It certainly would have made this easier."

"What the hell are you talking about?" His smile faded to a frown as his mind grappled with the meaning of her words.

"Complications." She shrugged. "At least I've managed to maintain the upper hand." She waved her gun, the motion adding emphasis to her words. "I wish it didn't have to be this way. I actually enjoyed our little interlude."

"Interlude?" he repeated. And then he saw the flash drive in her hand. "You're stealing the drive."

"You always were quick on the uptake," she said, her smile not reaching her eyes.

"But why?" He lifted his hands in supplication and

inched toward the bureau and his gun, thankful that it was hidden in the shadows. If she didn't know he had a weapon, he might just have a chance. "We're supposed to be working together. Our countries have an agreement."

"So they do," she acknowledged. "But, you see, I don't actually work for my government. And the people I do work for would very much prefer that the information on this drive not fall into the wrong hands."

"You're a double agent?" It was a blinding glimpse of the obvious, but he needed to buy himself a little time.

"More of a plant, I'd say. My work with Mossad gives me access to things I might never have had the opportunity to obtain. And your involvement"—she paused, her fingers tightening on the gun as something that might have been regret played across her face—, "well, let's just say it was serendipitous in more ways than I can count. But, unfortunately, all good things must come to an end."

"So you've been planning to kill me all along?"

"Those were my orders," she sighed. "But I'll admit you've made it more difficult than I'd anticipated."

"So don't do it," he said, turning slightly so that the gun was just behind him, within reach but out of her view.

"And what? Turn myself in?" Her laugh was hollow. "Please. You know as well as I do that's not the way it works."

"It doesn't have to be this way." He shook his head, still holding up his hands. "You admitted it yourself; there's something between us. Let me help you. Maybe there is a way out."

"Right. You're going to come over to the dark side." This time her laughter wasn't forced. "You're not the kind to turn traitor, Drake. And I'm not the kind to play noble.

So I'm afraid we're at an impasse, and since I've got the gun..." She shrugged, her expression resigned as she tightened her finger on the trigger.

Drake dove for the bureau as Cass's weapon exploded, the bullet grazing his arm as he grabbed his gun, hit the floor, and came up firing. His shot found the mark and Cass's eyes widened in surprise as she slammed back into the closet door.

For a moment, she held his gaze, and then with a soft exhalation she slid to the floor, the gun falling from lifeless fingers. His gut churning, he walked over to the body, kicking away the Walther. For a moment he stood, and then with a wave of self-revulsion, he bent over the body to retrieve the flash drive.

There should have been some other emotion. Regret maybe. Or some sense of loss. Not ten minutes ago he'd actually been thinking that there might have been something between the two of them. Something beyond the world of espionage. But clearly he'd been a fool to believe Cass was different. To let her lure him into thinking they'd had something more than just sex.

He should have known better.

Cass's betrayal only served to underscore what he already knew—women were liars.

It was as simple as that.

Di Silva Coffee, Bogotá, Colombia

Madeline was depleted. Bone-deep, soul-shatteringly hollow. Some days she wondered if there was any part of her left that was untouched by the things she witnessed every

day. The things she'd done. She'd become someone she
despised. And yet, she'd had little choice. Her sister's
life depended on her pleasing Jorge di Silva, or more
specifically his man Ortiz. But after three years, she had
to admit that she had her doubts.

The men continued to promise freedom. To hold it out
like a gold-plated carrot. One more job. One more piece
of information. But it never ended. They always wanted
more. And she had no choice but to acquiesce. After all,
they controlled Jenny.

Currently, Madeline's sister was sequestered in a
seaside rehabilitation facility in northern Colombia, but
it had been almost a year since she'd seen her sister and
almost seven months since they'd talked. Instead of leaving Colombia after Madeline's arrest, Jenny had sunk
deeper into the dark side of Bogotá. Penniless and desperate, she'd gone to work for di Silva—as a mule.

But in the end her hunger for drugs had rendered her
useless, so she'd bargained for her life using Madeline—
or more accurately her sister's connection to a prominent
diplomat living in New Orleans. Henri Marton had been
Madeline's first employer, the man who'd offered her a
way out of Cypress Bluff.

It had all seemed so easy sitting there across from Ortiz
in the dank holding room at San Mateo. Then, his request
had seemed simple. In return for Madeline's release all she
had to do was get information from Marton. Information
that would aid di Silva's organization. Once she'd accomplished the task, her sister's drug debt would be paid, and
the two of them would be free to return home. In the meantime, Ortiz promised, Jenny would go into treatment.

But men like Ortiz lied as easily as they breathed,

and Jenny hadn't been interested in rehabilitation, her need for a fix outweighing any desire for freedom. So Madeline had continued to work for di Silva, seducing other men into giving up their secrets, while Jenny, with her addiction, had kept digging them deeper into debt.

Madeline sucked in a breath and slipped into Ortiz's office. Officially, Jorge di Silva ran the drug cartel she worked for, his aristocratic roots giving him entrée into all levels of Colombian society, his name adding legitimacy to the most illegitimate of businesses. His family, ostensibly in coffee, had run drugs since the days when clipper ships provided the fastest mode of delivery. He was the old guard. And Hector Ortiz was the new.

It was Hector who'd shifted the cartel's focus from drugs to weapons, the former providing cover for the latter. What had been a profitable organization under di Silva had become an even more powerful force under Ortiz's influence. Basically, Hector made the money, staying under the radar, while Jorge took all the credit.

And Madeline hated them both.

Which was why she'd been stealing documents for the past two years. Ortiz had taught her well. Information was better than currency, and she'd managed to secure some pretty damning evidence. But as long as they had Jenny, her efforts were pointless. Still, her mother had always said it was best to be prepared.

Somehow Madeline didn't think working for a drug cartel was what Candace Reynard had had in mind. But then, her mother had been dead for more years than Madeline cared to remember. She'd left her girls when they'd needed her most. And Madeline was still struggling to fill the void.

Ortiz's office was quiet, the only sound the steady

ticking of the clock on the wall. It was early yet, only a few overachievers already hard at work. Ortiz had a breakfast meeting. She'd overheard him discussing it with di Silva, which meant that for the moment at least she had the office to herself. It was always a risk coming here. But she was so rarely in Bogotá, she wanted to make the most of the opportunity.

Usually, when she wasn't working, she spent her time at di Silva's compound near Cali. It was the center of operations, but he kept offices in Bogotá as well. And it was here that she hoped to find something to document the recent influx of munitions into the country. She had evidence to prove that the cartel had been buying arms, but nothing that documented their arrival in the country. She'd seen the stockpile herself—once or twice when there'd been no option but to bring her along. But if she was going to bring down the cartel, she needed more than her word. She needed proof. A paper trail.

Maybe her efforts were futile. Maybe she'd never find a way to get Jenny free. But hope was all she had. That and the burning need to make Ortiz pay for everything he'd put them through.

A noise outside the office interrupted her thoughts. If Ortiz caught her rifling though his things, she was dead. It was as simple as that. Madeline's heart beat staccato against her ribs as she ducked beneath the desk, holding her breath. Footsteps echoed as they approached and then faded.

Counting to ten, she waited to be sure the coast was clear, then pushed to her feet and sat in Ortiz's chair. The desk was a monstrosity, carved oak with drawers on either side. She pulled the first one open. There were the usual assortment of office supplies and a few harmless invoices. Nothing that would help. She reached for the bottom drawer, smiling when it refused to budge.

A locked drawer almost always meant pay dirt. At least she hoped so. Producing a pick from her pocket, she made short work of the lock and slid the drawer open. The files looked promising, and she reached for the first one, pulling it upward, dislodging an envelope in the process. Frowning, she bent and picked it up, the return address indicating a physician. Maybe Ortiz was sick. A girl could dream.

She glanced again at the door and then pulled out the sheets of paper inside, forcing her mind to translate the Spanish. She'd become quite fluent in the time she'd spent in di Silva's organization. Andrés would have been proud.

Her smile was bittersweet as she thought of her friend. She'd tried to get word of him, but to no avail. Most likely he was dead. But at least she'd always remember.

She shook her head, concentrating on the letter, the words forming into sentences, the sentences into a horror she couldn't begin to contemplate. Cold sweat broke out on her forehead, her eyes swimming with tears as her heart dropped to her stomach, her lungs no longer capable of taking in air.

With shaking hands she read the letter again, its meaning still the same.

Her sister was dead.

Dead.

Madeline shuddered. The word was so final. Drugs had ruled Jenny in life. And now it seemed they ruled her in death as well. She'd died from an overdose. No,

Madeline amended, her grief turning to burning rage, she'd died because Ortiz had killed her. As surely as if he'd administered the drugs himself.

She wiped away her tears, glancing at the document that accompanied the letter, a death certificate from a hospital in Bogotá, dated six months ago. Jenny was supposed to have been in a treatment center in Barranquilla on the other side of the country. Swallowing a sob, she slid the letter back into the envelope, her fingers still shaking. There was nothing to be gained by losing it here. She had to maintain control.

She put the envelope back into the drawer, and then carefully relocked it. It was tempting to run. She craved her freedom, but she wanted Ortiz more. And to bring him down, she needed the information she had ferreted away, the files hidden at di Silva's compound. Which meant she'd have to wait. Pretend that she didn't know.

But there *was* one thing she could do now. One thing to set the wheels in motion. There was nothing to hold her back anymore. Jenny was dead.

She pushed away from the desk, her mind made up.

It was time to play Andrés's card.

CHAPTER 2

Sunderland College, New York

T he air smelled like fall even though Indian summer was still holding court, the temperatures higher than normal for late September. Drake Flynn made his way across campus, his thoughts far away from students and classes. He'd been back for a couple of weeks, been going through the motions. Teaching. Working with friends and colleagues. But he still couldn't shake the image of Cass dead on the floor, her blood staining the carpet.

He hadn't had a choice. It had been her life or his. But even so, he couldn't let it go.

Not that he intended to share that fact.

He trusted his friends, but he wasn't a share-his-guts kind of guy. So he'd rebuffed all attempts to talk and thrown himself into his work. He nodded at fellow professors and students as he walked, forcing his thoughts to the lecture he'd just given. He'd always found the past a better place than the present. It was part of why he'd chosen archaeology as a profession.

At least until the CIA had come calling.

"Professor Flynn," a breathless coed called, her voice interrupting his thoughts. "Have you got a minute?"

He stopped, dutifully shifting his attention to the girl in front of him. "What can I do for you, Stacey?"

"I had a question about the degradation of ancient ruins," she said, glancing up at him coyly from behind lowered lashes. God, they started young. "You were talking about how much had been lost to deforestation and greed. And I was just wondering why it mattered so much. I mean, isn't it better to have progress? People working? Food on the table?"

"There certainly is an argument to be made for the modern world over the ancient one," Drake responded. "But I'm not sure that stripping the land of everything it harbors—trees, animals, artifacts—is truly a step forward. There's got to be a way for us to use our past to make a better future. And if we destroy everything that's old, we lose a valuable tool in understanding not just where we've been but where we're going. Look, Stacey, since you seem to be so interested, maybe you should consider the topic for your paper."

"Thanks, Dr. Flynn. I'll think about it. And you're right"—the girl licked her lips and flicked her hair provocatively, and Drake fought to keep his expression neutral—"not everything old is bad. I mean, look at you."

"Right. I'm positively decrepit." He nodded, shaking his head as she walked away. Maybe he was taking it all too damn seriously. It was a job, and Cass had been a distraction. Nothing more. She'd played him. But in the end he'd managed to come out on top. And he'd learned his lesson. He'd handle it better next time, and he had no doubt there'd be a next time. A-Tac wasn't about sitting on your ass and doing nothing. It was a war. Pure and simple. And sometimes the bad guys got a leg up.

But, push come to shove, A-Tac usually won the day.

The American Tactical Intelligence Command was an off-the-books arm of the CIA. Operating out of Sunderland College, it was cloaked under the guise of the Aaron Thomas Academic Center, one of the country's foremost think tanks. Members of the unit were adept at both academics and espionage, their unique abilities setting the stage for some of the CIA's most dangerous missions.

"Fraternizing with the coeds?" Nash Brennon asked, pulling Drake from his reverie. Nash was Drake's best friend, as well as A-Tac's second in command. He also chaired Sunderland's history department. An expert in covert operations, he was the go-to guy when something needed to be accomplished under the radar.

"Are you kidding me?" Drake asked, shaking his head. "She's like nineteen."

"If that." Nash grinned. "You on your way to Avery?" Avery Solomon was their boss. A hard-nosed ex-military man, Avery inspired fierce loyalty among team members. He'd successfully ridden out four political administrations, and maintained contacts at the highest levels of government, including the Oval Office.

"Yeah," Drake said, patting the beeper on his belt. "He paged."

"Me, too." Nash studied him for a moment, his eyes darkening with concern. "You doing all right?"

"I'm fine," Drake answered. "Just ready to get back to work."

"I can understand that," his friend said with a nod, thankfully not pushing any farther.

"So, any idea what the new orders might be?"

"Not a clue." Nash shook his head as they walked into the Center to a bank of elevators at the back of the lobby. Nash inserted a key into an elevator marked "professors only" and the doors slid open. They stepped inside, and Drake inserted a second key as Nash pushed a button behind the Otis Elevator sign.

The doors closed as the elevator started downward to the A-Tac complex hidden beneath the campus.

"Any luck convincing Annie to join the team?" Drake asked. Nash's wife was the exception to Drake's rule about women. She actually made his friend happy. They'd recently married, and although Avery had done everything possible to convince Annie, an ex-CIA operative, to join A-Tac, she was still holding out.

"Not yet. But I think maybe she's weakening. Avery asked her the other day for about the millionth time if she'd be interested in being reactivated. Usually she just says no. But this time she told him she'd think about it."

"Sounds like progress. I bet she won't hold out much longer. Hell, she's as much of an adrenaline junkie as the rest of us. She's got to be itching to get back into the saddle."

"Well, there's Adam to think about." Nash and Annie had almost lost their son a year ago. "I know he's safe here, but I worry about both of us being gone."

"So you split your time," Drake shrugged. "It's doable."

"Hey, I'm not the one saying no." He held up his hands in defense as the elevator doors slid open. They walked into what appeared to be a reception area, and Nash slapped his hand on a bust of Aaron Thomas, the Center's namesake. Then, palm identification completed, a panel in the far wall slid open, and Drake followed Nash into the A-Tac complex.

"I was wondering where you guys had gotten to," Hannah Marshall said, as the panel slid shut again. Although no one would ever guess it, Hannah was the team's intel expert. She looked more like one of her students than an expert in both political theory and ferreting out information. Her spiky hair was streaked with purple today, the glasses perched on the end of her nose a contrasting green. "Everybody's waiting for you in the war room."

"So what's the mission?" Nash asked.

"No idea." Hannah shrugged. "You know Avery doesn't like spilling the beans until everyone's together."

The three of them walked into the war room. With computer banks flanking the walls and LCD screens above and behind the oblong conference table, the oversized space was the heart of A-Tac.

Hannah moved over to the far end of the table, opened a computer console and flipped up the screen. Like Jason Lawton, who was sitting to her left, she lived on her computer. Jason handled the unit's IT needs, as well as computer forensics. A whiz with everything electronic, he was an invaluable asset to both the college and the team.

Jason lifted a hand in greeting as Nash settled in next to him. Across the way, Tyler Hanson was sitting on the edge of the table, talking with Avery, her long blond hair, as usual, pulled back into a ponytail.

Tyler was the epitome of the girl next door—with a definite twist. Drake doubted there was a bomb in existence that she couldn't put together or tear apart. She served as the team's ordnance expert. And, to add to the dichotomy, she was also the chair of Sunderland's English department.

Rounding out the team were Emmett Walsh and Lara Prescott. Emmett handled the team's communication issues. And Lara, a noted expert in biochemical warfare, served as the team's medical officer.

It was a diverse group. But they were all professionals. And Drake would have laid his life down for any one of them. And even though he was the newest member of the team, he knew that the sentiment was returned.

"You okay?" Lara asked as Drake dropped into the chair beside her. "I haven't had the chance to talk to you since you got back from Hungary." In the face of her open concern, Drake bit back his flippant retort. It wasn't her fault he'd acted like a fool.

"I'm doing better. Thanks. Like I told Nash, I'm ready to get back to work."

Lara nodded, her gaze speculative, clearly seeing far more than he wanted her to. But thankfully, before she had the chance to respond, Avery cleared his throat, signaling that the meeting was to begin.

"Now that everyone is here," Avery said, "why don't we get started. We've been charged with an extraction." He pressed a button in front of him and the screen filled with the picture of a woman. "Her name is Madeline Reynard."

"French?" Tyler asked, obviously going off the name.

"No. American," Avery said. "Although we don't know too much else about her. She seems to have sprung fully formed, so to speak. According to her passport, she's from a small town outside New Orleans. Cypress Bluff. But we couldn't find any record of her there at all."

"So she's lying about her name," Drake said, as he studied the woman's photograph.

She was tiny, her long dark hair curling wildly around her face. Her features were sharp, her chin a little long, her nose aquiline. But even so, she was still a looker, with full lips and a body that begged a man to touch her. Tottering on heels that should be declared illegal, she stood on a corner, arm held up as she hailed a taxi.

"Or maybe she's one of those people who just falls through the cracks." Emmett shrugged. "It happens."

"Either way, we're more interested in her present than her past," Avery said. "According to our intel, for the past three years, she's been associated with Jorge di Silva."

"The drug racketeer." Jason nodded, clearly recognizing the name.

"Actually, di Silva's gone a step beyond that," Hannah said, typing something into her computer. "They've even coined a new term—narcoterrorist. Not only is he producing and dealing cocaine, he's using the proceeds to buy and sell weapons to the highest bidders. No questions asked."

"Hell of a guy." Drake frowned. "So how does Madeline Reynard fit into all of this?"

"She says she's his mistress," Avery said. "And there's some evidence to support the idea. According to the briefing file I was given, he had her plucked out of a Colombian prison. Place called San Mateo."

"I've heard of it." Emmett nodded. "Some kind of fortress in the Chaco region. I thought it was reserved for political prisoners."

"And foreigners," Avery said.

"So what landed her in San Mateo?" Nash asked.

"No idea," Hannah said, still typing. "Most people don't even know the prison exists. Which is exactly how the Colombian government wants it. Anyway, as such, their security is top-notch and prisoner records aren't easy to come by."

"When has that ever stopped you?" Jason quipped.

"I'm working on it." Hannah frowned, her hair standing on end as she absently ran a hand through it. Drake smiled. If anyone could break into San Mateo's data banks, Hannah would be the one.

"So when was the photograph taken?" Tyler asked, as she studied the picture.

"About six months ago," Avery said, shifting so that he could see the photo as well. "In Bogotá. That's di Silva behind her." The man in the picture had his back turned, his attention on someone out of the frame.

"Here's a better one of him," Hannah said.

The chiseled, flat-nosed face that filled the screen was almost identical to the ones that decorated the burial mounds and ancient monuments of the pre-Columbian ruins scattered along the Cauca River. Generations of genealogy pooled into one man. His autocratic bearing, however, had no doubt descended straight from the conquistadors, Castilian arrogance at its best. Drake shook his head, pushing away his anthropological thoughts in favor of more practical details.

"Okay, so we know that the woman has a sketchy past." Drake frowned. "And that she's been living with a drug lord. But I'm not seeing exactly where it is that we come into this."

"Apparently, she went to the Embassy in Bogotá and asked for help." Avery hit a button and the photo of di Silva moved back to the one of Madeline.

"In return for?" Tyler prompted.

"Information on di Silva and his operations." Everybody broke into conversation at once, speculation running rampant.

"So why doesn't her contact at the Embassy handle the extraction?" Drake asked, ignoring the chatter, focusing instead on Madeline Reynard's face.

"Because the man's dead." Avery's pronouncement had the effect of silencing the room.

"Son of a bitch," Nash said, putting voice to the prevailing sentiment. "Anyone we know?"

"I don't think so. He was fairly new to the diplomatic corps. This was his first posting. Guy named Will Richardson."

"So what happened?" Lara asked.

"He was murdered. Gunned down outside his apartment."

"I take it Richardson's death is being linked to di Silva?" Nash asked.

"There's no hard evidence." Avery shrugged. "The police are blaming local gang activity. But if you play connect the dots it seems likely."

"That still doesn't preclude the Embassy from doing their own dirty work. They have assigned CIA personnel." Jason looked up from his computer with a frown.

"Yes, but Madeline isn't in Bogotá anymore," Avery said. "Shortly after Richardson's death, she was removed to di Silva's compound in the mountains." He nodded at Hannah, who switched the photograph again, this one depicting a sprawling stucco home. "This is di Silva's hacienda. Casa de Orquídea. The area's known for its orchids. Anyway, the house is part of a compound located about twenty miles due west of Cali. It's officially listed as a coffee plantation. But as we know, there are other, more lucrative crops that grow well in that part of the Andes."

"Like the coca plant," Emmett inserted.

"Exactly." Avery nodded.

"And that's where Madeline is?" Tyler asked with a frown. "Not going to be an easy in and out."

"That whole area is pretty inhospitable," Nash agreed. "I'm assuming he's got guards."

"Full-meal deal." Avery nodded again at Hannah, who switched to a map of the area. "Surveillance, perimeter rotation, and at least four men on duty in the house. He's also got eyes on all approaching roads."

"We can helicopter in," Drake said, frowning up at the map. "Then hike through the jungle and catch them by surprise."

"Makes sense," Nash agreed. "But we'll need to disable the cameras somehow."

"I should be able to do that from here." Jason shrugged.

"May not be as easy as you think," Avery said. "I'm going to need you on site as part of the team. Emmett and Lara are heading out to Russia in the morning. We've agreed to help neutralize a recently discovered stockpile of chemical weapons. And I'm not certain that Drake is ready for a new mission."

"What the hell are you talking about?" Drake said, his fingers tightening on the edge of the table. "I've been through the requisite debrief." He glanced over at Lara for confirmation. "And I've been cleared for duty. Besides, I'm the best you've got when it comes to extraction."

"Yes, but you've had a lot to deal with in the last few weeks. I just don't want you out there too soon." Avery paused, eyes narrowed. "Before you're ready."

"I could go," Emmett offered. "Drake can go with Lara."

"No dice." Avery shook his head. "Drake doesn't speak the language and your Russian is flawless."

"I'm perfectly capable of going into Colombia," Drake said, trying to contain his irritation. "For God's sake, it's not like I had an attachment to the woman." He hadn't meant to add the last bit; the words came of their own volition. Everyone stopped talking, eyes riveted on the table. "Jesus"—he blew out a long breath—"you'd think I was the first one to have to deal with a traitor. I'm telling you, I'm fine. I can handle this."

Avery studied him for a moment, and then nodded. "All right. But I want Jason to go anyway. He can fill in for Emmett handling communications. That going to be a problem?" The question was rhetorical but Jason answered anyway.

"Not from my end. Hannah's perfectly capable of dealing with things here, and if she runs into a problem, I'll just advise long distance."

"Okay," Emmett said, staring up at the photo, "so it sounds like we've got everything arranged. But I'm still not seeing why Langley would go to all the trouble to bring us in to retrieve her. She's just the guy's mistress— how much do you think she really knows? I'm thinking there's got to be something more to this."

"There is." Avery crossed his arms, a smile playing at the corner of his lips.

"Do tell," Nash prompted.

"As I mentioned earlier," Avery said, "di Silva's been suspected of dealing arms for quite some time now. But there's never been any tangible proof. There have been all kinds of rumors. Everything from a warehouse in Bogotá to a terrorist hideout in the mountains of Chaco."

"But nothing has ever been substantiated," Hannah added.

"Until now." Avery's expression turned grim. "According to the original source, Madeline Reynard knows the location of di Silva's weapons cache. And it's somewhere in the vicinity of his compound. So if she's telling the truth—"

"Then we'll be able to nail di Silva," Nash said.

"Exactly." Avery nodded. "Our task is to find the cache, document the site, and then blow it to kingdom come."

"After we extract Madeline Reynard and get her back to D.C.," Jason prompted.

"Not possible," Avery shook his head. "The only way to be sure she's on the level is to make her show us the site. If everything pans out, then Tyler blows the pop stand and we escort Ms. Reynard straight to Langley."

"And if she's lying?" Drake asked.

"Then," Avery shrugged, "we leave her to di Silva."

CHAPTER 3

Casa de Orquídea, Valle del Cauca, Colombia

Madeline Reynard paced back and forth in the confines of her bedroom. It seemed whatever decision she made it was the wrong one. She'd killed a man to save her sister. Confessed to keep Jenny out of the picture. And then she'd agreed to Ortiz's conditions—this time to buy her sister's freedom. But Jenny was dead. Which meant that everything she'd done had been for nothing.

Madeline had promised her mother, and now she'd failed.

And to make matters worse, she was little more than a prisoner here in Cali. Once they'd returned from Bogotá, she'd found that her bedroom had been moved from the first floor to the second. And at night there were guards outside her bedroom door. During the day she wasn't allowed even a walk on the grounds without an armed escort. Di Silva's men swore it was for her own protection, but Madeline didn't believe a word of it.

It had been almost three weeks since she'd heard

anything from the Embassy. And once she'd been sequestered here, there had been no way for her to contact
anyone. Someone was always watching her. She stopped
in front of the window, looking out across the manicured
lawns. The breeze caressed her face, the curtains lifting
lazily as the air was filled with the heady perfume of
orchids.

Casa de Orquídea was beautiful, its namesake flowers
coloring every nook and cranny in shades of pink and
purple. But beauty could be deceiving. The compound,
like San Mateo, was a prison. Only this time, Madeline
was fairly certain there would be no reprieve. In the end,
Andrés's playing card had amounted to nothing. She
hadn't wanted to believe it offered salvation. Only fools
bought into happy endings. And yet, some part of her had
hoped it was true.

She sighed, her hands closing on the bars that
obstructed the open window. They were a new addition,
another way to make sure she couldn't escape. Behind her
the door rattled as it was thrown open, and she whirled
around, composing her face as she struggled to maintain
at least an outward sense of calm.

"I see you've settled in here nicely," Hector Ortiz
said, his lithe frame filling the doorway. Hector was one
of those men who blended into the background. Neither
tall nor short, big nor small, handsome nor ugly. He was
every man. And it served him well. His dark hair was
always impeccable. Combed back in the Latin style, it
emphasized the angles of his face, and the dark obsidian
of his eyes.

She hadn't realized until now how much she truly
despised the man. "I liked my old room. I had access to

the courtyard and the grounds beyond. Now," she waved toward the window, "I'm little more than a prisoner."

"I'm sorry you feel that way." Although Madeline's Spanish was excellent, Ortiz, for some reason, preferred to hold their conversations in English. "But I have reason to believe that you've been considering breaking our agreement. And I don't have to tell you how dangerous that would be."

"I've done exactly as you asked me. From the very beginning." She shook her head. "But it's never enough."

Ortiz smiled. "I'm afraid it's the nature of the bargain. There's always something more. But your work isn't the problem. You've actually been quite a valuable asset. Which makes my discovery all the more disappointing."

Her heart twisted, but she lifted her chin, squaring her shoulders. "I've done nothing wrong."

"You contacted the American Embassy." He threw a photograph onto the bureau. She reached for it, fighting to keep her hand from trembling. "Is that not you?"

She glanced down at the picture. "I'm an American." She tossed the photo back on the chest. "And Will is a..." She hesitated, lifting one shoulder in feigned indifference. "Friend."

Actually, she'd only met him once before the picture was taken. At a political function. She'd been there with a prominent politico, a man with strong ties to the Latin American military-industrial complex. He'd been a pig. But Ortiz had insisted he had access to information no one else did. Anyway, it was that night that she'd met William Richardson, filing the name away as a possible ally should she ever need a way out.

"You're implying that the man was your lover?" Ortiz

actually laughed. "From what I've heard he was a devoted family man."

"That hardly stops di Silva," she said, determined to keep him from the truth. "Will had certain needs. And..." she trailed off. "Did you say 'was'?"

"Yes." He held out another photograph.

She took it, her stomach threatening revolt, as her brain struggled to process the scene depicted. Will lying in the street. His body crumpled like a rag doll, his blood staining the pavement. "Oh, my God."

"You left me no choice," Ortiz said, his voice devoid of emotion. "I had to clean up your mess."

"You killed him?" The words came out a strangled whisper.

"I gave the order." Ortiz shrugged, his gaze never leaving her face.

"But he hadn't done anything to you." She shook her head, the photograph falling from trembling fingers, drifting to the floor.

"Ah, yes, but if he'd helped you escape..."

"I told you he was my lover."

"And I'm telling you it's a lie." He slapped her hard and she jerked back, eyes wide as she covered her cheek with her hand. "I'm certain you were asking him for help. And I know why."

She froze, her heart threatening to break through her ribs.

"You were in my office." His voice was soft, but there was a thread of steel.

"I'm in your office all the time. I work for you, remember?" She clenched her fists, praying for a miracle— certain that none would come.

"Yes, but this time you were there without my permission. And you found the letter."

"I don't know what you're talking about."

"The hell you don't." He raised his hand again and she shrank back, but instead of striking her, he clenched his fist, his hand dropping back to his side. "Shall I spell it out for you? Your sister is dead. And you decided you wanted out. And you thought William Richardson would help you, but you miscalculated. And now he's dead."

"But I'm still alive. Why is that?" she asked, anger pushing away her fear.

"Because we believe you can still be useful to us." His gaze had turned speculative.

"And why would I want to help you? You killed my sister." She spoke through clenched teeth, hanging on to her control by sheer force of will.

"I did nothing of the sort." He waved a hand in dismissal. "Your sister killed herself. She was a junkie. And like all junkies, she simply couldn't stop."

Madeline swallowed her tears. "I should have been there with her. You should have told me."

"There was nothing you could have done," he said, his expression impassive. "And I needed you focused on your work."

"So you lied. You let me believe she was still alive."

"I did what was best for our operations."

"And now?"

"Now," he shrugged, "you will continue to pay off her debt. Besides the drugs, there is the small matter of the hospital."

"And if I refuse," she said, clenching her fists. "Then what?"

"Then I'll be forced to tell the authorities where you are. They still believe you're in San Mateo. And murder is a crime punishable by death."

She shivered but held her ground. "You're bluffing."

"I never bluff," he said, his gazed locked with hers. "And if that isn't enough to keep you in line, consider the information you've stolen. The men you've deceived. There are bound to be consequences for such duplicity."

"But I was working for *you*. If you bring me down, then you come with me."

"You always were naïve." His laugh was harsh. "There are ways of releasing your identity without involving the di Silva organization. We've been careful to insulate ourselves in case you failed. And that protection will only play in our favor should I choose to throw you to the wolves."

"You wouldn't." The words came involuntarily as she thought of the men she'd duped. Powerful men who'd like nothing better than to make her pay.

"Oh, believe me, Madeline," he said, jerking her forward, his fingers biting into her skin, "if you make any further attempt to betray us, one way or another, your life won't be worth a damn." He released her, and she stumbled backward. "If you don't believe me, have another look at the photograph of William Richardson."

"You in?" Nash asked, the communications device in Drake's ear crackling to life.

"Roger that." He frowned, surveying the dark room beyond the terrace door he'd just entered. "But there's no one here. Looks like there hasn't been for a while. The closet is empty and there aren't any sheets on the bed.

Any chance we're too late?" As he spoke, he rechecked the room, looking for something that might give him a clue as to Madeline Reynard's whereabouts.

"Negative," Nash insisted. "Hannah's got recent footage. She's there somewhere. They must have her somewhere else."

"All right, so what's my next move?" Drake asked. "In or out?"

"Got to be in," Nash said, his tone grim. "You've got incoming. Three of di Silva's men just took position on the terrace."

"Great. No package, no exit strategy, and I'm flying blind." Drake swallowed a surge of irritation. There were always hiccups in operations. It was part of the gig. The best thing to do was stay alert and roll with the punches.

"Hang on," Nash said. He and Avery were located just inside the compound's walls, but they were still too far away to give Drake needed backup. "Jason's patching us through to Hannah. She's working to get access to di Silva's internal security cameras. You guys there?"

"Yeah," Jason said. "We're still working on the feed. We're in, but Hannah's having a little trouble with the encryption."

"Hey, it's only been a couple of seconds," Hannah's voice crackled over the line. "Give a girl a chance."

"Not sure I have that option," Drake said, moving the drapes slightly so that he could see outside. "I've got two of the guards on the move. They're heading this way."

"Hold on." Hannah's voice was distracted. "I'm almost there."

Drake pulled out his gun and shifted position. "We're down to seconds."

"Got it," Jason said, as Drake released a breath he hadn't realized he'd been holding. "Hannah, can you see it?"

"Yeah," Hannah confirmed. "And I've got infrared as well. There's no one in the adjoining room."

Drake sprinted across the room and through the door, pulling it closed behind him, the sound of voices rising as they came in from the terrace, indicating just how close he'd come to being discovered.

"They still coming?" he queried, keeping his voice low.

"No," Hannah responded. "They've gone back outside. You're clear from that direction."

"What about the hallway?" Avery asked, his voice breaking up a little.

"I'm showing no activity in the immediate area," Hannah responded. "But there are people all over the house. Maybe ten or eleven. And the ones I can see on the security cameras are armed."

"Nothing like being outgunned," Drake said, his eyes on the doors opening off the hallway to the right and left. "What about the rooms up ahead?"

"They're not on the security cameras. But the infrared shows them as empty," Hannah replied.

"What about Madeline Reynard? Any sign of her?"

"Let me check," Hannah said. There was a moment of silence as they waited for her to cycle through the various security cameras. "I've got her. A bedroom upstairs. She's alone in the room, but I think she's got guards. Outside in the hallway. I can't actually see them; the security camera's angle is wrong. But I've got two hot spots on the infrared."

"So how do I get there from here?" Drake asked.

"Front stairs are out of the question," Jason said. "You've got two hostiles posted sentry with guns."

"Di Silva clearly isn't taking any chances," Tyler interjected. "You want me to move in and help out?" She and Jason were situated just outside the back of the compound.

"Not yet," Avery replied. "Hold position for the time being. You need to make sure there are no surprises for you and Jason. Nash and I will move to cover Drake."

"There's a small stand of mangos, surrounded by bushes, about thirty yards to your southeast," Hannah said. "The security cameras face out, so I can only see the vegetation, but it should be just under the bedroom window. And the bushes should give you enough cover to hold your position."

"Copy that," Nash said. "We're on our way."

"Drake," Hannah continued, "there's a second staircase just east of your position. And for now at least the coast is clear."

"What about the security cameras?"

"I'm rigging a looped feed," Jason said. "Give me a second and you should be good to go."

"It's going to be the second left," Hannah added. "Approximately fifteen feet down the hallway."

"Roger that," Drake said, cracking the door for visual confirmation that the hall was indeed empty.

"All right," Jason's voice crackled against the static. "I've got it rigged to loop the last five seconds of security feed. But I can't do it for too long or they'll figure out someone's in the system. You've got to move fast."

"No problem," Drake said as he swung out into the hallway, leading with his gun. The space was quiet, and he moved quickly, keeping tight to the wall. "I've got the turn in sight."

"Good," Hannah said. "The staircase is set beyond a doorway that should be immediately to your right after you make the turn. Still nothing to stand in your way."

Drake rounded the corner, passing through the doorway that led to the back stairs. They were narrow and uncarpeted, and Drake slowed his progress slightly to avoid making any noise. "What next?"

"Go right. And hold at the corner. The room will be immediately on your left, but as I said, there are two guards."

"Not to worry," Avery broke in. "Nash and I are in place. We just need some kind of distraction."

"You could rig an explosion," Tyler said. "Use the powder from a grenade."

"Hell, no need to rig it," Nash said. "We'll just throw the damn thing."

"And alert di Silva's entire security force," Drake responded. "Not a good idea. I can handle it myself with a hell of a lot less fuss."

"All right," Avery agreed. "But we're here. So don't hesitate to call for backup."

"No worries." Drake smiled. "Self-sacrificing heroics aren't my thing."

"We'll debate that another time," Nash said. "For now just be careful."

"Copy that." Drake stopped at the top of the landing long enough to make sure the way was clear, and then held at the corner, inching out to verify the positions of the two guards.

He checked the silencer on his gun and then, on an

internal count of three, swung out into the hallway, firing twice. He dove to the ground and rolled to his knees, gun raised for a second volley. But there was no need. Di Silva's guards were dead.

"I've got two down. But nothing to indicate anyone's aware of the fact," Drake said as he double checked the bodies for signs of life. "Hannah, you got anything?"

"Everything is clear for the moment," she said. "But I don't know how long that's going to last. Someone is trying to block our access. Which means they know we're in. Jason, can you stop them?"

"I'm doing everything I can, but, Drake, you need to move quickly. I'm not sure how long I can hold on to this link."

"All right," Drake responded. "I'm going in now. Keep your eyes on that hallway." As he opened the door, Madeline Reynard jumped, spinning around from her position at the window, a flash of fear quickly masked as she squared her shoulders, her gaze locking with his.

"Who the hell are you?" She stared at him defiantly, and despite himself, Drake was impressed.

Her photograph hadn't done her justice. Except for a purpling bruise on her left cheek, her skin was practically flawless. Milky white and soft. The kind a man wanted to taste and ultimately bury himself in. Her hair was almost black, with hints of russet and brown, the curls so tightly wound they seemed to have a life of their own.

He'd expected a pampered princess, but Madeline looked more like the girl next door. The one who could take on any guy and win. Despite her size, there was an air of bravado, a sense that she'd be up to any task, no matter the difficulty. And yet beneath all of that there was a hint of fragility—a paradox that Drake understood only too well. Strength came from pain. It was a lesson he'd learned a long time ago. And he had the feeling that Madeline Reynard was familiar with the primer.

"I asked who you are," she repeated, hands on hips, eyes flashing. Her sweats and camisole hugged her curves, illuminating her admittedly spectacular body.

"My name is Drake Flynn," he said, fighting against a smile. Maybe this operation wasn't going to be so bad after all. "And I'm here to rescue you."

CHAPTER 4

You scared the life out of me," she said, eyes still narrowed in anger.

"You and the two guys outside the door," Drake said, turning to check the hall again.

"You killed them?" she asked, moving to stand beside him, a frown creasing her forehead.

"Didn't have a choice."

"Who sent you?" There was a note of suspicion, as she closed and opened one hand, the gesture giving Drake the distinct impression she was wishing for a gun.

"Your friend Will Richardson."

"Will is dead," she said, a shudder rippling through her.

"I know." He nodded. "But not before he got word to the people that matter. I'm here to get you out."

"You and what army?" she asked, a bitter laugh coloring her words. "You look capable enough, but di Silva's men are everywhere."

"Yeah, well, at least there are two less to deal with." He

shrugged, moving to the center of the room. "Hannah," he spoke into the com mic, "tell me you've got a way for us to get out of here."

"You've got friends?" Madeline asked, moving to the door to check the hallway.

"Yeah." He nodded, tapping his earpiece. "A small army of them."

"Drake, we've got problems here," Hannah said, pulling his attention from the woman in the doorway. "We've lost access to the security feed. Which means no visual."

"And worse, they'll have been alerted that someone's on site," Jason's voice filled his ear. "Which means they'll be heading your way. Your best bet is to go out the window."

"No can do." Drake shook his head. "The window is barred. We'll need an alternative."

"And we'll need it fast," Madeline called over her shoulder. "Someone's coming."

"Did you hear that?" Drake asked.

"Affirmative," Hannah responded. "But everyone's still on the first floor. I've got them on infrared. So you've got a little time."

"So where do we go?" Drake barked into the mic, his fingers tightening on his gun.

"There's a window in the room two doors to your left," Hannah said. "I saw it when we had the live feed. It's unobstructed. According to the blueprint, the first floor juts out just below it. So you should be able to drop to the roof and from there make your way to Nash and Avery's position in the bushes."

"Roger that," he said, turning back to Madeline. "You're going to need shoes."

She nodded and bent to retrieve a pair of boots from

under her bed, the sturdy kind he wouldn't have expected her to own, let alone have at the ready. Clearly his initial impression of Ms. Reynard had been flawed.

She pulled on the boots and a shirt, then grabbed a waterproof courier bag. "I'm ready."

"You're not bringing the bag. It'll just get in the way," he said, eycing the little carryall.

"It goes. It's all I've got," she said, her chin jutting out in defiance.

"It's just going to cause problems."

"Please." She held his gaze, her eyes flickering with something he couldn't quite put a name to, but recognized just the same.

"Fine," he said, angry at himself for giving in so easily. "Take it."

"Thank you." She nodded as they turned toward the doorway.

"We still clear?" Drake queried into the mic.

"Roger that," Hannah affirmed, "but they're on the stairs, so you'd better move now."

"You know how to use a gun?" he asked Madeline, reaching into his jacket pocket for a second handgun.

"Point and shoot," she said, taking the weapon. "It can't be that hard."

"Look, I can use your help, but I don't need any more problems."

She took the gun, released the safety, and checked the ammo, her movements clearly not a novice's.

"I'd say you've had a little practice," Drake observed, his eyes narrowing in speculation.

"In the world I come from," Madeline said, shrugging, "it's a necessity."

He studied her for a moment longer, then moved to peer out the door. "On my signal, we're going to head to the right, down two doors."

"Di Silva's study." She nodded.

"And from there we'll proceed through the window, out onto the roof."

She nodded, tensing as he pushed the door open.

"We're clear," he said. "Go."

Madeline shot out the door and sped down the hallway just as two men emerged from the stairway. Drake sprinted forward, shooting behind him, managing to drop one of di Silva's henchmen before slamming shut the door to the study.

"They're right behind us," Drake said, as Madeline pulled back the heavy drapes to reveal a set of narrow French doors opening onto a Juliet balcony. "Hannah, how close are they?"

"You nailed one of them, but his buddy is still on the move. ETA less than a minute. And there are more coming up the stairs."

"Got it." He nodded once as he pulled the doors open, his attention shifting to Madeline. "We'll climb over the balcony and drop down to the roof below. You think you can handle that?"

"No problem," she said, already straddling the railing. With surprising grace, she dropped onto the roof. Drake followed suit just as the study door burst open.

"We're about to have company," he said as they scrambled across the roof. Seconds later gunfire erupted from the open French doors above them, two men silhouetted in the light from the study.

In front of him a terracotta tile exploded from the

impact of a bullet. Drake pulled Madeline down behind the cover of a chimney stack. One of the men had dropped onto the rooftop and was making his way toward their position, the other continuing to fire from the balcony. Below them, Drake could see a second group of men rounding the far corner of the house.

The edge of the roofline was just below them—maybe ten feet, but the angle of the roof was sharp here, the slant making their descent more difficult.

"All right," he said, popping up to slow the guard's pursuit with a shot that sent the man ducking for cover. "When I give the signal I want you to head down. Keep moving and when you get to the edge, drop to the ground. Jump if you have to. Then head for the mango trees over there. My team will be waiting."

"What about you?" she whispered.

"I'll cover you. Whatever happens, don't stop. Just keep going. Got it? I'll follow as soon as you're off the roof." He fired again. "Now go."

She paused for a moment, searching his face, then started down the roof as he continued to hold off di Silva's men with gunfire. There were three of them now. Two on the roof, and one positioned on the balcony.

What he wouldn't give for a rifle or machine gun. Popping up from behind the chimney, he fired at the man closest to their position. The man gasped and grabbed his chest. The second gunman fired in return, the bullet whizzing past Drake's ear as he ducked back behind the safety of the chimney blocks.

Below him, Madeline had reached the edge of the roof. As she dropped over the edge out of sight, he fired twice in the direction of the balcony and scrambled down the sloping roof, keeping low to avoid the bullets coming from behind.

As he neared the edge, he turned to fire again, and then flipped over the edge and dropped to the ground. To his left a group of guards were closing the distance, but still out of range. A shot splintered past him, coming from above, one of the men on the roof reaching the edge.

Drake spun around, dropping to his knee to fire, but before he could align the shot, the man grabbed his shoulder, and fell back. Madeline emerged from the shadows, gun in hand. "I wasn't sure your friends could make the shot from the trees."

"I told you to keep moving."

"And I decided you might need my help." Her stance was defiant. "Look, you're my only ticket out of here. So it's in my best interest to keep you alive."

"And it's my *mission* to keep you alive. So move. Now."

They sprinted toward the trees, the men on the ground close enough now to shoot. Reaching into his pack, Drake produced a hand grenade. Pulling the cap with his teeth, he tossed it toward the group of men, the resulting explosion sending two of them flying through the air.

Score one for the good guys.

"We're almost there," he said into his mic.

"Nice move with the grenade," Avery said, as they ducked into the cover of the mango trees. "Now we've just got to figure out how to make an exit."

"I'm guessing the way we got in is out of the question?" Drake asked, as Nash fired on the advancing group of guards.

"They've got the exits covered," Avery said. "Hannah

says they've got people on both the front and side gates. We'd never get past them."

"So we're trapped."

"I might know a way," Madeline said as she dropped down beside Drake.

"Welcome to the party, Ms. Reynard." Avery's smile was grim.

"Madeline," she corrected. "I think we're well past formality."

"So what's your idea?" Drake asked, cutting through the social niceties.

"There's a gate at the back of the property. It's an old service entrance. For gardeners and such. No one uses it anymore. It's mainly overgrown with weeds. I found it by accident when I was walking once. Last time I was there, it still opened."

"And that would be?" Drake asked.

"Around two months ago. Before di Silva's men started watching my every move."

"Hannah," Avery said into his mic, "can you verify the gate's location?"

"It's not on any of the plans I have. But they're recent and if the gate's not in regular use it might not show up."

"You're sure about this?" Drake asked Madeline.

"I told you it was overgrown. I don't even think di Silva knows it's there. It's really old."

"Look, we haven't got time to debate," Avery said. "Di Silva's forces are almost here. We need to move now. You two head out and we'll follow."

"Roger that," Drake said, pulling Madeline to her feet. "You ready?"

She nodded as they shifted away from the trees, moving across the manicured lawn, past a swimming pool, toward the deep shadows at the back of the property. Behind them Drake could hear gunfire as Avery and Nash worked to hold their attackers at bay, buying time for them to find and open the gate.

"So where is it?" he asked as they reached the safety of the overhanging trees, stopping in front of the back wall.

"Over here," she said, disappearing beneath the heavy undergrowth that covered this part of the wall. He ducked under the vines, the vegetation blocking out all sound, the sudden silence almost deafening. "This is it." She pulled back a few remaining leaves to reveal a small gate, its rusted metal rivets and splintering wood irrefutable evidence of its disuse.

Drake pressed the latch and pushed against the gate, but it refused to yield as the gunfire drew nearer. "It's not opening."

"It's probably swollen from the humidity. We've had rain for the last three days. Try harder. I know it'll open."

Drake slammed his shoulder into the gate. "They're bound to figure out what we're up to," he said, more to himself than to Madeline, as he shoved against the wood. "Even if they don't know about the gate, if I don't get this open, we're going to be in deep shit."

He pushed again and this time the gate swung open. Something on the other side shifted, and he raised his gun.

"Hold on," came a whispered response. "It's Tyler." She stepped out of the shadows, holding an M-60.

"As usual, perfect timing." Drake grinned at his friend.

"Hannah finally found a plan that showed the gate.

And it seemed like you guys could use a little reinforcement." Tyler shrugged. "Truck's over there."

"Take Madeline and get ready to roll," he said. "I'll cover Nash and Avery."

"Sounds like a plan," she said, handing over the machine gun and heading for the truck parked in the shadows, Madeline on her heels.

Drake stepped back through the gate just as Nash and Avery burst through the undergrowth, backs turned as they continued to fire at the oncoming forces. After positioning the M-60, he fired, satisfied to see two of di Silva's men go down. Under Drake's covering shots, Nash and Avery pushed forward until they reached the gate.

"Tyler's just outside with the truck," he said, as Nash took out another of di Silva's henchmen.

"And the package?" Avery asked.

"Safely stowed."

"Then I say we get the hell out of here." Nash grinned.

"You guys go first," Drake instructed. "I'll hold them off until you signal you're safe."

Avery nodded as he and Nash moved through the gate. Drake turned and opened fire on the still advancing group of men. There were ten, maybe twelve left. He ducked as a bullet passed a little too close for comfort and then fired, leaving three more men down.

"We're secure," Avery's voice crackled in his ear. "Move your ass."

Not needing further encouragement, Drake fired one last time and dove through the gate, rolling to his feet as the truck pulled up next to him. He threw the gun in the back and grasped Avery's hand as the big man hoisted him up into the tarp-covered truck bed just as a jeep roared around the corner, guns blazing.

"We've got company," Avery said into his mic.

"Copy that," Tyler said. "I can see them in the rearview mirror." She gunned the engine and Nash fired out the window.

Drake retrieved his gun and waved an arm in Madeline's direction as she made a move to join him at the open end of the truck bed. "Stay down."

She nodded, dropping to her knees, lowering her head protectively.

Drake and Avery opened fire, their bullets, combined with Nash's, forcing the jeep to drop back just out of range, while still keeping pace with the truck. "How much farther to the rendezvous point?" Drake asked.

"A couple of minutes," Avery said.

"You still think it'll work as planned? I mean, we weren't counting on this kind of a response from di Silva."

"We weren't counting on a response at all. It was supposed to be a simple in and out," Avery observed. "But we figured for the contingency anyway."

"I'm pushing it as fast as I can," Tyler replied over the com. "We should be there in less than a minute. And if Jason's on point, the plane should be waiting." The jeep moved closer and Drake fired another round, forcing it back again. "Sharp turn," Tyler called as she jerked the truck to the right onto a rutted road leading to a clearing and a weathered-looking landing strip.

As promised, the small Cessna was sitting at the end of the runway, engines running. As they approached the plane, Tyler hit the brakes and the truck skidded to a stop, fishtailing so that the back end was facing the plane, the body of the truck blocking the oncoming jeep's view of the plane's open hatch.

Madeline moved toward the plane, her obvious intent to get herself on board, but Drake stopped her.

"What? Aren't we getting on the plane?" Madeline asked.

"No," Avery said. "It's only meant as a diversion."

"I don't understand," Madeline said, securing her bag over her shoulder.

"Just stay with me," Drake said, as he helped her down. "We're going under the plane to that dump over there." He pointed to a tumble of old barrels and crates that littered the far side of the runway.

Madeline frowned, but followed behind him as he ducked beneath the humming fuselage. Behind him he could hear the jeep as its driver gunned the engine as it neared the runway. When they reached the abandoned cargo, Drake pulled her down into what appeared to be the open end of a crate. But once through the opening a small ladder led down into a dark cement-lined hole.

"What the hell is this?" she asked, her body tensing.

"Plan B." Drake said as Tyler and Nash moved into the bunker, Avery on the ladder above, disguising the entrance with additional pieces of discarded wood and metal. The small amount of light that had filtered through the opening vanished, swallowed by inky blackness as Avery closed a metal hatch.

Madeline reached out to grasp Drake's arm, her fingers cold, her nails digging into his skin. "I can't see."

Drake flipped on a flashlight, the beam seeming overly bright after the blackout. Above them, the roar of the plane's engines crested as the aircraft started its taxi down the runway.

The squeal of the jeep's brakes was followed by a volley of gunfire overhead, and then another, the shooters obviously trying to bring down the plane, but the engine sounds crescendoed as the little Cessna took to the sky.

"I don't understand," Madeline whispered, frustration cresting in her eyes as the engine noise began to fade and the gunfire stopped. "I thought the whole idea was to get me the hell out of Dodge."

"The whole idea was to liberate you and then destroy di Silva's weapons stash," Drake said, his gaze locking with hers. "Which means we're only halfway there."

CHAPTER 5

Di Silva Coffee, Bogotá, Colombia

So you're telling me that she's gone?" Hector Ortiz slammed a fist down on his desk as he listened to the man on the other end of the telephone. In his anger it was hard to hold on to his Spanish, but now wasn't the time for a slip. "How can that be possible?"

"There was some kind of commando attack. I don't know who. But they were definitely American." Caesar Vega had recently been assigned to head security at Casa de Orquídea. Clearly, however, he hadn't been up to the task.

"How many men did we lose?"

"Eleven so far. But three others are seriously wounded."

"Jesus, Vega, how many of them were there?"

The other man paused, silence stretching across the phone lines. "Three. Maybe four. At the end it was hard to tell."

"And you saw them board the plane?"

"I saw it fly away," the man confirmed. "Heading northwest."

"I didn't ask you about the fucking plane," Ortiz breathed, his voice almost a whisper. "I asked you about Madeline and the bastards who took her. Did you see them get on the plane?"

"No. It all happened too fast. But there was no one left behind. We did a thorough search."

Ortiz closed his eyes, clenching a fist. "Was it the landing strip to the west of the compound?"

"Yes. The abandoned one near the Cunida plantation."

"There's a bunker there. The resistance used it during the rebellion as a place to hide contraband. Did you search the bunker?"

"No. We didn't know it existed. But surely if we didn't know, then—"

"A stupid supposition. The Americans work with whatever side favors their politics. And for many years that meant siding with the guerillas." He released a slow breath, pushing aside his memories. "Anyway, the point is that it's possible they're still in-country."

"But why would they want to linger?" Vega asked. "They've already achieved their objective. They have Señorita Reynard. Surely there's nothing to be gained by staying in the country."

"You underestimate them. Madeline is a valuable asset, there is no question. But if they could find the weapons cache that would be icing on the proverbial cake. No?"

"I do not know what you mean by 'icing.' But if they do find the stash..." he trailed off, and Ortiz swallowed a sigh. If the Americans found the weapons, then everything he'd worked so hard to achieve would be at risk.

"Shall I call Señor di Silva?" Vega asked, sounding understandably nervous.

"No. I'll deal with di Silva." The last thing Ortiz needed was for his boss to try to take charge. The man had been no more than a figurehead for years now. Di Silva had no idea how much of his business had been shifted to the arms trade, or the exact nature of the partnerships Ortiz had orchestrated in his name. He'd made allies of many powerful men—men who would become dangerous enemies if they thought they'd been betrayed.

Damn bitch. He wasn't about to let her bring him down.

"It's better if we handle this ourselves," he told Vega, pushing away his anger. "I want you to take as many men as you can round up and head for the cache."

"If I find the *gringos*, what do you want me to do?" Vega asked.

"Kill them," Ortiz said, his voice without inflection, even though his mind was racing with possibilities. "Except for Madeline. Bring her to me. It'll be my pleasure to show her exactly what we do to traitors."

Drake paused at the top of a steep incline, leaning down to give Madeline a hand as she climbed over the last of the rocky escarpment. They'd made good time through the jungle, so far with no sign of di Silva or his men, but Madeline wasn't foolish enough to drop her guard.

The sky was beginning to lighten, which helped with visibility, but it also made them more vulnerable, particularly now that they were so close. For the last twenty minutes or so, they'd been following the path of a rushing stream cutting its way through the mountainous terrain.

"How much farther?" Drake asked, as the rest of the team made their way over the tumble of stones. She'd sketched out the rudimentary path for them in the bunker, but with every second moving danger closer, they'd headed out as soon as they were certain that di Silva's men had left the airstrip, leaving the details for later.

"We're almost there," Madeline answered, her breathing labored from the climb. The jungle was dense and the humidity made walking feel like swimming in quicksand. "It's just beyond that rise." She pointed to an outcropping of rock almost completely engulfed in the undergrowth. "The water cuts through the rocks up ahead. It forms a sort of natural gateway to the clearing hiding the ruins."

"What ruins?" Drake asked, a frown cutting across his face. His eyes were icy blue, his granite chin dark with stubble. Like the rest of the team, his clothes were dark. Black T-shirt with a flak jacket and camouflage pants. He had an edge that was hard to ignore. As if he'd crossed the line one too many times. Maybe it was all in her head, but there was something about him that called to her.

A kindred spirit.

And yet, even as she had the thought, she knew better. He and his friends might have rescued her from Casa de Orquídea, but she wasn't foolish enough to believe they truly gave a damn about what happened to her. She was merely a means to an end. And the feeling was mutual.

"I asked you a question," Drake said, his impatience pulling her thoughts back to the here and now.

"I'm sorry." She shook her head. "You asked about the ruins. I can't tell you anything specifically. But they're old. Like Machu Picchu in Peru. This area is littered with places like that. But what makes these particular ruins perfect for the cache is the location itself. The clearing is completely protected. It's surrounded by cliffs on three sides, and a huge dropoff in the back. The only entrance is the opening where the stream cuts through."

"The perfect hiding place." Drake nodded, his eyes narrowed in thought, as he studied the towering cliffs.

"Or the perfect ambush," Jason said, his gaze suspicious. Madeline wasn't quite sure what to make of Jason. More caustic than the others, he'd been located off site during the rescue, handling logistics and communications. "What's to stop her from leading us right into a trap?"

"Nothing," Tyler said, her smile at odds with her words, "except maybe the fact that she's the reason half the men at di Silva's compound are dead. Seems like a weird way to set up an ambush."

"Still, I think Jason has a point," Avery said, waving off Madeline's protest. "While I don't think that Madeline is setting us up, I wouldn't put it past di Silva. So bearing that in mind, we need to proceed with caution."

Madeline hadn't considered the idea that she was being played. She knew it couldn't be di Silva. The man wasn't astute enough to orchestrate something like that. But Ortiz was another matter. He knew she'd tried to get help. Maybe he'd lied when he'd said killing Richardson was the end. Maybe he'd had other plans.

"You think it's possible, don't you?" Nash asked.

Madeline blew out a breath. "I suppose. They knew about my meeting with Richardson. That's why I was sequestered at Casa de Orquídea. But I thought that was the end of it. Still, anything is possible." She stopped, knowing she had to be careful about how much she revealed. These people believed she was di Silva's mistress. And she needed for them to keep thinking that. It was the only way she'd avoid prison. If they knew about all the things she'd actually done...

"There's no way di Silva could have known that we were coming," Avery said. "The mission was secured. Clearance strictly limited. So, for the moment, at least, I think we've still got the element of surprise. You said there were usually two guards?"

"As far as I know." She nodded, ignoring her tumbling thoughts. "I've only actually been here twice. But I tried to make note of as much as possible. There should be one man at the opening and another near the temple. It's a kind of grotto, actually, built back into the cliffs. The stream bisects the clearing, then drops off the far edge to form a waterfall. There's a pool below it. It's quite beautiful, really."

"Pity we aren't here to sightsee," Nash observed as he lifted his field glasses.

"Yeah, well, you can't have everything." Avery shrugged with a grin. "Jason, I want you to stay here until you verify we've made it safely to di Silva's cache. Then you can proceed to the rendezvous point and handle logistics from there. Hopefully we won't need emergency evac, but after our scuffle at di Silva's compound I want to be sure we're ready for anything."

"Not a problem." Jason nodded, rotating dials on his handheld com device. "Although I'm having a little difficulty raising Hannah. I think maybe it's this damn canopy." He nodded at the thick trees towering overhead. "As soon as you're safely inside, I'll make my way to somewhere a little clearer and see if I can reach her. She ought to be able to get a satellite feed of the area."

"Just keep me informed," Avery said. "Tyler, you ready?"

"Everything I need is in here." She patted the large duffel she had thrown across her shoulder.

"Good." Avery checked his weapon and then turned to the team. "Drake, I want you and Nash to take the lead. Our first priority is to find and immobilize the guards. Tyler and I will follow, with Madeline."

"Me?" Madeline asked. "Can't I just stay here with Jason?"

"He's too damn busy to baby-sit," Drake said, irritation flashing. "Just follow orders, keep quiet, and everything will be fine."

"Not a problem," she snapped, surprised at how easily he managed to push her buttons.

Behind her Avery cleared his throat. "If everyone's ready? We move on my signal."

And with that, they were off. Nash and Drake on point, Tyler flanking Madeline, and Avery bringing up the rear. As they neared the opening in the rocks, Drake fanned to the left and Nash moved to the right, the two of them keeping low as they circled cautiously toward the gorge.

About fifteen feet from the entrance to the ruins, Drake stopped and held up his hand.

Avery touched his head, and Madeline nodded, reaching up to turn on the communication device they'd given her.

"I'm not seeing anyone," Drake said, his voice absurdly intimate as it resonated against her ear.

"Me either," Nash responded. "But that doesn't mean there's no one there. It's hard to see anything beyond the rocks." Madeline watched as they inched forward, guns at the ready, Nash crossing to the far side of the gorge as they passed between the rocky sentries.

The silence stretched out as they waited, and then her earpiece sprang to life. "We're clear," Drake said.

Madeline followed Avery and Tyler as they made their way through the gorge and into the ruins. Inside, the ground leveled out into a circular clearing paved with small beveled-edge stones. The stream cut through the middle, widening into a peaceful series of concentric ponds that formed channels leading to a central pool. The edges were adorned with carvings, forgotten images of a vanished culture.

To the left on the far side of the clearing statues stood silently along the edge of the enclosure, their faces worn and ravaged with time. On the right of the stream, jagged steps rose from the jungle floor to a platform leading to what must have once been a temple or tomb. Parts of the stone structure had collapsed, and there were vegetation-filled gaps in the masonry, but the doorway stood solid, its dark mouth gaping open. The sound of the waterfall punctuated the calls of the birds and somewhere in the distance the chittering of monkeys.

"Looks like we're definitely alone," Tyler said, as she and Madeline joined Drake in the main courtyard. Nash and Avery had moved to the far side of the stream, surveying the area for any sign of activity.

"I don't like it." Drake shook his head, his eyes narrowed as he turned to Madeline. "I thought you said there were supposed to be guards?"

"There were." She nodded, trying not to squirm under the heat of his gaze. "At least when I was here before."

"Maybe di Silva called them back to the compound,"

Nash said, as he and Avery joined them on the terraced paving. "There's no sign of anyone."

"It gives me the creeps," Tyler said, her gaze shooting around the clearing, still scanning for danger.

Drake moved away from them, kneeling beside the pool to examine one of the carvings. Without thinking, Madeline followed him. "Any idea what they are?" she asked.

"Petroglyphs," he answered, without looking up, his fingers tracing the curve of a spiral and then the scarlet-edged line of what appeared to be a crested bird. "Sacred ones, if I had to guess. Created by *jeques* or priests." He brushed off his hands and pushed to his feet, his gaze moving across the ruins. "This was definitely a ceremonial place."

"You seem to know a lot about it," she said.

"There actually isn't a lot known about the ancient peoples who inhabited this part of Colombia. But I know enough to recognize what we're seeing here."

"He knows a lot more than he's letting on," Tyler said, coming to join them. "When he's not out to save the world, Drake's a rather noted archaeologist."

"Tyler, as usual, exaggerates," he said.

"So what's with the stone over there?" Tyler asked, as Madeline tried to place this newest information in context with her earlier impressions of Drake Flynn.

Drake moved his gaze to a tilting table of rock near the steps leading to the temple. "Most likely a sacrificial altar of some kind."

"Maybe it's just as well we don't know the details." Nash frowned as he joined them. "Sounds like a bloodthirsty lot."

"And a long dead one," Avery said, bringing the

conversation back to the task at hand. "What's more important now is the fact that this place is deserted." His eyes narrowed. "Maybe I was right and di Silva's been playing us and the weapons have been moved."

"No," Madeline insisted. "They're here. I'd know if they'd been moved."

"For a mistress, you seem to have been privy to some pretty important information," Drake commented, his gaze dismissive.

"I told you I made it my business to keep my ear to the ground," she spat out, anger threatening her composure. Forcing herself to breathe, she turned to Avery. "The weapons are here. I swear it."

"Well, the only way to be certain," Nash said, cutting through the building tension, "is to check it out."

With a grunt and a nod, Drake agreed, moving up the steps. Madeline clenched her fists and then followed. Tyler and Nash followed behind her as they made their way to the top, Avery staying behind to watch the clearing. Inside the temple, they were faced with more petroglyphs and a crumbling interior. Fallen stones and broken statuary littered the floor.

"Avery was right." Tyler frowned as she shone her flashlight around the room. "There's nothing here."

"There's a hell of a lot here," Drake whispered, lost in his reverie again as he reached down to retrieve a small earthenware pot with tripod legs. "Just not the weapons."

"There's a doorway leading to another room behind there," Madeline said, aiming her flashlight at a half-tumbled-down wall. "The stash is inside."

She watched as Drake reluctantly set the pot down and then the two of them followed Tyler and Nash around the fallen wall. In front of them a doorway opened into a shadow-filled room, the carved lintel seeming ornate after the simplicity of the anteroom.

"Maybe you should go first," Tyler whispered to Drake, her voice tinged with reverence. "I feel like we're going somewhere we shouldn't."

"Whatever magic this place held, it's long gone," Drake said, sweeping across the room with his flashlight. Crates were stacked five deep, reaching almost to the ceiling, each stamped with the language of its original owner—Russian, English, Chinese.

Tyler pried open one of the closest crates, revealing a stack of machine guns nestled against packing material. A second crate revealed explosives—grenades and other incendiary devices—this one from the ex–Soviet Union.

"Jesus," Nash whispered, pulling out a digital camera, "there's enough here to fight a fucking war."

"I had no idea," Madeline breathed. "I've never actually been in here."

"Then how the hell did you know this was here?" Drake asked.

"I saw the boxes being carried in." She shrugged. "I guess they didn't think I knew what was inside." A blatant lie. Without the information she'd stolen, Ortiz wouldn't have been able to acquire half of the munitions here.

Drake eyed her for a moment, his gaze speculative, but before he could question her, Avery's voice crackled in her ear.

"Just checking in. You guys all right?"

"Yeah." Drake nodded, turning away from her to talk with his boss. "How about you? Any sign of intruders?"

"It's still quiet," Avery replied, "but I'd feel a hell of

a lot better if we could just be done with this thing. You
find the weapons?"

"They're here," Drake answered. "Just like she said.
One-stop shopping for terrorists. My guess is that
di Silva's been stockpiling for months. They're documenting it now."

"And, Tyler, you'll be able to take it out?" Avery
asked.

"Should be able to. But it's going to be a hell of a
blast. Which means it won't be much of a secret. We'll
have to be ready to move when it goes."

"You're going to blow it all up?" Madeline asked with
a frown. She'd known they were going to destroy the
weapons, but she hadn't realized that meant the ruins as
well. Her heart twisted.

"We don't have a choice." Drake's somber gaze met
hers. "There's no time to move them. And we can't risk
their being sold."

She nodded. "I just think it's sad. I mean, all of this—
it's survived for so long…" she trailed off, not sure what
else to say.

"Sometimes," he said, "we have to make sacrifices for
the greater good." The words were clipped but she could
hear the note of pain in his voice. Every action had a
price. And this one was costing Drake Flynn.

"Hey, Madeline," Tyler called, frowning down at the
duffel holding her equipment, "would you mind giving
me some more light over here?"

"Sure." Grateful for the distraction, Madeline nodded
as she grabbed a flashlight and headed over to Tyler.

"Avery?" Drake called into his mic. "You still there?"

"Roger that."

"Have you heard anything from Jason?"

"Yes," Avery replied, his voice thready in Madeline's ear. "He's in place. But he still hasn't been able to contact Hannah. Between the mountains and the trees there's just too much interference. Hopefully he'll be able to rig something. But in the meantime, we're on our own."

"Shouldn't be a problem as long as it stays quiet," Nash said as he snapped another photo.

Madeline lifted the flashlight and held it over Tyler's shoulder, illuminating the duffel's contents. Tyler sorted through her equipment, sighing as she pulled out several of the components.

"Is something wrong?" Drake asked, moving over to join them.

"Yeah," Tyler sighed, lifting her gaze to meet his. "Someone's had a go at my bag. Everything's been tampered with. The equipment's totally fucked. There's no way this stuff is going to blow anything."

CHAPTER 6

"How the hell could the explosives have been compromised?" Avery asked, as Drake joined them at the mouth of the clearing. Madeline had been uneasy ever since they'd left the airfield, but now suddenly the weight of what she was doing hit her full force.

If Ortiz caught up with her, she was a dead woman.

She glanced around the clearing, sizing up the opportunities for escape. If things went well, she'd let them get her out of the country, and then make her move. But if things went south—and it was beginning to look as if that was going to be the case—the only choice she had was to make her escape on her own.

She owed these people nothing.

"I've got no idea. Tyler says she checked everything before we left. So your guess is as good as mine. Anyway, the point is that all of it's trashed," Drake was saying. "And if Jason can't get through to Hannah, it's going to be the blind leading the blind as far as knowing if di Silva is in the area."

"I'm going to go talk with Tyler," Avery said. "Drake, you stay here with Madeline."

"But I..." she started, but Drake cut her off with a crooked smile.

"Not a problem. I'll be happy to keep watch." His gaze swept slowly from her head to her toes, leaving a trail of heat as it passed. "Over everything."

Madeline sucked in a breath, hardly noticing as Avery walked away, her eyes locked on Drake's, her stomach clenching in anticipation of something she wasn't even certain she wanted to define. He reached out, the pad of his thumb running gently below the line of the swelling beneath her eye.

"So how did you get the bruise?"

She lifted her chin, trying to ignore the spirals of pleasure emanating from his touch. "I colored outside the lines."

"Why am I not surprised," he said, his fingers moving to cup her chin, his gaze probing. She swallowed, but held her own, determined not to let him see how easily he'd gotten to her. "Still, I never would have figured you for a drug lord's mistress."

Her mind cleared, and she jerked away, anger flashing. "Sometimes there isn't a choice. You do what you have to do." And sometimes the price paid was too high. But she wasn't about to share that fact. Instead, she tilted her head, studying his face. "You don't think much of me, do you?"

"I don't know you well enough to have an opinion. But if there's one thing this job has taught me, it's that everyone is working an angle. I just haven't figured yours out yet."

"It's simple," she shrugged, reaching up to highlight her bruise. "I want out."

"Nothing's ever simple, darlin'." His smile didn't quite reach his eyes, the lines around his mouth turning harsh. "Believe me, that's a fact." He turned his back then, staring out at the rocks flanking the entrance of the clearing. The air hummed with insects and in the distance Madeline heard the plaintive cry of a macaw.

She started to retort and then shook her head. There was no sense in arguing. And besides, it was perfectly clear that he didn't want to talk. So with a pointed sigh, she made a play of exploring the upper terrace, trying to ignore the man behind her. But after about fifteen minutes, she couldn't take the silence.

"If the situation is compromised"—Madeline frowned, coming to a stop in front of him—"wouldn't it be better to cut our losses and get out of here? Maybe it's better if you just finish documenting the site and then come back and destroy it when you have the right equipment."

"We can't take that chance," Drake said, still not looking at her. "By the time we organized a second mission, di Silva would have had the opportunity to move everything. He's certainly going to be on high alert with you gone. Which means it won't be long before he sends his people back in here."

"All the more reason why we should leave," she said. "Especially when you add in the bit about sabotage. That most certainly didn't come from di Silva. Which means someone else wants this mission to fail."

"Like maybe you?" he asked as he spun around to face her.

"Are you out of your mind?" she spat, forgetting all

about keeping her cool. "Sabotaging your efforts would be like signing my own death warrant. Do I look like I want to die?"

"I told you, I don't know what to make of you." His eyes were the palest blue she'd ever seen—like ice—cold and potentially deadly. "But you're as likely a suspect as anyone else."

"You love thinking the worst of people, don't you?" she prodded, even though she knew it was dangerous to goad him. For some reason the man seemed to bring out her baser instincts.

"Maybe it's just you," he said, stepping closer, his breath warm against her cheek. "Or maybe Jason was right. Maybe this was the plan all along. Isolate us in a narrow-necked gorge with no other means of retreat."

"God, you're an ass," she said, her face hot with anger. "Figures I'd ask for help and they'd send you."

"If I'd known what a treat it was going to be to rescue you, believe me, I'd have stayed in New York." His jaw tightened, a muscle twitching in his cheek, and she was surprised by the urge to reach up and soothe him.

"If wishes were horses..." she said instead, turning away, fighting her rioting emotions.

"Look, maybe I was a little quick to judge." The words weren't exactly an apology, but it was pretty damn close.

She turned back to face him. "I didn't set you up." Something flickered in his eyes. "But you don't really believe that, do you? You're just angry, and lashing out at me is the easiest way to deal with it."

"Yeah, right." His expression shuttered, but not before she had the chance to see that she'd hit a nerve, and then he turned away, cupping a hand over his ear as he listened to someone on the other side of his earpiece. "Copy that."

"What?" Madeline asked, hands on hips. She'd left her earpiece in the temple. Damn thing hurt. "What did they say?"

"Tyler's managed to salvage some of her equipment. She's jury-rigging the explosion now."

"So what's with the face?" Madeline queried. "You look like you want to hit something. Clearly everything's not all right."

"The original plan was to make our way to the rendezvous and blow the weapons cache remotely from there. That way we'd be out of the area before di Silva had the chance to mount any kind of response."

"And now?"

"Tyler's going to have to blow it from here."

"Which means if di Silva's men are anywhere in the vicinity, he'll know where we are."

"Yes." He nodded, his expression grim. "Jason's trying to arrange an evac from here—"

"But he can't contact your people in the States to change the plans."

"Exactly. Not the best of situations." For a moment he looked almost human, but then his jaw tightened again, and his eyes flickered with resolve. "But everything's going to be fine. We'll get you out of here."

She nodded, biting back a retort. Sometimes it was better to stay silent.

"You've told us everything, right?" He rounded on her, apparently intent on resuming hostilities. "The only way out of here is through the opening in the rocks?"

She pulled her bottom lip between her teeth, considering for a second telling him the truth about the other path—the one down to the pool. But she'd learned long ago that she was better off establishing her own back door. If necessary she'd come clean later. For now, she'd keep the information to herself.

"Right," she said. "There's nothing else. Unless you can climb over those cliffs." She nodded toward the stark walls of rock on the two flanking sides of the clearing.

He stared at her a moment, his gaze intense, and she fought to keep from flinching. Then he shrugged. "We could do it if we had to. Believe me, we've climbed worse."

She had no doubt that he was telling the truth. Whatever else she might think of the man, he'd proved himself more than capable. "Did they say anything about how long—"

"Sssh." He shook his head, his voice a whisper, his attention centered on the trees at the mouth of the gap leading from the clearing to the jungle. "Stay here." He started forward, leading with his gun, and she waited a second and then followed.

"Madeline," he hissed.

"I'm coming with you," she answered, careful to keep her voice as low as his. "You might need my help. And if not, I might need yours." It was as close as she was going to get to admitting she was scared. "You took away my gun—remember?"

"Fine. Just stay quiet." His response was terse, his eyes still fixed on the trees. One of them shifted and the undergrowth beneath it quaked as something moved.

Madeline sucked in a breath, her heart hammering in her ears.

"We may have company," Drake whispered into the mic attached to his earphone.

In front of them trees moved again, this time a few feet closer. Drake lifted his gun, his eyes never moving from the undulating greenery.

Madeline moved closer to him, hating herself for her fear.

The bushes beneath the trees waved violently and then a black and silver monkey swung up into the tree, his wizened face turning toward them for a moment before he scrambled into the upper branches and disappeared into the overhanging leaves.

"Thank God," Madeline sighed, heart still pounding.

"Be still." Drake's words were barely audible and she froze, her eyes scanning the opening for some other sign of danger.

A shadow detached itself from behind a tree, holding position for a second before melting back into the jungle.

"We've definitely got hostiles," Drake said, still talking into his mic. "Only one verified so far, but I've got a bad feeling." He frowned at the trees and then motioned her backward.

To her right, Nash and Avery appeared on the terrace, both with guns at the ready as they made their way down the stone steps.

"How much longer?" Drake asked as his friends joined them in relative security behind one of the large stone statues.

"She's almost got it ready," Nash said.

"And Jason?"

"He hasn't managed to establish radio contact." Nash

shook his head. "But he says he's close. Piggybacking on a satellite, I think."

"Any idea who's out there?" Avery asked.

"None at all," Drake said. "Just saw something definitely human. I figure he was on recon. Which means he'll need to report back."

"And you're sure he saw you?" Nash frowned as he searched the perimeter for signs of life.

"Not definitely, no. But I'd say the odds are that he knows we're here."

Madeline sucked in a ragged breath and glanced surreptitiously across the courtyard at the ancient rain tree that marked the beginning of the steep steps that led to the pool below. She knew that she should tell them about it now. Give them another way out. But Drake had made it clear that their primary objective was to see the mission through, no matter the cost.

And Madeline wasn't interested in the greater good. All she cared about was escaping from Ortiz. Better to go now while she could and let Drake and his team provide unwitting cover. They'd hold off Ortiz and she'd make her break.

She'd seen Drake and his friends in action. They'd been amazing, actually. But she'd worked for Ortiz a long time. And she, more than anyone, knew what he was capable of. He was a dangerous man, especially when he was feeling threatened. And he'd made it more than clear what he'd do to her if she betrayed him.

The hard cold facts were that if Ortiz was coming, not even Drake Flynn would be able to stop him.

"Jason, any luck reaching Hannah?" Avery asked, while Drake kept an eye out for further signs of life.

"Not yet. But I think I'm almost through," Jason said, his voice sounding miles away. "If you're right and there are hostiles in the area, you're not going to be able to make it to the rendezvous."

"Roger that," Nash said, moving across the stream. "The easiest area for a chopper to land would be the terrace by the temple."

"You're going to try to land a helicopter in here?" Madeline said, moving closer to try to hear the other side of the conversation.

"It may be our only alternative," Drake responded with a shrug.

"Are you out of your mind?"

"Look, Madeline, you're just going to have to trust us." He frowned down at her. "In the meantime, I want you to head for the temple and help Tyler."

She opened her mouth to argue and then with an exasperated sigh headed up the stone stairs toward the building.

"She okay?" Avery asked.

"I have no idea. The woman's impossible to read." Impossible period, not to put too fine a point on it. "Where's the helicopter going to put down?"

"I've vetoed the terrace," Avery said. "It's too close to the weapons cache. Tyler is going to have to blow it without benefit of computer remote, which means she'll have to be right on top of it. The chopper, and anyone in it, would just be collateral damage."

"So we'll use the basin." Drake nodded toward the concentric rings of the pool. "It's not ideal, but it should be far enough from the blast to keep the helicopter safe and close enough to allow Tyler to detonate."

"Did you hear that, Jason?" Avery asked.

"Yeah," he replied. "It just might work."

"Hang on," Nash whispered into his mic. "I think we've got company." Almost before the words were out, the little clearing exploded with gunfire, shots coming from the top of the cliffs on adjacent sides of the clearing.

"Snipers," Avery called, wheeling around to return fire. "Coming from both the north and south. Fall back to the temple." He waved at the steps behind him, still holding his position. "Jason, if you're going to call Hannah, now would be the time."

Nash moved back across the stream, Drake providing covering fire.

"I've got her," Jason said. "I can't patch her through, but she's got satellite, and the situation is not good. The area's crawling with di Silva's men. They've got you boxed in."

"Well, that much we already knew," Drake said, moving to follow Nash up the steps as Avery fired at the cliffs. "How many of them?"

There was a burst of static as he stepped inside the temple.

"She says a couple of dozen," Jason replied. "Maybe eight stationed on the rocks above you. And the rest heading toward the opening to the clearing."

"No way we can pick them off," Avery said, as he dove through the open doorway, bullets ricocheting against the cobblestones outside. "As long as the snipers are up there, we're sitting ducks."

"Then I suggest you get the hell out of there," Jason's voice cut in and out, the static building.

"You'll get no argument from me," Drake said. "But we've got a job to finish first."

"Well, you're going to have to move quickly. Hannah's just confirmed the change of plans with the chopper pilot. He'll be there in less than ten."

"Sounds like we've got company," Tyler said, stepping into the room.

"And then some." Avery nodded. "You ready to go?"

"More or less," she said. "I still need to make the final connections, but that won't take too long. Better to let you all go first, though. That way you can clear the path and give me a little cover."

"What about Madeline?" Drake asked, realizing the other woman wasn't anywhere in sight.

"What about her?" Tyler frowned.

"She's supposed to be in here helping you."

"I haven't seen her since you all left the temple."

Avery swung around, eyes searching the shadowy room. "Madeline?" he called, keeping his voice pitched low but still loud enough for her to hear. No one answered.

"Damn it to hell," Drake grated out.

"Well, we know she didn't go out that way." Nash nodded toward the narrow opening to the gorge. "We'd have heard them open fire."

"Which means that she's making a run for it." Avery shifted so that he and Nash were standing on either side of the door, their positions as much for recon as for defense.

"But there's no other way out," Tyler objected.

"That we know of," Drake sighed, anger warring with frustration. He should have known better than to leave her on her own. "But if she's still in the compound, she's out there somewhere. I saw her heading up the steps. And if she'd come back down, we'd have seen her."

"All right. So what do we do?" Nash asked, as another volley of bullets shattered the stones paving the terrace. "It's not exactly the optimal time to send a search party."

"I say we leave her and get the hell out of here," Drake said.

"Not really a choice when you consider she's the mission." Tyler shrugged, leaning down to straighten out some filament wire she'd strung from the room behind her. "Or at least a major part of it."

"How long until you're ready?" Avery asked.

"A couple more minutes."

"All right." Avery nodded. "Do what you need to do."

"Then we'll have to go dark," she said, her eyes shooting to the clearing outside. "I've got the explosives rigged to give us a little more distance. Should be enough to make the helicopter. But I can't risk any kind of interference. Radio waves can be hell on electronic ignitions."

"Right then." Avery shrugged. "We've got no choice. Jason, you got everything ready from your end?"

"Yup. Chopper is here, and I'm on board. ETA eight minutes. Good luck." Drake reached up to disconnect his com, the other team members following suit.

"Drake, I want you to find our missing package." Avery nodded toward the doorway. "I doubt she's gotten too far."

"I wouldn't be too sure about that," Drake said, lifting the Glock as he dropped into a crouch beside the door. "Madeline Reynard may be a lot of things, but helpless isn't one of them."

"Regardless, I want you to find her." Avery's tone was grim.

"Roger that," Drake said.

"And then, once Tyler's ready, we'll all meet at the basin," Avery said, "and, with any luck, blow this place to smithereens."

CHAPTER 7

Madeline paused midway down the ragged steps leading from the temple to the pool below the falls. The pathway was barely discernible, ferns and vines covering the ancient stones. In places the steps had given way altogether, giant rain tree roots and other vegetation dislodging them, making the way all but impassable.

She skirted a fall of scree, rocks tumbling to the floor of the canyon below her. For a moment she froze, trying to remember the way. It had been months since she had last been here, and then she'd had the luxury of di Silva's men guiding the way.

There was no doubt in her mind that if Ortiz managed to win the day, she was as good as dead. So she'd bolted, heading for the safety of the jungle—a laughable thought when one considered there were deadly predators hidden in the lush overgrowth. Both animal and human. But the jungles of the Valle del Cauca were vast, and despite the threat, no one there was specifically targeting her. And that was at least an advantage.

All she had to do was keep low and let the two factions battle it out. Then when it was safe, she could circle back to Cali and freedom. It was an imperfect plan at best, but gunfire from the terrace above had decided her course of action.

She felt a twinge of regret, thinking of Drake. He'd risked his life for her, after all, but the hard truth was that if she wanted to stay alive—and free—this was the best course of action.

Moving gingerly down the broken path, she stopped as she reached a bromeliad-covered wax palm, the parasites beautiful even as they sucked the life from the palm's branches. Here the stones stopped, the path continuing downward into the jungle and then cutting over to the pool beneath the waterfall.

Sucking in a breath, she hurried on, gingerly picking her way over gnarled roots and lichen-covered stones. It was a difficult climb at best, and with the recent rains, parts of the path had been completely washed away. Still, it was her best chance.

The air was heavier here, under the canopy. Hot and humid. Her hair plastered itself against her skin and her clothes were quickly drenched from perspiration. Orchids clung to the sides of trees and poked their elegant faces out of crevices in the rocks. The heavy overgrowth muffled the sounds from the ruins, the silence broken only by the plaintive calls of the birds above her and the soft sound of the falls off to the south.

She picked up her pace, moving more surely now as

the ground began to level out. Just a little bit farther and she'd be out of danger, at least for the moment.

At the base of a giant saman tree the path angled sharply left, the tree's massive roots making forward progress seemingly impossible. Cursing nature in general, and Hector Ortiz in particular, she stepped back into the relative protection of the tree's umbrella-shaped canopy as she tried to figure out the best way to get past the protruding roots.

Above her, a parrot shrieked and took to the air, its feathers a brilliant gold against the green of the overhanging trees. Across the way, the ferns edging the path shimmied as another bird shot out of the tree, its startled cry sending Madeline's heart racing.

Something was coming.

Moving with an agility she hadn't known she possessed, she dove under the massive roots, squirming her way beneath them. Her shirt caught against the rough bark, pulling her backward, and with an angry growl she ripped it off, then reached upward to grasp the base of the root and pull herself through to the other side, grabbing her bag as she slid to her feet.

Behind her, a man broke through the vegetation, stepping onto the path. She recognized him. One of di Silva's house guards. He smiled, a gold tooth glistening in the light, as he raised his rifle.

Madeline stumbled as a bullet winged past her. The man's laughter echoed through the trees as she fought to regain her balance, tumbling forward as gravity won the day. She hit hard on her knees, and then pushed back to her feet, heading off the path for the cover of the jungle. Branches tore at her camisole and hair as she ran, panic taking sway over any sense of purpose or direction.

Dodging rocks and trees, she tore through the undergrowth, her breath coming in ragged gasps. She could hear him behind her, and knew that he was closing in fast. She pushed herself into a sprint, intent only on increasing the distance between them. Ahead of her, a pile of rocks loomed out of the shadowy darkness, their slick faces covered with moss and heliconias.

She slid to a stop, her heart hitting her throat as she realized she was standing on a precipice. Two hundred feet below her, the jungle floor mocked her with the promise of freedom. Frantically she searched for a way down, but she was trapped.

She whirled around as the man burst through the undergrowth, his eyes turning feral as he realized he had her cornered. Raising the gun, he circled closer, even as she edged backward, the sharp edges of the rocks digging into the back of her legs.

"Venga aquí," he called, crooking his finger.

She shook her head. No fucking way was she going anywhere with him.

He advanced a step, and she slid sideways against the rocks, looking for a way around him. "Your bosses wouldn't appreciate your threatening me this way." She bit the words out, overenunciating every syllable. Her Spanish might not be perfect, but she could see that her words had given him pause. His eyes narrowed as he considered her, and then with a tight-lipped smile he slid closer, his gaze falling to her breasts.

"They are not here," the man said, and then lunged forward, pushing her back against the rocks, his heavy body pinning her in place as his lips descended.

She screamed and fought against him, raking her

fingernails down the side of his cheek, but the pain only seemed to spur him onward as he grasped her breast, his breath putrid against her face. Blind fury raced through her as she swung her knee up into his groin.

He groaned with pain, but his grip only tightened. "You'll pay for that," he whispered, his fingers twisting her hair as he pulled her closer. "But first I will make you mine."

"I belong to no one," she spat, struggling against him as she tried to break free.

His laughter was vicious as he pushed her down to her knees.

For a moment, she pretended to acquiesce and then with a violent shove, she pushed him back, springing to her feet, intent only on escape. But he grabbed her hair and swung her around, until he had her pinned again against the rocks. "You are a fighter." He smiled. "I like that."

Panic threatened, and she pushed it away. If she was going to survive, she couldn't give in to her fear. She forced herself to smile and lick her lips, deflecting his attention, as she reached behind her, her fingers closing around a loose stone.

He leaned forward, eyes cloudy with lust, and she swung with all of her might, the rock hitting his skull with a satisfying thwack.

The man spun backward, holding his head, blood dripping into his eye. *"Puta pendeja."*

She launched herself in the direction of the jungle, but he was faster, his fingers biting into her shoulder as he slammed her back into the rocks. Her head hit the stone hard, her body jerking as pain cascaded down her neck and arms.

Her vision blurred as she tried to fight, but he was too

strong, his hands closing around her neck—tightening, cutting off the precious supply of blood to her brain. She struggled to breathe, to stay conscious—to stay alive—but somewhere inside her, she knew it was a losing battle.

"I don't think we can hold them off much longer," Nash said, ducking back inside the temple as bullets slammed the walls outside. "They're better equipped and they've got us outmanned. It's just a matter of time."

"Still no sign of Drake?" Avery asked, looking up from the relay he was helping Tyler assemble.

"No. And by my count we've only got a few minutes until the chopper's here." He glanced down at his watch with a frown.

Drake was always pushing it too far. Testing the boundaries. Thumbing his nose at death one bullet at a time. Not that Nash would have done it any differently. Truth be told, he was as much of an adrenaline junkie as his friend. Although now that he had a son, he had to admit that he was a little bit more likely to err on the side of caution. Adam deserved the chance to have a real family, and Nash was determined to give it to him.

"Well, everything's ready here," Tyler said, standing up and brushing the dust off her shirt and pants. "I'd just feel better if Drake were back."

"I know, but Nash is right." Avery frowned. "We can't afford to wait any longer. And it's not like we don't have a contingency plan. Drake knows to head for the coast if something goes wrong."

"Don't worry." Nash reached out a hand to reassure Tyler. "He'll make it back. He's just waiting for the right moment. You know how he likes to make an entrance."

They all laughed, but despite the effort the tension still stretched tight. They'd been in worse situations, but Nash still didn't like the odds. They were surrounded by di Silva's men, and someone, most probably someone they knew, had fucked with Tyler's equipment.

This wasn't the first time the team had come up against deliberate sabotage. They'd had problems on at least three of their last missions, twice with almost deadly results. And it was hard to ignore the very real possibility that it was someone with a connection to A-Tac. Nash drew the line at suspecting his friends. It was impossible to even consider the idea. But with this latest episode, he knew it was going to be hard to convince the powers that be that no one from the unit was involved.

"We'll figure it all out," Avery said. "We always do. But right now, we've got to focus on blowing the explosives and getting the hell out of here."

Nash nodded, pushing away his unsettled thoughts. Avery was right—they needed to focus on the now.

"How do you want to do this?" Avery asked, pushing to his feet to eye the area immediately outside the door.

"They've got men positioned on the cliffs to the north and south. And unfortunately, people at the mouth of the clearing. They haven't been able to get any farther than that because the opening is so narrow that even with cover from the cliffs I can still pick the bastards off. So far I've gotten five."

"But you won't have the same advantage when we move into the open," Tyler said.

"No." He shook his head, joining Avery at the mouth of the temple. "And thanks to Madeline's defection, we've lost Drake. Which leaves only the three of us."

"Not the worst of odds." Avery shrugged.

"All right," Tyler said, "give me a second to get things set, and then we're out of here."

"You're going to wait to blow it until we're aboard, right?"

"Yes," she affirmed. "With everything di Silva's got sequestered here, it's going to be one hell of a bang. I want to give the chopper a chance to take off before the reverberation from the explosion hits."

"And we want to give Drake as much time as possible to make it back."

Tyler's expression turned grim. "Once that thing blows, no one is going to make it back to the courtyard from that direction."

"Son of a bitch," Nash whispered, anger coloring his voice. "We shouldn't have let him go after her."

"Delivering Ms. Reynard to Washington is a primary directive of our mission. If it hadn't been Drake, someone else would have had to go," Avery said. "Let's just concentrate on doing what we have to do and trust that Drake will take care of himself. You ready?"

Nash nodded as Tyler began to activate her improvised incendiary devices. The danger was that some other source—a stray radio wave, a cell phone frequency, or even the reverb from gunfire—would inadvertently provide the right signal to detonate the jury-rigged bombs before the team could reach the rendezvous spot.

Nash and Avery came through the doorway firing, bullets exploding at their heels as they zigzagged across the terrace toward the steps leading down to the courtyard. Tyler followed a few seconds later, the modified detonator cradled in her hand. The three of them moved down the steps one at a time, alternating as they provided each other with covering fire.

At the bottom they huddled behind a fallen statue, Tyler checking her watch as Avery searched the sky for the helicopter and Nash watched anxiously for some sign of Drake.

"I think I hear it," Avery said. "Either way it's time for us to move." He nodded toward the entrance to the ruins where several of di Silva's men had managed to take up position behind fallen masonry. "It's going to be a hell of a gauntlet."

"You and Tyler go first; I'll cover you." Nash nodded, waving his gun toward the pool at the end of the courtyard.

Tyler nodded, and, after a silent count of three, she and Avery sprinted off toward the rendezvous. Nash popped up with his submachine gun, spraying bullets across the opening of the gorge. Two of di Silva's men went down and another retreated into the relative safety of the jungle.

Tyler and Avery dropped behind another statue, this one fully intact, providing solid cover. Avery motioned Nash forward, and with one last look behind him, Nash pushed away from the fallen statue and made his way toward them. Bullets whizzed past him as Tyler and Avery worked to keep the shooters at bay.

From somewhere behind him he heard movement, and acting purely on instinct, he swung around and fired. A man about ten feet away dropped to his knees. Moving off an extra burst of adrenaline, Nash ran forward, diving down beside Avery and Tyler. Above them, Nash could hear the sound of the chopper approaching.

"There's our ride," Avery said, nodding toward the

helicopter. "He's not going to have much time before they get a fix on him. We need to get a move on now."

Again, Avery and Tyler made the first foray out into the open, Nash keeping them covered as best he could. The gunmen above on the cliffs had increased in number, which meant that di Silva's forces were strengthening. If they were going to make it, they had to get out now.

Nash shot another look up toward the terrace, but saw no sign of Drake. It was tempting to go after him. To discard everything else but the need to find his friend. Drake would do the same for him. He was certain of it.

He popped up from behind the statue, shooting another round, already anticipating his sprint back up the steps. Then, off to his right, he heard a cry. Spinning around, he saw Tyler clutch her side.

Avery had already made it to the pool, taking refuge behind the altar stone. In front of him, Tyler fell to her knees, just as the chopper broke through the clouds above the clearing.

Moving almost as one, Nash and Avery sprang into action, the two of them meeting at Tyler's side. Nash provided covering fire as Avery scooped Tyler into his arms and the three of them moved back to the relative safety of the altar.

Tyler's breathing was labored, her chest stained dark crimson, and there was already a bluish tinge to her lips. He'd seen enough field wounds to know that if they didn't hurry there was a chance she'd bleed out.

"We've got to go. Now," Nash yelled above the sound of the helicopter hovering just out of gun range, awaiting their signal.

Tyler moaned and shook her head, her lips moving but

the resulting sound not strong enough to carry her words. Nash bent closer. "The detonator," she whispered, her voice raspy, almost inaudible. "I dropped it."

"It doesn't matter," Nash said, alarmed at the amount of blood seeping into her shirt. "Right now we just need to get you out of here."

"No dice, Nash," Tyler said, struggling against Avery. "I didn't go through all this to fail. Please. Go back for the detonator."

Nash recognized the determination in her eyes. "All right. I'll go. But you two get on the chopper and if I can't make it back, you get the hell out of here anyway."

Avery frowned, his face tight with worry. "You think you can do it?"

"I've got to try."

Avery nodded, and Nash sprinted out into the open, keeping low to avoid the bullets strafing across the cobblestones. When he reached the place that Tyler had fallen, he crouched to have a look, rolling twice to miss incoming shots, but the detonator was nowhere to be seen. As the shooting increased, he dove behind the fallen rubble of a wall, still searching the area in front for signs of Tyler's missing equipment.

Off to his right, he could just make out Avery behind the altar, flashing a small mirror, signaling the chopper above.

There were only seconds left, and Nash still couldn't see the detonator. He recreated Tyler's fall in his mind, tracing the possible trajectories for the device as she fell, his gaze following the newly directed paths. And sure enough, there it was, jammed between two of the beveled cobblestones.

As the helicopter descended, he ran out from behind the rubble, bending to snatch the detonator as he passed, but the thing refused to budge. In front of him, he could see Jason leaning out of the chopper helping Avery to get Tyler safely inside as the pilot worked to keep the helicopter steady while the copilot opened fire on di Silva's men, who were now swarming into the clearing.

Gritting his teeth, Nash felt a bullet graze his back as he bent again to try to pull the detonator out of the crevice. This time it slipped free, and on a dead run he made his way toward the chopper, stopping when he reached the safety of the altar.

Nash lifted his gaze to the helicopter, waiting as Avery climbed inside. Then, with a last look back at the terrace, Nash pressed the button on the detonator, the resulting flash of light and sound almost instantaneous.

The chopper shook ominously as the blast waves radiated across the courtyard. The bird started to move as Nash jumped for the door, Avery reaching out to pull him safely inside.

Below them the temple and its terraces burned, rocks and debris raining down, the sky black with smoke. Tyler lay in the back of the chopper, eyes closed, as Jason worked to stanch the bleeding.

Anger washed through him as Nash turned his face toward the jungle. Below him, he searched the terrace and the jungle behind it for some sign that Drake had survived. Jorge di Silva had a lot to answer for. And Nash had every intention of making sure he paid.

CHAPTER 8

Drake stopped near an ancient tree, scanning the jungle for some sign of Madeline. Thanks to the recent rains, he'd managed to follow her footsteps most of the way. But the last hundred feet or so her prints had been obscured by a second set—a man's.

Frowning, he settled his gaze on something blue caught on one of the tree's roots. Dropping to his knees, he reached under the twisted wood to free the garment. Madeline's shirt.

Just beyond the tree, the ferns and plants by the trail were trampled. With a silent curse, he made his way over the roots, stopping on the other side to examine the broken stems and leaves. The trampled trail stretched off to the south, the second set of footprints also visible in the thick mud that covered the jungle floor.

Drake drew his gun and moved forward, keeping to the deep shadows of the trees, searching the area as he moved. Somewhere ahead of him, the shrill sound of a scream broke through the silence. But it could have come from anything. A bird, a monkey—Madeline.

He started forward, then skidded to a stop as the world behind him quite literally exploded. A dark plume of smoke spiraled into the air, debris and ash raining down on the jungle. For a moment he let his gaze fix on the pillar of smoke, eyes searching the horizon for signs of a helicopter, something to prove that his friends had made it out alive.

"Is anyone there?" he asked, switching on the com unit.

Static filled his ear as the reverberations of the explosion rocked the ground beneath his feet. Above him, silhouetted against the rising sun, he could just make out what looked to be a helicopter. Releasing a breath, Drake allowed himself a second of relief. Tyler had clearly managed to blow the weapons cache. Which left only one thing undone.

Finding Madeline.

With renewed determination, Drake pushed forward through the thick undergrowth, continuing to follow the path of broken leaves and branches. Additional explosions rocked through the area as the weapons continued to burn, but his mind was focused now on what he was going to find ahead of him.

No matter how angry he was at her for running away and putting the team at risk, he knew that if di Silva got his hands on Madeline again, she probably wouldn't live to talk about it. "Avery, can you hear me?" he whispered again into his com device.

There was static and then silence. Even though he had visual proof that his friends had escaped, his gut clenched at the idea that somehow di Silva's men had managed to bring the helicopter down. If they were dead—

The thought was interrupted by another scream.

Sprinting now, he crashed through the jungle, heedless of how much noise he made, every instinct he possessed telling him he had only seconds to act. Bursting through the undergrowth into a clearing, he saw Madeline pinned against an outcropping of rock, the ragged edge of a cliff only a few feet behind her. The man who held her had his fingers around her throat.

Without stopping to think, Drake lifted the gun and shot, the bullet hitting the man's right shoulder. Gasping in surprise and pain, the man released Madeline, swinging around to face Drake as he simultaneously reached for his gun.

Madeline's eyes widened as she recognized Drake, and then with a little nod, she dropped to the ground, rolling away from the stranger. Drake took the shot as soon as Madeline was out of range, cutting to the left to miss the assailant's bullet.

The impact of Drake's shot drove the man backward, and for a moment he teetered on the edge of the cliff, gun raised as he tried to shoot again. But Drake was faster, his gun's report filling the clearing, the third bullet driving the man over the edge of the precipice.

"You all right?" he asked as he moved to the edge of the cliff.

"I'm better now," Madeline replied, scrambling to her feet to stand beside him. "Is he dead?"

"Yeah," Drake said. "Two hundred feet will do that to a guy. Not a friend of yours, I take it?"

"No. Although he was definitely interested in getting

better acquainted," she said. "Until I kneed him in the balls."

"Takes the romance out of it every time."

"I don't think romance was ever part of the equation." She shook her head, and for the first time, Drake noticed the bruises on her shoulders and neck.

"Jesus," he said, reaching out to touch the purpling skin. "I shouldn't have made light of the situation. Looks like the bastard really hurt you. Are you sure you're okay?" He felt gently along the line of her collarbone. "I don't think anything's broken."

"I'm fine," she said, pulling away, the loss of contact oddly disarming. "It's just bruises. Believe me, I've been through worse. But if you hadn't gotten here when you did..." She stopped, and then shrugged. "Seems that I owe you—again."

"It's just part of the job." He shook his head, studying her for a moment, then with a frown, he turned back to the cliff edge. "Is he one of di Silva's?"

Madeline nodded. "I recognize him from the grounds of Casa de Orquídea. Just a low-level flunky."

"With an appetite for taking what doesn't belong to him." Drake's jaw tightened as he considered what had almost happened here, surprised at the depth of his anger.

"But I'm okay," she said, laying a hand on his arm, her fingers warm against his skin. "He didn't hurt me. Not in any way that matters." She waited for a moment, and then stepped back, shading her eyes as she looked up at the smoky sky. "I heard the blast."

"Fireworks courtesy of Tyler." He nodded. "She managed to blow the cache."

"Di Silva and his people are going to want blood."

"Without a doubt," he said. "And, at the moment, we're sitting ducks. We made enough noise to draw out an army, so if your man down there has got friends, they're probably on their way. "

She frowned, scanning the surrounding jungle. "I thought you guys had an evacuation plan."

"Past tense. I'm afraid that ship has sailed—or flown, as the case may be. I saw the helicopter take off just after the weapons blew."

"So they just left us?"

"You didn't give them much choice. Your defection cost both of us our chance at an easy way out. If you'd stayed put like I told you—"

"I did what I thought was best," she said, her tone defensive. "I figured I'd be better off on my own."

"Right," he said, irritation swelling. What was it with the two of them? They couldn't seem to hold on to the peace for five fucking seconds. "That'd explain the maniac with his hands around your throat."

"I hadn't counted on di Silva's men coming from this direction," she admitted. "Anyway, I would have figured a way out."

"Look," he ground out, his hands clenching, "if I hadn't arrived when I did, you'd be dead."

She blew out a breath, shoulders slumping. "I know." The admission was almost too soft to hear, but even so, Drake understood what the words had cost her. "But they didn't have to leave us behind."

"They had no choice. I asked you if there was a second way out. If you'd told me the truth we could have planned our exit differently. And more safely. As it was, your omission put my entire team at risk. They had to blow the cache and then make a run for it straight through the line of fire."

"But you said they made it out all right."

"I said I saw the helicopter. There's no way of knowing if everyone was on it."

"So we'll go back and check." It was a noble gesture, and from what he could see sincerely offered.

"Impossible." He shook his head. "When Tyler detonated the explosion, it cut the ruins off from this part of the jungle."

"So the only person I really hurt—was me," she said with a little sigh of relief. "And you, I suppose."

"You're not listening. If you'd told us the truth, we'd have all been able to use the lower path, and Jason could have brought the helicopter to a clearing like this one instead of having to make a landing in the middle of a firefight."

"So why didn't you just leave me?" she asked, her troubled gaze lifting to his.

"Because we were charged with getting you out of here alive. And while I might not understand what the hell is so important about saving some drug lord's mistress—"

She flinched as if he'd hit her. "I'm sorry I'm not worth the sacrifice."

"I didn't mean—"

"The hell you didn't." She rounded on him. "And for your information, I have never been di Silva's mistress. His whore, maybe—if you consider what I did for his organization—but *never* his mistress." She stopped, eyes wide as she realized what she'd just said. "I didn't...I shouldn't…" Tears welled in her eyes, and Drake wasn't sure that he'd ever felt as much like an ass as he did standing here right now.

"Look, Madeline, I was totally out of line. Your relationship with di Silva and his organization isn't any of my business. You'll have to tell the suits in Washington everything, but you sure as hell don't owe me an explanation."

She blew out a breath, squaring her shoulders. "But you're the one who got stuck with the short straw."

"Come again?" He frowned.

"You had to risk your life to come and find me."

He shrugged, relieved to be back on familiar ground. "It was no big deal. I was the best suited for the situation."

"Retrieving me, you mean." She was frowning now, too, their momentary détente evidently at an end.

"If that's what you call saving your life," he snapped.

"I already said thank you."

"Actually you didn't," he said, fighting his growing irritation. "You just admitted that you needed my help."

"It's the same thing."

"Yeah, right," he said, bending down to retrieve her bag, the vinyl carryall wedged between two rocks. "Anyway, now that you're secure, the trick is going to be getting you out of the jungle alive. As I said, this place is going to be crawling with di Silva's men."

She shivered, for a moment looking almost lost and a little vulnerable. "So you knew your friends were going to leave you?"

"It seemed the most likely outcome."

"I see," she said, chewing on her lower lip. "Can't you

call them? I mean now that they've gotten away. Can't they come back to get us?"

"My com link isn't working. We're probably out of range."

"But weren't you talking to someone earlier? At di Silva's house?"

"Yes, but Jason was using a relay. And he's not here now. So that's no longer possible."

"So what do we do?" she asked.

"We get the hell out of here." He handed her the bag. "Do you know where the pathway leads?"

"To the pool by the falls. I don't think it goes anywhere beyond that."

"Which direction did the guy who attacked you come from?"

"From behind. So back toward the ruins. Maybe he came from there?"

"Not possible." Drake shook his head. "We had the entrance covered. There must be a way down from the cliffs to the north. A second path."

"So we just have to find it." She made it sound so simple.

"Yeah. And avoid di Silva's men in the process." He reached into his backpack and pulled out a laminated map, spreading it on the largest of the rocks, ignoring the smear of blood staining the granite. "We're somewhere in this vicinity," he said, pointing to an area to the south of the little river. "The ruins are here and the cliff path, assuming there is one, should branch off somewhere between the steps and the tree where you veered off-path."

She nodded. "So we backtrack and try to find it. I mean, it's our only alternative, right?"

"We could just work our way through the jungle. But I don't like the idea of doing it without benefit of a detailed map. Worst case we could follow along the water." He traced the squiggly line marking the stream. "It dumps out here, into the Rio Negro. From there we could make our way down to the coast."

"Why the coast?"

"That's where the team will be looking for us. We always have backup plans in case things go south."

"Plan B."

"Exactly." He smiled, admiring her resilience.

"But if we can get back up the cliff to the head of the ruins, there's a chance we can make it back to the road."

"Yeah," he said. "And assuming we can avoid di Silva's men, we could commandeer a vehicle and make our journey a lot quicker. There's more chance of our being detected that way, but it's a hell of a lot better than being forced to make our way through the jungle without provisions."

"Okay, so the path it is." Her response was a little too bright, but Drake appreciated the fact that she kept her misgivings to herself.

"All right, then," he said, folding the map and stuffing it into the backpack. "You stay here, and I'll do some recon. Check out the path to make sure we don't have unwanted company."

"No way," she said, crossing her arms over her chest. "I'm not staying here on my own."

"I thought that's the way you liked it." He was goading her and he knew it, but he couldn't seem to help himself.

"I do," she admitted. "Most of the time. But just at the

moment, I think I'm better off with you. At least as long as di Silva's men are out there."

"Well, don't be afraid to tell me how you really feel," he said, blowing out a breath, frustration threatening to drive him over the edge. "Okay. Fine. You win. Let's go."

CHAPTER 9

I want you to do whatever I tell you," Drake said, already regretting his decision. "No questions asked. Understood?"

"I promise." She held up two fingers, Boy Scout style, and despite himself, he smiled.

"All right then, we're agreed," he said, reaching down for the dead man's gun. "If you're coming, you might as well be armed."

She nodded, taking the gun and sliding it between the small of her back and her sweats. Then, without further discussion, she followed as he began to move back through the jungle. The air had grown ominously still. No birds chirping. No chatter from the monkeys. Just the faraway sound of the falls, and the quiet drone of insects in the undergrowth.

He motioned for her to stay behind him, and they made their way back to the path without incident. Pulling her down behind the roots of the old gnarled tree, he grabbed his field glasses and swung them in a circular pattern, checking the area for signs of life.

"Everything seems quiet," Madeline whispered.

"Too quiet," he said, his senses on high alert. "But I still think we're better off trying to find the path your attacker used."

She nodded.

"If I give you a boost, do you think you can make it over the roots?" he asked.

"Beats going under them," she replied, her eyes dropping to the place where she'd crawled through.

His hands circled her waist and for a moment, he froze, his mind trotting out less-than-virtuous thoughts as his hands dropped down to cup the sweet curve of her ass. Her muscles tightened beneath his fingers, her sharp intake of breath indicating that he wasn't alone in his thoughts. Had the situation been different he might have been tempted to pull her back into his arms, to satisfy the sharp hunger racing through him.

But even as he had the thought he recognized the sheer stupidity of it. Angry at himself for his own weakness, he shoved her upward, ignoring her gasp of surprise.

"Use the branches above you," he commanded, the words sounding sharper than he'd intended.

There was a moment's hesitation, and then she grabbed a low-lying branch, using it to pull herself up and over the twisted roots. On the other side, neither of them spoke, Drake taking the lead as they set off up the trail. There was no excuse for his reaction other than that it had been purely physical. A man reacting to a woman. *Any woman.*

He shook his head, forcing himself to focus on his surroundings. The jungle on either side was still abnormally quiet, probably a reaction to fallout from the explosion. In front of them they could now make out the dancing flames of the still-burning ruins, the remaining temple stones stark white against the inky backdrop of the smoke-filled air.

"It's totally destroyed," Madeline whispered, coming to a halt as they stared up at the ruins.

"Tyler didn't have a choice. The only way she could rig it to work was to use the stash itself as part of the explosion. What started out as a surgical strike ended up as full-out obliteration."

"I'm sorry," she said, her voice soft. "I know you didn't want to see it demolished."

She was right. There was a part of him that couldn't abide the destruction. But there was another part that understood the necessity of the sacrifice. "Collateral damage," he said, his gaze still locked on the ruins.

"It's like you said, it's for the greater good."

"That's what they want us to believe, anyway." He hated the edge of cynicism in his voice, but years of walking in the shadows, of straddling the line between right and wrong, had left him with little to believe in.

"Will the fire spread to the jungle?" she asked, pulling him out of his bitter reverie.

"Hopefully not. This kind of explosion tends to burn hot and fast, which means it won't last long. And between the cliffs, the water, and all the stonework, it's a pretty insulated situation."

"I'm glad it's limited to the ruins." She shot a look at the canopy above her. "After all my time in Colombia, I've sort of fallen in love with the rainforest. I'd hate to think I'd played a part in its destruction."

"Come on," he said, gruffly. "We need to keep moving."

She nodded. The ground had begun to slope upward, the sound of the falls increasing as they drew closer to the stone steps that led up into the ruins.

"I don't see anything that would indicate another path," she said as they continued the upward climb.

"The guy's got to have come from somewhere." Drake paused in front of a tree stump covered with moss and bromeliads, his eyes coming to rest on a half-buried stone off to his right. "Hang on." He knelt, fingering the broken trunk of a young wax palm directly behind the stone. "There's something beyond this tree." Stepping around it, he pushed aside a clump of ferns to reveal more half-buried cobblestones.

"You've found it," Madeline said, her voice rising with excitement.

Drake held his finger to his lips, shaking his head, and she immediately clamped her hand over her mouth, her eyes apologetic.

He waited for a moment, listening; then, satisfied that they were still alone, he motioned her forward, and together they began to work their way up the second path. The ground here was broken by outcroppings of rocks and gnarled tree roots, the ancient stones themselves at times blocking the way. Above them the soft patter of rain hit against the leaves of the trees, the canopy protecting them from the worst of it.

They'd gone about a hundred yards when the jungle suddenly opened out onto a clearing of some kind. Drake pulled Madeline down into the shelter of a small stand of trees and grabbed his field glasses. Just across the clearing he could see the path angle sharply upward, the beveled stones jutting out of the craggy cliff like the plastic handholds on a modern climbing wall.

But of even more concern was the group of men at the base of the cliff. There were fifteen or so, all of them armed, the front-runners already moving toward them as they crossed the clearing.

"We've got to hide," he whispered, shoving the glasses back into his pack.

"Why," she asked. "What did you see?"

"Di Silva's men. More than I can possibly take out. And they're moving our way."

"Can't we just cut around them somehow?"

"Not possible," he said, urging her upward as he drew his gun. "The only way out is up." He motioned toward the cliff. "And we'd be doing it in plain sight of them. We might as well paint targets on our backs."

He grabbed her by the arm, yanking her into the heavy undergrowth, then pulled her down behind the moisture-slick face of a boulder, motioning her to stay silent. Although they couldn't see the path clearly from this vantage point, they could hear the men as they approached.

"This is *loco*," a man said. "There's nobody else out here. The *gringos* escaped on the helicopter."

"We have to make certain," a second man said. "If we miss someone, the boss will have our heads."

"Who's to know?" the other man queried.

"*Silencio,*" a third man whispered. "Something's moving over there."

There was a moment's silence and then a twig or branch broke somewhere off to their right, the noise seeming overly loud. Drake shifted so that he could better see the path. Di Silva's men were already moving into the jungle, weapons drawn, as they searched for the source of the noise.

Again, the bushes rustled, and a white-tailed deer stepped into view, its head raised in alarm.

"Over there," di Silva's man called. "It's coming from over there."

Three men burst through the bushes, and the deer, startled, ran directly toward Drake and Madeline, pausing at the rock, and then veering away to disappear into the undergrowth.

"It was only a deer," one of the men said, lowering his weapon.

Drake could feel Madeline tense beside him. He covered her hand with his, signaling her to be calm. Two more seconds and they'd be gone.

"*Sí,*" the second one said, shrugging. "I told you it was nothing to worry about. We should be getting back."

"*Momento,*" the third man said. "I need to take a leak."

"And what?" the second man laughed. "You need us to hold your hand?"

Still laughing, the two men turned and left their friend to his business. But before he had the chance, the deer reappeared, running past the startled man, who jumped back, spinning around in surprise as he moved into their line of sight. His gaze locked on Madeline as he aimed his gun, but Drake was faster, firing before di Silva's man had time to pull the trigger. The shot reverberated through the jungle.

"Oh, my God," Madeline breathed, the words hardly more than a whisper.

"Come on," Drake urged, pulling her to her feet. "Focus. We've got to move. Now."

Together they sprinted through the undergrowth, pushing through the heavy leaves and vines, running back the way they'd come. Behind them, the sound of di Silva's men carried across the whispering silence of the jungle.

Just ahead, the undergrowth thinned as it opened out onto the main pathway. Drake pulled Madeline down. "Stay here," he whispered. "They won't see you, and I need to make sure there's no one coming from the other direction."

She opened her mouth to argue, but he shook his head, and she nodded once, her expression resigned. Leading with his gun, he stepped out onto the pathway, searching both directions for di Silva's men. When he was certain the way was clear, he motioned for Madeline to join him and they started back down the pathway, moving as quickly as they dared.

As they came up on the leftward turn, Madeline suddenly stopped, grabbing his arm and pulling him into the shadows of the trees.

"Down there," she said, motioning toward the curve. "I think there's someone coming."

Drake pulled out the binoculars and focused on the bend, the glasses revealing a second group of men, also armed, heading their way.

"Damn it," he whispered, more to himself than to Madeline. "We're caught between the two groups. We'll have to make a break for it."

"No." Madeline shook her head. "There's another way. We can head for the stream. Use the water to cover our tracks. You said it leads to a river."

"Won't work," he said. "They'll be able to track us to the stream, which means they'll know what we're up to."

"Not if we don't leave a trail." She glanced down at the ground beneath their feet. "Look, the rain's washed away most of our footsteps from earlier. So if we disappear here, they'll have no idea where we've gone."

"And how do you suggest we do that?" he asked, the sound of di Silva's men growing closer.

"We go up," she said. "That way there are no tracks and then when we're sure we're clear, we can make our way to the stream."

"And how do you propose we do that?"

"The saman trees." She nodded toward a grove of ancient rain trees stretching down toward the distant stream. "If we use the roots, it'll give us a buffer between the pathway and any signs we've left behind us in the jungle." She leaped across the path onto a large, twisted root. "Come on, it's easy."

The noise level grew as the two groups drew closer. Drake nodded, already following Madeline as she crossed the thick roots of the tree, the ancient wood providing crude but workable stepping stones. Leaping from root to root and tree to tree, they managed to traverse the jungle for fifty yards or so before the enormous rain trees gave way to smaller mata ratons and fledgling wax palms.

Drake stopped to listen. In the distance, muffled by the trees, he could still hear di Silva's men, but it was obvious that they hadn't yet picked up their trail. And the vegetation in this part of the jungle was too dense for them to be able to see them, even with scopes or field glasses.

"It might just have worked," he said, as he dropped down beside Madeline onto the jungle floor. "How the hell did you know to do that?"

"I grew up on a bayou. And the cypress trees that

lined our swamp weren't that different from samans. My sister and I used to make a game of it." Something dark passed across her face, but before he could comment, she'd already moved off in the direction of the water. "If memory serves, it should be just up ahead."

They worked their way forward another ten yards or so, the vegetation so thick here that every step was an effort, the humidity bearing down on them as if it were corporeal.

"It can't be much farther," she said, her breathing labored as she ducked under a low-hanging tree branch. "I can hear the falls."

"Which might not be a good thing," Drake responded, as he used his knife to cut away the tenacious stems of some kind of overgrown thorn bush.

"What do you mean?" she asked, her brows drawing together in concern.

"Probably nothing," he was quick to assure. "It's just that we don't want to come out too close to the ruins."

"It shouldn't matter." She shook her head. "As long as we can get to the water."

He nodded, not willing to argue further. Besides, wherever they wound up, it was a far sight better than being caught by di Silva's men. With a last slice, he cleared away the thorns to push through the overgrowth, Madeline following on his heels.

On the other side, the jungle gave way suddenly to a rock-strewn escarpment ending in a sheer cliff wall rising out of the jungle. Orchids and heliconias clung to its crevices, while some kind of vine stretched upward, its red-veined leaves disappearing into the overhanging trees. In the center, a thin stream of water splashed down from somewhere far above them.

"It's a dead-end," Madeline said, sinking down onto a boulder.

"No." Drake shook his head. "There has to be a way out. Can't you hear the falls? They've got to be just beyond the cliff wall." He pointed toward the right, as he walked over for a closer look.

"Well, even if you're correct," she said, "we can't very well move through solid rock."

"Who said it's solid? There's an opening here." He smiled at her and then stepped into what amounted to the narrow mouth of a cave, surprised to find that there was dappled light at the far end of what appeared to be a natural tunnel.

"What is this place?" Madeline asked, coming to stand beside him.

"Hopefully a way out." They moved underneath the rocks, stopping for a moment to accustom themselves to the gloom.

The passageway was about three feet wide and mostly tall enough for them to pass without bending over. At the end it opened into a wider cavern with three solid walls and the sheer curtain of the waterfall forming the fourth.

"I was right, it is a dead-end," Madeline sighed, reaching out a hand to cut through the water. "We'll have to go back and figure out another way down."

"There's no time," Drake said. "By now there's a good chance they'll have seen through our ruse with the saman trees, and if they've discovered our tracks they'll have figured out which way we're headed."

"So what do you want to do?" She frowned up at him, hands on her hips. "Surrender?"

"Not likely." He shook his head, resisting the urge to smile.

There was little sign of the cultivated woman he'd first encountered at di Silva's hacienda. Her hair was matted with leaves and twigs, her camisole stained with dirt and mud. Her shiner had turned a lovely shade of green, and the sweats sported holes in both knees. Any other woman would have been whining and complaining, begging him to get them out of here. But Madeline Reynard was giving him attitude. And quite surprisingly, he found that he liked it.

"All right," she said, lifting her hands with impatience. "So what's the plan?"

Drake looked back down the tunnel, satisfied to see that it was still empty. "How deep is the pool below the falls?"

She shook her head, clearly surprised at the question. "I don't know. I only swam in it the one time. Nine, maybe ten feet? It's deeper near the falls and then starts getting shallower as the pool narrows and becomes the stream again."

"And the current?"

"It's really fast. Almost too fast to swim there. The stream is wider and deeper here than it is above in the ruins. More of a river. Why?"

"Because I think it's our best way out," he said, watching the confusion play across her face. "I assume you're a good swimmer?"

"Of course." She frowned. "I told you, I grew up on a bayou. But I don't see what the hell that has to do with—" She cut herself off, understanding dawning. "You've got to be kidding. You want us to jump?"

"Yeah, and then ride the stream. It'll be like tubing."

"Only without the inner tube." She glanced doubtfully at the sheet of falling water. "You're out of your mind."

"Maybe," he acknowledged. "But I still think it's our best option. All we have to do is jump, push off the bottom, and let the water carry us forward."

"Right into a school of piranhas or crocodiles."

"Crocs don't school, and even if they did you won't find them up this high. Piranhas either. The worst that can happen is that you'll bang into some of the rocks."

"And drown."

"I won't let you."

Madeline searched his face and for a moment there was nothing in the world that mattered but the two of them—and her believing in him.

Then she shook her head and walked to the edge of the ledge. "I must be crazy to even be considering this."

"Well, if you'd rather, we can always go back the way we came..." he trailed off, knowing that she wouldn't be able to resist the gauntlet.

"Fine," she sighed. "We'll jump."

CHAPTER 10

U.S. Military Hospital, Eloy Afaro Air Base,
Marto, Ecuador

How're you feeling?" Nash asked as he settled in the
chair beside Tyler's hospital bed.

"Like someone shot me." She smiled. "But since I'm
lying here talking to you, I'm figuring the prognosis is
good."

"The doctors worked their magic," he said, returning the
smile. It had been touch and go, as the bullet had lodged
perilously close to her aorta, but after long hours in sur-
gery, the doctors said she'd make a full recovery.

"So where are we?" she asked.

"Ecuador. It was our closest base. We couldn't risk
landing in Colombia, since technically, we weren't even
supposed to be in-country. And for the same reason, we
couldn't risk using a civilian facility."

"Hey, I've got no complaints. And no memory of what
happened after I got shot. Everything's a big blur. Did
you manage to detonate the explosion?"

"Yeah, went off like a charm. Created some pretty amazing fireworks, too."

"Between my jury-rigging the explosives and the amount of ordnance di Silva had stockpiled, I'm not surprised. I'm guessing the explosions were visible for miles. So what's the fallout? Have you talked to Hannah?"

"So far the chatter has been minimal, but she said it's still too soon. Overall, though, she seems to think that it'll be downplayed. The ruins were fairly remote, and di Silva isn't going to want to draw any more attention than necessary to what happened. And since his network in Colombia is pretty extensive, I'm guessing that downplaying the explosion won't be that much of an effort."

"So where's everyone else?" she asked.

"Jason's on his way back to Sunderland to debrief the rest of the team. And Avery's in an office down the hall. Conference call with the brass."

"Glad it's him and not me."

"No kidding. After everything that went wrong out there, I wouldn't want to be in his shoes," Nash agreed.

"At least we destroyed the weapons stash."

"Yeah, but we lost Madeline Reynard."

"So what about Drake?" she asked, wincing as she shifted positions in the hospital bed. "Did you guys manage to get him out?"

"No." Nash shook his head. "I kept thinking he'd show up. But once we blew the stash there wasn't much chance he'd make it back. And it was probably just as well; the evac was dicey enough as it was."

"Thanks to me," Tyler sighed.

"It's not like you shot yourself." Nash's smile was gentle.

"So do you think something happened to Drake?"

"Obviously there's no way to know for sure." He shook his head, sobering. "But he's resourceful."

"But you haven't heard anything." She frowned. "I thought maybe he'd call in after the explosion. When it was safe to communicate again."

"I had the same hope. There was some static—Jason said it could have been Drake, but it could also have been nothing. Anyway, my guess is that if he did try, the mountains and the jungle would have interfered with reception. Anyway, now even if Drake does manage to find a clear spot, with us gone, he's out of range."

"And I guess there's a very real possibility that even if he figured out a way to try to contact us, he couldn't. I mean, di Silva's men were crawling all over the place. We can't ignore the possibility that he's been captured."

"Hannah thinks she'd have heard something. And so far nada. So I'm betting Drake's moving cross-country even as we speak."

"Through some really rugged terrain. That part of the Andes is pretty remote. Some of it hasn't even been accurately mapped."

"He knows what he's doing. We've just got to keep the faith."

"And Madeline Reynard?" she asked. "You think he found her?"

"My money's on Drake. If anyone can run her to ground, he can. Although he might be better off without her. Especially trying to make it through the jungle. Besides, none of this would have happened if she hadn't bolted. Hell, this whole fiasco's on her head."

"Well, regardless of who's at fault, we can't just leave

them out there," she said, reaching for the glass of water on her bedside table. "Maybe we can call on someone in-country. Someone who knows the area."

"No can do," Avery said, striding into the room, his frown fierce. "Langley wants the whole thing to stay off the books. As far as anyone in Colombia is concerned we were never there."

"But we can't just leave him," Tyler protested.

"I didn't say we were going to." Avery shook his head. "I just said we can't call in outside help. In fact, I'd prefer that whatever we decide to do, it doesn't go beyond this room."

"I'm not sure I'm following." Nash frowned. "What about the rest of the team?"

"For the moment, I want to leave them out of it, at least beyond generalities. Look, you two are my next in command. You've both been with me since the beginning and I know I can trust you."

"And you don't think you can trust the rest of the team?" Tyler asked, shooting a questioning look in Nash's direction.

"I'm not saying that either." Avery held up his hands. "I'm just saying that something doesn't feel right here. And until we figure out what it is, I think the fewer people in on it the better."

"You're talking about the sabotage," Nash said.

"In part. It's definitely something we need to get to the bottom of."

"But you just said you didn't think it was one of us?" Tyler shook her head, her eyes narrowing in disbelief.

"For the moment, no. I don't. But there are people at Langley who think it's possible."

"I wasn't aware anyone else knew about our incidents." Nash studied his boss's face, trying to figure out what the hell was going on.

"There were questions about the last few missions. Mistakes made. I had to give them an explanation."

"And so now they're pointing fingers. You'd think after what happened with Annie they'd be more cautious about that sort of thing." Homeland Security had been the leading voice in suggesting that Annie was a traitor, but the CIA hadn't been far behind. Hell, for a little while even he'd believed the worst. In the end, however, they'd all been proven wrong. And Nash, at least, had learned a lesson.

"Look, they're just trying to make sense of what happened. And in light of Drake's disappearance—along with Madeline's..." he trailed off.

"The heat's on." Nash blew out a breath.

"The suits at Langley are definitely on high alert. What should have been a simple operation has turned into a nightmare scenario. So they're circling the wagons. And we've got to be careful not to get caught in the fallout. This thing with Madeline is bigger than they're letting on. There's something more here than them just wanting to question the mistress of Jorge di Silva."

"So what the hell is it they want with her?" Nash asked.

"I don't know. And it's going to take a little digging to find out. In the meantime, we've got to find Drake and keep him out of sight until we can figure out what's what. And we have to do it on the QT."

"None of this makes any sense at all to me," Tyler said. "Drake aside. We've got three definite instances of sabotage and a couple more questionable incidents. And, at least in the three confirmed cases, access to the equipment in question was limited to members of the team."

"And certain ancillary staff," Avery added. "Everything was shipped. Through secure channels of course, but there were certainly people outside the team that handled the items involved."

"True. But at least in my case," Tyler said, "I checked the equipment before we left."

"In detail?" Avery queried.

"Absolutely. And everything was fine."

"And in Colombia?"

"I only did a cursory examination, but if something was wrong I would have seen it."

"Sometimes we see what we expect to see." Nash shrugged.

"And you didn't check the equipment again?" Avery asked.

She shook her head. "It never occurred to me that I'd need to."

"Which is no doubt what someone was counting on. The truth is that there·were opportunities for someone with the proper motivation to access and manipulate our equipment."

"All of them CIA or military personnel." Nash shook his head. "And all of them with proper clearance."

"People can be bought," Tyler said. "And Avery's right, there are always ancillary personnel involved in a mission."

"But there's not much crossover. At least when we're in the field," Nash said, turning the idea over in his mind. "What about the earlier incidents?"

"Same situation, really. There are always people who

handle our munitions, whether we're in our country or on foreign soil." Tyler shrugged.

"So how do we narrow it down?"

"When I get back to New York, I'll start seeing what I can dig up," Avery said. "And maybe Tyler can help once she's back on her feet. We can cross-check personnel lists and see if anything pops. In addition, I want to see what I can find out about Madeline Reynard. There's got to be some connection to the CIA that supersedes her relationship with di Silva."

"And while you guys are playing supersleuth, what am I doing?" Nash asked.

"When the timing is right, I want you to go to Puerto Remo. That's where Drake will surface if he makes it through."

"With Madeline, if he found her," Tyler said, her worried gaze encompassing the two of them. "And I'd lay odds that he has."

"Look, at this point all of this is just conjecture," Avery sighed. "I mean, as far as I know, no one outside the immediate team is even aware that he'll be heading to the coast. But if the unit has truly been compromised it's possible that the information's been leaked."

"Meaning di Silva could know."

"We may have bigger problems than di Silva," Avery said. "Look, if I'm right and there's something big connected with the retrieval of Madeline Reynard, then someone out there may believe that the easy solution is to take her out. And if whoever's involved is connected to Langley, then they may very well be looking for a scapegoat to cover their actions."

"Drake."

"Exactly."

"Well, if someone is gunning for Drake and/or Madeline, isn't Nash going to need someone to back him up?" Tyler protested, shooting Nash an apologetic look. "I mean, not that you're not capable, but we have no idea what you could be walking into."

"I appreciate the thought." Nash smiled at her. "But I can handle it. Besides, who could go? Avery already said that we need to keep this limited to the three of us. You're in no shape to go anywhere, and Avery's disappearance at this point would certainly bring up questions."

"Well, so will yours," Tyler said, a stubborn note in her voice. "You can't go out there on your own. Come on, Avery, you know I'm right."

"He won't be going anywhere on his own," Avery said. "And he won't be missed. It's all been arranged."

"But I don't..." Nash began.

"You've been complaining about not having time for a honeymoon," Avery said, with a slow smile. "And the tropics are a perfect place for young couples in love."

"Annie," Nash said, his heart lifting at the sound of his wife's name.

"Yes." Avery nodded. "I know she hasn't wanted to get back into the game. But she understands the importance of our finding Drake."

"I'm not surprised she agreed to help," Nash said, feeling a surge of pride. "You'll watch out for Adam?" As much as he needed to help his friend, he also needed to make certain his son was protected.

"No worries," Avery said. "We'll all keep an eye out."

"Then it's perfect," Nash said, with a grin. "I mean, hell, what good is a honeymoon without a little espionage?"

*   *   *

Café Amarillo, Bogotá, Colombia

"Thanks for coming so quickly," Hector Ortiz said as he leaned back to allow the waiter to refill his coffee cup. "I apologize for getting you involved in so difficult a situation. I thought I had it handled." He drew in a breath, waiting for the man to answer.

Michael Brecht was a major player in the arms industry. The owner of Mossler-Brecht, one of Germany's largest producers of munitions, he held the respect of people on both sides of the law. It was Brecht who had first approached Ortiz about the prospect of his taking control of di Silva's enterprises and expanding the old man's business into the illegal arms trade. And it was Brecht who had introduced him to prominent men within the market.

Which meant the older man had as much to lose as Ortiz if Madeline Reynard was allowed to talk.

"Clearly you hadn't counted on CIA involvement," Brecht said, eyes narrowed as he watched Ortiz from across the table.

"And you're sure they're the ones who freed Madeline?" He frowned, tearing the corner off a packet of sugar.

"Positive," the other man answered. "A black ops group called A-Tac. I assume you're familiar with them?"

"I've heard of them. Never come up against them, though." He shook his head, thinking that it hadn't been out of the realm of possibility, but thankfully their direct involvement wasn't a threat—except as it related to Madeline.

"As you know, I've developed an extensive network

of contacts," Brecht continued. "On both sides of the law. And one recent acquisition is someone with intimate knowledge of A-Tac and their movements."

"So you know where they are now?" The damned operatives had managed to blow up the munitions stash and escape by helicopter. And despite Ortiz's best efforts, he'd been unable to obtain information on their whereabouts.

"Yes," Brecht said, his gaze still speculative. "Most of the team is currently recovering at a military hospital in Ecuador. It seems despite their ultimate failure, your men managed to do some damage."

"And Madeline?" Ortiz asked. "Is she there as well?"

"No," the older man said. "She was left behind. And is most likely making her way to the coast with a man called Drake Flynn."

"Did you say Flynn?" Ortiz asked, the words out before he could stop them, his surprise momentarily getting the better of him.

"Yes. Do you know him?"

"Only by reputation." It was a partial truth. He hadn't ever met the man, but he'd certainly heard all about him—ad nauseam. "I'm afraid he'll be a formidable opponent. Although his route is probably predictable. I'm guessing he'll head for one of the smaller coastal villages."

"I'm one step ahead of you on that," Brecht said, taking a slow sip of his tea. "According to my sources, the most likely place for them to surface is Puerto Remo. It's at the mouth of Rio Negro, which isn't far from your weapons cache. So all they'd have to do is make it downriver."

"Makes sense." Ortiz nodded. "I'll get my men on it immediately."

"No need for that. I've already hired experts. Men I've worked with before. Of course I did it in di Silva's name. You realize that if we can't stop this, then di Silva is going to have to take the fall."

"And me?" Ortiz asked hesitantly, afraid that Brecht was going to cast him out for his mistakes.

"You're too valuable to dispose of. Although, make no mistake, should it become necessary, I've no problem at all letting you take the fall as well. I knew it was a risk when I took you on. But I've always believed your talents exceed your liabilities."

"And these men you've hired," Ortiz asked, "they'll find Flynn and the girl?"

"I learned long ago that there's no such thing as a certainty. There are always variables that one can't possibly predict. But yes, I'm confident that my men will handle the situation. They're both single-minded and rather competitive. And to take advantage of that, I've made it a competition. First man to find and eliminate the two of them—wins."

"And the fallout from the destruction at the ruins? How do you want me to handle that? A hell of a lot of the weapons had been sold and were prepped for shipping. I've already had calls."

"Again, worst case, the blame will have to be shifted to di Silva. But in the meantime, you have the secondary stash, and whatever you can't make good on, I can probably procure replacements."

"Why are you doing this for me?" Ortiz asked, shaking his head as he considered the enormity of Brecht's involvement. "Basically, I totally fucked up."

"Yes, you did. But as I explained to you when I first

recruited you, we're in the process of building a consortium, a group of like-minded individuals who want to make certain that the world's confrontations continue to escalate."

"So that you can make money."

"It's the entrepreneurial way." Brecht shrugged. "Although there are certain political gains as well. Anyway, I've worked hard to integrate you into my network, so it's in my best interest to make certain that the girl isn't allowed to talk. Particularly to the Americans. That doesn't change the fact, however, that you shouldn't have put yourself in this position in the first place."

"But she's done excellent work. Without her, we'd never have had access to the information we needed. And I thought holding her sister hostage would keep Madeline in line."

"Except that the sister died."

"Yes. But it was strictly a fluke that Madeline found out."

"You should have killed her then," Brecht said, returning his cup to the saucer, his gaze inscrutable. "You're not going soft on me, are you?"

"No," Ortiz denied. "Just overconfident. I really did believe I had it handled. And she was truly an asset when I had her under control."

Brecht paused for a moment, still studying Ortiz. "There isn't anything else, is there? Something she knows that's more dangerous than the workings of your day-to-day operations?"

"Of course not," Ortiz said, his stomach knotting as he considered the real truth. If Madeline Reynard was allowed to reach Langley, there was a hell of a lot more at stake than his illegal activities on behalf of di Silva and Brecht.

"You're certain?" Brecht queried.

"Yes. Absolutely." Ortiz nodded. "But there's no question it will be better for all of us when Madeline Reynard is dead."

CHAPTER 11

The water was cold, and deeper than Madeline remembered, the current tugging her along with anxious fingers, the weight of her clothes sucking her downward. She had no idea how far she'd come. It could have been inches or feet; there was no way to know for sure.

The only thing for certain was that the river wasn't going to let her go. The farther they traveled the more it held on to her, as if she were some kind of water sprite infrangibly bound to the rushing river. She struggled upward to break the surface for much-needed air, but the water refused to let her go, pulling her deeper instead, the stream agitated now, pebbles and stones abrading her skin.

She struggled against the current, her lungs contracting as she fought against the urge to breathe. The water spun her around as the current picked up speed, and she lost all sense of direction, up and down ceasing to have meaning. Panic threatened as the desperate need for air overcame everything else.

Her heartbeat echoed in her ears, amplified by the water around her. And finally, she gave in to the urge, opening her mouth even as the river pulled her deeper. Water flooded her lungs as a preternatural calm descended, her mind accepting the inevitable.

This was what it felt like to drown.

It was almost laughable—after everything she'd survived, for it to end like this.

She closed her eyes, but the river wasn't through with her yet, pushing her back to the surface. Coughing and sputtering, she felt a hand close around her arm.

Drake.

Her mind was fuzzy, moving in slow motion, but she felt him yank her upward, his other arm grasping her around the waist as he hauled her out of the water and onto the muddy bank. She could feel his hands as he pressed on her chest, the motion forcing the water up and out of her lungs.

She gasped once, and then again, drinking in the air, oxygen filtering through her blood, relief singing through her body.

"Are you okay?" Drake asked as he helped her to sit up.

"Yeah, I think so," she said, still coughing up dribbles of water. "Next time we decide on a river adventure I vote for inner tubes and ice chests full of beer."

"Sounds like a plan," he said, running his hands over her legs and arms, checking for injury. "I'll bring the beer. But first we've got to make it to the coast. Our adventure, as you so aptly called it, sped things along nicely, but best I can tell we've still got a ways to go until we reach the Rio Negro. You think you can walk?"

"I can give it a try," she said, accepting his hand as he pulled her to her feet. Her legs wobbled for a moment, the world going wonky.

"Hang on," Drake said, his voice calming. "I've got you."

"I'm okay," she said, sucking in a breath and finding her balance. "I can make it on my own."

"You're sure?" He frowned, pale blue eyes studying her.

"Yes." She squared her shoulders. No way was she falling apart now. She'd come too damn far. "I'm positive."

"Good." He nodded his approval, and she grimaced at the little surge of joy that accompanied his praise. He'd saved her life now—twice—but that didn't mean there was anything to be gained in getting attached to the man.

"How far have we come?"

"I'm not certain. But we were in the water almost fifteen minutes, and the water's moving fast this time of year, so it's possible we're about a mile or more downstream."

"I don't think I'd have made it much farther," she said, looking down at her feet. "Thanks for pulling me out when you did."

"I told you I wouldn't let you drown."

"Although you did let it go to the absolute last possible moment." The words came out of their own accord, and she was immediately ashamed of them, but Drake just laughed.

"Any sign of di Silva's men?" she asked, lifting her chin as her gaze met his.

"No. But I expect it'll take them a little time to figure out what happened. Although they will figure it out. Which is why, if you're up to it, we really should get a move on."

"I told you I'm fine." Her jaw tightened on the words.

"Well, humor me and have a little water," he said, handing her a canteen.

"Where did you get that?" She eyed the metal canister dubiously.

"Standard issue. I had it in my backpack. Filled it with water from the stream at the ruins when I started after you."

"Thanks, but no thanks." She held up a hand, shaking her head. "I think I've already had more river water than I can handle in one day."

"Believe it or not, you need the hydration."

"What about contamination? Aren't we supposed to avoid drinking the water? Parasites or worms or something?"

"There's always a concern with water in the tropics. But I've got purification tablets. So we're good to go. Now drink."

She took a sip and then gulped some more, surprised to find that she actually was thirsty.

"So what else have you got in that bag of yours?" she asked, handing him back the canteen.

"Not nearly as much as I'd like, but there's enough to keep us alive for the next couple of days, if we're lucky."

"I'm guessing you're not talking a four-star hotel with room service."

"Sadly, no. But I do have chocolate. Although you'll

have to wait until we're farther downriver to get your share."

"The proverbial carrot." She smiled. "I'll let you lead the way." She waved a hand toward the rushing river as he slipped the canteen into his backpack, the movement jostling Madeline's memory.

"My bag," she whispered, her heart slamming in her chest. "It's gone. I can't go anywhere until I find it." She started for the bank, eyes searching frantically for the little carryall.

"Easy," Drake said, reaching out to pull her back. "It's right here. I snagged it when I pulled you out of the water."

"Thank you," she whispered, relief making her giddy as she grabbed the bag from him, pulling open the zipper. Everything inside was just as she'd left it. And remarkably dry, considering. She flipped through the file on Ortiz and di Silva, then pulled out a second plastic bag. Inside were the only things that really mattered in her life. Her passport, an old photograph of Jenny, a tiny gold cross, and the playing card. It was a sad testament of a life, but it was all that she had.

"I don't suppose you'd care to share with the class?" Drake asked, his eyes alight with speculation.

"No." She shook her head, dropping the plastic bag back into the carryall. "I wouldn't."

Their gazes locked for a moment, his probing. And then he shrugged. "Fair enough," he said. "I know it's important to you, so I'm glad it didn't get lost."

There was an invitation in his words, but Madeline wasn't in the mood to open up to him. Instead she slipped the bag over her shoulder and started walking. "So do we keep following the stream?"

"Yeah, I still think it's our best course of action. Once we reach the junction with the Rio Negro I'm hoping we'll be able to commandeer a boat."

"Doesn't that seem a little unlikely?" she asked. "I mean considering this isn't exactly the hub of civilization. The jungle around here is basically uninhabited."

"Yeah, but there are still indigenous people around. Their settlements are scattered throughout the region."

"Great, a dugout canoe will do wonders."

"Beats walking," he said, hacking at a thorn bush barring their path. "But I'm hoping for something a bit more modern. There's an outpost where our river feeds into the Rio Negro—or at least there was one the last time I was in the area."

"Rescuing another damsel in distress?" she asked, only half kidding.

"No." He laughed, the sound warming her from the inside out. "I was working a dig. In college. Anyway, the place isn't much more than a dock and shack, but it's open to anyone in the area who wants to use it. I think it's owned by the University of Colombia."

"And you think there might be a boat."

"I think it's possible. But don't get too excited. As I said, it's been a long time. For all I know it isn't even there anymore. In any case, we're definitely not going to find it today." He nodded at the canopy above, a small opening in the trees allowing them to see a patch of pink-tinted sky. The day was well past its zenith, the sky already fading as the sun sank behind the horizon.

"Meaning we'll have to spend the night out here?" The thought was unsettling.

"I know we've got a lot of ground to cover, but we're better off not trying to move at night."

"Because of the animals," she said, carefully stepping over the remains of a fallen tree.

"Not just them. Although pumas and bears are nothing to sneeze at. There's still FARC activity in this area as well."

"You're talking about insurgents." She frowned, her thoughts turning to Andrés. "But haven't things quieted down in the past few years?"

"They have. But that doesn't mean the threat is gone. FARC is still somewhere between six and eighteen thousand strong, depending on whose statistics you want to believe."

"The government or the revolutionaries," Madeline finished for him.

"Either way it's more than we want to deal with. Finding two Americans roaming around the jungle would be like found treasure as far as they're concerned. And I'm sure di Silva's people would be more than happy to pay for your return."

"So that they can kill me." She blew out a breath, fighting a surge of fear. "So basically, we're stuck in the jungle trying to make our way to an outpost that may or may not exist, in hopes of finding a boat to take us downriver while we work at avoiding the drug cartel from the north and the terrorists to the south. Sounds like great fun."

"Glad to hear you're up for the challenge." His grin lacked any real humor, but she appreciated the effort. It was easy to blame him for their predicament, but the honest truth was that she'd dealt her own hand, starting with the Queen of Hearts, and now she had to accept the fallout.

All of it.

Including her growing dependence on Drake Flynn.

They walked in silence for the next hour or so, all their energy spent on hacking through the jungle in order to stay with the river. And if that weren't enough the river itself made their efforts even more difficult. There were fallen trees, thorny undergrowth, moss-slick stones, and always the cold rushing water. A second waterfall proved almost impassable, with a dicey series of fallen boulders bordered with jagged rocks that protruded at awkward angles, their sharp edges threatening to cut right through the soles of their shoes.

After managing to pick their way safely down to the bottom of the falls, Madeline was drenched in her own sweat. The idea of going farther was almost beyond comprehension. But Drake had produced the promised chocolate, giving each of them a square. And after a few minutes' rest, they'd started out again, following alongside the rushing water.

The trees were thicker here, the hot humid air weighing down on them like a living, breathing thing, smothering in its intensity. The jungle itself had grown quiet, the only sounds the rush of the water and the occasional squawk of a bird high over their heads. The sky, when she could see it, had grown ominously dark, and the smell of rain pervaded her senses.

And then, as suddenly as if God had turned on the taps, the rain came, torrential sheets of it that cut through the trees, lashing against them as they worked their way through the river of mud created by the downpour.

Despite the heat, Madeline found herself shivering violently as the rain pelted down. Rivulets of water coursed down her cheeks, running into her nose and mouth as she tried to shelter her face and protect herself from the onslaught.

Drake was walking in front of her, using his knife to clear a path through the overgrown vegetation. Clearly unfazed by this latest turn of weather, he kept the pace fast, forcing her to push herself to the limit just to keep up.

Finally, when the shivers turned to shudders and she could hardly walk for shaking, she stopped to give herself a moment's respite from the relentless fall of rain. What she wouldn't give for a hot bath and a warm bed, but the only way that was ever going to happen was if she kept moving.

So with a grimace, she straightened up, startled to see that Drake had disappeared into the gloom. The jungle around her had grown noticeably darker, the rain lessening to form a fine mist. She tried for forward motion, but her legs refused the order, buckling instead, sending her headfirst into brush.

"Hang on," Drake said, appearing by her side, his breath warm against her ear as his arms closed around her. "I've got you."

He pulled her upright, and she leaned against him, her teeth chattering as she tried to control the shuddering. "Sorry," she mumbled. "Can't seem to stop."

"You're going into shock," he said, his voice still gentle. "I should have seen it coming." He rubbed her shoulders, the resulting warmth seeming almost heaven-sent, but the shudders were still winning, so violent now that her muscles were visibly twitching.

"I need to start a fire. Get you warm. Will you be all right if I leave you for a minute?"

She wanted to tighten her hold. To mold herself to him permanently. But she knew that the desire sprang from her exhaustion. So she nodded against his chest. "I'll... I'll be okay. Ju...just help me sit down."

He lowered her carefully onto a grassy tuft of the riverbank. "I'll be right back," he said. "I've just got to get some wood. Okay?"

She nodded, her tongue too thick for words, her body still racked with shudders. Wrapping her arms around herself, she closed her eyes and waited, minutes passing slowly, like the molasses her mother used to pour on pancakes. She'd made the best pancakes. They were Jenny's favorite. Madeline smiled, the image of the two of them at the table, their mother flipping pancakes at the stove—her father passed out in the next room.

It was the only time there was peace. She let herself drift on the encroaching darkness.

"Madeline? Come on, you've got to stay with me."

Drake.

"I've got the fire started," he said. "We've just got to get you warm. Everything's going to be all right."

She shook her head, denying the words. Nothing was ever going to be right. Her mother was dead. Jenny was dead. She was alone in the jungle.

With Drake.

Her eyes flickered open as he lifted her into his arms, carrying her away from the river. Out of the mist an

outcropping of rock rose behind a stand of mata ratons.
In places, the trees literally sprang from the rocks, and
the overhanging branches formed an umbrella of sorts,
a quiet copse that, for the moment at least, promised
refuge. In the center a little fire danced against the green-
gray backdrop of foliage.

He carried her over to the fire and set her down on a
mat made from palm leaves, kneeling beside her. "We
need to get you warm," he said, "and that means getting
rid of those sweats for now. They're soaked."

She nodded, and with gentle fingers he peeled them
off, then pulled her into his lap, her body cradled against
his warmth. She closed her eyes again as his arms tightened around her. It felt so nice to be taken care of.

She couldn't remember the last time someone had just
held her.

It had been years.

She nestled closer, her shudders slowing to shivers,
his body heat radiating into her skin, seeping down to her
bones. He smelled like leather and shaving cream. Which
seemed absurdly funny in the middle of the jungle. But
then again maybe this was all a dream. Her brain was
having a hard time separating fact from fiction.

She could feel his heart beating against her hand, his
even breath soothing her in a way nothing else possibly
could have. Tears seeped from the corners of her eyes, and
though the sign of weakness angered her, she couldn't seem
to find the energy to lift her hand and brush them away.

He pulled her closer, stroking her hair, and she buried
her face in his chest, great gulping sobs breaking through
her carefully constructed façade.

He stroked her hair, murmuring nonsensical nothings,

and Madeline cried, releasing the terrors of the past few days. Ortiz's threats. Their narrow escape from the compound, the man in the jungle, the waterfall—everything—all of it. He wrapped himself around her, rocking her gently, surrounding her with warmth and at least the illusion of safety.

She knew it couldn't last. Knew it was predicated on the moment, with little or no bearing on reality. And yet, she couldn't let go. The feel of his heart beating against hers became the cadence of her breathing, his life tied inexorably to hers.

She lifted her head, opening her mouth to thank him, but the words stopped in her throat as she met the dark heat of his gaze. Suddenly she wanted nothing more than to feel his skin against hers. To seek a completely different kind of comfort.

Her lips parted, inviting his kiss, her heart pounding, praying that he'd understand—that he wouldn't reject what she was offering. And then he was there, his mouth against hers.

At first it was a gentle kiss. Tender almost. But Madeline wanted more. She opened her mouth, drinking him in with the desperation of a woman who'd been without water too long. Her body burned for him, the fire licking at her, building deep inside until she thought it might incinerate her. His tongue traced the line of her teeth, sending tiny waves of desire coursing through her, chasing away the shadows that threatened to consume her.

She twined her fingers through his hair, drawing him closer, knowing she was treading on dangerous ground. Drake Flynn wasn't the kind of man to start something he wasn't prepared to finish. The kiss deepened and sensations exploded inside her, his mouth branding her with nothing more than his lips.

She knew she should stop him, but here in the warmth of his arms, she didn't want to pull away. The toll of the past few days was beyond measure, and just for a moment, she wanted to forget. To escape into the silent seduction of the kiss. She pressed closer, not sure what it was she needed but absolutely certain that he was the only one who could give it to her, and that she wanted it with every fiber of her being.

His lips moved to her cheeks, then to her eyes, his calloused fingers framing her face. Tremors of pleasure raced through her, building with each touch, each caress. Then he moved again, taking possession of her lips, his kiss demanding now—possessive.

A hint of worry rippled through her, but was gone before she had time to think about it. Her hands were trapped between them, his heart beating wildly against her fingers, the syncopated rhythm matching her own. She traced the line of his lips with her tongue, smiling against his mouth when he groaned with pleasure.

There was power in knowing that she aroused him— that the seduction was mutual, her strength matching his. And on that thought, she let go of any doubt, intent instead upon riding the wave.

His intake of breath was audible and he reached out, skimming a palm along the contours of her breasts, his touch so light, she almost couldn't feel it. With a sigh, she closed her eyes and leaned forward, forcing the pressure. His fingers fluttered slightly and then he tightened his hold, teasing each of her nipples until they were hard, the sweet pain pooling between her legs.

She threw back her head for another kiss, but instead her heart skittered to a stop as a low, menacing growl cut through the still night air. Just off to her left, two golden eyes gleamed in the firelight as a big black cat crouched low, muscles bunched, ready to attack.

CHAPTER 12

Don't move," Drake ordered, eyes on the puma as he carefully released her and slowly reached for his gun.

The big cat moved forward, its teeth bared, sharp incisors white against the black fur of its muzzle. It sprang into the air, and she opened her mouth to scream, but the only sound she heard was the sharp report of Drake's gun. The panther hit the ground, twitched once, and was still.

"Is it dead?" she asked, her breathing ragged, her eyes locked on the puma.

"Yeah." Drake nodded as he knelt beside the body, using his knife to cut away several hunks of meat. "You okay?"

"I am now," she said, her voice still thready. "It could have killed us both."

"But it didn't." He shook his head, eyes narrowed. "Unfortunately, that shot was probably audible for a couple of miles. Which means we've got to get moving."

In the panic of the moment, the intimacy between them had vanished. Probably a good thing, all in all. But Madeline couldn't help but feel a tiny niggle of regret over the possibility of what might have been.

"You going to be all right?" he asked, the question perfunctory, as he wrapped the meat in palm leaves and then doused the fire.

"I'm fine," she said, lifting her chin, feeling as if something precious had slipped away. She pulled on her sweats—thankful that the cotton was already beginning to dry—and grabbed the carryall. "Let's just get the hell out of here."

The new fire leaped and crackled as Drake turned the makeshift spit with the meat from the panther. They'd walked a half mile or so farther downstream, and then he'd doubled back to make sure that no one was following them. Even with the reassurance that they were alone, it was important to stay vigilant.

Firelight flickered across Madeline's face as she stared into the flames. They hadn't said much since he'd set up the new camp, just to the north of the river at the mouth of a small cave, the rocky canopy keeping the smoke from giving them away. Madeline was exhausted, he could see it in the slope of her shoulders and the circles under her eyes. But she hadn't complained. Not once. Except for the brief interlude of tears, she'd gamely met every challenge that had been thrown at them.

He knew it shouldn't sway him one way or the other. Cass had been a strong woman, too. Hell, so had his mother. And they'd both betrayed him. He'd be a fool to put any trust in a woman like Madeline Reynard. The facts spoke for themselves. Whatever she was to di Silva, she'd been part of his organization, which put her on the wrong side of the equation as far as he was concerned.

Still, he couldn't shake the feeling that there was something more. Some part of her that connected to him. At first when they'd kissed, he'd just been reacting, taking her because his body demanded it. But then, something had shifted, and he was kissing *her*—Madeline. And if he were honest, he'd wanted to take her then and there.

Maybe he should be sending thanks to the puma. Sleeping with her would have been crossing a dangerous line. Whatever the reason.

"I'm sorry," she said, breaking into his thoughts as she lifted her face to meet his gaze across the fire. "About before. I don't usually lose it like that. And we shouldn't have…I mean…it was a mistake…" She looked down at her hands, chewing on her bottom lip.

"It was just shock." He shrugged, turning the meat. "It can happen to anyone. You've been through a lot today and your body's had enough."

"Maybe that explains breaking down." She shook her head. "But I kissed you."

"And I kissed you back." He allowed himself a small smile. "Sometimes we just need to prove to ourselves we're alive. You had some close calls today. It would be surprising if you hadn't had a reaction."

"So we're okay?" she asked, her question oddly endearing. Her eyes were huge, her teeth still worrying her bottom lip "I mean, we aren't exactly friends, but we're stuck here together, and we were doing okay before I…before we…"

"We're fine," he said, removing the meat from the fire.

"Besides, we're almost out of here. Once we reach the coast, we'll contact my team and they'll get us back to the States in no time. Then this whole thing will be nothing more than a bad memory." He cut the mcat into pieces and offered her some on a makeshift palm leaf plate.

They ate in silence, lost in their own thoughts. Beyond the fire, the jungle lurked in the darkness. It felt almost primordial. Man, woman, fire. His imagination flared as he remembered the feel of her lips against his. The dark could do strange things to a man. Especially here in the heart of the Andes.

He shook his head, banishing his mutinous thoughts, concentrating instead on the makeshift meal.

"Are you sure it's all right for us to have a fire?" she asked, her gaze shooting to the surrounding jungle.

"It's a bit of a risk," he acknowledged. "But we've got the overhang to protect from too much smoke and light. And if di Silva's men are out there, they're not going to be traveling by night for the same reasons we aren't. So I figure we're safe for now. Besides, the fire holds other predators at bay."

"You're figuring our puma has relatives?"

"Got it in one." He nodded. "Is the meat okay?"

"Delicious. The best takeout I've ever had." She smiled, popping another bite into her mouth, and he was reminded again of her bravery. "Although I don't think I could possibly eat any more," she said, watching as he slid another piece of meat onto the spit.

"In this kind of humidity raw meat goes rancid fast. So I'm cooking food to take with us tomorrow as well."

"So where'd you learn to be a Boy Scout? This rescue unit of yours?"

"Actually, I started as a Cub Scout in California," he admitted with a grin. "Redlands. Didn't make it as far as the Boy Scouts, though. I discovered girls."

"I can see how that would be a distraction. So what came next?"

"A stint in college baseball."

"Let me see," she said, with an exaggerated frown. "First baseman?"

"Pitcher. I had a hell of a slider. Even managed a year in the minors. But I wasn't good enough for the majors, so I went back to college and finished my studies. Majored in archaeology." He finished the last of his meat, tossing the leaf into the fire. "I've been interested since I was a kid. My dad took us to La Brea when I was six."

"So that's where you learned all this. On digs?"

"Some of it, yeah. But I've also picked up a tip or two since joining the unit."

"And I guess you can't tell me what exactly the unit is. Or who you work for?"

"Not without killing you, no." He pulled out a knife, and she actually shrank back from him. His laugh echoed across the clearing. "I work for the government, Madeline. But you already know that."

She blew out a breath and cocked her head to one side, studying him. "So why the switch from preservation to destruction?"

"In both cases, you're oversimplifying, but the real truth is that I'm an adrenaline junkie."

"I think there's more to it than that." Her eyes glittered in the firelight, her gaze speculative. "But whatever your reasons, I'm glad you made the choices you did. Otherwise, I might be dead."

"So earlier," he said, taking advantage of the fact that she seemed to have lowered her guard, "when you said you were never di Silva's mistress—were you telling the truth?"

She paused for a moment, clearly considering a lie and then, with a little sigh, nodded. "I said that to protect myself. I actually worked for the organization."

"Doing things you might be prosecuted for," he finished for her.

"Yeah. Last I heard there was nothing illegal about being someone's mistress." She stared down at her hands for a moment, then lifted her gaze to meet his, her expression unapologetic.

"So why did you do it?" he asked, careful to keep any hint of accusation from his tone. "Go to work for someone like di Silva, I mean."

At first he thought she wasn't going to answer, but then she shrugged. "I was trying to protect Jenny." She laughed, the sound harsh against the soft silence of the jungle. "But in end, it didn't matter; she still wound up dead."

"Jenny?" he asked, curiosity roused.

"My sister." She stumbled over the words. "She was two years younger than me."

"I had a brother," he said, surprised at himself for sharing. "Three years older. He died, too."

Her smile was sad. "Then you understand."

And he did. Tucker's death had hit hard. As if someone had cut a part out of him. The good part.

"How long ago did he die?" she asked, pulling him away from his thoughts.

"It's been almost five years," he said, closing his eyes,

remembering. "It was an accident. He was doing flight training in the desert in Nevada."

"It must have been hard on your parents."

Drake shook his head. "No. My dad's dead. And my mom doesn't give a damn. Short version is that my mom ran off and left us when Tucker and I were just little. My dad did the best he could. But he wasn't ever the same after she was gone. He died about ten years ago. Cancer."

"I'm sorry." She tilted her head, the firelight enhancing the beauty of her face. "You said it was a training flight. Your brother's accident. Does that mean he worked for the government, too?"

"Yeah," he nodded. "The military."

"Were you close?" she asked.

"He was my best friend. Especially when we were kids. Like I said, our family went through a rough patch, and Tucker's the one that held us together. What about Jenny? Were the two of you close?"

"When we were little it was the two of us against the world. Especially after my mother died."

"But things changed?"

"Not the way we felt." She shook her head. "But my father was a drunk—a mean one. When my mother was alive, she kept him away from us. But after she was gone…" She paused, considering her words. "I was the only thing standing between him and Jenny."

"Why didn't you just leave?" he asked.

"I was ten. Jenny was eight. Where were we supposed to go? Social Services doesn't exist in backwater places like Cypress Bluff. We only had each other. Jenny used to say that as long as we were together we could handle anything."

"So what happened?" Drake asked, the question hanging between them in the dark.

"I broke my promise. I left. And she got addicted to drugs. It was her way of dealing with my dad, I guess. Anyway, things went from bad to worse and she wound up in Colombia. She'd been working as a mule to support her habit."

"Di Silva."

"Yes, she worked for his organization, and she got in over her head. I stepped in to help. But it was too late. Six months ago she died from an overdose."

"God, I'm sorry," he said, wanting to reach out, to try to comfort her, but knowing firsthand that there was nothing he could do to take away her pain. "No wonder you want to bring down di Silva. You must hate him."

"I hate myself more," she said, her shoulders slumping with the weight of her grief. "I'm the one who deserted her. I'm the one who drove her to drugs. If anyone is responsible for my sister's death—it's me."

"It doesn't work like that. I've been around enough to know that people can't be saved unless they want to be. You weren't responsible for Jenny's choices."

"Yes, I was," she said, her voice cracking a little. "I promised my mother I'd watch over her. And I didn't."

"You came to Colombia."

"It was too late. She was in too deep. And nothing I did was enough. I couldn't turn back the clock. I couldn't make it okay."

"But you tried. That's why you agreed to work for di Silva."

Her head jerked up, as if she'd only just realized how much she'd revealed. "I told you before, I did what I had to do." She pushed to her feet, stumbling in the dark as she moved away.

"I'm not trying to pry, Madeline," he said, his hands resting on her shoulders as he moved to stand behind her.

"I know." She nodded. "And I know I have to tell all of it sometime. But I only just found out that she was dead. And it hurts so goddamned much."

He pulled her back against him, wrapping his arms around her. The move was instinctive. He understood her agony. Hell, he shared it. He could feel her tense beneath his touch. And then, with a ragged little sigh, she relaxed against him. They stood for a moment in silence, the physical contact enough. But then she pushed away, turning to face him.

"I seem to be falling apart on you a lot tonight. I'm sorry. It's just still so fresh. I found out by accident. Ortiz kept it from me. He knew that if I discovered the truth he wouldn't have control over me anymore."

"Ortiz?" Drake asked, taking her hand and pulling her back to the fire. She dropped down on a boulder, and he moved to sit across from her. "I haven't heard that name before."

"Hector Ortiz," she clarified, seeming relieved to have moved away from talking about her sister. "He's di Silva's number-two man. Although for all practical purposes, he's really the one running things. It was his idea to expand the organization into dealing arms."

"And what did you do for him?"

"I stole things. From influential men. Information mainly. Details about arms shipments, arms agreements, government research and development," she said, wrapping her arms around herself. "Anything that would facilitate access to the weapons and technology Ortiz needed. He, or sometimes di Silva, introduced me to prominent men with the right connections and I used whatever means necessary to gain the materials they required. I'm not proud of what I did. But I did it to help my sister. Ortiz promised that if I worked off her debt, he'd let us go. I should have known he was lying."

"And when you found out about Jenny, you contacted the Embassy."

She nodded. "Will Richardson. I met him at a function Ortiz took me to. I was supposed to chat up the Chilean ambassador. Anyway, I figured since I'd met him, he might be willing to help." She frowned, as if considering something, her teeth worrying her lip again.

"And he agreed?" Drake prompted.

She nodded, pulling herself from her thoughts. "Yes, but Ortiz was watching me. And he figured out what I was up to."

"And killed Richardson."

"Another death on my conscience." Her laughter was brittle. "He was such a nice man. He had a wife and a baby on the way. Did you know that?"

"You couldn't have known Ortiz was following you."

"I should have. If I'd been paying attention. I know the way he works."

"I'm sorry," he said, knowing the words were inadequate. There was nothing he could say that would assuage her guilt. But he wished to hell he'd get a shot at Ortiz. The man was a real piece of work. Preying on people like Jenny and Madeline to advance his own ambition and greed. He clenched his fists, anger rocketing through him with a strength that surprised him.

"It is what it is," she said, her voice sharp, her pain reflected in her eyes. "My mother always said that you make your own bed. I guess now it's time for me to lie in it." And with the words, her mask slipped firmly back into place, her secrets locked safely away. "Anyway, I think I've said more than enough for tonight. I'm tired. And I suspect you'll want to get going as soon as the sun's up."

He pushed to his feet, reaching over to a stack of mat-sized leaves he'd brought back with the meat. "These should make a fairly comfortable bed. Not exactly four-star, but better than sleeping in the mud." He fanned them out next to the rocks, under the canopy. "You go ahead. I'll keep watch."

She nodded, pausing for a moment, as if she wanted to say something more. But the mood had been broken, and with a sigh, she said good night and walked over to the improvised bed.

Drake crossed to the other side of the fire and picked up the gun, then sat down on a large rock, back turned, as Madeline settled in for the night. The fire had died down, coals glowing, so he stirred it with a stick, the flames immediately licking upward again, sending shadows dancing against the ground.

Out in the dark, he could hear movement, nocturnal animals out looking for a meal. The temperature had dropped—the air almost chilly. It had been a hell of a day. He didn't even know if his friends had all made it out alive.

And he sure as hell didn't know what to make of

Madeline Reynard. One moment tough as nails, the next crying in his arms as if her heart had broken.

Which made her exactly like every other woman.

Only, somehow—and this was the part that was probably going to keep him up all night—she wasn't.

CHAPTER 13

It seemed as if they had been walking forever. According to her watch, which was iffy at best since their jaunt down the river, it was just after two. Which meant they'd been at it for over half the day.

There hadn't been much chitchat, Drake intent on his map and the compass in his watch. Unlike hers his gear was equipped to withstand river racing, which at the end of the day benefited them both. She hadn't said anything about last night. And neither had he.

Maybe he was right and her emotional outburst had just been caused by the stress of everything that had happened. But that didn't explain the way she'd felt this morning, waking to see him sitting next to the fire keeping watch. She wanted to reach out and touch him. Feel his arms around her, his lips against hers. And none of that made any sense at all.

She'd told him things she'd sworn never to tell anyone. She could blame it on the circumstances. Blame it on the jungle and the dark. But she was afraid it was all about the man. He just inspired trust. Despite the fact that at times he infuriated her, push come to shove, he was a decent man. And she had a feeling that underneath his rough-and-tumble exterior, there was a good heart.

And inexplicably, the thought frightened her.

Anyway, at least he'd let it go. Allowed her to regain her tattered dignity. And there'd been moments when she'd thought he'd truly understood. Although that was probably just wishful thinking. After all, they were in this predicament because of her. There'd have been no jungle heart-to-heart if she hadn't run away.

But last night, he hadn't seemed to hold that against her. He'd actually listened. Even talked about himself a little. She smiled, thinking of his talk about baseball and archaeology. And his love for his brother. His *dead* brother. It might be macabre, but it was a thread of connection. A loss they shared.

She knew it couldn't amount to anything more. She was his charge. Nothing more. And once they were safely out of danger, she'd be on her own again. But for now at least, she was willing to admit that she needed him. Her mind turned again to the memory of their bodies pressed together. If the puma hadn't attacked...

She cut herself off with a muffled curse. After everything she'd been through, now was not the time to go soft. Entertaining any thought about personal feelings for Drake Flynn was definitely a mistake. And she'd made too many of those already.

Pulling her thoughts away from the man in front of her, she focused instead on the jungle. It was getting hotter as they descended toward the Rio Negro and the plain leading to the coast. The monkeys had grown more numerous, their chattering almost becoming white noise as they catapulted through the trees above her head. The birds, on the other hand, had all but disappeared, moving higher up in the canopy, their calls muffled by the heavy vegetation.

So far the morning had been uneventful. No sign of di Silva's men. But that didn't mean they weren't out there somewhere. Ortiz wasn't the type to give up easily. And now that his weapons stash had been destroyed, she had no doubt that he was out for blood.

Principally, hers.

Which meant that the sooner she disappeared the better. She had no faith whatsoever in the U.S. government's promise of protection. She was a means to an end. And nothing, not even Drake's icy blue eyes, was going to persuade her otherwise.

"How you holding up?" Drake asked, as they stopped for a moment to refill the canteen.

"I'm fine," she said. "Finally, dry. Although I'm not sure I'll ever be truly clean again." She gestured to her mud-spattered face with a grimace. "What I wouldn't give for a bar of soap and a shower."

"I promise you can clean to your heart's content as soon as we arrive in Puerto Remo."

"Is that where we're going?" She frowned. "I figured we'd head to somewhere bigger. Like Buenaventura." The coastal town was the largest on Colombia's Pacific coast. Noted for its frontier mentality, it nevertheless provided its citizens with all the conveniences of a modern city.

"Too obvious," Drake said. "Better to keep to the unexpected."

"And uninhabitable," she sighed. Most of the so-called "towns" on the coast were in actuality little more than mud-drenched outposts, many of them without running water or electricity.

"I wager it'll be a damn sight better than this."

"Point taken," she acknowledged, taking the canteen from him for a long drink. "Anything beats sleeping on leaves in the mud. Although I'll admit after yesterday's adventures, it wasn't as bad as it could have been. I actually slept pretty well, all things considered."

"It's amazing what a little adventure will do for you." His smile was disarming, especially set against the black shadow of his beard. "You ready?" He screwed the lid on the canteen.

"How much farther do you think we have to go?"

"Hard to say for sure." He shook his head. "We're kind of short on landmarks around here. But unless I'm way off on my calculations, we should be fairly close to the river. And from there it's another day's walk to Puerto Remo."

"But you said we might find a boat, right?" The idea of another day in this steamy hot jungle was almost more than she could contemplate.

"If we're lucky."

"And assuming we are, then how long do you think it'll be?"

"There's a chance we could be in Puerto Remo tonight."

"I'll keep a good thought." She pasted on a smile, fostering an enthusiasm she most certainly didn't feel. "Still no sign of di Silva's men, right?"

"Nothing so far. But this is a big place. It's possible we're paralleling each other."

"Comforting thought."

"I said it's possible, but not probable. They've no idea which way we went. Other than toward the ocean. And as I said it's a big area. My guess is they'll be far more likely to try to intercept us on the coast."

"At Buenaventura. Unless they figure out you're opting for somewhere less likely."

"It's a calculated risk, I know. But it's the right one under the circumstances. Besides, the coast is dotted with settlements, and there's no way for di Silva's men to cover all of them."

"So we just pray that they don't choose ours."

"And if they do, we take solace in the fact that we won't be alone once we get there."

"You really believe your people will be waiting?"

"Yeah, I do. They'll have to maneuver a bit, considering we weren't supposed to be in-country in the first place. But Avery will figure out a way. Like I said, if one of us got separated, the plan was always to head for Puerto Remo."

Just for a moment, Madeline considered what it would be like to be part of something like his team. To have someone who'd always have her back. Someone who'd care what happened to her no matter what. It was a lovely thought in theory, but in reality, she suspected the price would be too damn high.

"Well, for both of our sakes," she said, "I hope they're there."

They set off in silence, the terrain becoming more rugged as they transitioned from mountains to river basin. Two hours later, the ground leveled and the stream, which was more of a river now, widened even further and slowed slightly as if resisting the upcoming merger with the Rio Negro.

"We must be getting close," she said.

"I think it's just ahead." Drake nodded, pushing through a stand of tall grass, the prickly edges catching at their clothes.

"And the outpost?"

"If memory serves, it should be right at the point where the two rivers join. On the northwest side. But like I said before, the place might not even exist anymore."

"Well, the only way to verify for certain is to get there," Madeline said, pushing ahead of him, suddenly anxious. The prospect of finding a boat and potentially food and some sort of shelter had kept her going all day, and the idea that it might not be there was almost too overwhelming to contemplate.

"Wait," Drake said, pulling her back. "We need to be careful. We don't know what's up there. Even if the outpost is where it's supposed to be, we don't know if it's occupied, and if so, if the residents will be friendly."

She blew out a breath and nodded. He was right. Hell, he was always right. Damn the man. She dropped back to follow as they moved cautiously forward, the stream picking up again as it gave in to the inevitable, the sound of the rushing river filtering through the thick undergrowth.

And then suddenly, there it was. The Rio Negro, its raging waters swollen by the rains. The smaller river tumbled over a fall of rocks, one last cliff separating the tributary from its parent. Below them, the waters eddied as the two rivers joined, the clear stream dissipating into the mud-blackened Rio Negro.

"I see it," Madeline whispered, pitching her voice low to be heard beneath the roar of this newest set of falls. "The outpost. It's down there."

To the right of the converging rivers a silt-covered bank extended from the foot of the cliff, and on its farthest edge, a ramshackle building stood, its weathered walls so overgrown with moss and vines it almost disappeared into the surrounding vegetation.

"Okay," Drake said, studying the outpost through his field glasses, "our first order of business is to get down there without alerting anyone inside. Which means we have to find a way to traverse this cliff."

"I'm not going over the waterfall," she insisted, shooting her gaze over to the tumbling water. "Once is most definitely enough."

"No." His lips quirked at the corners. "I'm thinking we'll try the terra-firma route this time. But we need to make sure they can't see or hear us making our descent. So we should make our way upriver a little ways, and then look for a way down."

She nodded, and followed as he led the way back into the undergrowth. They worked their way northwest until the outpost was safely out of sight. Then, working on a diagonal, they began to move downward. The slope was littered with rocks and scree, and covered with thick black mud. Each step was an effort, either to avoid sliding on the rocks, or slipping in the mud.

At first there were tufts of some kind of coarse grass, and she used them as vegetative stepping-stones. But about halfway down the grass disappeared, and there was nothing but rocks and mud. Using a stick to balance herself, Madeline kept her eyes trained on the ground immediately in front of her feet, concentrating on every step she took.

About three-quarters of the way down, she slipped, falling forward, landing on her knees in the muck.

"You okay?" Drake asked, making his way back up the slope to where she'd fallen.

"I'm fine," she hissed, hopping to her feet, her pants plastered with the wet sticky mud. "Couldn't be better."

Frowning, he studied her face, no doubt to reassure himself that she wasn't going to lose it, and then, with a nod, headed back down again.

She stood her ground for a moment, cursing Drake, herself, and the world in general, and then resumed her trek downward, this time using the bigger rocks to brace herself against further unwanted tumbles. In what seemed like hours, but was far more likely to have been minutes, she reached the bottom and sighed with relief.

"So what next?" she asked, almost afraid to hear the answer.

"We do a little recon."

The idea of trudging through more of the black sucking mud held little appeal, but the idea of being left on her own was equally repellent, so she followed as he led the way into the reeds and rushes that bordered the river.

In truth, she wasn't sure whether she felt more like laughing or crying. Or, quite frankly, running as fast as she could in the opposite direction, but then she'd already chosen that course with disastrous results. No, the facts were simple—she needed Drake and his somewhat unusual skill set to survive this journey. Once she was back on familiar ground, all bets were off.

Up ahead, the weathered gray wood of the outpost shone through the mottled greens of the undergrowth.

"Wait here," Drake said, coming to a stop in front of her. "I'm going to check out the window and see if there's anyone inside."

Madeline nodded, fingering her bag as Drake pulled his gun and moved forward using the river plants for cover. She squatted behind a rock to wait, letting her gaze sweep over the surrounding area for signs of life. Just beyond her a small turtle basked in the sun on a rock, and two bottle-green dragonflies hovered over a small lily of some kind.

Suddenly the grass parted, and Drake was dropping down beside her.

"What did you see?" she asked.

"There's definitely someone inside. A man. Indeterminable age. Hispanic. Could be local. It's hard to tell. There's no sign of a weapon, but that doesn't mean there isn't one somewhere. It's just not in plain sight. At the moment, he's got his back to the door. So if I move quickly, I can intercept him from the front before he has a chance to do anything. Shouldn't be a problem to neutralize him."

"Kill him, do you mean?" she whispered, with a frown. "What if he's not a danger?"

"Obviously, I intend to find out before taking any drastic action. The point is that I can get to him before he can get to me. Which means that either way, we're good to go. So you stay here, and I'll see what I can accomplish."

"But what if something happens to you?" She hated that she had to ask the question, but she couldn't seem to help herself.

"I'll be fine. Stop worrying. You're probably right and he's got no connection with any of this."

Or she was wrong and Drake was walking into some kind of trap. She opened her mouth to argue, but instead settled for "be careful." His smile indicated that for him this kind of thing was a walk in the park. Routine procedure. She grimaced and waited for him to disappear into the brush, then moved forward so that she could see in the window.

The man inside was sitting at a table, looking at his laptop. A pot-bellied stove sat in the corner, something bubbling in a pan on the top, an old-fashioned percolator directly behind it. Madeline's mouth watered. It had been hours since they'd had anything to eat, and that had only been cold puma. Not exactly the breakfast of champions.

If the man turned out to be friendly, maybe he'd ask them to share his meal. And if he wasn't inclined, well, she had the feeling Drake would find a way to convince him. As if on cue, Drake appeared in the doorway.

"Don't move," he said. The man at the table tensed, his fingers tightening into a fist and then releasing. "Turn around slowly."

The man turned, one hand still on the table. His face was congenial enough, his brown eyes guileless. He looked to be somewhere between thirty and forty-five. His hair was long, and in need of a good wash. His clothes were serviceable, his shoes caked with the black mud that was everywhere.

"Not exactly a friendly greeting," the stranger said.

"A man out here can't be too careful." Drake shrugged, not sounding the slightest bit apologetic.

"True enough," the other man nodded. "But that goes both ways. Can I ask what you're doing here?"

"I'm a botanist. I've been cataloging plants in the area." He nodded out the door at the waving vegetation. "Lost my supplies in the rain. River surged and swamped my camp."

"It can get dicey out here," the man agreed. "Who do you work for?"

"University of California."

"American?"

"Yeah." He smiled, still holding the gun. "I guess it shows."

"I've been around, recognized the accent." The man lifted his hands. "Why don't you let me get you a cup of coffee?" He nodded toward the pot on the stove, and Madeline's stomach rumbled so loudly she was certain they'd be able to hear it. "Assuming you're willing to put down the gun."

"Why don't you tell me who you are first?" Drake asked.

"Jacques Ormond. You might say I'm a distributor of sorts. I collect animal specimens. There's quite a market for them. Especially zoos." He nodded toward a couple of cages stacked against one wall.

Drake eyed the man warily, but lowered the gun. Madeline felt a niggle of concern. Something was off. He'd said his name was Jacques. French pronunciation. But his accent wasn't French and Drake had been right, his features were definitely Hispanic.

"This your place?" Drake asked, walking over to lean against the table.

"Yeah, at least for the time being," the man said. "This outpost is basically here to serve whoever needs it. And for the moment, I guess that's me." He stepped over to the stove, his back to Drake as he poured a cup of coffee. "How long you been out here?" He turned to hand the cup to Drake.

"Only a couple of weeks. It's my first time out. I'm working with a team, but we split up in Buenaventura. Figured it would be easier to cover more territory if we worked on our own."

"So you're alone?"

"Yeah." He shrugged. "You?"

"Prefer it that way." The man smiled, and again Madeline felt a tug of uneasiness. He crossed back to the stove and reached up to grab another cup, then turned to pour more coffee. "I've been out here a month or so."

"Catch much?" Drake asked, his eyes shooting toward the door. At least he had finally remembered she was out here.

"I beg your pardon?" the man asked, half turning back from the stove.

"Animals?"

"Ah, sorry, wasn't following your drift. Couple of monkeys and a toucan. I've been stalking a leopard, but so far no luck."

Madeline shifted a little so that she could better see the room, her foot dislodging a small pile of stones propped against the edge of the house in the process. Holding her breath, she waited to be certain that no one had heard, and then glanced back down at the ground, to be certain she wouldn't do it again.

The falling stones had uncovered something blue. She reached down to pick it up, and was surprised to find a mud-splattered bandana.

Curious, she knelt, peering into the shadows underneath the pier and beam building. It took a moment for her vision to adjust to the dark, but when it did, her heart leaped to her throat as her brain registered what her eyes were seeing. A man lay prostrate, his head turned to one side, his mouth lolling open, his eyes rolled back in his head. His hand was outflung as if in entreaty.

Madeline had the distinct feeling she was looking at the real Frenchman. Jacques Ormond. But regardless of whether she'd pegged his identity, his presence meant that Drake had most likely walked into a trap.

She popped back up in time to see the stranger grab a gun from the shelf beside the stove and swing around, leveling it on Drake. "Toss me your gun," the man said as Drake grimaced, his muscles tightening.

Instinct surged, and Madeline reached into her bag, her fingers closing on the gun Drake had given her in the clearing. After wrapping the bandana around her left hand, she gripped the gun, and then smashed her fist through the window's glass.

The man swung around, surprised. And Drake dove for his gun. But Madeline didn't wait, firing instead through the hole, hitting the stranger dead-on, the bullet driving him backward into the shelves, boxes and cans going every which way.

Shaking now, she lowered the weapon, her eyes meeting Drake's through the window as he went to check the body. Adrenaline still cresting, Madeline ran around the corner, up onto the porch and into the building. "Is he dead?"

"Yes," Drake said, eyes narrowed as he stared at the gun in her hand. "Nice shot."

"There's a dead man under the house," she said by

way of explanation. "I think it might be the real Jacques. And then when I looked through the window again he was holding you at gunpoint. So I figured I'd catch him by surprise."

"Well, you did that." He nodded toward the body.

"I was afraid the guy was going to blow you away," she said, her breath still coming in ragged gasps.

"I would have managed."

"Now where have I heard that before?"

The corners of his lips twitched and she let out a slow breath, relief flooding through her, the power of the emotion surprising her. The idea of losing him was almost more than she could bear. After all, she needed him to stay alive so he could help her make her way out of here. He was her ticket to freedom. Without him...

She stopped, her gaze moving to his. And suddenly, with complete certainty, she knew that her relief stemmed from far more than self-preservation. She actually cared about the man. What that meant in the grand scheme of things, she had no idea. But there was no escaping the fact that in the moments before she'd fired, the only thing on her mind—the driving force behind her actions—was the urgent desire to make certain that Drake was okay.

Clearly, she'd lost her fucking mind.

CHAPTER 14

"So if the real Jacques Ormond is outside," Drake said, as he rolled the dead man over, "who's this?"

"I've no idea." Madeline shook her head. "If he's one of di Silva's men, I've never seen him before. Does he have any kind of ID?"

"No," Drake said. "The body's clean."

"Maybe there's a backpack or something?"

"Yeah. It's possible. But before we look, let's get him out of here. If any of his friends arrive, I don't want to tip our hand."

"Dead bodies do tend to raise questions." She nodded, shifting around to the dead man's feet.

Again, he was impressed by her control. She'd just killed a man, and while he'd expect this kind of calm from Tyler or even Hannah, he'd have thought she'd have been more affected. Then again, this was *Madeline*—and she always seemed to surprise him.

He bent and grabbed the guy under his armpits. "All

right, let's do it." Together they lifted the body and started to move toward the door.

"Where are we going to put him?" Madeline asked. "Under the house with Jacques?"

"No. We'll throw him in the river. Jacques, too, actually."

"That seems a little callous." She frowned at him. "I mean, maybe not for this guy. But Jacques deserves a little more respect."

"I'm just trying to keep us alive," Drake said as they moved out onto the jetty. "The current will carry the bodies downriver fast. And between the fish and the caimans they'll be gone before they they the hit the coast."

"I thought you said there weren't any crocs in these waters?"

"I said none in the upper altitudes. Down here they flourish. Except when people like Jacques Ormond poach them for the leather."

"How do you know that's what he was doing?" she asked.

"There are carcasses in a shed just beyond the jetty."

"Oh. Well, I suppose that does change things a bit. Still, they're crocodiles. Not exactly warm and cuddly."

"Yes, but they're a threatened species. At least certain varieties. And people like Jacques use the societal demand for purses and shoes to justify what they do. There's a hell of a lot of money in it, actually."

"I wouldn't have taken you for a member of PETA," she said as they came to a stop at the end of the pier.

"I just don't like bottom feeders." He shrugged. "We'll drop him on three. All right?"

Madeline nodded and he counted down as they swung

the body out toward the water. It hit with a splash and then bobbed underneath the surface, disappearing as the current dragged it downriver.

"You think someone else is going to come here looking for him?" she asked. "Or for us?"

"I think it's possible. And either way we're better off leaving nothing to indicate any of us were here. Even Jacques."

"What about the crocodile skins?"

"Those we can leave as is. But we'll need to sanitize the room. And make sure we cover our tracks."

"Somehow I don't think my slide down the cliff will be all that easy to cover up."

"You'd be surprised." He smiled down at her. "You're handling all of this really well."

"I don't really have a choice," she said, the corner of her mouth tugging upward. "You don't seem like the kind of man who tolerates hysterical females."

"I think I've proved I can be understanding when the situation calls for it." Their eyes met and held, and then she ducked her head, the pink stain of a blush washing over her cheeks.

"I already apologized for that."

"And I told you there was no need." He framed her face with his hands, her breath catching on a little whoosh at the contact. "And I still think you're handling things really well, all things considered." Their eyes met, gazes dueling as the conversation moved to a level beyond words. The words chemical combustion came to mind.

But this wasn't the time, and reluctantly, he let her go.

"We need to move Jacques."

She nodded, stepping back, what looked suspiciously

like regret flashing in her eyes. "No time like the present."

The two of them walked around to the side of the outpost, and Drake bent to drag Jacques from underneath the house. The man's body was already starting to decompose in the heat, the smell overwhelming. "You might want me to handle this one," he said, turning so that his back obstructed her view.

"No worries," she replied. "I've already been up close and personal with him." She sucked in a deep breath and reached for his feet. "Let's just get it over with."

They hauled the body up onto the jetty and swung him out into the water.

"If the caimans get him," Madeline said, shading her eyes as she watched the body floating downriver, "it's sort of poetic justice, in a macabre kind of way. Circle of life and all that."

They stood for a moment just watching the river.

"Does it ever bother you?" she asked, turning to face him. "All the killing, I mean?"

"Yes and no. I suppose after a while you kind of get used to it. Or maybe I'm just built that way. I don't know. My dad was military. And my brother. So maybe it's in my genes."

"So then it's just all in a day's work?"

"No. It's more than that. I mean, I respect the sanctity of human life as much as the next person. But sometimes, it's necessary to take a life to save one. And in the long run, most of what we do is about keeping people safe. People who won't ever even know they were in danger."

"You make it sound noble."

"Hardly. It's just a game of us against them. And my

job is to make sure we win more than we lose. And for
the most part, I honestly believe that what I do is for
the greater good." He shrugged, hating that the words
sounded so pretentious. "I know that sounds like bullshit.
Hell, the truth is, maybe I just like the ride."

"I suspect that's part of it. But you didn't have to come
after me. And when you did, you didn't have to put yourself out there to protect me. I'm not one of the good guys,
Drake. And still, you saved me. As far as I'm concerned
that's pretty damn noble."

"Or maybe it's just part of my job."

"To get me to D.C., I know." But her smile said that
she believed otherwise. "So what next?" she asked, as
they walked back into the outpost, her no-nonsense tone
thankfully signaling an end to all the philosophizing.

"We need to search the room and see if we can find
something that identifies our shooter."

"So what am I looking for?" she asked as she thumbed
through a stack of stuff on a shelf in the corner.

"A backpack or a wallet, anything that isn't related to
Jacques Ormond. Assuming that really was his name."

"It was." Madeline nodded, pointing at the computer.
"We must have interrupted the killer going through
Jacques's files. Look, his name is on the account screen."
She clicked on a document and whistled. "You were right.
There's money to be made in smuggling crocodiles"

"Hang on. I might have something here," he called
over his shoulder as he bent to retrieve a duffel that had
been shoved into the corner under a table.

"What have you got?" Madeline asked, coming to
stand beside him as he put the bag on the table and
unzipped the main compartment.

"A couple of guns," he said, lifting out a sniper rifle. "Whoever our guy was, he was ready for action. Ammo"—he pulled out a couple of clips and put them on the table—"and a scope. And night vision goggles. This guy was definitely a pro."

"As opposed to?"

"A revolutionary or even a drug runner. This guy's got top-of-the-line equipment here. I'm betting a mercenary."

"You think di Silva hired him?"

"I don't know," he said, pulling open a Velcroed pocket tucked into the inside of the bag, "but maybe this will tell us." He extracted a thin nylon pouch, the kind internationals used to protect their papers, and pulled out a passport.

"So what's it say?" Madeline pushed close in her eagerness to see, and despite the gravity of the situation, Drake felt his body respond to her proximity, pheromones overriding good sense.

Ignoring the stirrings, he opened the passport, thumbing through it. "The passport was issued in Portugal. His name is Paolo Montague." He sorted through the rest of the stuff in the pouch. Some Columbian currency, about a hundred dollars American, and an international driver's license. "License has the same name. Does it mean anything to you?"

"No. It's not a name I've heard Ortiz mention. Or di Silva, for that matter. But the organization is large. And I certainly don't know everyone."

"Which means we can't rule out his having been sent by Ortiz or di Silva. And if he was, then we've got bigger troubles than I anticipated."

"I don't understand," she said, shaking her head.

"I told you I expected di Silva to come after you, but this guy beat us to the punch. Which means they expected us to take this particular route."

"Seems a fairly obvious choice. I mean, you said yourself that following the river was the easiest way to get to the coast."

"Agreed." He frowned, trying to sort through conflicting thoughts. "But there's no way they could have known for certain what we'd do. And between the rain and our river ride, tracking us should have been difficult to impossible. Meaning that even if they worked it out and found a way to follow us, there wouldn't have been time for this guy to have beat us here. Especially coming from downriver."

"Maybe he's not affiliated with di Silva," she said. "Maybe he's working for FARC. They do hire mercenaries. And you said they still have people in this area."

"I suppose," Drake said, rummaging further into the bag. The bottom was loose, and he lifted it to reveal a second Velcroed pocket.

"It makes more sense, really. It explains his being here before us. And it also explains his need for advanced weaponry. Maybe FARC is planning some kind of attack."

"He's not FARC." Drake shook his head, holding out a photograph he'd pulled from the hidden compartment.

"It's me," she whispered.

"No question."

She lifted her head, her gaze locking with his. "I didn't have anything to do with this. Whatever *this* is," she said, punctuating the thought with a wave of her hand. "I swear."

"I know."

She looked so surprised by his immediate acceptance that if the next photograph hadn't been so alarming, he'd have smiled. Instead he held it out for her.

"I don't understand." She shook her head, a frown creasing her forehead as she stared down at the second photo.

"It's simple, actually. There's no way di Silva could have known that I was the man traveling with you. And even if there was, there's absolutely no way he'd have access to my photograph."

"Maybe he pulled it off his security cameras?"

"Hannah and Jason disabled them while I was inside the hacienda. And besides," he said, looking down at the picture, "this was taken two years ago. At Sunderland. The only way this guy could have known that I was here—with you—is if someone from my organization told him."

"So what are you saying?" she asked.

"That Nash was right. Someone on the inside is selling information. And it's probably someone I know."

CHAPTER 15

Eloy Afaro Air Base, Marto, Ecuador

figure if Drake is making his way to Puerto Remo, he'll head for the river and then use it to access the coast." Avery used a light pen to trace the line of the Rio Negro as it wound its way down from the mountains. "Of course that's only one of any number of potential routes."

"Yes, but if possible, he'll choose the most straightforward option," Nash said, studying the map.

"Agreed." Annie nodded. "But if di Silva's men are in pursuit, he might avoid the river for exactly the same reason."

"Bottom line is that we have no way of knowing where the hell he is." Nash sighed. "Have we got any kind of intel?"

The three of them were holed up in a conference room at the air force base hospital. Tyler was still recuperating, waiting for the doctor's official okay to travel. So they'd decided to meet here to finalize plans for Nash and Annie's trip into Colombia.

"Not much," Avery said. "If the Colombian government suspects, they aren't talking. And we know di Silva isn't going to want anyone knowing that his operations have been compromised."

"It's also possible that they don't know Drake's there, right?" Annie asked.

She'd arrived only hours before, coming without question when Avery had requested her help. Since Adam's rescue, Annie had chosen to stay at home with her and Nash's son, her need to be a mother overriding her desire to be part of the action. But this was different. Drake was their friend. And at the moment, Annie and Nash were the cavalry.

"Unfortunately, it's looking more and more like they do." Avery hit a button on his laptop and the map changed into a photograph of a couple of men Nash didn't recognize. "This photograph was taken thirty-six hours ago. Outside the di Silva Coffee offices in Bogotá. The men are a couple of contract players. Paolo Montague and Alexander Petrov."

"I've heard of Petrov," Nash said, studying the man's profile. "Wasn't his name linked with the assassination of that French foreign minister in the Congo?"

"Yes." Avery changed the slide to a new photograph, this one a close-up of Petrov. The man had the hardened look of a killer. "Nothing was ever proven, of course, but then Petrov's known for his invisibility."

"And Montague?" Annie asked. "I'm assuming he's cut from the same cloth?"

"Yeah." Avery switched to yet another picture, this one a close-up of Montague, his lips curling into a sneer. "He contracts out to whomever for whatever as long as the price is right. Only he's a little pickier about the work. Word is that he's the guy you call when you want to have someone taken out."

"Have you seen him before?" Nash asked Annie. She'd spent her time in the CIA working as an assassin. And since it required a very specialized skill set, there was a tendency for operatives to know their counterparts, no matter whose side they were on.

"No." Annie shook her head. "But I've been out of the game a long time. I'm guessing they've been called in to eliminate the problem?"

"Unfortunately, that seems to be the case. We've got solid evidence that Montague arrived in Buenaventura shortly after we were airlifted out, and anecdotal intel that Petrov's also in the area."

"They move fast."

"Yes, well they'd have to, wouldn't they? Di Silva is bound to know we'll be trying to get to them as well. And they'd want to strike before we get there, if at all possible. Keep the odds in their favor."

"So Drake and Madeline could be walking into an ambush," Nash said, his jaw tightening in anger.

"It seems possible." Avery nodded, his eyes reflecting Nash's ire. "Although they'll still have no idea where exactly Drake will be headed. We picked Puerto Remo specifically because it isn't the kind of place one would choose for a rendezvous."

"That should at least buy us some time," Annie said. "What about di Silva's men? Are they still in pursuit?"

"Yes. According to Hannah's sources, we've got activity in the area near the explosion as well as sightings of men along the roads leading to Buenaventura."

"And di Silva?" Nash asked.

"He's still in Bogotá. Acting for all the world as if nothing's amiss."

"But, in reality, he's got all the bases covered," Nash noted. "At least the activity would indicate that di Silva doesn't have Drake. No need to call in mercenaries if you've already captured the quarry."

"True enough," Annie mused, eyes narrowed as she considered the possibilities. "So is it possible Drake could already be on his way out?"

"No. If he'd made it to the safe house, we'd have heard." Avery shook his head. "There's a secure phone there. He'd know to use it first thing. Although it's still possible that we'll have heard from him by the time you get to Puerto Remo."

"Which would make our job a heck of a lot easier," Annie said. "But on the off chance that he's not there, how do you want us to proceed?"

"If he's not in Puerto Remo, then the primary objective is to figure out where the hell he is, and get him out. I figure the most likely scenario is that he's still upriver, working his way toward the coast."

"So we head in that direction, and hopefully intercept," Nash said.

"Unless Montague and Petrov beat us to it." Annie was still studying the photographs on the wall. "And we're assuming of course that Drake isn't alone. In all probability, he's found Madeline."

"I think the very fact that di Silva's brought in hired guns indicates that she's still alive," Avery said. "And if she is, then I think we can be fairly sure that Drake found her. And either way, di Silva's got to know that if she makes it out of the country his entire operation will be blown. I mean, ostensibly anyone who controls Madeline has automatic leverage over di Silva."

"Which is why he wants her dead."

"Well, at least if she's with Drake, she's got a chance," Nash said. "There's no way he'll go down without a fight."

"And besides, it's not like he's out there waving a banner." Annie shrugged. "They've got to find him before anything can happen. And I'm betting he's not going to make that easy. He's bound to know there'll be someone looking for them, even if he doesn't know specifically about Montague and Petrov. Which means he'll be on his guard."

"And hopefully this time tomorrow you'll be on the ground ready to offer support when he surfaces."

"What about you and Tyler?" Nash asked.

"She's been cleared to leave, so we'll head back to Sunderland. And as far as anyone knows, you've already left to meet Annie in the Caribbean for a little R&R. We need to do everything we can to foster the belief that we're sticking to Langley's directive."

"I still don't understand why they'd order you to leave a man behind," Annie said, shaking her head. "Not to mention a valuable asset. It just doesn't make any sense."

"Politically, the relationship between our countries is tenuous at best. If the Colombian government finds out that we ran an operation against di Silva without their consent, there will be all kinds of trouble diplomatically."

"So Drake gets sacrificed." Nash crossed his arms, thinking that as always the price was too high.

"Well, we're not going to let that happen."

"I know. It just chaps me that the suits in D.C. expect us to deal with operations that nobody else wants to touch, but then when we get into trouble, they're all about protecting their precious politics, the unit be damned."

"It's just part of the game. You knew the score when you came on board," Avery said. "Hell, Annie knows firsthand what the cost can be."

"And I also know that if it hadn't been for you guys' going off book to help me, I'd probably be sitting in a jail cell somewhere. Or worse—I'd be dead." Annie's somber gaze encompassed them both. "I don't want that to happen to Drake."

"It won't—because we're going to find him and bring him home," Nash said.

"You're awfully quiet," Drake said, as he directed the boat down the river. They'd been lucky to find the damn thing. Montague had hidden it well, but with a little perseverance they'd found it concealed in the reeds behind the shed.

"I'm fine," Madeline said.

"You're sure?" he asked, his eyes following the shoreline as the skiff moved past. So far they'd seen no sign of anyone following them, but that didn't mean there wasn't somebody out there.

"More than fine," she insisted with a bright little smile. "I mean, this is almost over, and I'll be away from all of this." She waved at the jungle, then her hand dropped back into her lap, and she sighed, her smile fading. "It's just that so much has happened."

"You're talking about killing Montague. That's what's bothering you, right?"

"I didn't have a choice." She shrugged, but he could see the tension in her shoulders, the regret in her eyes. "It was him or you."

"I'm glad you chose me." His words were meant to reassure, but he knew there was nothing he could do to alleviate her pain. "I know it was necessary, but that doesn't change the fact that you took a life. And that's never easy. Particularly not the first time."

"Except that it wasn't the first time," she said, still looking out at the passing landscape.

Silence held for a moment, the only sound the soft whoosh of the water and the birds calling from the trees.

"Do you want to tell me about it?"

"It was in Bogotá." The words were barely above a whisper. He hadn't really expected her to answer, but maybe there was something about being here on the run that made it easier to talk. To confess.

"What happened?"

"I told you I followed Jenny to Colombia. To try to get her to come home. To get help. But she was really far gone. We argued and she ran away. It took me about a week to find her. She was in this really run-down part of Bogotá. There were prostitutes and pushers. It was a nightmare."

"I can imagine," he said, wishing he could do something to make it easier for her, but also knowing that it was important for her to get it out.

"There was this building. An abandoned apartment building. It was like you see on television. People everywhere, shooting up, smoking crack. I'd brought a gun. But it didn't really make me feel any safer."

She swallowed once, then lifted her head, her gaze colliding with his. "Jenny was in a room on the second floor. And there was this man...he had her pinned to the wall, he was tearing at her clothes, and she was screaming for him to stop. I didn't even stop to think. Jenny was so frightened. I just pulled out the gun and shot him."

"You didn't have a choice."

"I know." She nodded, her chin jutting out. "But after that it got complicated. I told Jenny to run, and she did, but before I could get out of the building the police came. The man I shot was a politician of some kind. I never worked out exactly who. I tried to tell them my side of the story but they wouldn't listen."

"And you wound up at San Mateo."

Her eyes widened in surprise. "You know about that?"

"It was in your profile. We didn't know why you were there. Just that di Silva sprang you."

"It was Ortiz, actually. He offered me my freedom in exchange for my going to work for him."

"To pay off your sister's debt. But it seems like there'd be easier ways to get his money back."

"There was something more. Something unique I brought to the table. I had a relationship with a man who had information Ortiz wanted. I was working for Marton when I first went after Jenny."

"Henri Marton, the former ambassador?"

"Yes. Ortiz wanted me to steal the documents he needed from Henri."

"Using whatever tactics required," Drake said, understanding dawning. "That's what you meant when you called yourself di Silva's whore."

She nodded. "Only in truth it was Ortiz pulling the strings. And there were more men after Marton. But I did all of it to protect Jenny. And to get out of San Mateo. It was an awful place. I probably wouldn't have survived at all if it hadn't been for Andrés."

"Andrés?" he repeated, curiosity roused.

"He was my friend," she said, simply, a shadow passing across her face. "But friendships don't work out so well in a maximum-security prison. So mostly I was on my own."

"Couldn't the American authorities help you?"

"I wasn't given the chance. Apparently the man I shot had a lot of powerful friends. There wasn't anything even resembling due process. Anyway, the point is I've been through all of this before. Shooting someone, I mean. And even though I regret taking a life, I'd do it all over again if it meant saving my sister—or saving you."

She swallowed again and looked down at her hands, her teeth worrying her lower lip.

"Well, for what it's worth, I'm really glad you came to my rescue."

"You could have managed on your own, I'm sure," she said, but her lips moved into a tiny smile, and he felt as if he'd just won some kind of prize. "The truth is that if I'd just stayed in Cypress Bluff, if I'd never left Jenny, none of this would be happening."

"You can't second-guess yourself like that. You did what you thought was right at the time. And that's the best anyone can do."

"Yeah, but you wouldn't have made a mistake like that."

"The hell I wouldn't have," he said, his mind turning

to Cass. He'd believed in her. Thought there was a future for the two of them. And all the while she'd been leading him down the proverbial path. And in the end he'd killed her. "I've done unspeakable things. And believe me, I've made more than my share of mistakes. And for what it's worth, I'm sure wherever your sister is, she knows how much you loved her."

"Do you believe in an afterlife?" she asked, her eyes hopeful.

He started to lie, then thought better of it. Somehow the moment demanded truth. "No. I don't. In my line of work you see a hell of a lot of atrocities. And if there was really a God, surely he'd never let them happen."

"But it'd be nice," she whispered. "You know? A place where all the pain is gone. I want Jenny to have something better than she had here on earth."

"She had you," he said, his voice quiet. "And I think that probably meant more to her than you'll ever know."

"I hope that you're right." She sighed, pushing back her hair. "Did you ever tell your brother? How much he meant to you, I mean?"

"We were guys. We didn't talk about stuff like that."

"Not even after you grew up?"

"Especially then. But we didn't know we were on borrowed time. You always think you have forever. And now, I guess I'm like you, I'd like to think his spirit is out there somewhere."

"Maybe they're together." She smiled, the expression lighting up her face. "It's a nice thought anyway. I bet they would have liked each other."

"Maybe so," Drake said, covering her hand with his, the gesture meant to be comforting. But instead he got lost in the warmth of her eyes, something igniting deep inside him, and somehow he knew that in this moment, on a rushing river in the middle of the rainforests of Colombia, something had changed and there'd be no going back.

CHAPTER 16

Madeline relished the feeling of his hand against hers. She was acting like an adolescent, and she knew it, but then she'd never really had the chance to be young and carefree. And just for a moment, despite the situation, she felt something stirring. Something different from the usual rush of anger and resentment that dominated her life.

Hope.

She started to smile, then sobered, pulling her hand free as reality slammed home with a sickening jolt. "There's someone behind us. Another boat." It wasn't a whole lot bigger, but based on the roar from the engine, even at this distance, she had the feeling it was faster and probably more efficient.

"Don't borrow problems," Drake said, revving the outboard motor, the gesture in direct opposition to the thought. "We don't know that they're hostile."

"We don't know that they're not," she countered. "And

at least so far in this little adventure of ours, company has meant gunmen."

"Well, whoever they are, they're closing fast."

The boat was still trailing a good distance behind them, but Madeline could see that they'd already cut the distance by at least a quarter. "What are we going to do? We're not going to be able to outrun them."

"We're going to give it a try."

"And if that fails?" she whispered, her voice carrying under the sound of the straining motor.

"There's always—"

"Plan B." She nodded, her heart hammering, her gaze riveted on the boat behind them. "I know. Let's just hope this one doesn't involve jumping over a waterfall."

"Whatever keeps us alive," he said, turning to check out the boat behind them. "Looks like a cruiser."

"Is that good or bad?" she asked, not certain she wanted to hear the answer.

"Good in that it's slower than a jet boat. But bad in that it's going to hold more people."

"I don't suppose there's any chance of your friends riding to the rescue? A helicopter or something?"

"Grab the com link out of the bag. I don't think it'll work, but it won't hurt to try."

Madeline fumbled with the zipper in the backpack and then rummaged through the contents until she found the tiny earphone and corresponding transmitter. "I just talk into it, right?"

"There's a button by the earbud."

She pushed the button and stuck it into her ear, wincing as static vibrated through her head. "Hello?" she asked. "Is anyone there?" More static.

"Try switching to a different channel. Three maybe."

She twisted the button to the requisite number and tried again. Still nothing. "There's just static."

"It was worth a try." Drake shrugged, moving the skiff in a dizzying zigzag pattern through the water.

The cruiser behind them was closing fast. She could see people moving on a sun-shaded platform above the main deck. One was pointing. Another maybe steering. It was hard to tell for sure. But there was no mistaking the man by the railing with a gun.

"Grab the glasses," he said, nodding toward the pack again.

She tossed in the com link and pulled out the field glasses. "I can see a gun," she said. "The man above the deck. There are two others up there with him, but I can't make out whether they have weapons." As if on cue, the second man shifted and the fading sunlight hit the barrel of his gun. "Make that two of them armed."

"Handguns or something more?"

"Rifles. At least I think so. They're too long to be machine guns."

"You recognize any of them?"

She turned the knob to tighten the focus, her heart hammering. "Yes. Definitely di Silva's men. I recognize two of them."

"Damn bastards are everywhere," Drake said, his eyes back on the river in front of them. "Any sign of the old man or Ortiz?"

She moved the glasses in a slow arc. "I don't see them. And it wouldn't be like Ortiz to come on the hunt. He likes to keep a low profile. Always letting other people do his dirty work." Like her. She pushed away the thought as the cruiser's engine changed timbre, the boat picking up speed. "They're getting closer."

"Then we need to get ready."

"I'm not sure what we can do to beat the odds," she said. "They have a decided advantage. If nothing else, there are more of them and their boat is faster."

"Yes, but we're smarter."

It was a nice thought, but judging from the expression on his face, she wasn't certain that he actually believed it.

"So what do you want to do?"

"For now I want you to get your gun and take over the motor. I assume that bayou of yours required using boats?"

She nodded. "We had one a lot like this."

"All right then, I want you to take over. But I need you to stay down. As low as you can and still see to navigate. No matter what's happening I need you to keep your eyes on the river in front of us. You think you can do that?"

"No problem," she said, pulling the gun from the waist of her pants. "What are you going to do?"

"Give you cover when the time comes, and in the meantime try to figure a way out of this mess."

"Assuming there is one." She hadn't meant to sound so negative, but she was bone tired and the threats just never seemed to stop.

"Come on, now," he cajoled. "I didn't figure you for a quitter."

She lifted her chin, pushing aside her fear. "I'll be fine. You just work on getting us the hell out of here." Dropping onto the floor of the little boat, she shifted so that she could more easily control the motor and guide the skiff.

Drake moved to the other side, keeping the boat in balance as he eyed the cruiser behind them. Madeline concentrated on the river in front of her. The current had slowed, the banks widening as the Rio Negro moved closer to the sea.

"Try to keep the boat moving in a zigzag pattern. Not so much that we lose additional ground, but enough so that it's harder to figure trajectory." As if to verify his words, shots rang out, one of them ricocheting against the side of the boat. She veered to the left and then back to the right in response.

"That's the ticket," Drake said, the quirk of a smile lifting his upper lip. "At least we know now where we stand."

"Definitely not friendlies," she said, using his terminology, as another round of bullets cut into the water beside them.

"Just keep down, and keep the boat moving."

"Not a problem," she said, swerving again to the right and then back to the left, the little boat lurching as it moved through the water. Ahead of them the current picked up as the river grew more shallow, rushing across a group of boulders stretching from one side to the other.

"There are rocks ahead," she said. "I'm going to have to slow down. Make sure I don't hit anything."

Drake nodded, bracing himself against the side as the cruiser pulled closer, the hail of bullets finding purchase in the sides of the boat. Lifting his gun, he fired a couple of times in rapid succession, and one of the men fell over the railing and into the water.

"One down," he said, still firing, as she slowed to navigate the rapids.

The current grabbed the boat, sending it spinning forward, as Madeline fought to maintain control. Behind them the other boat slowed as well, recognizing the danger that lay ahead.

Drake dropped down beside her, reaching into his bag for a clip to reload. "We're down to three. Two shooters and the guy driving."

"I'd say that narrows the odds," she said, gritting her teeth as the boat scraped against the jagged side of a boulder.

"One more and I'd say we've got an advantage." He grinned and popped up to resume shooting as bullets slammed into the seat behind her, the other boat powering through the rapids. "Stay down," Drake called, a bullet just missing her hand.

She nodded, keeping her focus on the river and the skiff, passing the last of the boulders with a sharp release of breath. "We made it past the rocks, but the skiff took a hit, and the motor is running hot. There's no way we're going to outrun them."

"I know," he said, as the cruiser cleared the rocks and began firing again, this time one of their bullets finding its mark. Drake gasped, his face going tight with pain, his shoulder blossoming crimson.

"Oh, my God," she gasped, her heart stuttering to a stop. "You've been shot." She started toward him, her mind fixed only on making sure he was okay.

"No." He held up a hand. "Stay where you are. We've got to keep moving. I'll be okay. It's a through-and-through and it didn't hit the bone."

She hesitated for a second more, and the other boat

took advantage, moving closer, their gunfire audible now as bullets chased through the water.

"Madeline, move. Now."

She gunned the motor, pulling back ahead of the cruiser, keeping the little boat moving in an irregular pattern. Beside her, Drake popped up to fire again, the line of his jaw letting her know that he was not okay. Forcing herself to push all thoughts of him out of her mind, she concentrated instead on the water in front of them.

Ahead she could see a bend in the river, and just beyond it, the beginnings of what looked to be an island. Madeline squinted as she studied the curve, memory tugging, presenting a different body of water.

The bayou.

She'd been twelve. Jenny ten. And they'd been frog-gigging. It was really late and they were heading home when the lights of another boat had approached from behind. The bayou wasn't the safest place, especially at night, and even if the other boat proved not to be a threat, there was still the fact that they'd snuck out, and there'd be hell to pay if their father were to find out.

At first they'd tried to outrun the other boat, but when it had become apparent that they were losing ground, Madeline had doused the lights and pulled into a small cove. She could still feel Jenny's fingers closing around hers. Hearts pounding in unison, they'd waited. The other boat had roared past them, the darkness keeping them safe.

"Maybe we can use the island," Madeline said, pulling her thoughts back to the present, her memory giving her the germ of an idea. "If I take the narrow side, I don't think the cruiser will be able to follow." She nodded toward the tree-covered strip of land as they made their way around the bend.

Drake narrowed his eyes as he swung around to study the possibilities. "They'll cut us off on the far side, but maybe we can turn that to our advantage. Do it," he said, the stain on his shirt already turning dark as the blood oxidized.

The other boat was so close now, she could read the call letters on the side. Bullets slammed into the skiff and strafed the water. She pulled the boat to the right, giving every indication of following the current along the wider side. The cruiser followed suit, and the two boats careened through the rushing waters.

Then, just as they reached the point of the island, Madeline pulled the little boat hard to the left, the skiff skipping across the water like a giant stone. In seconds, they were behind the shelter of the trees, leaving the other boat no choice but to continue forward along the opposite shore.

"Are you okay?" she asked.

"I've had worse." He grimaced. "We'll deal with it when we get out of this."

"All right," she said, accepting his assessment. "I've bought us a couple of seconds. What do you suggest we do?" She slowed the boat slightly, as they continued to move forward, with an occasional glimpse of the other boat through the trees.

"I've got an idea, but it's going to be tricky. I want you to pace the boat so that the gap between us is infinitesimal. Then as we hit the end of the island I want you to slow down so that we're behind them as we come out from cover."

"But we'll be trapped. There's no way this engine can outrun theirs going upriver."

"I don't want to outrun them," he said. "I want to take them out. One shot to the gas tank and they're history."

"You think you can manage that? We're sitting a lot lower than they are, and being that close will make us sitting ducks. And besides, you're hurt."

"That has nothing to do with it." He frowned. "Timing is the key. You've got to make them think you're coming out in front until the very last second. Then you've got to kill the engine so that they pass us and I can get off a shot. Then you're going to have to gun us into reverse so that we don't get caught in the blast."

"Piece of cake," she lied, praying that she was indeed up to the challenge. "Just be sure you hit the tank the first time. I doubt we'll have a second chance."

"Roger that," he agreed. "Which means that I need to up our odds. Give me your gun."

She passed it across to him, frowning. "What are you going to do?"

"Pull a Rambo. Two guns are always better than one."

"Just be careful," she whispered, surprised at the emotion in the plea.

"Not a problem." He shot her a smile, checking the clips in both guns. "I'd say we'll ETA in less than a minute. Remember, timing is crucial, so wait for my go to kill the engine."

She nodded as he moved into place at the front of the boat, aligning himself for the best possible shot.

Beside her through the trees, Madeline could see the white of the cruiser as it moved along the river. She slowed a little to let it pull ahead slightly, and then gunned the engine again as they moved toward the far point of the island.

The two boats pulled out from behind their respective sides of the island almost running parallel. Madeline held her breath as she watched the other boat, her brain focused on the task at hand as she waited for Drake to signal.

Time seemed to slow to a crawl, everything moving in slow motion. Then suddenly it sped up again as Drake called "now," and she killed the engine, the little skiff jumping forward, then hitting the water hard, the cruiser so close, she could almost reach out and touch it.

On board the men scrambled to realign themselves as their boat shot past.

The skiff was rocking violently, caught in the cruiser's wake, but, somehow, Drake managed to keep his balance, rising to his feet, as he fired both guns simultaneously at the stern of the cruiser.

One second everything seemed to go silent, and then the world exploded in a cacophony of light and sound. Flaming bits of the cruiser rained down on them as Madeline jolted the engine back to life, the little boat skimming backward into the shelter of the leeward side of the island.

Madeline killed the engine again, the boat bobbing as the river absorbed the reverberations of the explosion. Adrenaline peaked, then ebbed, as the smoke cleared and the pale blue of the evening sky glimmered overhead, an early star twinkling among the leaves of the trees.

Ahead of her, beyond the island, she could just make out the remnants of the burning wreckage. "You think they're dead?" she whispered.

Drake nodded, grim satisfaction spreading across his face. "A fast ticket straight to hell."

CHAPTER 17

The river had grown so wide it was difficult to make out the far bank in the fading light. But the lights of Puerto Remo twinkled in welcome, and Madeline felt her heart soar. "Is that it?"

"Yeah. We're almost there. I think we need to ditch the boat, though, and walk the rest of the way. No telling who might recognize it and we don't need questions right now."

What they needed was an emergency room and the Four Seasons, but based on the shacks they'd passed in the last few minutes, Madeline was guessing Puerto Remo didn't actually lend itself to such accommodations.

The town was set at the mouth of a shallow bay, the Rio Negro emptying itself into the Pacific Ocean. High on a ridge towering over the town were the tumbled remains of what appeared to have once been a commanding building.

"It's a cathedral," Drake said, following her line of

sight as he headed the boat for shore. "Or it was supposed to be. It was never actually finished. Fifty or sixty years ago, some bishop decided that this was going to be the next great city in Colombia. He commissioned the cathedral and renamed the town after himself."

"Bishop Remo, I presume?"

"Exactly. But as you can see"—he waved at the ramshackle houses and palm-frond huts bordering the river—"the idea never took off. Buenaventura became the go-to spot, and Puerto Remo pretty much stayed the sleepy village it had always been."

"And the bishop?"

"Died here, actually. Malaria. So much for his grandiose dreams."

"But he must have accomplished something. I mean, you said there was a port?"

"Nothing to write home about. It provides harbor for the local fisherman, a day trip for more adventurous tourists, and valuable access to shipping lanes for the upriver drug trade. Look, we're almost to shore. Why don't you head for the bank while I take care of the boat."

She nodded and then climbed out of the skiff, wading through the shallow water to the edge of the river.

Drake wrapped a tattered piece of canvas around the barrel of his gun and shot twice into the bottom of the boat, the material muffling the gun's report. Then he pushed it back out into the current, the little boat already riding lower as it filled with water.

"Kind of feel like you just shot a friend," Madeline said, watching as the boat drifted into the current, the stern riding considerably lower now than the pointed bow. "How long before it sinks?"

"Ten or fifteen minutes, I'd think."

"So what happens next?" she asked as he joined her on the shore. The area where they'd landed was deserted, but there was a beaten path beside the river leading down into the town.

"We see what we can do about finding you that shower."

"And getting you bandaged. How are you feeling?"

"Nothing I can't deal with. Like I said, I've been through worse. The bleeding's stopped," he shrugged, "which is a good sign. It's only my shoulder. Nothing a little astringent and a bottle of rum won't cure."

"And some hot food and a bed." Her stomach growled, just thinking about it. "Will we be safe enough to stay the night?"

"I don't think we have a choice. We need the time to regroup."

"Any chance that it's over?" she asked.

"I don't think we can go that far. We know our friend at the outpost didn't have time to radio anyone. But I think we have to assume that the men on the boat had the chance to let Ortiz know where we were. Which means they know we'll probably head to Puerto Remo. But I'm thinking we've got a small window before they can possibly launch a new attack. And hopefully by then we'll be long gone."

"Sounds like a plan." She tried for a smile, but couldn't quite muster it.

"Look, we're going to be okay. We've made it this far. All we have to do now is keep our eyes open and make sure the safe house lives up to its name."

"Is it really a house?" she asked, glancing at the huts

and shacks starting to pop up in the dusk as they walked
along. So far they hadn't encountered any inhabitants, but
the wisps of smoke curling from the rooftops indicated
that someone at least was inside.

"More of a cottage, I suppose. A hacienda. It's situated
in the center of town, which makes it an unlikely choice
for our purposes."

"Like hiding in plain sight?"

"That's the general idea, yeah."

They turned onto a graveled street, the houses beginning to look a little less ramshackle, some of them
painted bright colors, the pink and yellow standing out
against the lush greenery and bright red of bougainvillea
and bromeliads.

A woman sat on a blanket at the corner, baskets piled
around her. She smiled as they passed, the smooth lines
of her face reflecting both her South American and African heritages. A block farther on, they'd moved into the
center of the village, an open-air market filling the central
square. Brightly patterned clothes and mouth-wateringly
fresh foods filled the stalls, and it was everything Madeline could do to resist running across the street and buying everything in sight.

As if recognizing the train of her thoughts, Drake's
hand tightened on her arm. "It's not much farther now," he
said, keeping his voice low. "Try to look like a tourist."

"A tourist stranded in the jungle, maybe." She swallowed a bubble of laughter, relief making her giddy as she
tried to imagine what she must look like.

"This is it." He nodded at an ochre-colored building. The front yard was full of swaying palms, flowers
blooming in the gardens that bordered steps leading to

an internal courtyard. A fountain gurgled, the heady fragrance of hibiscus filling the air.

"It's beautiful," Madeline whispered, her eyes feasting on the riot of color and smell. "Like paradise before the fall."

"Literally," Drake said, as he pushed aside a decorative tile to reveal a keypad. He punched in a number and the lock clicked open. "Wait here." He pulled his gun, his face hardening as he pushed open the door and swung over the threshold.

Madeline stood, frozen to the spot, her breathing shallow, as her hands closed around her own gun. The breeze ruffled through the little garden, and she strained into the silence for some sound to indicate that Drake was all right.

Emotion surged as she fought against memories of the past few days. So much had happened. They'd even established a fragile sense of trust. Madeline closed her eyes, reliving the feel of Drake's mouth against hers, their tongues dueling, bodies throbbing with desire. She shivered, the involuntary movement having nothing whatsoever to do with fear.

It would be so wonderful to let down her guard. To open her heart just a little. Surely there was nothing wrong with grabbing happiness, even if it was only for a night.

Life was to be lived in the moment.

And there had never been more reason to celebrate than their safe arrival in Puerto Remo. Tomorrow was another day. She'd deal with it when it came.

And in the meantime...

She smiled as Drake beckoned from the doorway.

*   *   *

Drake walked down the hallway toward the living room, noting that the door to Madeline's bathroom was still closed. She'd made a beeline to the bathtub, stopping only long enough for him to reassure her that for the time being at least they were safe.

He could hear her humming, and his brain immediately projected an image of her naked in the tub, the soap sliding down her body, over her breasts and between her legs. His body tightened and he took a step toward the door. It was tempting to join her, to finish what they'd started in the jungle. But there were more important things at stake. And for the moment at least he had business to tend to.

He walked into the main room and knelt in front of the vent—using his knife to work the grate off. Inside, as expected, he found a wrapped package containing a secure satellite phone and an extra handgun with ammo. There was also several thousand dollars. He tossed the money and gun onto a table.

After checking to make certain Madeline was still in the bath, he walked into his bedroom, closed the door, and dialed Nash's number. The phone rang twice then flipped over to voice mail. With a muttered curse he left a message and headed across the room to his bathroom and a shower. His wound, though not dangerous, was starting to throb, and infection was always a risk.

Fifteen minutes later, he emerged from the bathroom, rubbing his head with a towel. God, it felt good to be clean. He grabbed the phone, dialing Nash again. This time the phone picked up on the first ring.

"Where the hell have you been?" Nash barked. "I've been calling you back every couple of minutes."

"Sorry," Drake said, dropping down to sit on the end of the bed. "I needed a shower."

"Where are you?" Drake could hear the relief in his friend's voice.

"We just made Puerto Remo. Had a little adventure on the way."

"So you've got Madeline?" Nash queried. "Was she much of a problem?"

"Actually, she proved herself a hell of a traveling partner. Go figure. Anyway, we're here and safe, but I wouldn't count on it staying that way too long. We had a couple of run-ins with di Silva's people. Although Madeline says it's some guy named Ortiz pulling the strings. You ever heard of him?"

"Got a first name?"

"Hector. Came into the picture four, maybe five years ago."

"Doesn't ring a bell, but di Silva is notoriously secretive about his organization, so it wouldn't be hard for him to have stayed under the radar. I'll pass the info on to Avery. See what he can come up with."

"Good. Maybe then we can figure out how these people always seem to find us."

"You think maybe there's a bug?"

"No. I checked. Madeline's got a bag with her. But it's clean. I'm pretty sure we'd know if it was on her. She's definitely not playing on di Silva's team. Besides, we killed a guy upriver who was carrying photographs."

"Of Madeline?"

"And of me. An old photo taken at Sunderland." He waited, letting the significance of his words sink in.

"Sounds like we've got a bigger problem than just di Silva."

"Yeah, first Tyler's gear is fucked up. And now this guy's got a picture of me. Which means he knows we were behind the rescue."

"And the only way he could have known that," Nash continued the thought, "is if someone on the inside tipped him off."

"Could have come from Langley," Drake said. "Or from inside our operations. The whole team knew what we were up to. Including ancillary staff."

"Avery and Tyler are working that angle. And until we can be sure what's what, Avery decided we'd go eyes-only. Just him, Tyler, Annie, and me."

"Annie?"

"Well, Tyler's not exactly up to traveling." It was Nash's turn to pause.

"What the hell happened?"

"She's fine. But she took a bullet at the ruins. It came really close to her heart. It was pretty dicey there for a while."

"I saw the explosion. And the helicopter. At least I knew that some of you had gotten out. Jason okay?"

"Yeah, he's good. Already back at Sunderland. Avery's fine, too. He and Tyler flew home this morning. Anyway, with everything happening, we figured it was better to keep our little operation under the table, so to speak."

"I'm assuming when you refer to 'our operation' you're talking about me."

"Yeah. And Madeline. We're en route to you now. Annie and I." Drake could hear her saying something to Nash. "Annie wants to know if you're okay."

"Took a bullet myself, but it was nothing. Just nicked my shoulder. More blood than bite. I'll be fine."

"What about Madeline?"

"Like I said, amazingly resilient."

"I take it you've changed your opinion of her."

He paused, surprised to find just how far he'd come. "She's all right. The journey could have been a hell of a lot harder than it was. Like I said, she rose to every occasion. Even took out the guy I was telling you about."

"The one with the pictures."

"Yeah. Guy named Paolo Montague. You know him?"

"He's a mercenary out of Portugal. Contracts worldwide. We have intel that indicates he's working with di Silva, and I guess your run-in is confirmation."

"Well, he's not working for anyone anymore."

"Was he alone?"

"As far as I could tell. He'd killed the guy who was staying at the outpost, but there's no way they were together. Why?"

"Because we think there's another mercenary working for di Silva. Alexander Petrov."

"I've heard of him. A seriously bad hombre."

"That's what Avery said. Any sign of him?"

"We blew up a boatload of bastards about six miles upriver. Definitely di Silva's men. Madeline recognized two of them. But I didn't get a close look."

"Well if Petrov is still out there he's a dangerous man. And blowing up a boat is a hell of a calling card."

"We didn't have much choice. I disposed of Montague, though. And his victim. Figured it was better not to leave anything behind."

"Well, that's something. Anyway, just be careful."

"So where the hell are you anyway?"

"On a boat out of Santiago. We took a transport out of Ecuador this morning. Bit of a circuitous route, but if someone's watching we don't want them to catch on to what we're doing."

"Which would be?"

"Sailing to your rescue. Although it doesn't sound like you need the cavalry."

"Well, I could use some help getting out of here."

"That I can arrange. Avery's got people on standby."

"I thought this one was off the books."

"It is. But Avery's got friends in some pretty interesting places. People he trusts. And since I trust him—"

"Me, too. And I gotta tell you it's good to hear your voice. When do you think you'll be here?"

"Hopefully sometime tomorrow morning. Depends on if we encounter any problems coming in from international waters."

"You expecting something?"

"No. But the Colombians can be a picky lot. Anyway, the guy who's captaining is a national, so that should help. You're at the safe house, right?"

"Yeah. We'll stay put until you get here, unless something happens."

"Just hang on to the sat phone," Nash said. "I don't want to lose you again."

"You and me both, brother."

"All right. We'll see you in a few. Watch your back."

"Roger that." Drake smiled as he hung up, then sobered. The idea that someone within the CIA was jeopardizing their missions was hard to swallow. Especially the idea that it was someone within A-Tac. But it was hard to ignore the rapidly expanding stack of evidence.

Anyway, for the moment, he needed to concentrate on keeping Madeline out of harm's way. They could figure out the rest once they were safely out of Puerto Remo.

He walked into the hallway, noticing that Madeline's bedroom door was ajar. He knocked and then called her name. But there was no answer. Frowning, he pushed open the door only to find the room empty. There was a towel on the bed, and some of her clothes wadded up on the floor.

Moving with stealth now, he crossed into the living room to pick up the gun on the table, noticing, when he did, that the money from the stash was gone. Damn it to hell.

The bitch had played him.

•

CHAPTER 18

He tore for the front of the house cursing Madeline, himself, and womankind in general. He should have known better. A leopard never changed its spots. Hell, she'd probably made up all that stuff about the dead sister and the man she'd shot. Not to mention the abusive father.

Sympathy card—worked every time.

He'd never learn.

Yanking the heavy door open, he tried to calculate where exactly she'd have tried to run, and skidded to a stop. The tiny courtyard was full of light, candles glowing everywhere—like little pinpricks in the velvet darkness.

"There you are," Madeline said, lighting a candle and then blowing out the match. "I was just coming to look for you." Her eyes met his, but her smile faded when she saw the gun. "Is everything all right?"

"Just being careful," he lied, stepping out into the courtyard. "Where did you find the candles?"

"I bought them in the market. Clothes, too," she said, spinning around to show him her skirt. "It's an improvement. Don't you think?"

"Yeah. You look great." He nodded, still trying to shift gears. In point of fact, she looked beautiful. A far cry from the torn sweats and camisole she'd been wearing. Her skirt was fluid and gauzy, the brightly colored material sparkling in the candlelight. The white peasant blouse draped softly over her breasts to gather at the waist, the effect emphasizing just how small it was. Her face, freshly scrubbed, looked young and alive. And her hair had been tamed into a thick braid that she'd tied with a red satin ribbon.

His fingers itched to free the strands and tangle his fingers in the soft curls.

Obviously, relief was making him crazy.

"You shouldn't have gone out," he said, knowing he sounded peevish, but it beat sounding horny.

"I was careful." She shrugged. "And the market is just across the street."

"You could have been seen."

"But I wasn't," she said, moving to stand in front of him, her head tipped up so that she could look him in the eyes. "And I wanted to do something to say thank you . . ." Her voice faded as she picked nervously at the material of her skirt. "For all that you've done for me."

"It's a nice gesture." He nodded at the candles. "I just don't want anything to happen to you."

"I'm fine. I swear. I'm sorry if I worried you." Her gaze dropped to the gun in his hand. "I just went out to buy a few things."

"There was a couple thousand dollars on the table,

Madeline." He wasn't sure why he was goading her. Maybe because the idea that she'd left him had mattered more than he wanted to admit, even to himself.

Her eyes flashed with understanding. "You thought I'd run again."

He nodded.

"I see." She sucked in a breath, her fingers lacing together. "Well, for the record, I grabbed the stack without realizing how much money was there. And the bulk of it is on the kitchen counter. Next to a change of clothes— for you. Mine aren't the only ones that have seen better days."

She let her gaze run up and down him, and despite the fact that he was still angry with her, he suddenly wanted nothing more than to take her right here in the candlelit courtyard.

"Look, Madeline, I…"

"It doesn't matter." She shook her head. "Nothing matters tonight except that we're here and we're safe. Everything else will keep until the morning. All right?" Her gaze was hopeful, and he felt guilty for believing the worst of her.

"I'll go change," he said, turning to leave, still feeling as if he'd let her down somehow.

"Wait," she said, her hand on his arm. "What about your wound? Do you want me to help you dress it?"

He sucked in a breath, knowing it was a stupid idea— letting her touch him. "I did it myself."

"And I'm sure you did a fine job." She nodded. "Except that it's difficult to bandage yourself. Especially a shoulder." She reached for the neck of his T-shirt, pulling it down. "Not bad. But you need more padding."

"So what? Now you're a nurse?"

A shadow crossed her face, and he wished the words back. Hell, everything he said was coming out all wrong.

"When my father was on a tear he could do a lot of damage," she murmured. "So I guess the nursing skills are a product of necessity. Cypress Bluff didn't offer much in the way of medical care."

"I'm sorry," he said, lifting a hand to caress her face. "I can't even imagine."

"Just as well," she said, her gaze meeting his. "I wouldn't wish my life on anyone. But tonight isn't about the past—or the future. It's about now. About letting go and enjoying the moment. So let's go back inside and I'll rewrap this and then we can have our dinner."

"There's food?" he asked, as she shoved him toward the door. Living in the now had a hell of a lot of appeal, and not just on the sensual level. He wanted her. There was no denying the fact, but he also craved something more. A sense of normalcy. And the idea that if even for a night, the two of them could pretend to be regular people leading regular lives—well, it was a hell of a fantasy.

"Yes, of course," she was saying. "That was actually the point of going out in the first place. Your safe house might be safe, but it's poorly stocked."

They walked back into the house and for the first time he noticed the smell of something wonderful bubbling on the stove.

"That smells amazing," he said, as she pushed him toward the bedroom.

"Just some stuff I bought in the market," she said, tossing the clean clothes on the bed and indicating that he should sit down. "Take off your shirt."

For just a moment his imagination went into over-drive, but he pushed the images aside as she picked up the medical kit, her intent clearly business. With a wince, he lifted his arms and removed the shirt, noticing that his makeshift bandage had already come loose.

She carefully peeled it off. "It hasn't started bleeding again. Which is a good sign. And it looks like it's clean." She probed the wound, and he winced again. "Sorry. I'm not trying to hurt you. I just wanted to make sure the bullet was gone."

"No worries there." He twisted so that she could see his back. "There's an exit wound."

"Right. I forgot." She ripped several strips from the pillowcase, folding them into two small pads, one for the front and one for the back. "At least that should help it heal. I'd say, all things considered, you're a pretty lucky man."

"And you really do know your way around a bandage," he said, as she spread antibiotic on one of the pads.

"Yeah, well, as I said," she said, keeping her eyes on her work, "my father wasn't keen on doctors. Too many questions." He opened his mouth to reply, but she shook her head. "It was a long time ago. Water under the bridge." She shrugged, using some tape to secure the bandages. "There you go." She stepped back to admire her handiwork. "All done."

"I don't suppose you bought any aspirin when you were out in the market?" he said, rotating his shoulder to test the bandage, the pain bearable but still uncomfortable.

"No. But I did remember the rum." She smiled. "Put on your new clothes and then we'll have a drink while I finish heating our dinner."

She walked out the door and he shook his head,

wondering how someone could come through all that she'd endured and still be able to smile like that. He understood the will to survive. But with Madeline there was something more. As if somehow she'd been able to keep a part of herself separate from all the ugliness.

He shook his head, pushing the thought aside, almost before it was fully formed. Women lied, used whatever tools necessary to obtain what they wanted. It was a cynical view. But it was the only way to protect his heart. Better to take a step back than risk getting hurt again.

He changed into the pants and shirt she'd bought, grateful for the feel of clean cotton next to his skin. Then, after tucking the gun into the back of the pants, he walked back into the living room to find Madeline behind the counter, stirring the pot and humming softly to herself.

"The clothes are great," he said, sliding onto a barstool, careful to keep his tone neutral. "So what am I smelling?" he asked, moving the subject to safer ground.

"It's called *sancocho*. A fish stew. Ingredients vary by location, but I figured since we're on the coast it's probably going to be good. And I bought *arepas*— these are corn. They're sweeter than tortillas you'll find at home, but I find they offset the stew nicely."

"I'm impressed."

"Don't be. I've lived in Colombia for over three years now. It'd be impossible not to have gained a little knowledge about local specialties. The rum's over there." She nodded toward the far end of the counter. "I didn't know how you liked it. So there's fruit juice—or if you prefer, just some fresh lime."

"What are you having?" he asked, walking over to the makeshift bar.

"Rum and *feijoa*. It's a kind of guava. Really sweet. I like it."

"Think maybe I'll stick with the lime."

"I suspected that might be more your style. You don't seem like an umbrella drink kind of guy."

"Actually, I prefer scotch. Straight. But when in the tropics—" he said, squeezing a lime into his glass, then raising it. "Cheers."

"To better days." She lifted her glass and then took a sip, the muscles in her throat working as she swallowed, their gazes locking for one long smoldering moment.

Drake took a long drink, clamping down on his surging hormones, while Madeline put her glass back on the counter, making a play of stirring the stew. At least his wasn't the only libido on overdrive.

"I think it's done," Madeline said, lifting a spoon to her lips, to verify. "Why don't you grab the *arepas* and I'll bring the stew. The table's already set outside."

He grabbed the basket with the tortillas and his drink and followed behind her, his eyes locked on the soft swaying of the skirt as her hips moved beneath it. After placing the food on the table, they sat down, and Madeline ladled the stew into earthenware bowls.

"Enjoy," she said as they began to eat.

Drake wasn't sure if it was the company or the fact that he hadn't eaten real food in days, but the stew was heavenly. "This is great," he said, reaching for a tortilla and dipping it into the broth.

"So you're not mad anymore that I went to the market?" she asked, a little frown cutting across her forehead.

"I wish you'd told me," he said, taking another bite, "but no, I'm not mad. This is perfect."

"I'm glad," she said, with a crooked little smile. "I wanted to do something nice. And they do say that the way to a man's heart is—" she cut herself off, the smile fading. "I'm sorry that didn't sound right. I just meant that I'm grateful for everything you've done."

"Well, it's not over, until we're safely out of here. Which means we have to stay alert. And you can't go running off without telling me."

"I know. I should have said something. But you were in the shower, and I really wanted to surprise you. Anyway, I won't do it again," she promised, solemnly. "Did you talk to your friends?"

"I did. And they're on their way. They should be here early tomorrow morning."

"So soon?" She frowned.

"I thought you'd be pleased. I mean the sooner we're out of here, the less likely it is that di Silva will find us. And you'll be free."

"I know," she said, her face shuttering. "I guess I was just enjoying this respite. I mean, once you get me back to D.C., it's going to be all about protective custody and testifying. Not exactly freedom in the true sense of the word."

"I guess I can see that," he said. "But it's got to be better than being forced to work for di Silva's organization." He nodded toward the fading bruise beneath her eye and self-consciously she reached up to touch it.

"Absolutely. But there's a part of me that wishes I could go back. Do it differently. Somehow keep Jenny alive."

"I think you did everything you could," he said, reaching out to cover her hand with his. "Given the situation, you made the right choices. Sometimes that just isn't enough."

She studied him for a moment, her eyes sparkling with

unshed tears. "Thank you for that. It means more than you can possibly know."

"Hey, I thought we were supposed to be living in the moment," he said, purposefully shifting the mood. "So no more thinking about the past."

"Or the future." She nodded. "At least until tomorrow." They sat for a moment listening to the sounds of the night. And then she smiled. "Do you hear that?"

He shook his head.

"Oh, come on. The music. It's coming from the market." She closed her eyes, swaying a little as the melodic sound of drums and guitars carried on the breeze. "When I was little my mother played her records and my sister and I would dance. And in that moment, nothing could hurt us."

"Then we should dance," he said, holding out his hand. "Although I should warn you I'm not that good at it."

"Doesn't matter." She smiled as he pulled her to her feet. "There's no one here to see you but me." She pulled close, their elbows bending between them, and then moved back again, arms straight, following the infectious Latin beat.

They moved around the courtyard, his feet miraculously following her movements. And as the music swelled to a crescendo, he whirled her around, his hand at the small of her back, dropping her into a deep dip at the end of the turn.

"I thought you said you couldn't dance," she said, eyes wide with pleasure and surprise as he pulled her upright again.

"I can't." He shook his head. "I was just winging it."

"Well, I liked it." She swayed gently as the band started a new tune, this one soft and slow. They stood in silence as the tune drifted across the courtyard, and then she lifted her arms. For a moment he considered refusing her, knowing that they were playing with fire. But in the end desire trumped reason and he pulled her close as they began to move together to the sweet, seductive sound.

She laid her cheek against his chest, her breathing slowing to match his, their bodies moving in sync as if they'd danced together often. She sighed, and he tightened his arms around her as they swayed back and forth, letting the music carry them around the courtyard.

He rested his chin on her head, the fragrance from her hair teasing his senses. The breeze brushed against them as they moved, carrying the sweet scent of hibiscus and the pulsing sound of the music. It circled them like a cocoon, keeping reality at bay. There was nothing here but the two of them. And for the moment at least, that suited Drake just fine.

They rocked together slowly, back and forth, no longer moving, just holding each other. The music changed, the tempo faster, but they stayed together, neither willing to break the spell.

Finally, Madeline mumbled something against his shirt. "It's not a slow dance anymore," she repeated, her voice clearer as she lifted her head.

"I know," he said, still not willing to let her go.

"Then maybe we should—" she started, but broke off as her gaze met his, her breath coming in an odd little gasp.

With a groan, he bent his head, slanting his lips over hers as he took possession of her mouth. It started as a gentle kiss, a counter note to the melody drifting over from the market, and then like a variation on a theme it became more sensual. More hungry.

She opened her mouth, welcoming him inside, and he relished the thrust of her tongue as they tasted each other. Thrusting and parrying. The tactile sensation becoming their own private language, both of them advancing and retreating. Giving and taking. A prelude of things to come.

His hands moved in slow, languid circles across her back, his breath lifting the tendrils of hair around her face. She moved closer, her hands twining through his hair, and the kiss built in intensity, passion coiling deep inside him. He wanted her. More than he'd wanted anything in a long time. Maybe it was the music, or hormones—hell, maybe he was just a fool.

He reached behind her, loosening her braid, and her hair cascaded over her shoulders. She laughed and tipped back her head. And he kissed her ears, her nose, his mouth trailing kisses along the line of her throat to the valley between her breasts. Her skin was soft and supple, smooth as silk.

His pulse pounding in his groin, he kissed his way back to her ear, dipping his tongue inside, sucking on the lobe, using his tongue to tease her, building the sensation until she squirmed beneath his touch, her breath shuddering in gasps of delight.

Madeline couldn't remember the last time a man had made her feel like this. As if anything were possible. She turned her head, taking his mouth again with hers. Loving the feel of his lips against hers, his beard rough against her face. She pushed closer, feeling his erection hard against her stomach. Her thighs clenched as her body demanded more, and she stood on tiptoe, pressing her heat against his.

His hands dropped, cupping her rear, the heat from his skin burning through the thin gauze of her skirt. The wind whistled as it picked up, singing through the little courtyard, and he swung her into his arms, his mouth finding hers again as he carried her into the house. With a groan built on desire, he lifted her up onto the kitchen counter, sending dishes crashing in his haste, his mouth crushing hers, his need for her laid bare with his kiss. Passion rose inside her, and she gave it to him freely, wanting him as much as he wanted her.

His hand brushed against the embroidered trim on her blouse, loosening the ties that held it closed. Then his fingers dipped inside, cupping her breast, his thumb rasping against her nipple, the sensation igniting the heat between her thighs. Gasping with pleasure, she arched back, offering herself to him. And with a wicked smile, he trailed hot kisses down the slope of her breast, the soft silk of his hair adding torment to the already unbearable heat.

When his lips closed around her nipple, tugging gently, she whispered his name, urging him on. His tongue circled, sucking softly as he drew her breast farther into his mouth. Bracing herself on her elbows, she leaned back, her body responding with a fervor she hadn't known she possessed.

Still licking and teasing her breast, he reached for the hem of her skirt, easing the gauzy cotton up her thigh. She trembled in anticipation as his fingers teased, moving higher, then higher still, until all that separated his fingers from the throbbing junction of her thighs was the soft satin of her underwear.

She held her breath as his fingers slid between her panties and her skin, circling lazily, slowly, until she thought she might explode. Then suddenly he was there, caressing her, stroking her, sending flickers of pleasure pulsing inside her. Swallowing a cry, she arched upward, forcing his fingers deeper, and he obliged, the internal rhythm increasing as he suckled her breast.

His mouth and his hands possessed her, driving her higher and higher, until there was nothing but the feel of him burning against her, inside her. He moved down, raining kisses along the smooth skin of her abdomen, crossing the divide marked by her bunched skirt, the heat of his lips making her writhe against him.

With amazing finesse he slid down her panties, removing them, lifting her legs over his shoulders as he bent to take her in his mouth. With a soft cry, she abandoned all decency, pushing against his head, urging him on, balanced on the edge of a precipice that scared and excited her beyond anything she'd ever imagined.

His mouth found her, his tongue driving deep inside her. He tasted her, drinking her in, pulling her soul from her body into his. The darkness surrounded her, caressing her as his tongue moved in and out, in and out, driving her higher and higher, until the darkness exploded with light, and she screamed his name, reaching to hold him, to anchor herself in the spinning vortex he'd created.

She arched against him, her body vibrating under the power of his touch. And she knew suddenly that it wasn't enough to find this heaven. She wanted more. She wanted him—inside her, needing her as much as she needed him.

Taking a shuddering breath, she pulled back, and, eyes still glazed with passion, pulled him up, wrapping her legs around him, feeling his hardness pulsing against her heat.

The sensation almost sent her over the edge again, but she knew what she wanted. She reached for the buttons on his shirt, her fingers trembling with desire as she pulled them free one by one. With a sigh of pure delight, she pushed his shirt off his shoulders, her breath catching at the sheer beauty of his hardened muscles and velvet skin.

She leaned forward, bending to kiss the edge of the bandage, her fingers gentle as she traced the line of his chest and shoulders. And then he pulled her hard against him, his mouth opening, accepting what she offered, raising the ante with the fervor of his kiss.

He pulled her off the counter, her legs still wrapped around him, tongues tangling together with need. They moved backward, into her bedroom, and after removing the rest of their clothes, he sat down on the bed, pulling her with him.

Pushing him back against the sheets, she leaned down, wanting to taste him as he'd tasted her. So she ran her tongue along the edge of one nipple, pleased when it tightened under her touch. Then she dropped her hand, first stroking the hard ridge of his stomach and then letting her fingers slip lower.

His skin was hot, and she closed her hand around his penis, stroking and squeezing, establishing a rhythm.

"Oh, God, Madeline," he rasped, his voice hoarse with emotion. "I want you."

"Good." She smiled, her eyes locking with his. "Because the feeling's mutual." She slid slowly downward, letting her breasts cup his penis, the sensation sending white-hot heat pooling inside her. And then she moved even lower, taking him in her mouth, sucking on his velvety strength.

And then with a growl, he took control, pulling her up and flipping her beneath him, his powerful body lifting over hers. "Are you sure?" he asked, his eyes dark with passion.

"I've never been more sure of anything," she whispered.

He smiled, and then bent to kiss her, his mouth branding her—claiming her as his. Madeline ached inside, wanting only to feel him fill her, two parts coming together to make a whole. She tipped back her head, welcoming his hands and mouth. He explored every inch of her, leaving nothing untouched, unloved. Trembling with the sheer power of the feelings he evoked, she opened to him, catching his gaze.

"Please, Drake. Now. I want you, now."

His smile was slow and sure, and with one swift move he buried himself deep inside her, filling her with his heat. The pleasure was exquisite, and she pushed against him, taking him even deeper.

There was desire and triumph reflected in the depths of his eyes—and something else, something so tender it almost took her breath away. She lost herself then, in his strength and passion.

Eyes still locked together, they began to move, slowly, almost languorously at first, each slow thrust tormenting and delighting. Up and down, in and out, the movement creating exquisite agony. He let her set the pace, and she kept it slow, relishing the delicious torture of her own desire. Her body strained to find release, even as her mind fought to control it. And she lifted her head to brush her lips across his. His fingers twined through her hair as he pulled her to him, deepening the kiss. And with the contact, the power shifted.

He grasped her hips, forcing his own rhythm, thrusting harder and deeper, faster and faster, the friction of their bodies moving together ratcheting her need higher and higher, until she felt as if she might explode.

And still he thrust, her muscles tightening around him, holding him inside her, until she could no longer tell where he ended and she began, in a kaleidoscope of emotion and sensation that seemed beyond endurance. And yet she wanted it—needed it—more than anything she could possibly have imagined.

His hands tightened hard against her hips, and then the world exploded, combusting into feelings so intense she felt as though she might be ripped apart. Wave after wave washed through her, pleasure and pain so intricately bound that her body shook with the impact.

Then she felt his arms close around her, heard the sweet whisper of her name as he kissed her face, and she let go, allowing herself to soar, to fly, and in that moment she felt invincible. As if she'd never fall.

But deep in her heart, she knew there would be a price to pay—for only fools dared to defy gravity.

CHAPTER **19**

The first pink fingers of dawn were stretching across the sky. Madeline sat at the end of the bed watching Drake sleep. She knew she should go. Knew that it was better to make a clean break. But still she stayed, watching him breathe. She so seldom trusted anyone. It seemed odd that she felt so comfortable with a man she'd known only a few days. Maybe it was because in some ways he reminded her of herself. Guarded. Cautious. Not the sort to suffer fools lightly.

And yet, he had a confidence she'd never known. Hers was strictly bravado. But Drake was the real thing. A man's man with a heart. A rarity for certain. And as unobtainable as the elusive gold at the end of a rainbow.

At least as far as she was concerned.

It was the captive falling for the jailer, and that was always a strategic mistake. He'd said it himself, she was just an asset. And when it came time to turn her over to the authorities in Washington, there'd be no hesitation. Mission first, last, and always.

He might regret the fact, but he'd never shirk his duty. His honor was his life. It was part of what she admired about him. What had drawn her to him, made her open up, share herself. But now, the time had come to take care of herself. It was a cold, cruel world. And she knew better than to believe in happy endings. Instead, she'd take the memory and store it away with the others. Jenny's laughter. Andrés's smile. Drake's eyes. His hands. His lips...

She shook her head, rising to her feet and turning her back. No last lingering look. It was simply too tempting to crawl back into bed—to pretend that tomorrow would bring more of the same. But it wouldn't. It couldn't. Drake's bosses didn't care about her. She was simply a means to an end. And Ortiz had already proven his determination to find and eliminate her.

Her only option was to disappear.

She slipped out of the bedroom, angry at herself for her tears. Good things happened to people who deserved them, but she wasn't foolish enough to think that included her. *You reaped what you sowed.* It was as simple as that.

The living room was still shadowed, and she crept into the other room, retrieving one of the guns, the sat phone, and Drake's wallet—still fat with cash. It wasn't as if he needed it, she justified. His friends were coming. But still she felt a tug of guilt, and after tossing a couple of bills on the table, she grabbed a torn slip of paper and scribbled the word "sorry." It wasn't enough. But anything more and she'd be blubbering like a baby.

And for all she knew, he'd be laughing at her anyway. A one-night stand. Probably the norm for a man like him. Any woman would be all too happy to grace his bed. And yet, even as she had the thought she decided it did him an injustice. Drake was more than that. Or at least she wanted him to be. One thing about riding off into the sunset—or sunrise, as the case might be—she got to leave with all of her fantasies intact.

They'd carry her a long way.

Shouldering her bag, she slipped out the front door, her throat tightening as her gaze caught on the remnants of last night's meal. It had been a perfect evening, one she'd never forget. But morning had come, bringing with it the harsh cold light of reality. So, with a determination borne of years of practice, she walked away from the hacienda without so much as a backward glance.

The market was just beginning to see signs of life, vendors arranging wares, calling out morning greetings to each other. She slipped by them, ignoring their curious stares, making her way through the little village to the harbor.

The port, like the rest of the town, was run-down, but here there was also a hint of malice, a wash of something less than savory. She squared her shoulders, asking a passing man for directions to the harbor master. His leer sent concern lancing through her, and she closed her hand on the gun in her pocket.

But she'd been stared at before. And with a haughty look she thanked him and headed for the building the stranger had·indicated. The office was little more than a palm-frond shack, and she fought against trepidation as she approached the door. Inside, at first, she thought the room was empty, but then a wizened little man rose from behind the counter. His dark eyes were speculative as he watched her approach, and she swallowed convulsively, for the first time questioning the wisdom of her decision.

It had all been so much easier knowing that Drake had her back.

Still, she'd handled herself in far more dangerous situations. And she had the advantage of a gun. Bolstering her courage and calling on every ounce of femininity she possessed, she lifted her hands and gave him a smile. "I'm sorry to intrude, but I'm afraid I need your help."

"The office is closed," he said, eyes narrowing as he continued to study her. His Spanish was difficult to follow, his sentences laced with Chocoan dialect. Words from the ancient language blended into the modern-day Spanish. But she was determined to persevere.

"I don't mean to intrude so early in the day. It's just that I've missed my boat," she improvised with a smile. "I'm traveling with friends, but they weren't interested in coming to Puerto Remo. I wanted to see the cathedral." She tipped her head toward the massive structure perched on the rocks above them. "Anyway, I'm supposed to be meeting them in Esmeraldas this morning. In Ecuador. And I'm hoping that you might know of someone going in that direction?"

"I have no knowledge of the boat you say you missed," he said, his expression hardening.

"It was a yacht. You can't have missed it. American. A lovely couple. They offered me a ride from Buenaventura." She slipped a folded wad of money into her hand. "We anchored just beyond the harbor." She waved toward the sea, in the process displaying the money, praying that he would buy the ruse or at least let his greed override his doubt. "Anyway, they must have assumed I'd decided to stay on. And now they're gone. So I'm hoping that you can help me find another way out." She opened her hands, shrugging as if in dismay, the money again openly displayed. Then she dropped her hands to the counter, waiting to see if he'd take the bait.

"It is not wise for you to travel alone." He frowned, his eyes dropping to her hands.

"I'll be fine," she soothed. "I'm used to being on my own." There was too much truth in the statement, and she winced, her thoughts winging back to Drake and the night they'd spent together. "Please," she said, pulling her thoughts to the present. "I need your help."

The man studied her for a moment, then took the money with a shrug. "There is a trawler leaving in a few hours. I believe it is headed for the port you seek. You'll find it tied off of the third quay. It is called *Princesa*. The captain's name is Valdez."

"Thank you," she said with a nod as she walked from the office. The wharf outside was quiet, the rising sun hidden now behind clouds, the wind picking up, whistling eerily through the masts of the anchored boats, the tethered rigging clanking in counterrhythm.

She glanced down at her watch, surprised to find that she'd managed a lot in a very short time. Now all that remained was to find the *Princesa* and convince its captain to let her on board. She fingered Drake's wallet, confident of her success, knowing that in this part of the world money could guarantee one almost anything.

Still, she had to keep moving. She had no doubt that once Drake realized she was gone, he'd try to find her. She was his package, after all. Chattel to be traded for information. It was a crass way to put it, but it did the trick, reminding her that last night hadn't been real. Passion wasn't the same as love. And she wasn't about to let one night of amazing sex trick her into believing something different.

The path along the waterfront was only partially paved with shells and pebbles, making it difficult going in places where the rains had washed the paving away and turned the ground to mud. She picked her way carefully, ignoring the occasional catcall from men working on the piers.

The boats, for the most part, were small ones, meant for fishing or hauling local goods up and down the coast. Since it was still early, there was little activity. All the better for her purposes, but she remained wary as she passed into the shadow of a warehouse sitting adjacent to a long wooden jetty, a burst of wind sending dirt and pebbles skittering across the ground.

Sucking in a fortifying breath, she cast a look behind her, and satisfied that she was not being followed, sped up her pace, less mindful now of the mud beneath her feet. The sooner she found the *Princesa,* the sooner she'd be out of this cursed place.

A sign at the far side of the warehouse pointed toward the third quay, and she sighed with relief as she spied the trawler, its empty hull riding high in the water, its nets rigged and ready for the day's run.

A dark man with a heavy beard was working on the deck, his attention on the rope he was coiling. She turned onto the pier, making her way past abandoned barrels and crates to the gangway leading to the *Princesa.*

"Hello," she called. "I'm looking for Mr. Valdez?"

"You've found him," the man said, his scowl less than inviting. Again, she had a moment's doubt. But the gun in her pocket brought clarity.

"I'm hoping you can give me a lift? The harbor master said that you were headed for Esmeraldas. I'm supposed to meet my friends there, but I missed my boat."

"This is a working vessel," he said, shading his eyes with his hand. Thankfully, his Spanish was easier to follow, his accent less guttural than that of the harbormaster.

"I'd be more than happy to pay," she offered. "I'll give you a thousand. Half now. And half when we reach Esmeraldas." The idea was a bit ludicrous, since once she was on the boat, she'd be at his mercy, more or less, but beggars couldn't be choosers and all that.

"Two thousand," the man said.

"I'm sorry, but a thousand is all I've got," she lied, wishing she'd thought to separate the money, hiding some of it. "But I promise not to be a bother." She gave him her most beguiling smile.

"All right, then." He nodded his acceptance. "I'll take a thousand."

"When do we leave?" she asked, moving toward the gangplank.

"As soon as I finish with the rigging," he said. "Half an hour, maybe less. You can go below if you like. Until we're out of port." He lifted an eyebrow, his gaze knowing. "And I'll take the first half of the money now."

"Fine," she said, reaching into her bag for the wallet as she stepped onto the gangway, losing her footing on the slippery metal, her bag flying into the mud as she fell to her knees. "Damn it to hell," she muttered, as Valdez

stood watching, making no effort to help. Swearing
again, she pulled herself back to her feet, leaning down to
rescue her bag, eyes searching for the wallet.

It had tumbled off the gangway into a puddle of water,
flipping open, some of its contents scattered across the
pier. She bent to retrieve some money and a plastic sheath
that had fallen out of one of the wallet's compartments.
After safely stowing the currency, she turned the plastic
sleeve over, wiping it clean, her heart stuttering to a stop
as she stared down at the photograph encased inside.

"Are you coming?" Valdez asked, his tone impatient.

She lifted her head, her mind whirling. She needed
to go. Now. This was her best chance. If she went back,
Drake would see to it that she never had another opportunity to escape. But if she boarded the boat, she'd be
betraying him in the worst possible way.

Indecision whirled inside her, baser instincts warring
with common decency.

"So make up your mind," the man said, his expression
fading back into a scowl. "Coming or going? I haven't
got all day."

She looked down at the photo again, her hands trembling. It shouldn't be a debate. Self-preservation should
always win the day, even over something as monumental
as this. But she could see his face. Hear the pain in his
voice. And she knew suddenly that there was no choice.
She had to go back.

She had to tell Drake.

Drake stood in his bedroom staring down at Madeline's scrawled message. "Sorry," he read. "What the hell
does that mean?" Was she sorry about running out on

him? Sorry about last night? Damn the woman. He should have known better than to trust her.

For all he knew the whole thing had been a setup. Lure him in and make him believe in her, then wham, she's gone—just like that. And even if he put aside his personal feelings—which, considering the circumstances, was probably the wiser thing to do—there was still the matter of the mission. He was responsible for delivering her to Langley. And without a second thought he'd surrendered to his desire and as a result let her slip right through his fingers.

He grabbed his gun and the two hundreds she'd left him and headed into the living room, determined to run her to ground. She couldn't have been gone that long. The sun was barely over the horizon. And they'd been up until the wee hours—he closed his eyes, cursing his own stupidity.

Damn, but she was good. Played him like a fucking violin.

He leaned down to pick up his pack, the scattered plates and cups reminding him of their foray onto the counter. How stupid could a man be? Using sex was the oldest trick in the book, and he'd fallen for it without even a backward glance.

Pulling an extra clip from the bag, he stuck it in his pocket and turned for the door, just as the screen opened and Madeline walked in, her face blanched of all color.

"What the hell are you doing back here?" he asked, fighting the urge to pull her into his arms.

"I have something I need to tell you," she said, her voice coming on a whispered gasp as she struggled for air.

Instantly his senses went on high alert. "What's happened? Is it Ortiz? Di Silva?" He moved to the door, drawing the gun, his gaze sweeping across the courtyard.

"No," she said, shaking her head. "Nothing like that."

"Then what the hell is it?" He hadn't meant to sound so angry, but he couldn't seem to help himself. "I got your note. So I know you didn't just step out for breakfast. You were running. Again. So tell me, Madeline," he taunted, "why the hell did you bother coming back? Did you need more money? Or maybe you wanted more of me? Is that it? A quickie before you hit the road?"

She winced, but held her ground, her breath coming more easily now. "I *was* leaving. I found a boat to take me to Ecuador. In fact, I'd be gone now except that I found something—and if I'm right, then it's a big deal. And I couldn't go. Not without telling you first what I found." She held out the photograph.

"So what? You're telling me that you had an attack of conscience over a picture of my brother?" He stared down at the photo, at Tucker's crooked grin. They'd been fishing in Colorado, the trip a gift from their dad. It had been the three of them for a week on the Rio Grande.

The picture had been taken high in the mountains after a three-hour hike into a box canyon fabled as the home of enormous trout. They'd fished away the morning catching absolutely nothing and finally, exhausted, they'd stopped for lunch.

In the picture, Tucker was holding an eggshell, his eyes crinkled with laughter. Drake smiled at the memory. They'd brought hard-boiled eggs for their lunch. But somehow when Drake had gone to retrieve them, he'd picked up the fresh ones instead, so they'd started the long trek home with both their stomachs and their creels empty.

And their father had laughed so hard, Drake thought he'd split a gut. And then he'd made them scrambled eggs for supper. It was a precious memory.

"So it is your brother in the picture?" she asked, her brow furrowed as she contemplated something.

"Yes. Of course it is. But I still don't understand why that would cause you to do a complete about-face."

"You don't think very highly of me, do you?" she snapped, her eyes flashing with anger.

"Hey, I'm not the one who snuck out of here without even saying good-bye."

"You said you got my note." At least she had the decency to look uncomfortable.

"Right. 'Sorry.' What the hell was that supposed to mean?"

"That I'm sorry. For a lot of things. Most principally ducking out on you like that. But I had to do what I thought was best. And if I let you take me back to Washington, there's no telling what would happen to me. So I found a fisherman who agreed to take me to Ecuador. He had a trawler. And I was all set to go. Only then I dropped the wallet."

"My wallet."

"Yes. Yours. And the photograph fell out. And as soon as I saw it, I knew I had to come back. I owed you that much."

"You don't owe me anything."

"Yes, I do." The words were quiet, and some of his anger dissipated at her tone. "Look, I wouldn't be alive if it weren't for you. There's no questioning that fact. And you said you were close with your brother."

"So you brought back the photograph?"

"No. I recognized it."

"What?" He frowned, trying to make sense of her words.

"I've seen the man in this picture." She waved at the photo in his hand. "Your brother. I know him. Or at least I knew him," she amended. "Three years ago."

"That's impossible. Tucker died five years ago."

"That's just the point, Drake. He wasn't dead when I last saw him. He was very much alive." She paused, her gaze locking with his. "In San Mateo. Drake, your brother is my friend Andrés."

CHAPTER 20

That's insane," Drake said. "I don't know what you think you're seeing in this picture, but it's not your friend Andrés. I told you my brother died five years ago in Nevada when his plane went down."

"That's impossible." She shook her head, hands on her hips. "Your brother was standing in the exercise yard talking to me three years ago. Very much alive. He's the reason I'm here with you now. If he hadn't helped me, I'd never have gotten Washington's attention."

"Madeline, you're not making any sense." He frowned, still fighting against the idea that Tucker was alive, even as hope began to blossom.

"Look, I can prove it, " she said, fumbling through the plastic envelope she carried in her bag. "Andrés gave me this." She held out what appeared to be a playing card.

"The Queen of Hearts?" he asked. "This is your proof?"

"Yes. He gave it to me the last time I saw him. Made me swear that I'd use it if I had the chance."

"Use it to do what exactly?"

"Get out. He meant prison at the time, but then Ortiz came and I had to help Jenny. So I kept the card. And when I found out my sister was dead, I took Andrés's advice. I went to the Embassy. And I showed Robertson the card. Don't you see? That's why you were called in to rescue me."

"Because you gave him a playing card?" He frowned, shaking his head. "Do you have any idea how crazy you sound?"

"Well, does it make sense that I would come back here, risking your anger and my freedom on a whim? I'm telling you that Andrés and your brother are one and the same. Believe it or don't. I just thought you had the right to know."

"Considering everything you've done, why the hell should I believe you?" The words came out of their own accord and she flinched again, this time pain cresting in her eyes.

"Because whatever's happened in the meantime," she said, her chin lifting, "there was something between us last night. Something good. And because I loved my sister as much as you loved your brother, and I couldn't stand the idea that you would go on thinking he died in Nevada. And because I owe it to Andrés to let his brother know that he might be alive."

"You just said 'might,'" he spat out. "I thought you were sure."

"I'm certain that your brother was my friend," she said, dropping her eyes to look at the photo in his hands. "But when he gave me the card, I asked why he didn't use it himself. And he told me that it was too late. That he was marked for death. And I know that they killed people there. I'd hear them shooting sometimes late at night." Tears rolled down her cheeks as she remembered her friend. "So I can't tell you if he's still alive. But he was when I saw him last. That much I'll swear to."

"Three years ago." None of this made any sense. It had to be a con. Another game she was playing. But he'd be damned if he could see what she stood to gain.

"Look, I know this is hard to swallow. Especially coming from me. Now. Right after I ran out on you. But don't you see? That's what makes it plausible. Why the hell would I come back here if I didn't honestly believe what I was telling you?"

"If you thought it would get you something you want, I believe you'd say anything."

"But I don't want anything from you. If I had, I would have stayed. I'd have used what happened between us last night. I didn't need to invent a story about your brother. Besides, you're missing the point. If your brother was in San Mateo three years ago, then he couldn't have been killed in the desert. Which means that the government lied to you."

"Yes, but—" he broke off suddenly, holding his hand up to signal quiet as a noise outside caught his attention. Drawing the gun, he signaled Madeline to get down and moved toward the door. There was a sharp knock, and then the handle turned. Drake pressed his back to the wall, waiting as the door swung slowly open.

"Drake? Are you in there?" Nash called as he inched forward into the room, his own gun drawn.

"Jesus, Nash, I could have shot you," Drake said, his breathing still coming in short gasps. "Why the hell didn't you call first?"

"We did," Annie said, following her husband into the room. "No one answered the sat phone."

Madeline stood up, a guilty expression on her face as she produced the phone from her bag, laying it on the counter. "I took it with me when I left. I didn't think you'd need it and I wanted backup. Just in case. But I didn't have it on."

"She ran again," Nash surmised, frowning over at Drake.

"First thing this morning," he acknowledged with a tired sigh.

"But I came back," she said, her tone defiant.

"Annie," Nash said, "this is Madeline. The woman who put us all through hell."

"It was never my intention..." she started, then trailed off. "I was just doing what I thought best. Anyway, the point is I'm here now."

"Which is interesting in and of itself," Annie said, her gaze speculative. "I know Drake's charming and all that, but I'm guessing you had another reason for coming back?"

Madeline shot him a look and then ducked her head, her cheeks turning red. "I found out something I thought he should know about."

"She says that Tucker is still alive."

"Your brother?" Nash frowned. "But I thought he—"

"—was dead. So did I. But she swears he was in San Mateo prison. Same time she was." As much as he wanted to believe her, he couldn't keep the note of cynicism from his voice. "He even gave her a get-out-of-jail-free card. She swears this is what caught the attention of the brass at Langley." He held out the card.

"The Queen of Hearts?" Nash scoffed.

"That's what she says."

"It's true," Madeline said, crossing her arms over her chest as she glared at all of them.

"Can I see the card?" Annie asked, a funny expression crossing her face. "What did your friend say when he gave it to you?" She studied the front, then turned it over to look at the back.

"That if I presented it to the American Embassy, they'd help me. No strings attached."

"And you believed him?" Drake queried.

"Actually, I didn't. I thought maybe he was crazy. I mean San Mateo isn't exactly an easy ride. But because I cared about him, I couldn't bring myself to get rid of it. And then later, after I..." She stopped, her eyes meeting Drake's. "After I found out the truth about my sister, I just wanted out, and I figured the card might be my ticket. So I arranged for the meeting and you know the rest."

"Except that we don't, obviously," Nash said, looking over at his wife. "Does the card mean something to you, Annie?"

"Yeah." She nodded. "I think it's related to the CIA's divisions. Deep black ops," she added for Madeline's benefit. "They're referred to by number. I worked with a guy from D-2 once. An operation in Eastern Europe. Anyway, everything they do is deep cover. Even more than A-Tac. They're considered totally expendable. But in the event that things go south, each division member is given a playing card. Like this one. There are different colors and patterns for each division, and every member has a number. In this case the Queen. The higher the card the higher the rank within the division. Assuming this card is legit, your friend was the second in command."

"And if they get into trouble," Madeline finished for her, "they can use the card to get through to people who can help. Oh, my God, it *was* a free ticket out."

"If that's the real thing," Nash pointed out.

"It has to have some significance," Annie responded. "Otherwise why would Langley have agreed to pull Madeline out?"

"Because she could turn evidence on di Silva," Drake said.

"Yeah," Nash said, "but something had to have gotten their attention initially. And besides, we've all had the feeling something else was going on here. This could be it."

"But it doesn't prove that Andrés is or was Tucker." Drake sighed. "Tucker was in the military. If he'd been with one of the CIA's divisions I'd have known it."

"Would you?" Annie asked. "Did you tell Tucker about your work with the CIA?"

Drake shook his head. "No. I didn't tell him anything."

"So it's possible he wouldn't have told you. Look, your cover is being a professor. Tucker's could have been serving in the military. I mean, it's perfect for someone who's spending time working deep under cover. It's an easy explanation for absences, injuries. All kinds of things."

"But I was told he was dead." Drake sat down, his head spinning. "Why would the government do that?"

"Because, like Annie said, we're expendable," Nash said. "If his division *was* here in Colombia, you know that it wasn't officially sanctioned. Which means that if something went wrong, there'd be no easy way to extract survivors."

"Better to just let them all die?" Madeline asked, her eyes widening with disbelief.

"The greater good and all that." Nash shook his head, his own anger reflected on his face. "They almost sacrificed Annie for that same ideal."

"But they didn't." She reached out to cover his hand with hers.

"Look, all of this is just conjecture. We don't know that any of this is true," Drake said. "I mean, all we've got is Madeline's word."

"I wouldn't lie about something this important," she said. "Andrés was my friend and you're..." she stopped herself, shaking her head instead. "I'm telling the truth."

"What if there was a coverup?" Nash suggested.

"But we don't have any—"

Nash cut Drake off with the wave of his hand. "Just speculate for a minute with me. What if there was a coyerup—some mission here in Colombia gone south. The team is killed and the powers that be don't want anyone to know we were even there. What better way to cover it up than a training exercise in the desert? No one to verify it. And no reason for civilians to disbelieve the facts as stated."

"But I wasn't a civilian," Drake protested.

"No, but you had no reason to believe it wasn't the truth." Annie shrugged.

"Anyway," Nash said, pulling attention back to his conjecture, "let's assume that the plan works. The operation is covered up, the missing people are accounted for, and no one is the wiser. But what if not everyone was dead? What if one of the team members found himself in prison?"

"Andrés," Madeline said.

"Exactly. He stays with the role, knowing that he can't risk coming out and admitting who he really is. But he brings the card with him, thinking that maybe he'll be able to get it out to someone to let them know he's alive."

"So why didn't he use it?" Drake asked. "If he had the power to escape, why wouldn't he?"

"The mission," Madeline said, her face torn with anguish. "You people seem to care more about completing your operations than anything else. That's why Drake risked his life coming after me when I ran the first time. And that's why you all left him behind. Because the mission demanded it."

"So you're saying that Andrés"—he couldn't bring himself to call the man Tucker, not yet—"knew that it would be problematic if he surfaced. That he sacrificed himself for whatever it was they'd hoped to have achieved."

"Maybe," Madeline mused. "Or maybe there were still other people to protect. Maybe Andrés wasn't the only one who lived. All I know is that when I asked him why he didn't contact his family, he told me that they thought he was dead. And that it was better that way. I thought it was because he was a revolutionary. That they'd be either ostracized or threatened because of his associations. But now that I think about it, he never really said he was a guerilla. I was the one who suggested it. He just never denied it."

"But you had to know he was an American," Nash said.

"No. He spoke fluent Spanish, and his English, though good, was heavily accented."

"Any one of us could pull something like that off," Annie said. "And division personnel are even more adept. Sometimes their entire careers are spent pretending to be something or someone they're not."

"So you think this man she knew in prison *was* my brother?" Drake asked, looking from Nash to Annie.

"I think it's possible," Annie answered. "Madeline obviously believes that it's true. So much so that she came back here to tell you."

"We need to take this to Avery," Nash said. "He's the only one with the clearance to figure out what the real truth is. Bottom line, if there's a chance that your brother is still alive, we have to do something to get him out of San Mateo."

"So you believe me?" Madeline asked, her attention on Drake, her eyes filled with more than just the question.

"I believe *you* believe it," Drake acknowledged, fighting against the feelings she aroused in him. Lust. Irritation. *Hope*. "And for now, at least, that'll have to be enough."

CHAPTER 21

Madeline had never felt so alone.

Whatever tenuous connection had existed between her and Drake, it had been severed when she'd run out on him this morning. She hadn't thought it would matter. But then she hadn't counted on coming back. And with the appearance of Drake's friends, they'd closed ranks, leaving her to her own devices while they contacted Avery with the news about Andrés. It shouldn't have bothered her. But it did. Partly because she was worried about her friend, but also, if she were honest, because she was concerned about Drake.

She couldn't imagine how she'd feel if she found out that Jenny wasn't dead. That the whole thing had been a scam. A coverup to keep her from the real truth. It would be wonderful, of course, but also mind-blowing in that it inverted reality, turning everything on its ear.

She sighed, moving restlessly around the living room. Inactivity had never been her strong suit. She preferred taking action. Doing something. Anything, really, just to keep her mind from replaying the past seventy-two hours.

The obvious choice was to exit stage left. Pay off the captain and get the hell out of Puerto Remo. After all, she'd done what she'd set out to do. She'd told Drake about his brother. And now, clearly, her part in this little drama was over.

And if Nash's suppositions were true and Madeline had somehow stumbled into a long-buried secret of the CIA's, then her status had most definitely changed from asset to liability. And she had no illusions about what that might mean. These people meant business, and if her knowledge was a threat, then so was she.

She needed to go. Now.

But she knew that she couldn't. She'd run out on Drake twice already. She simply wasn't going to do it again. Maybe not the wisest of choices, but it was what her heart told her to do. And sometimes it was important to have a little faith.

But even so, that didn't mean she had to stand here and stew. She'd go to the market. When they got out of their meeting they'd need to eat. It wasn't the same as being part of the inner circle, but at least it would make her feel as if she were contributing something.

She grabbed some money from Drake's wallet and headed out the door. The clouds had dissipated, the sky turning an azure blue. A lazy breeze stirred through the mangroves, as heat shimmered across the partially paved road. Across the street, the brightly colored awnings over the booths gave the market an air of gaiety.

Any other time she would have stopped to appreciate the simple beauty of it all, but somehow in light of everything that was happening, she just couldn't find the energy to care. It was easier to focus on the mundane. Coffee. Food. Anything but her conflicted feelings about Drake, and her worries about Andrés.

She knew that there was a very real chance that her friend was dead. That last day, in the exercise yard, he'd told her that he was a marked man. And that was three years ago. But even so, some part of her believed that he was still alive. Or maybe she just wanted it to be so. For Drake. The idea of his having to lose his brother twice was beyond contemplation. Surely fate couldn't be that cruel?

She stopped at a booth to buy some fruit, haggling with the man behind the counter over the price of some mangoes. From there she moved on to buy *arepas*, *empanadas*, and some *chorizo* on sticks—Colombian street food at its best. Maybe not the most well-balanced meal, but at least she felt as if she were doing something to help.

The coffee stand, with its white paper cups of sugar-laced Colombian coffee, was at the northernmost corner of the market. She remembered seeing it the night before when she'd made her first foray into the maze of stalls.

She'd wanted so much to create a special evening, a moment separate from the reality of all that they'd been through—a way to repay Drake for everything he'd done. What she hadn't counted on was falling for the man.

The words hit her hard, and she shook her head as if by doing so she could banish them. She didn't care for Drake. At least not like *that*. It was a ridiculous notion. She was attracted to him, most definitely. The man aroused a need so powerful it had almost brought her to her knees. But the reaction was physical. Not emotional.

Strictly chemical. Her pheromones calling to his.

She wanted that to be true. And in part maybe it was. But chemistry couldn't explain her sudden bout of self-lessness. She'd actually thrown away her best chance at freedom because she'd wanted to help Drake. Of course, she wanted to help Andrés, too. But if she were truly honest, her first thought on seeing the photograph and recognizing its significance had been to find Drake, to tell him that his brother hadn't died in Nevada.

Angry at herself and her musings, she tucked the food packages under her arm and headed toward the coffee stand. Vendors called to her, hawking their wares, but her smile was empty, her mind reeling with the horrifying realization that she had violated her number-one rule.

She'd lowered her defenses and allowed herself to care. She'd put someone else first. And by so doing, she'd put herself right back into the line of fire.

Damn it all to hell.

The smell of coffee pulled her out of her maud-lin thoughts, and she stopped at the counter, debating whether to try to carry cups or to simply buy ground coffee and make her own. The former would be easier, but this wasn't Starbucks. There were no lids and no carrying containers, which meant figuring out how to balance both the cups and the food.

Finally, she settled on the ground coffee, praying that there was something at the hacienda that could serve as a percolator. Adding the package of coffee to her other purchases, she turned to go but was stopped short when something hard shoved into her back.

"Don't do anything to call attention to yourself," a voice behind her said. "One wrong move and you're dead. Do you understand me?"

She nodded, her mouth going dry, her heart pounding so fast it was difficult to breathe.

The man shifted, his gun digging into her side, his profile familiar. It was the captain from the *Princesa*. Valdez.

"Look, if it's the money you're after, I don't have it with me," she said, looking frantically for a way out. If he managed to get her back to his boat, there was practically no chance for her to escape. And in her haste to get to the market, she hadn't left a note, or anything to let Drake know where she'd gone. He might work it out, but it would be too late. Which meant she was on her own. And the thought sent panic rocketing through her.

"I don't need your money," Valdez responded, with a shake of his head. "Turns out you're worth ten times as much. The man said he'd pay cash. All I have to do is hand you over to him."

Her body went cold. Ortiz was the only one who would possibly offer that kind of money. And she had no doubt what her fate would be if he got his hands on her. "I can pay you more," she offered, hating the note of desperation in her voice. "All you have to do is let me go."

"Nice try." Valdez laughed, the sound harsh. "But if you had that kind of money, you wouldn't have needed to bargain with me for a ride."

"Maybe I'm just a bargain hunter." She tried to wrench free of his grip, but he held tight, the gun digging deeper into her ribs.

"Easy now," he hissed, his fingers tightening on her arm. "I'd hate to have to kill you. But if you give me any more trouble, I promise you, I will."

"Somehow I doubt that," she said, her bravado strictly

for show. "If I'm dead, I'm no longer worth anything to you."

"Now that's where you'd be wrong." He smiled, his eyes narrowing speculatively. "You see, I get paid either way. Granted, I get more if you're alive. But I'm not opposed to cutting my losses if you prove to be more trouble than you're worth."

She nodded, holding her tongue. There was no sense antagonizing him. Instead, she poked her finger into the paper bag holding the coffee. It wasn't as good as a trail of bread crumbs, but it was better than nothing. And maybe if she was lucky, Drake would see the coffee and know which way she'd come.

"My friends will come looking for me," she said, still working to keep her panic at bay. The only way she was going to get out of this was to keep her head.

"Not if you're counting on the coffee." He laughed, nodding at the muddy street. "Black coffee against black mud. No one will see that." He grabbed the packages, throwing them into a pile of garbage on the corner as they turned into an alley leading to the pier where the *Princesa* was moored.

So much for the Hansel and Gretel approach.

A dilapidated warehouse ran the length of the alley on the left-hand side. To the right there were several smaller buildings, all of them seemingly deserted. Still, her gaze moved back and forth across the street looking for some sign of life, someone who could help her. But there was nothing except the soft whistle of the wind as it blew through the empty alley.

As they moved farther down the street she could see the mast of the *Princesa* over the top of the warehouse, and she knew that if she was going to make a move it had to be now. Once the captain had her on his boat it would be next to impossible to escape.

Heart pounding, she scanned the alleyway, searching for something that might offer sanctuary. The warehouse, made of aluminum siding, was windowless, access limited to a series of sliding doors, all of them securely padlocked. Then, just as they were nearing the end of the building, she saw her out. A small door, at the top of a metal staircase. All she had to do was break free and make it up the steps.

It was risky, but bottom line, it was better than doing nothing. And if she could buy herself some time, she still had hope that Drake would find her. And if not, then she'd damn well have to figure out how to save herself. But first things first.

As they approached the staircase, she was careful to keep her eyes away from the door. No point in telegraphing her intentions. She'd have only one chance, which meant she had to get it right.

Sucking in an audible breath, she stumbled, then bent over, grabbing her chest. "Asthma," she wheezed, sputtering for air. "Can't breathe."

Valdez, caught by surprise, loosened his grip, and she seized the opportunity, yanking free and driving an elbow into his ribs. Cursing, he staggered backward and she sprinted for the stairs, her feet ringing against the metal as she took the steps two at a time.

Adrenaline pushing her onward, she pulled on the door, to no avail. Behind her, she could hear Valdez clambering up the stairs. Summoning all her strength, she grabbed the door with both hands, yanking it open as it screeched in protest.

She slipped through the door as a bullet embedded itself in the metal above her head. Racing across the mesh metal floor, she dove behind an abandoned metal drum as another shot ricocheted past her.

"There's nowhere to go," Valdez called, his footsteps growing closer. "And I can promise it'll go better for you if you give up now." His tone was cajoling, but she could also hear the underlying anger.

She glanced around her, trying to figure out her best move. She was on a narrow walkway that circled the perimeter of the warehouse. Only about six feet at its widest, the catwalk offered little protection—a couple of pillars and some piles of abandoned crates.

Still, she knew she couldn't stay put. Valdez was closing in, and he had the lethal advantage, especially at close range. At the far end of the platform, she could just make out a second staircase leading down to the main floor. She needed to make a run for it, but first she needed to buy herself a little time.

Reaching down beside her, she grabbed a piece of rusted metal and hurled it back the way she'd come. The fragment hit the floor with a loud clank and Valdez, still about ten feet away from her, spun in the direction of the noise.

Madeline pushed off the floor, sprinting down the catwalk toward the second set of stairs. Valdez responded with a hail of bullets, exploding at her feet as they ricocheted off the metal flooring. Ducking behind one of the pillars, she pressed her back against the cold steel.

The staircase lay about twelve feet away, tantalizing in its offer of freedom. But to get there, she'd have to step out into the line of fire. And he was closing the distance, which meant his shots would be more accurate. Fighting against panic, she searched for something that might give her a way out.

But there was nothing.

Valdez's footsteps were coming closer now. Time was running out. She shifted slightly, trying to see around the pillar without giving herself away, and in so doing, her foot brushed against something hidden by the shadows. Dropping to her knees, she felt along the floor, her hand closing on something cold and hard. A piece of rebar. Three feet in length, the twisted bit of iron seemed a gift straight from heaven.

Pushing to her feet, back to the pillar, she waited, holding the rebar like a baseball bat. Valdez moved closer, turning in circles as he searched for her. Madeline sucked in a breath and waited. Three feet. Then two. And then he was there. She could hear him breathing, as he searched the shadows, trying to find her.

Her heart pounding, Madeline stepped out from behind the pillar, swinging the rebar for all she was worth. It caught him across the chest, sending him flying backward to slam against the railing. He stumbled, then caught his balance, lunging forward again, his hand just missing her arm as she sprinted past him, running full-out for the staircase at the end of the catwalk.

Another bullet whizzed past her and she grabbed the railing on the stairs, using it to propel herself downward. Behind her, she could hear Valdez, still in pursuit. The stairs curved to the right, and she slowed only slightly, shifting her weight to maintain balance, as she flew down the steps. She hit the landing hard, her muscles protesting as she moved off the stairs onto the cold concrete floor of the warehouse.

She ran forward, following a narrow hallway, grateful when it opened into a larger space. But something felt off and she skidded to a stop, turning in a slow circle as her eyes telegraphed a frantic message to her brain. She wasn't on the main floor of the warehouse. Between the murky shadows and her haste to escape, she'd somehow missed the first-floor landing, winding up instead in some kind of basement.

The small cement room had no windows or doors, no egress from any direction except the way she'd come. She turned back to the hallway leading to the stairs, heart pounding. She could hear Valdez coming off the steps. Spinning around again to face the room, she prayed she'd missed something. That there was a door, or some other means of escape. But there was nothing—no way out.

She was trapped.

Valdez appeared in the doorway, leveling his gun, a slow smile of satisfaction spreading across his face.

CHAPTER 22

Drake made his way cautiously down the last of the stairs into a hallway leading to the warehouse basement. Keeping his back to the wall, he inched forward, leading with his gun. When he'd realized Madeline had gone missing—again—he'd guessed that she'd headed to the market. He'd learned enough about her to realize that she wasn't good at sitting idle. She needed to do something, even if it was only buying food.

And when he'd seen her at the coffee stall, he'd been certain his assumptions were correct. But before he could get to her, she'd done a one-eighty and left with a stranger, heading for the docks. It had appeared that she'd gone willingly, so Drake figured the man must be the captain she'd convinced to take her out of Puerto Remo.

Anger had warred with disappointment, but he'd followed her anyway, knowing that he had to stop her. Had to take her back to D.C. It wasn't until they'd turned into the alley that he realized the man was holding a gun. And then, before he could do anything about it, Madeline had somehow managed to pull free, heading for the warehouse, her captor hot on her heels.

There was no sign of either of them now, but he'd heard gunfire, his blood running cold. Then he'd seen someone disappearing down the stairwell at the end of the catwalk. So he'd followed, keeping back out of sight to avoid discovery, heart twisting as he tried to keep from imagining the worst.

But when a second round of gunfire split through the silence below him, he threw caution to the wind, starting to run, skipping steps as he wound his way down the stairs, past the first landing to the bottom, and into the shadowy hallway he hoped would lead him to Madeline.

Immediately ahead, a doorway loomed out of the darkness, and he heard voices.

"I told you it was no use running." The voice was male, but Drake couldn't see the man, his line of vision obscured by a structural support.

"So what?" Madeline queried. "You expected me to just give in and let you hand me over to Ortiz?" She was crouched in a corner, holding an iron rod as if it were a sword. Her voice was calm, but he could see that her hand was shaking.

"Ortiz," the man repeated. "Is he the one who offered me the money?"

"Someone who works for him, more likely," Madeline said, with a practiced shrug. Drake recognized the gesture—her way of whistling at the dark. "Ortiz isn't big on getting his hands dirty."

"I can't say that I blame him," the man said. "Although with a pretty little package like you, I can see where it would be tempting." Anger surged, but Drake managed to keep his control. He had to wait until the angle was right.

Madeline's fingers tightened on the rebar. But the man only laughed, brandishing the gun as he lunged for her, moving into Drake's line of sight.

Drake stepped forward, leveling his weapon. "Drop it or I drop you right where you stand."

The man lifted his arm, holding his gun out to the side in seeming surrender, but as Drake took a step toward him, the man swiveled, dropping down to take the shot. Drake moved on instinct, diving to the side and firing once. The man careened backward as Drake's bullet ripped through his shoulder, his hand spasming as the gun dropped to the floor.

Drake moved closer, keeping his weapon trained on the man. "Madeline, are you all right?" he asked, his eyes never leaving the man on the floor.

"I'm fine," she assured him.

"Good. Get the gun."

She inched forward, snatching the gun away and handing it to Drake, then retreated to her corner, her gaze locked on her captor.

"What's your name?" Drake asked.

"Marco Valdez."

"And who do you work for?"

Valdez frowned up at him, one hand clasped over his bleeding shoulder.

"If you want to live, you're going to tell me everything you know."

"He's the captain of the trawler," Madeline said. "The one I tried to hitch a ride on this morning."

"Is that the truth?" Drake asked. "Or did you lie to her?"

"I told her the truth. It's my boat." He lifted a hand in surrender. "She asked for my help and then she changed her mind. A woman's prerogative, no?"

"Except that you apparently can't take no for an answer."

"It wasn't as if I was looking for her. I simply ran into her in the market. And since there was a bounty on her head, I decided to take action. It was providence."

"For you, maybe," Madeline said, her hands still clenched around the iron pipe.

The man shrugged. "I never wanted her dead. But then she hit me."

"Believe me, I'm going to do much worse if you don't start talking. Who offered you the money?"

"I swear I don't know," he said, holding up both hands. "A man came by the trawler asking about a woman. Said she'd run away from her husband. He told me there would be a substantial reward for any information."

Madeline made a choking sound, but Drake kept his attention focused on the man. "And you were only too happy to help."

"Sí. It was a lot of money. Ten thousand. American."

"Is this the man?" Drake held out the photograph of Alexander Petrov that Nash had given him.

"It looks like him. Only his hair is shorter. Like in the American army."

Drake nodded, filing this newest bit of information away. "So what did you tell him?"

"The truth. That she'd asked me to ferry her out of the country, only she ran off before we could finish the deal." He shifted, wincing from the pain. "The man threw a couple hundred my way, and I thought that was the end of it. Until I ran into her in the market."

"And you figured you could turn a tidy profit if you grabbed her and took her to Petrov."

"It seemed like a plan," the man said, shrugging, "only I wasn't taking her to him. He said he'd check back, so I thought I'd just hang on to her until then. Hadn't planned on her being such a livewire." He shot a heated look in Madeline's direction. "Bitch almost got me killed."

"Yeah, well I wish I'd hit you harder," Madeline said, lifting the rebar.

Valdez growled something unintelligible, his eyes narrowing as he reached for his pocket.

"Gun," Madeline yelled as Valdez dove for the cover of the pillar, shooting at Madeline.

Drake fired as he dove between Madeline and the bullet, then rolled to his knees and fired again. Valdez's body slid down the pillar, his lifeless eyes still wide with surprise.

"Did he hit you?" Drake asked, turning to Madeline, searching for any sign that she'd been injured.

"No." She shook her head, reaching out to touch his hand. "I was afraid he'd hit you."

"I'm fine," Drake said, his fingers squeezing hers. "Bastard never had a chance."

"Is he..." Madeline whispered, her eyes moving to the body.

"Dead? Yes." Drake nodded, reaching over to check the pulse and retrieve the little handgun. "Should have guessed the guy had a second piece. Anyway, we need to get out of here before we have company. If I heard the shots, someone else will have heard them, too."

"Petrov," she said, running a hand through her hair, still staring at the body. "So who is he?"

"One of two mercenaries we think di Silva hired. Montague was the other one."

"The guy I killed," she said, her lips tightening into a thin line. "How long have you known this?"

"Since I first talked with Nash. The night we arrived in Puerto Remo. There's been a lot going on. I didn't have the chance to tell you. I thought maybe we got him when we blew up the boat."

"But we didn't." She shook her head, clasping her hands together so tightly her knuckles turned white. "And even if we had, Ortiz would have just sent someone else. It never stops. Like a nightmare I can't wake up from. They just keep on coming."

"Now's not the time, Madeline," Drake cautioned. He held out his hand to her, but she pushed it away.

"I'm sorry. I'm fine," she said, pulling to her feet. "Really. What's a little kidnapping after everything else I've been through?"

"It's almost over. And you've been amazingly strong. You've just got to hang in there a little longer."

"Until you can turn me over to your buddies in Washington. The ones who covered up your brother's disappearance. Sounds peachy keen to me. Just what the doctor ordered." She was just this side of hysteria; he could see it in her face.

He reached out, his hands closing on her shoulders. "Madeline, I'm not going to let anything happen to you."

"It's a lovely promise. But you know that it isn't one you can keep. Besides, you've got your own problems to deal with."

"Right now, all that matters is making sure you're safe."

She nodded, and he started for the door, but she put her hand on his arm, and he turned back. "Look, I know you had to save me again. And I know I've been a real pain in the ass. But I also need for you to know that I wasn't trying to run. I was trying to help. I was feeling left out, so I went to the market. I wasn't trying to get away. I swear it."

"I know," he said, intent on reassuring her. "I saw your bag. On the counter. You'd never have left it behind."

"I wouldn't have left *you*, not after everything that's happened," she whispered, her gaze holding his. "I was wrong to have left this morning. I can't take that back, but—"

"We can't do this now," he said, shaking his head.

"But I don't know what I'd have done—"

"You'd have figured out something." He shrugged, his tone dismissive. "You always do."

Hurt crested in her eyes, but he turned away, resisting the urge to pull her into his arms, knowing that allowing himself to care was a mistake. Things between them were already too complicated.

"Come on," he said, his tone brusque as he forced himself to focus on the task at hand. "We need to move. As long as Petrov's in Puerto Remo, you're in danger. Which means we have to get you out of here. Now."

"I'm not going back to the States until someone can assure me that I'm not walking into some kind of trap." Madeline crossed her arms, turning to look out the window at the red and pink hibiscus in the courtyard. The fountain gurgled merrily, the soft sound comforting, the normalcy almost seeming to mock her fear.

"You'll be safer in custody than anywhere else," Drake argued, eyes narrowed as he watched her from his perch on the sofa. Annie sat across from him, sipping a glass of fruit juice. Nash was in Drake's bedroom talking with Avery. Reporting, no doubt, on Madeline's latest brush with death.

She squared her shoulders, turning back to face Drake and Annie. "Unless the whole reason Langley wanted A-Tac to get me out of di Silva's grasp was to make certain that I don't tell anyone about the card and its significance."

"But you didn't understand what it meant," Drake said, frowning. "So you weren't a threat even if there was a coverup."

"Maybe, but they had no way of knowing that. And even if I didn't know, I do now." She crossed her arms over her chest, leaning back against the windowsill.

"I think Madeline has a point," Annie said. "Until we know what really happened with Tucker—or Andrés—we can't be certain what's motivating Langley. Or more specifically, the people who may or may not have something to lose."

"I wasn't trying to throw you to the wolves." Drake shook his head, his troubled gaze meeting Madeline's. "After everything we've been through, you know that I don't want anything to happen to you."

"It's just that you trust your bosses." Madeline sighed. "I get that. And taking me to Virginia would mean mission accomplished." She hadn't meant to sound bitter, but the sentiment came just the same.

"Look," Annie said, cutting through the building tension between them, "I've had firsthand experience with the suits making up their minds without any effort to distill the truth, so I tend to side with Madeline on this. But the important thing here is that we have evidence of wrongdoing. We know that someone on the inside is supplying di Silva's organization with information. There's simply no other way his people could have known Drake's identity, not to mention your location."

"Agreed," Drake said. "But it's still a leap to assume the leak is related to the possibility that my brother may still be alive."

"True." Annie nodded. "but that doesn't mean we can afford to ignore the possibility. The way I see it there are two potential sources for the leak. Either someone in the upper echelon of the Company, someone with access to our movements, or someone within the unit. And given what we suspect about your brother, it seems credible to believe it's coming from over our heads."

"Someone with the motivation to cover up the truth about what happened to Tucker's division five years ago in Colombia." Madeline moved to perch on the arm of a chair, her eyes on Drake as he considered Annie's words.

"But the evidence also supports its being someone from A-Tac." Drake frowned. "I mean, we've had issues with sabotage for several operations now, including the equipment Tyler used to blow the stash."

"I'm not arguing with you, Drake. I'm just saying that as long as there's a chance that someone at Langley is trying to silence Madeline to avoid revealing a coverup, we can't risk taking her in."

Madeline shot a grateful smile in Annie's direction, her heart twisting at the thought that Drake was so intent on getting rid of her. She knew he'd never intentionally put her in harm's way, but clearly he was ready to move on. While the notion wasn't anything new, the intensity of her disappointment came as a complete surprise. Somewhere along the way, she'd started to count on Drake.

She blew out a breath, running a hand through her hair, her muscles protesting the movement, the pain reminding her all over again of the danger she was still in.

"I have to agree with Annie," Nash said, snapping his phone shut as he strode into the room. "Until we figure out what's what, Madeline stays with us."

"You're making me sound like the bad guy here," Drake said, his frown deepening. "I just want Madeline to stay safe. And so far, I haven't done the best of jobs."

"You saved my life more times than I can count," she protested. "You're the only person I *do* feel safe with." Again the thought came as a complete surprise. And Madeline bit her bottom lip, wishing the words back.

"You're not the only one," Annie said, with a smile. "Drake saved my life once, too. Hell of a shoot-out, and I wasn't on the winning side—until he showed up."

"Okay, enough with the Drakefest," Drake growled, pushing restlessly away from the sofa and walking over to the window. "What else did Avery have to say?"

"Is he going to tell Langley you found me?" Madeline cut through Drake's question, putting voice to her worst fear.

"No." Nash shook his head. "Avery considers it need-to-know. And until things get straightened out it'll be easier if the folks at Langley believe you're still missing. Not to mention di Silva's thugs."

"Good, then it's settled," Annie said, her eyes darting to Drake.

"I told you I only want what's best for Madeline," he sighed, spreading his hands in acceptance. "And if that's staying with us, then so be it."

It wasn't exactly a ringing endorsement, but Madeline was relieved nevertheless. She lifted her gaze, intending to encompass them all, but instead her eyes settled on Drake. "Thank you," she whispered. "I can't tell you what it means to know that you're on my side."

He held her gaze for a minute, then shrugged, leaning back against the sill as he turned his attention to Nash. "I assume there's still no confirmation that Andrés is Tucker?"

"No, but Avery's going to keep digging."

"What about getting out of here?" Annie asked.

"The boat's waiting in the harbor," Nash said. "Or it will be by the time we get there. So the only thing left to decide is where we're going."

"Well that one's not up for debate," Drake said, pushing to his feet, his expression resolute. "We're going to San Mateo. Because if there's even the slightest chance that my brother's alive, I'm damn sure not leaving Colombia without him."

CHAPTER 23

Magdalena, Colombia

E verything appears to be secure," Drake said, as he
joined Nash, Madeline, and Annie on the front porch
of the house Avery had secured for them in the village.
It was a ramshackle building of indeterminate age, its
exterior suitably nondescript.

"Yeah, well, I think we've got company inside," Nash
said, drawing his gun as he nodded at the front door
standing slightly ajar.

"Get behind me," Drake whispered to Madeline, and
for once she obeyed, stepping behind him as he and Nash
stepped in tandem through the doorway.

"Christ, Hannah, I could have blown your head off,"
Nash said, lowering his gun.

"Now you know how it feels," Drake said, smiling
over at Hannah. "I wondered if you'd show up."

"You know me." Hannah grinned, her dark hair spiking
every which way, a bright streak of red framing the right

side of her face as she peered over the tops of her leopard-framed glasses. "Never could resist a good mystery."

"Nosy Nellie is more like it," he said, his tone teasing as they all joined Hannah in the living room.

"How long have you been here?" Nash asked.

"I got in a few hours ago. I was actually just starting to wonder where you guys were."

"We had to be sure that no one was following us," Drake said, as he sat next to Madeline on the sofa.

"Sounds like you've had quite an adventure," Hannah said, smiling at Madeline.

"An understatement actually. But I was lucky. I had Drake along for the ride."

"Definitely a man you want around in a crisis."

"You're in charge of intel, right?" Madeline asked. "Drake mentioned you. But I thought our location was supposed to be—"

"Eyes-only?" Hannah nodded, sitting back down. "It is. Except that intel is my thing. And Avery's been acting really weird. Tyler, too. It didn't take much to tap into my sources and work out what was what. I never thought for a moment that we'd actually leave you and Drake out there, no matter what Langley said."

"So, does Avery know you're here?" Nash asked.

"He was very particular about keeping our presence here 'need to know,'" Annie added.

"He made that more than clear, when he told me to butt out. But me, being me—I ignored him. And kept digging. And finally he gave in and here I am."

"You know that the threat to Madeline is very real," Drake said.

Hannah sobered, her gaze encompassing them all. "I

do. And I've done everything in my power to make certain no one can track my movements coming here. And I brought my personal computer." She waved at the laptop. "It's got everything I need, but it isn't networked through Sunderland or Langley. Which means any work I do stays off the grid. And thanks to Jason it's encrypted as well. There's absolutely no way to trace it. And I swear no one knows I'm here."

"The best-laid plans..." Nash shrugged.

"Well, Avery's got things covered from his end as well," Hannah said. "He's created alibis for Nash, Annie, and me, but we don't have much time. Langley's already on edge and they're going to get suspicious if we're out of the loop for too much longer."

"What about Tucker?" Drake asked, his heart rate ratcheting up at the thought of his brother. "Any news?"

"They're still stonewalling at Langley. Of course Avery's inquiries have all been off-book. But they're basically sticking with the original story. Tucker wasn't CIA and he died in Nevada with the rest of his military unit. Anyway, Avery isn't buying. But so far he hasn't found anyone who is willing to contradict the party line."

"The suits are closing ranks," Annie said. "Not surprising."

"Yeah, well, they weren't counting on me." Hannah smiled. "I've been at it nonstop since I first heard that Tucker might be alive. And since digging for dirt is second nature to me, it wasn't long before I started to unearth things that make it look like Langley has been playing fast and loose with the truth."

"So what have you got?" Drake asked, leaning forward, his body tightening with anticipation.

"Well, first off," Hannah said, "Tucker Flynn wasn't in the military. I hacked into army files, and there's no record of his ever enlisting. Or training or anything. He just pops up, a full-fledged soldier. On the surface it wouldn't appear hinky, but the deeper you go the more obvious it is that his service record is a fake."

"And what about the CIA's divisions? Could you hack into them?"

"Didn't have to." Hannah shook her head. "I have a friend with the proper clearance. Just took a couple of drinks and a pissing match about the best code words. She uses Billboard Top Ten."

"Songs?" Madeline questioned, her tone incredulous.

"An alphanumeric combination of the song title and its placement in that week's chart," Hannah said. "It's only the personnel files. And an outsider would never have access, so there's no need for fancy encryption. Anyway, the point is that your brother was most definitely a member of D-5. And I cross-checked the others who died in the alleged plane crash. They were D-5 as well."

"What about their missions?" Annie asked.

"Unfortunately, that *is* an encrypted system. And the fail-safes there are a much tougher nut to crack. So far I haven't been able to get in. I did find a reference in some old chatter reports of suspected U.S. activity in Colombia around the right time period. But there's no verification, and nothing to indicate that it was in fact D-5."

"So we've got proof that Tucker was working for the CIA. And some anecdotal information that might indicate his division was in Colombia. But nothing else that proves definitively that he was there. Or that he might have been captured and imprisoned at San Mateo."

"But there wouldn't be evidence of that," Madeline protested. "I mean, he was still playing his undercover role. As far as the Colombian government was concerned he was an insurgent named Andrés."

"Exactly right." Hannah beamed at her as if she were a prized pupil. "And that's why I decided to go at it the other way round."

"You started looking for Andrés."

"Yes. First step was to try to find a last name," Hannah said. "I was able to dig up a prisoner roster from three years ago. Approximately the time when Madeline was there. She's listed as an American. A political prisoner."

"Yes, but what about this Andrés?" Drake asked impatiently.

"There were two, actually," Hannah said. "One of them with the last name Diaz and the other Castillo."

"Either of those names sound familiar?" Drake asked, turning to Madeline.

"No." She shook her head. "I'm sorry. He never told me his last name. And it wasn't the kind of thing one asked."

"Doesn't matter," Hannah said. "You said your friend was a revolutionary. And only one of the two men tracks to FARC. Castillo. It took some digging but I found some government records—Colombian—that verify a sweep they did of a jungle stronghold just south of Cali. According to their incident report the entire base was destroyed, most of the insurgents killed in the process. But there were three survivors. One of whom was Andrés Castillo."

"And he was imprisoned in San Mateo," Nash said, eyes narrowed as he considered this latest revelation.

"Yes. Around the time of Tucker's alleged death."

"But that's still not enough to prove that Tucker and Andrés are one and the same," Annie said.

"What about Madeline's playing card," Drake asked. "Did you find anything to verify its authenticity?"

"Well, without the actual card, I can't vouch for it completely," Hannah said. "But I did uncover information about the cards and each division's color coding. Division personnel are definitely issued playing cards. Langley has been using them since the inception of the division program. And according to my intel, the card Madeline described was definitely associated with D-5."

"So if Andrés had the card, then we know he at least had contact with someone from D-5," Nash said.

"But since he's also a ringer for Drake's brother," Madeline insisted, "it seems likely that the card was his."

"I agree with Madeline," Hannah said. "Based on what we've got, I'd say that we can be pretty damn certain that Andrés is Tucker."

"You used the present tense," Drake said, his heart pounding. "Does that mean you think he's alive?"

"Actually, yeah." Hannah shook her head emphatically. "I do. I managed to access the San Mateo files with prisoner records. And Andrés Castillo is definitely alive and kicking."

"Oh, my God." Drake swallowed, his mind reeling. "I didn't think...Hell, I was afraid this was just some kind of cosmic joke."

"But it's not," Madeline said, reaching over to cover his hand with hers. "Tucker is alive."

"And I think I've got the working elements of a plan to rescue him," Hannah said, turning the laptop so that everyone could see. "This is a view of the prison from here in Magdalena." She pointed to a picture of the prison rising out of the jungle, perched at the top of a tree-studded rise. "It was originally built by the Spanish as an area fortification. In the 1800s it was used as a hospital. And about fifty years ago it was converted to a prison."

She switched to a new photo, this time an aerial shot of San Mateo. "Okay, so you can see the prison here. It's basically a U-shaped building with two wings, each containing a cell block. There are also a couple of outbuildings. And the whole complex is surrounded by an eight-foot stone wall."

"With barbed wire on top," Madeline added. "And two guard towers built into the wall. You can just see them through the trees." She pointed to the spire of one tower breaking out of the canopy.

"How many guards in the towers?" Drake asked, studying the photograph, memorizing the layout.

"No more than two," Hannah said.

"But they're usually only in the towers during the day," Madeline said. "Particularly when people are in the yard, since it backs right up to the wall."

"What about security cameras?" Nash asked, making notes on a white legal pad.

"There aren't any except at the front gate," Hannah said, shaking her head. "Overall, external security is pretty rudimentary, principally because of the location and the wall. Basically the only way in or out is through the front gate."

"Or over the wall," Drake mused with a frown.

"Maybe from inside, but definitely not from the outside," Hannah said, switching pictures again to show a section of the fence. The dropoff was immediate, the rocks making it almost impossible to maneuver. "It's just too steep."

"She's right." Nash nodded. "The gate is our best opportunity for access."

"Okay, so what's security like at the gate?" Annie asked.

Hannah switched pictures again, this one depicting a gated opening in the wall. "The guardhouse has external cameras and it houses central security for the entire complex. Best I can tell, it's manned twenty-four/seven. Easiest way in is for you to convince them to let you through."

"Somehow, I'm thinking they're not going to be too keen on the idea of us just waltzing in." Drake frowned.

"They will if they think you're there to repair a problem," Hannah said, moving to another photo. "This is a picture of the local electrical company's repair van. It's in a lot about five blocks from here. Assuming I can access the electrical grid, it shouldn't be too hard to interrupt service. Meanwhile, you guys can secure the van and use it to convince the guys at the gate to let you save the day, or night, as the case may be."

"She's right," Madeline agreed. "There's less personnel at night, and security should be a little more lax when everyone inside is securely locked down."

"It just might work," Drake speculated, considering their options. "But it'll have to play out as realistically as possible. Which means we'll need the proper gear to convince them we are who we say we are."

"I'm already on it," Hannah said, "Avery gave me

some names, people who've agreed to help us for the right price."

"Okay, so far so good," Annie said, "but once we're inside the gate, where do we go from there?"

Hannah hit a key and the computer screen dissolved into a diagram of the prison's buildings. "There's an out-building just past the main gate that serves as the utility hub. That's where they'll expect you to go. Fortunately for us, that same building also provides access to what used to be the main structure's septic system, a cesspit underneath the prison that connected to chutes inside that originally served as conduits for... well, you can guess."

"Tell me you're not asking us to climb through shit," Nash said, his distaste apparent.

"I'm not." Hannah shook her head. "The system was abandoned eighty years ago. But sometime in the sixties when the place was converted to a prison, they widened the chutes and turned them into maintenance crawl spaces. They provided an easy way to access wiring and so forth without having to disrupt security within the prison."

"Seems to me like it would have accomplished just the opposite, the crawl spaces providing the perfect exit for the discerning inmate." Annie frowned.

"Never would have worked," Hannah said. "The cell blocks are separated from the rest of the building by security gates. And the only access to the crawl space from the interior of the building is through a small service closet near the southwest corner, here," she said, switching to a diagram of the prison's floor plan.

"So even if a prisoner knew about the crawl space,

he wouldn't be able to access it without getting past the gate," Annie said.

"Exactly," Hannah agreed. "And from what I can tell, prisoners aren't allowed off the block all that often."

"Hardly ever," Madeline concurred. "The doors to the exercise yard are at the end of each cell block. And meals, if you can call them that, are served in the inmate's cell. The only time I was ever out of my cell block was when they took me to the infirmary—which has its own security."

"So which wing were you in?" Drake asked, nodding at the floor plan.

"I was here," Madeline said, pointing to the east cell block. "About halfway down. The prisoners on my side were mainly older men and a few women. People deemed less dangerous."

"And the west cell block?" Nash prompted.

"That's where they keep the stronger men. And the inmates who caused problems or were marked for execution. Not that they ever used those words, mind you. But we all knew it happened." She shuddered, and Drake remembered she'd told him once that she'd heard them shooting at night. "Andrés's regular cell was in the west block."

"Do you know which one?" Annie asked.

"As a matter of fact, I do," she said, her face tight as she worked to control her emotions. "The solitary cells are at the end of the west block, so to get there you have to walk along the corridor. And unfortunately, I made the trip a couple of times."

"And you saw Andrés while you were there?" Hannah asked.

"No. He was in the infirmary then. But we talked about

it later. And he told me where his cell was. My having been on the block made it easy to visualize what he was describing. And besides, the two wings are basically mirror images. His cell would have been right around here." She pointed to a spot about two-thirds of the way along the west cell block. "Of course, there's no guarantee he's still there. People got shifted around all the time."

"I'm trying to get a firm location," Hannah said. "But to do that I've got to end-run the prison IT system's safeguards. It's slow going, but I'll get in, and when I do, I'll have access to the current inmate roster."

"Okay," Drake said, still sorting through all the details, "so let's assume that we make it through the front gate and into the service passage. Then what?"

"Like I said, you'll come out here"—Hannah pointed to the floor plan again—"in a storage closet. The opening to the crawl space has been sealed off for years, but you shouldn't have any problem getting through. The good news is that by coming in this way, we're circumventing the first security gate."

"What's the bad news?" Annie asked, her brow furrowing as she studied the drawing.

"You still have to get past the second," Madeline said. "Like Hannah said, it's keyed electronically. Operated through some kind of central system."

"Which means in this day and age it'll be computerized," Hannah said. "So I should be able to open it remotely."

"After we deal with the guards." Nash frowned. "Any idea how many?"

"It varies," Madeline said. "But never more than two on each side. And at night there should only be one."

"And if I can rig their security cameras," Hannah continued, "the right hand will never know that the left has been immobilized."

"The whole thing is going to have to happen really fast," Drake said, running through the entire scenario in his mind. "Before anyone has time to clue in to what's what."

"I agree, timing is going to be important," Annie nodded. "So, are the interior cell locks electronic as well?"

"No," Madeline said. "They're all mechanically keyed locks. Or at least they were when I was there."

"But the good news," Hannah said, "is that there's just one master key. And although each of the guards carries his own, the keys are checked in before the men leave the premises and they're kept at the guards' station."

"Okay, so let's say we've managed to make it to Tucker's cell and free him." Drake walked over to the window, crossing his arms as he leaned back against the sill. "How do you propose we get out of there?"

"Same way you got in," Hannah said. "If we've done everything right, you should be able to get Tucker out of the building and into the van while I restore the power. Then you simply drive through the gate and we're home free."

"In my experience," Nash frowned, his tone dry, "operations never go quite that smoothly."

"He's got a point." Annie nodded. "But I should be able to handle the tower guards if necessary. Assuming you can do without me on the inside."

"I was already thinking that might be a good idea," Nash said. "So Annie will handle external complications, and Hannah, you'll coordinate and deal with the technical aspects of the mission. I'll hold the fort at the utility hub, maintaining the façade of our repairman gig. And in the meantime Drake will break into the prison to find and liberate Tucker. "

"What about me?" Madeline asked. "What do I do?"

"You stay here and help Hannah," Drake said.

She nodded, her expression inscrutable.

"So when do we go?" Nash asked.

"There's no time like the present," Hannah said. "And the faster we move, the less chance we'll run into interference. So assuming we can get everything put together, I'm thinking we should be ready to go just after midnight."

CHAPTER 24

Moonlight spilled across the front porch of the hacienda, the trees swaying in the silvery light. *Hunter's moon*. Madeline wrapped her arms around her knees as she sat on the steps, looking out at the lights of Magdalena. So many things had happened in so little time. It was hard to deal with it all. Most especially the way she felt about Drake.

It was confusing at best, depressing at worst. In some bizarre way, the whole thing reminded her of summer camp. Relationships intensified, normal social barriers gone, the magnification making everything seem exaggerated. More important somehow. But when it was over, and reality returned, the intensity faded, and the feelings passed. A moment's enchantment—gone.

She sighed, staring out at the moonlit night. Palm trees swayed in the gentle breeze, the sweet fragrance of mango and coconut filling the air. Stars dotted the velvet sky, their twinkling light dimming against the brightness of the moon. The soft sound of bleating drifted across the road from the field on the other side, a herd of goats settling in for the night.

Behind her, the screen door squeaked as it opened, but she didn't turn to see who it was. She already knew.

"I wondered where you'd gotten to," Drake said, dropping down beside her on the steps.

"Where's everyone else?" she asked.

"Nash and Annie are trying to get a few hours' sleep and Hannah is holed up in her bedroom with her computer."

Madeline nodded, standing up to lean against the railing, her eyes still on the moonlit sky.

"You okay?" he asked.

"Just thinking," she said. "About everything that's happened."

"Well, for the moment at least, things seem to be going our way. That's something."

"Yeah, you guys have everything under control?" she asked.

"We have a plan, if that's what you mean." He shrugged. "And for what it's worth, while we're gone, you'll be safe here with Hannah. We've taken every precaution. There's no way di Silva's people are going to find you here. It's the last place they'd expect you to come. And no one at the CIA knows about any of this. So you don't have to worry."

"I'm not worried," she said, swinging around to face him. "I just don't want to stay here." She stopped, the idea surprising, the truth hitting her full-on.

"I thought we'd been through this already." He frowned, coming to his feet. "You can't afford to go off on your own right now."

"You're not understanding me," she said. "I don't want to leave. More specifically, I don't want to leave *you*. I want to come with you. To San Mateo. I want to help you free Andrés."

"That's out of the question," he responded, his tone brooking no argument. But she wasn't in the habit of letting other people tell her what to do.

"It most certainly is not," she said, hands on her hips. "I'm the only one you've got who's been inside. I know the guards' routines as well as the prisoners' schedules. I know the building. And I know the layout."

"Hannah's got blueprints."

"Old ones. I had a closer look at them. They're not accurate. Four years ago they did some remodeling. Things aren't exactly the same. But I've been there. And I know the changes they made."

"So you can show me."

"Yes, but what if I don't remember everything? You need me on site. Timing is crucial. Which means things will go better with an inside man—*or woman*."

"I can't let you go. It's too dangerous."

"But this is something I have to do. Can't you understand that? Look, Drake, you need me. And I want to help. Please let me." They stood for a moment, toe to toe, their gazes dueling.

And then Drake shook his head with a soft laugh. "You're a stubborn woman. You know that, don't you?"

"I can be a little single-minded," she admitted. "But I'm right this time. You need me. And after everything you've done for me, it's the least I can do."

"It won't be easy."

"Neither was jumping over the waterfall. Or killing

that man on the river. But I did it. And I can do this, too. Please, Drake," she said, reaching out to touch his arm. "Let me go with you."

"You're sure?"

She nodded, lifting her gaze to his. "Look, I know I've said it before, but for what it's worth, I'm really sorry about this morning. I could have handled it better. I guess I just panicked."

"In all honesty, if I'd been in your position, I can't say that I wouldn't have done the same," he said, the ghost of a smile chasing across his face. "But you know at some point you have to stop running, Madeline. You have to stay and fight."

"Maybe that's what I'm trying to do," she whispered.

He reached out to tuck a strand of hair behind her ear, and she trembled as his fingers brushed her skin. A truck rumbled down the gravel road in front of them, blaring its horn at a wayward goat, and she stepped back, the moment broken.

She wanted there to be an underlying meaning to his words, for him to be talking about something beyond Ortiz and the CIA and plastic-coated playing cards. But she knew that there wasn't. At least nothing that would change the situation at hand.

"So where were you going to go?" he asked, the question cutting into her tumbling thoughts as they settled back onto the front porch steps. "When you left this morning, I mean."

"I don't know," she said with a shrug. "Somewhere new, I guess. Someplace I could start over."

"But you'd still always be looking over your shoulder."

"Maybe. But it's got to be better than all of this, right?"

"I don't know; this hasn't been so bad," he said.

"So says the adrenaline junkie."

"There's truth to that, certainly. I'm not exactly the poster boy for settling down. My job doesn't lend itself to minivans and picket fences."

"But you wouldn't really want it to, would you?" she asked, already certain of his answer.

"No." He shook his head, the moonlight highlighting his profile. "I guess I wouldn't. I've never been a nine-to-five kind of guy."

"It obviously runs in the family." The minute the words were out she regretted them, the specter of his brother rising up between them.

But he smiled, the breeze dispelling any negative feelings. "My mom certainly had the wanderlust. Although I'd never thought about my craving for adventure coming from her. I guess maybe it did. Funny to think that as much time as I've spent hating her, I actually turn out to be just like her."

"You'd never desert your family," Madeline said.

"No," he agreed. "I wouldn't."

"Do you ever wonder what might have happened if things had turned out differently? I mean, like, if your mother hadn't run off?"

"When I was a kid, all the time. But as I grew older I guess I accepted the situation for what it was. I realized that there was nothing I could do to change it. What about you? Would your life have been different if your mother had lived?"

"It's hard to say. She wasn't a strong woman. But she did try to protect us from my dad."

"Did she ever try to leave? Get you away from him?"

"Once," she said. "She woke us up in the middle of the night, and we snuck out of the house. I thought we were going on an adventure. We made our way to town, and I think we were at the bus stop. I don't know; it was a long time ago, and I was little. But I remember my father finding us. It was the first time I was really conscious of being afraid of him. He hit my mom, and I tried to hit him back, but she grabbed me and told me to take Jenny and run home. I can still see her face." She paused, the memory heavy as it settled around her. "Anyway, I ran. And I guess in some ways I've been running ever since."

"I'm sorry," he said.

"Don't be. It is what it is. And with Jenny gone, the worst of it's over."

"But it still haunts you."

"Yeah, some nightmares are hard to get rid of." She stopped, staring out into the night. "What about your mom? Is she still alive?"

"I don't know. I tried to find her once. When I was in college. But I kept hitting dead-ends, and Tucker told me that maybe there was a reason."

"Like you weren't supposed to find her."

"Something like that." He nodded. "Anyway, I never tried again." Silence stretched for a moment, but it was comfortable, the palms gyrating in the breeze, casting eerie shadows against the house. "Tell me about my brother," Drake said finally, his voice soft against the whisper of the wind.

Madeline paused, knowing that this was the reason he'd come out to talk with her, and wanting to get it right. "He was sick. That's the only way I would ever have had the chance to meet him. The sick and the infirm took the yard with the women."

"What was wrong with him?" he turned to face her, his eyes turning silver in the moonlight.

"They thought it was malaria. But he was already getting better when I met him. It was my first time outside. I'd been in solitary, and I wasn't exactly the best of company. But your brother can be quite persistent when he's of a mind."

She could see Drake smile. "Yes, he can."

"Anyway," she continued, "he was a little scary looking. His beard was matted and he was filthy. I was actually a little afraid of him. But then he offered me a square of chocolate. I've no idea where he got it, but I hadn't eaten in days and it was amazingly good. And he just sat with me. Waiting until I calmed down. Until I wasn't afraid anymore."

"Sounds like my brother." Drake nodded. "I remember when I was a kid, I used to believe there were monsters under the bed. I'd make my dad let me keep the bathroom light on to keep them from coming out. Anyway, one night in the middle of the night, the lightbulb burned out. I was too scared to get out of bed. So I just lay there freaking out, certain that I was about to get eaten. Tucker heard me, and he came in and sat with me all night. Even after I fell asleep."

"He was that way with me, too. A guardian angel. At first he only talked in Spanish, but my command of the language was basically limited to curse words and totally useless sentences like '*Te gusta invierno*?' "

"Do you like winter?" he repeated.

"Yeah, for some reason my fifth-grade teacher thought the question would be useful for a kid growing up in the Louisiana heat. We learned the appropriate responses, too, but that's about as far as it went. So finally, Andrés tried his English. Which was surprisingly good, although occasionally flawed. I can see now that it was part of the act. But his friendship wasn't a lie. It was a lifeline. I don't think I'd have made it in there without him."

"You're stronger than you think you are."

"Yes, but San Mateo isn't the kind of place that's easy to survive. The prisoners are people the Colombian government wants to pretend don't exist. It makes places like Abu Ghraib look like Disneyland. Most people who go into San Mateo never come out. It's easy to lose hope. I think that's what happened with your brother," she said, thinking about that last day.

"I think he decided to give me the card because he knew no one was coming for him. And he thought maybe I still had a chance. I begged him to keep it. But he refused. He said it was too late, that he was on borrowed time." She sucked in a breath, tears threatening. "Then the guard called for him. He'd recovered from the malaria, so he was being transferred back to his original cell. I stood there, watching him go, feeling like my whole world was leaving with him. I never saw him again."

"Did you ever try to go back? To check on him?"

"No. I guess I was too busy with my own problems." She sighed. "Not very commendable, is it?"

"It's what he wanted you to do. Get the hell out of San Mateo. Get on with your life."

"Yeah, well, I don't think he meant signing on with Hector Ortiz."

Madeline held her breath, wondering if she'd gone too far, said too much. She had no experience with real relationships. Her only friend in the last three years had been a fellow prisoner she'd talked to once a day for fifteen minutes, and most of that had turned out to be lies. So what the hell did she know?

"Probably not," he answered, his eyes filled with tenderness. "But considering the circumstances, I think he'd have understood."

She nodded, tears welling again. She'd never met anyone who made her feel so vulnerable and so safe all at the same time.

"Madeline," he said, his eyes searching hers, "I don't know what's happening here. And I can't make any promises. I don't know what's going to happen tomorrow or the day after that. I only know that right here, right now, I want you."

She wanted him every bit as much as he wanted her. It was as if she'd never really lived before. As if somehow he'd breathed new life into her. And it scared her to death. Yet she couldn't walk away.

"I want you, too," she whispered, the words raspy as her breath caught in her throat.

With a crooked smile, he swung her into his arms and carried her inside to his bedroom, letting her body slide against him as he released her, the friction only heightening her building desire.

After closing the door, he framed her face with his hands, his mouth slanting over hers, his lips taking possession, slowly, as if savoring the taste of her, cherishing the union. And with a little murmur, she opened to him, all signs of gentleness disappearing as their passion ignited, consuming them in a fire so hot she could feel her skin flush with desire.

She felt her nipples tighten as her body demanded

more, and with a groan she threaded her fingers through his hair, drawing him closer, her tongue dancing against his, thrusting and withdrawing, taking and giving.

Reaching for the hem of her cotton sundress, he pulled it up and over her head, the thin material billowing as it fell to the floor. His shirt followed and then his pants, the two of them coming together again, their mouths greedy as they explored each other with lips and hands.

She tipped back her head, gasping, as he took her breast into his mouth. His teeth closed around her nipple, sending spirals of heat coursing through her, tightening until she burned with need. He sucked slowly, his thumb and forefinger stroking the other breast as she closed her eyes, the soft silk of his hair caressing her skin.

His tongue circled hot and needy as his hand slipped down her belly, stroking, teasing as his fingers circled the soft hair at the apex of her thighs. And then they dipped inside, the contact sending her arching against him, struggling to breathe. And still he sucked and stroked, holding her against him, playing her like a cherished instrument, the strings pulled tight as each carefully chosen note built upon the others.

Then, just when she thought she couldn't stand it a moment longer, he lifted her up, and she wrapped her legs around him as he thrust against her, teasing her with his heat and his strength. Her body contracting with need, she pressed closer, gyrating her hips, sliding against him, up and down, up and down, until her muscles contracted in ecstasy, the building friction making her moan against his throat.

"More," she whispered. "I want more."

Shifting so that his hands were under her legs, he

carried her to the bed and laid her against the sheets, their momentary separation sending need pulsing through her. And then he was there beside her, throbbing and hard, and she took him in her mouth, pulling and sucking, her tongue tracing the length of him, feeling him grow harder as she caressed him with her lips.

Then, with an earthy growl, he pulled her up, her body sliding against his until his hands framed her face as he took control. His kiss was hard and demanding, his body arching against hers. And with a smile, she sat up, running her hands down her breasts, over her stomach, and between her legs. Then she slid her body onto his, letting him watch as she started to move, still caressing her breasts, smiling as she felt the familiar tension begin to grow.

This man made her crazy. She wanted him more than she'd ever wanted anyone—ever. She needed him like breathing, and the idea should have frightened her, but instead she found it empowering. She moved slowly, laving him with her body, each stroke driving her higher, closer and closer to the edge. She tightened around him as she slid up and down, feeling him grow harder inside her. Cupping his balls with her hand, she squeezed gently as she rode him, watching his eyes flash with pleasure.

And then he grabbed her hips, rolling the two of them over, straddling her as he drove inside her, taking control, their rhythm increasing as he began to move faster. She lifted her hips, taking him deeper, her passion reaching a fever pitch. Without breaking rhythm, he reached between her legs, his thumb rasping against her clitoris, the added friction sending her bucking against him, forcing him deeper still.

Pleasure built until it was almost unbearable, and she teetered on the brink. Wrapping her arms around him, she opened her legs wider, wanting more, needing more. And as if sensing her need, his thumb moved faster as he thrust harder and harder.

She screamed his name as she felt his muscles tighten, as he thrust against her one last time, and then her body exploded into spasms of release. Sensation rocked through her, stripping her of everything but a pleasure so pure it was almost more than she could bear. And then suddenly he was there, his hand closing around hers. And there was nothing but the two of them. One body. One soul. Two halves of a whole.

Later, much later, she drifted on the edge of sleep, her contractions subsiding until they were only gentle undulations, their bodies still connected as he held her cradled in his arms. She wanted to hold him inside her forever. To stop time and engrave this memory in her heart.

She, of all people, recognized how precious their connection was. But nothing lasted forever. And there had been no promises made. No covenant between them. It was just one night.

One incredibly special night.

With a sigh, she nestled her head against his chest, letting the soft sound of the breeze lull her into sleep.

It was dark, and although he could hear the ocean, he couldn't see it. He turned in a circle, trying to verify position, to remember where exactly he was. The jungle was thick here, the trees twisted and bent, making forward progress difficult. From somewhere off to his right, monkeys chittered, their cries angry and alarmed. His senses were on high alert, and he pushed through the under-growth, heedless of the branches and thorns.

Then suddenly the trees started to thin, the floor of the jungle opening out into a statue-lined clearing, an ancient altar standing sentry in the center. He walked forward, slowly, eyes searching for signs of danger, while another part of his mind tried to place the architecture. Chibcha, maybe Muiscas. Definitely Pre-Colombian.

He walked forward slowly, the eyes of the statues seeming to follow as he moved. The altar stone was placed on the back of a carved jaguar, golden eyes glowing eerily in the half-light. As he got closer he realized with a start that someone or something was lying on the stone. His heart slammed in his chest as he inched his way closer, his mind struggling to make sense of what he saw.

The body was lifeless, lying on its stomach, one hand thrown carelessly over the side of the altar stone, blood dripping from the fingertips. Stepping closer still, Drake recognized the hair, the shape of the head, and his stomach dropped as his mind presented the irrefutable conclusion.

Tucker.

Anger mixed with pain as he ran forward, praying that he was wrong. He reached out, hand trembling as he clasped the shoulders, turning the body over.

And then suddenly everything shifted, masculine features turning to feminine. Cassandra's eyes mocked him, blood dripping from the wound where he'd shot her. "There's no such thing as a happy ending," she taunted. And then she was gone. Instead soft black curls spilled over the stone altar, lifeless brown eyes staring up at the overhanging canopy of trees.

"Madeline," he screamed, his heart twisting as bile rose in his throat. "Madeline. No."

Hands tore at him, and he tried to fight them off; he wouldn't let them hurt her. Whirling around, he tried to find his enemy, but the clearing was empty, the wind whispering his name.

"Drake . . . Drake . . . *Drake*."

His eyes flickered open, the altar and the ruins vanishing into the shadows of the bedroom.

"Drake, it's me. Madeline. Can you hear me?" She shook him gently, her face creased with worry. "You were having a nightmare. But it's over now. Everything is okay."

He sucked in a ragged breath, the vision of her body, beaten and bloody, still etched into his brain.

"We're safe," she whispered, reaching for his hand. "In Magdalena. Remember?"

Reality came flooding back. He sat up, running a hand through his hair, pushing away the last vestiges of the dream.

"Are you okay?" she asked, her eyes still wide with concern.

"Yeah," he said, still feeling a little shaky. "I just thought . . . I thought . . ."

"Whatever you thought, it wasn't true," she soothed as she squeezed his hand. "It was just a dream."

He nodded, recognizing the truth, but unable to let go of the images. "I thought you were dead. I was in the jungle, trying to find something, and I wound up in a clearing with an altar. And there was a body and I thought it was Tucker but when I turned it over it was you."

"But I'm here," she said, reaching up to stroke his face. "And I'm fine."

"I know. It's stupid."

"No. It's not. You're just going through a lot right now."

"Yeah, well, we're leaving in a couple of hours, so I don't think now's the best time for a meltdown." He hated himself for his own weakness, and even more for having shown it to her.

"Drake"—her smile was gentle—"even superheroes have their moments. It's just your mind's way of coping."

"You make it sound so clinical." He smiled, beginning to feel a little better.

"Well, when you think about it, it is. I mean, dreams are just the mind's way of letting off steam. Dealing with issues we can't or won't deal with in real life. Only sometimes the subconscious can get a bit carried away."

"You're right. It was just a dream. And I'm fine." He leaned back against the pillows, suddenly feeling uncomfortable.

"Well, I'm here, if you need me," she said, her hand still cupping his face.

And suddenly he felt guilty. There were so many reasons why there couldn't be anything permanent between them. Her situation. His job. She was an asset and he'd allowed himself to get involved. To care. But it couldn't go any further and she deserved to know the truth.

"Look, Madeline," he said, summoning his courage, "we need to talk."

"No." She shook her head, her fingers moving to cover his lips. "We don't. I understand that this isn't anything more than what it is. I needed you and you needed me.

And nothing else matters. So for now, let's just leave it as it is. Okay?"

Her eyes pleaded with him, and with a guttural groan, he gave in to his own desire, rolling over and pinning her to the mattress. Their gazes met and held, the worry in her eyes replaced with something more primitive. Passion. Basal and earthy. Chemistry at its most elemental.

His mouth slanted over hers, his kiss possessive. He wanted her. And she opened to him. Asking nothing in return. It humbled him. And excited him. And created feelings he wasn't even sure he understood. But he knew one thing; he needed her. And he'd be a fool to turn away from so precious a gift.

He pulled her back into the soft comfort of the bed, determined to show her with his mouth and body and hands all the things he couldn't find voice to say. And she answered him in kind, the two of them delighting again in the discovery of each other, tasting and exploring, kissing and teasing, his body responding to hers as the fears and anxiety about his brother were pushed aside in the wake of their rising passion.

He braced himself above her, marveling at the beauty of her face, the brown depths of her eyes, the tiny mole at the corner of her mouth. This was a woman a man could lose himself in. And at the moment, that's all he wanted.

With a single thrust he was inside her, his body establishing a rhythm. She arched against him, taking him deeper, her body rising to meet his, their movements building in tempo and complexity until there was nothing but the two of them.

He closed his eyes, and let himself go, surrendering

to the moment. And together they found release, the
world breaking apart in a frenzy, his climax beyond anything he'd ever believed possible. And in that moment
of ecstasy, he found sanctuary, and rejoiced in the fact
that, at least for the moment, she'd helped him hold the
monsters at bay.

Bogotá, Colombia

"Montague is dead, and Petrov failed to run Madeline to
ground," Ortiz said, grinding his teeth as he stared out
into the rainswept streets of Bogotá. On the other end of
the telephone line, Michael Brecht was silent. "Did you
hear what I said?"

"Yes. Of course." There was a rebuke in his tone, the
master reminding the student of the nature of their relationship. "I was already aware of the situation."

"And are you aware that she's disappeared? Probably
on her way back to the States? If she makes it there, not
even your network can get to her." Agitated, Ortiz crossed
over to the credenza in his office and poured himself a
drink.

"Must I remind you," Brecht said, "that she's your
problem, not mine? As I told you in the beginning, I've
arranged things so that no one can possibly trace your
activities to me or my organization."

"So what are you saying?" Ortiz tightened his fingers
around the glass. "You're cutting me loose?"

"No. Quite the opposite. I still consider you an asset,
Hector. And because of that I'm calling to let you know

where she's gone. Although I'll admit it makes no sense at all to me."

"Where is she?" He slammed the glass down, the liquid inside sloshing the papers on his desk.

"She's gone back to San Mateo. At least, she's in Magdalena."

"Are you certain?" Ortiz asked, his stomach tightening with dread.

"Absolutely. I told you I have an inside source. And even though they've ostensibly gone dark, he can still track their location. Any idea why she'd want to go back to that hellhole?"

"None at all," Ortiz lied. "Maybe to clear herself. I don't know."

"Well, whatever the reason, it's a godsend for you. A final chance to remove her from the equation once and for all. Shall I send Petrov?"

"No." Ortiz shook his head, even though the other man couldn't see him. "He's already failed once. I'll handle this myself."

"Just be careful," Brecht said. "These people are clearly playing for keeps. And I'd hate to see you become a liability."

"Don't worry. I've had dealings with the CIA before. It won't be a problem."

"See that it isn't." Brecht hung up, and Ortiz stood staring down at the receiver. He'd need to call di Silva. Apprise him of this newest development. And then he'd head for Magdalena. This time there was no room for failure. There could only be one reason Madeline was going back to San Mateo.

Tucker Flynn.

She might not know the whole truth. But she was well on her way. And if she and her cohorts managed to spring Tucker from prison, everything Ortiz had worked to accomplish would be destroyed.

He lifted his glass, then downed the contents.

Madeline Reynard had to be stopped.

CHAPTER 25

Magdalena wasn't much more than a collection of ramshackle houses and a half dozen rutted roads. Its municipal services were limited to water, electricity, and a rickety bus that traveled to Quibdo and back twice a week. All vehicles owned by the village were kept on a small lot behind the town hall surrounded by a chain-link fence.

Standing beside the fence, Madeline looked up at the prison towering over the town like something out of a horror movie. She'd never thought she'd be this close to San Mateo again. She shivered even though the night was warm, the cold metal of her gun pressing against her back, and she couldn't help but think about how much her life had changed over the past few days.

It had taken a little convincing on Drake's part to get Nash and Annie to agree to allow Madeline to be part of the rescue attempt. But in the end, they'd given the okay, agreeing that Madeline's firsthand knowledge of the prison could come in handy should they hit a snag.

At the moment, Drake and Nash were busy at the parking-lot gate working to open the padlock holding it shut. Annie had already gone up the mountain to do a little recon. And Hannah was locked inside the hacienda doing her cyber thing, trying to finalize preparations to hijack the prison security systems. She'd already managed to tap into the electrical grid and deal with the warden's phone lines.

Madeline stood for a moment, feeling useless, and then Drake motioned for her as the gate swung open. Her gaze swept the darkened buildings surrounding the lot, looking for something to indicate they'd been spotted. But the neighborhood remained quiet, the only movement the silent swaying of the towering palms.

Following Drake and Nash, she slipped inside the gate. The parking lot was shadowed, the only light coming from the single street lamp at the gate. There were four vehicles parked on the broken asphalt: a battered police cruiser, a taxi, the aforementioned bus, and the Energia Electrica van.

"While you guys get the van going, I'll disable the other cars," Nash said, loping off into the darkness, his pack slung over his back.

Drake reached up to open the driver's side door, dumping his backpack onto the seat as he stepped up into the cab.

"What are you going to do?" Madeline asked. "Hotwire it?"

"It's a possibility. But if Colombian utility workers are anything like Americans, we may not have to." He reached up and flipped the visor down, a key falling into his hand. "Told you." He grinned, sliding the key into the ignition, the van's engine springing to life.

"I guess Magdalena isn't all that different from Cypress Bluff," she said as she pulled open the passenger door and climbed inside.

She climbed into the back of the van as Nash hopped into the front seat next to Drake. "Everything's good. Those cars won't be going anywhere anytime soon."

"All right then, I guess it's time to head up the mountain." Drake drove the van out of the lot, keeping the headlights off to avoid drawing unnecessary attention. Madeline stowed their gear under a tarp that they'd brought, as Drake turned onto the mountain road, switching on the headlights as he followed the mountain's twisting curves. "Hannah," he said, activating his mic. "You there?"

"I am," she said, the line full of static.

Madeline watched as Drake's hands tightened on the wheel. "You get a bead on Tucker's location?"

"Nothing but what Madeline already told us," she said, regret coloring her voice. "The west cell block. But I'm still working on it. Hopefully by the time you make it inside, I'll have the information we need."

"Listen," Nash reassured, "all we're asking right now is that you get us past the front gate."

"As far as that goes I've done my part. The rest is up to you." She paused, the com going silent for a moment, and then she was back. "Hang on," she said. "Let me patch you through to Annie."

"Hey, guys." Annie sounded farther away than Hannah, but her voice was clearer. "Everything going okay?"

"Right as rain," Nash said, his voice more ebullient now that he was talking to his wife. Madeline fought against a wave of envy. It was hard not to want what they had. "And we're coming your way. Any activity at your end?"

"Nothing much at all. There are two guards on the gate. And one in the back tower. Other than that I haven't seen anyone else on the perimeter."

"How about inside?" Drake asked.

"Can't see anything. The only windows are on the back side, looking out into the yard. So there's no way to tell who's on the inside. But from what I can see, I'd be surprised to find more than a couple of people on the cell blocks. I can see a light on in the warden's building. But again, I haven't seen anyone. Could just be a night light. But figure it's better to be prepared."

"What about your angles? You going to be okay if you have to take out the tower guard?" Nash asked.

"Shouldn't be a problem. Same for the guys at the gate. I can take them out, too, if necessary."

"Fingers crossed, it doesn't come to that," Nash said. "And in the meantime, keep your head down."

"I promise," she said, her voice tight with emotion. "Same to you."

"All right, Hannah," Drake said as they slowed to approach the prison gate. "We're here. You're sure the lights are on the fritz?" As if on cue the lights in the gatehouse flickered off and then on again.

"Damn," Nash said. "You're good."

"I aim to please." Hannah laughed, then sobered. "Good luck."

"Roger that," Drake said. "Madeline, get under the tarp."

Grabbing the gun, she slid underneath the canvas, adjusting her position so that she could still see Drake and

Nash. Drake slowed as he approached the guardhouse, rolling down his window.

"Hear you guys are having some trouble with your electricity," he said, his Spanish passing for local. "The company sent us to fix it, pronto."

"Where's José?" the man asked, his eyes narrowed speculatively. "He's always the one who comes when we've got problems."

Drake hesitated, Hannah's voice filling his ear. "José Mendez was born and raised in Magdalena. Still lives with his mother. He's worked for the utility seventeen years."

"Sorry." Drake shook his head. "José's mother's been sick. So they called us up from Quibdo to cover for him. But if you don't want our help, I'll just turn the van around and head back to town."

The lights in the guardhouse dimmed again, actually going out for a moment.

"Looks like it's the transducer," Drake said with a sideways glance at Nash, who nodded his agreement.

The guard frowned, then relented as the lights flickered again. "Just let me call and check." He reached for his cell phone, speaking quietly into the receiver, then shrugged and waved them forward. "The electrical box is in that building over there." He waved toward a cement structure abutting the west side of the prison. "You can park in back."

Drake pulled the van past the gate, behind the utility building.

"What the fuck is a transducer?" Nash said, his face breaking into a grin.

"I don't know." Drake said. "I just made it up. Figured

he wasn't the kind to know what the hell I was talking about."

"Well, it worked," he said, still laughing as he helped Madeline out from under the tarp.

"Amen to that," Drake added, cutting the engine off.

Grabbing their gear, they walked into the utility shed and down the stairs to the room below. There was a huge electrical panel against one wall, and a generator adjacent to it. Nash flipped on a light, the single bulb flickering a little, then shining true.

"Very funny, Hannah," Nash said, pulling a gauge out of his pack, along with a screwdriver and a pair of needle-nosed pliers.

"That wasn't me," she responded. "Probably just an old bulb."

"We've got plenty of extras in the truck." Drake frowned, turning to survey the room.

"I think I can see the door over there," Madeline said, squinting into the shadows, her eyes focusing as they adjusted to the dark. "It's boarded shut."

Large planks had been secured across the door, the wood rotting and the nails rusty. Pulling a small crowbar out of his backpack, Drake went to work on the door. "Can you give me a little more light?"

She flipped on the flashlight, shining it at the door as he worked to pull the planks free, tossing the debris into the corner. Behind her Nash made a play of hooking the gauge to a port on the panel. The gauge clicked and hissed, and Nash, satisfied with his work, set the little machine on a ledge by the panel.

"Keeping up appearances," he said. "I'll just go up and make sure we don't have company."

Madeline nodded as Drake jerked the final piece of wood, the last few nails yielding and the door coming free. Tossing away the plank, he reached for the handle and yanked the door open.

Damp, dank air flooded into the room, and Madeline swallowed as her stomach heaved.

"Hannah, are you sure this isn't still an active septic system?" Drake asked, covering his mouth and nose with his hand.

"Dry as a bone," she replied. "Or as dry as anything in the jungle ever is. But definitely no longer in use as a privy. It ought to dissipate pretty quickly."

"Everything's clear on the outside," Nash said, coming back down the stairs, holding another gadget. "The guards are still at the gate, and there's no sign of any other activity. So we should be good to go." He wrinkled his nose, the odor sinking in. "What the hell is that smell?"

"Old prison," Drake said.

"Or old shit."

Madeline wrinkled her nose, staring at the dark opening to the tunnel.

"Are you sure you want to go through with this?" Drake asked, recognizing her discomfort. "I can handle it on my own."

"Or I can go with him," Nash said. "And you can hold the fort here."

"Not a chance." She shook her head. "I'm going with Drake. I don't fancy a one-on-one with the guards. Been there and done that. Besides, I know my way around inside."

"If you're sure," Drake said, his gaze holding hers.

"I am." She nodded. "And Hannah's right, the smell is almost gone."

Drake picked up his bag and switched on his flashlight, the beam cutting through the dark as he stepped inside the tunnel. Madeline followed behind him, her own light bouncing off the floor. The passage sloped down slightly, the walls covered with moss, the ceiling dripping with water, little pools forming in patches at their feet. The smell was better here, or maybe she'd just grown used to it.

The tunnel widened, then petered out, opening into the large, cavernous area beneath the prison that had once served as a cesspit. The floor was lined with brick, channels cut into the paving marking its previous use. There was no moss here, only sediment and stain from mineral deposits and something that looked a lot like crusted salt.

They moved quickly, sweeping their flashlights ahead of them as they looked for the ladder reaching up into the crawl space. It was hidden in a dark corner against the far wall, the rungs rusted with age, trails of red running down the wall where the water had leached away the iron.

"I'll go first," Drake said, already starting to climb.

Madeline fastened her flashlight to a ring on her belt and followed behind him, the chute narrowing as they moved higher up, her heart racing as the walls closed in. She'd never liked enclosed places. Too many memories. The closet under the stairs. Solitary. All of it more than she could bear. But the only way out was up, so she kept moving.

"I think I've reached the top," Drake said, disappearing into an alcove, his flashlight making an eerie canopy of light against the roof.

Madeline reached for the next rung, her mind on

Drake at the top, her fingers closing around the rusty iron as she began to pull upward. Suddenly, the rung broke free of the wall on one side and she careened out into the dark. Heart threatening to break through her chest, she grabbed the rung with both hands, holding on for dear life as she scrambled to find purchase with her feet.

"Hang on, sweetheart," Drake called from above, his voice laced with worry. "I'm coming."

Adrenaline surging, she swung her body back toward the ladder, her foot finding the edge of a rung as she pressed herself hard against the wall. "I'm okay," she said, securing her balance. "I'm okay." And she closed her eyes, willing herself to breathe in and out. In and out.

Finally, bracing herself against the wall, she stretched upward, fingers closing around a higher rung, and she pulled herself up and on to the top. Crawling into the alcove, she collapsed against the floor, her breath coming in short gasps.

Drake pulled her close, his heart beating almost as wildly as hers. "Are you sure you're all right?"

"I'm fine," she said, embarrassed by her clumsy display.

He studied her face as he ran his hands along her body, checking for injury. "Are you sure?"

"I banged up my knee and scraped my elbow, but I swear that's the worst of it. I'm just glad I made it to the top. Was Hannah right? Is there access to the service closet?"

Drake pointed the flashlight at a metal plate screwed to the floor in the corner. "I think that's it. I'd just started working on the screws when I heard you fall."

Shifting to her knees, she shone her flashlight on the plate as he worked. And in short order, he had removed it, leaning it against the wall, the dark cavity of the service closet revealed below them.

She looked down into the hole, her mind rebelling. She'd escaped from San Mateo once and she'd never thought she'd see the place again. Certainly not by choice—not like this. Her throat tightened, her stomach threatening mutiny. And then her eyes met Drake's, her heart remembering why they were here.

She'd come to help him find his brother. Nothing was more important—certainly not her fear.

And in that moment, she had a horrifying revelation. The God's honest truth was that she'd do anything for Drake. Follow him into hell, if that's what he asked of her. Because somewhere along the way, as they'd battled Ortiz and di Silva's henchmen, she'd made a fatal mistake— she'd allowed herself to fall in love.

CHAPTER 26

Drake dropped down to the floor of the service closet, thinking about Madeline. He'd seen the look on her face and known what it was costing her to come back here. She was such an odd mixture of strength and vulnerability, the combination marking a complexity that was at the same time both frustrating and fascinating. He'd never met anyone quite like her.

She'd been through so much and yet she'd managed to survive. Her father, San Mateo, her sister's death, and everything involving Ortiz and di Silva. Most people worked off ulterior motives. And when he'd first met her, he'd believed she had more than most. But then he'd gotten to know her. And his opinion had changed. And now she'd come back to the prison, risking everything to help him find his brother.

Still, he was under no illusions. He knew that she was doing all of this for Tucker. His brother had been there during a time when Madeline had needed a friend. And now she was returning the favor. Drake felt a swell of envy—jealousy raising its ugly head.

He shook his head, pushing aside his rioting emotions. There'd be time to examine his feelings later, after they were all safely out of Colombia.

Or maybe not.

Some things were best left unexamined. The important thing now was to concentrate on getting them in and out in one piece. For that much, at least, she was truly counting on him.

Turning on his flashlight, he reached up to help her down. Then, after lifting a finger to his lips, he cracked open the door and, leading with his gun, stuck his head out. The hallway was empty, the first gate visible to his right.

"Hannah, can you hear me?" he asked, after stepping back into the closet. "We're about to head out into the hallway. I'm not seeing any security cameras, but wanted to verify that there aren't any there."

"Perfect timing," Hannah said, her voice crackling in his ear. "I've just gotten access to the security system. You're good to go. But I still haven't been able to locate updated blueprints."

"Roger that," he said. "But we're still okay. Madeline should be able to fill in any blanks." He motioned Madeline to follow, and then swung back out into the hall, careful to keep his back to the wall.

The two of them worked their way to the left along the far wall, moving toward a corner leading to a second hallway. "So according to what you remember, the second electronic gate is still just around the corner, right?"

"Yes," she whispered. "The one that leads to the

western cell block. They moved the security station, though. It should be just on the left. And there's a second room on the right—used for clerical staff. There shouldn't be anyone in there this time of night."

Drake nodded and signaled for her to stay back, then inched forward until he reached the edge of the wall. After a silent count of three, he risked a quick look out into the corridor, gratified to find that it was also empty. The room on the left was open, light spilling across the hall, the one on the right, dark, the door closed.

"Looks like we're in the clear," he said, as they rounded the corner. Madeline opened her mouth to respond, but he shook his head, the sound of voices carrying from just beyond the far side of the electronically keyed gate.

Grabbing Madeline's hand, he yanked open the closed door and pulled the two of them inside, just as the locks clicked and the gate opened. Pressed flat against the wall, he waited as the guards drew closer.

"All I'm saying is that it's a sure thing," the first guard said in Spanish as they moved through the gate and into the hallway. "I mean it isn't like she can say no."

"But what if the warden finds out?" the second man protested.

"He won't. That's the beauty of working nights."

Beside him, Drake felt Madeline tense, and he fingered his gun, wanting nothing more than to wipe the smug tone from their voices. But nothing was ever gained by acting in anger, and their success depended on their remaining undetected.

"What the hell," the second guard was saying. "There's no reason why I shouldn't get a little enjoyment from my job."

"Just think of it as a perk," the first man agreed, their voices trailing off as they moved down the corridor.

Madeline started to move, but Drake held out a hand, shaking his head. She pressed back against the wall and they waited for the telltale clanking of the far gate as it opened and then shut again.

"Did that happen to you?" he asked, anger burning as he turned to face her. "Did the guards hurt you?"

"Not like that. No." She shook her head. "I was lucky. *Gringas* are considered less than desirable. But there were other women. Sometimes, I could hear them." She shuddered, remembering. And he marveled again at the fact that she'd managed to survive. She'd been through so damn much.

"I'm sorry." His voice was low, emotion rocking through him.

"It doesn't matter. It's over," she said, laying her hand on his arm. "None of it can hurt me anymore. So what do you say we get that gate open and go find your brother?"

He nodded, centering his mind on the task at hand. "Hannah?" he said, flipping his com link on again. "You still with us?"

"Yes. I'm here. Have you made it to the gate?"

"We have. But not without a little company. Two guards. I'm guessing they were doing rounds. Anyway, they've headed to the other side of the building now. And they definitely didn't see us."

"Good," she said.

"Have you figured out how to alter the security camera feed in the west cell block?" he asked, while Madeline kept watch at the door.

"I have," Hannah said, sounding pleased. "I've got a loop of an empty hallway ready to plug in as soon as you can locate the appropriate monitor. I want to be certain the transition goes smoothly, but once I set this thing up, you guys should be as good as invisible."

"Any word from Nash or Annie?" They'd opted to keep the channel between them closed unless it was an emergency, using Hannah as their link, reducing the chance of one of them tipping off the location of the others in case of discovery.

"Everything's quiet. Nash and I have been playing 'screw with the electric grid.' I'm guessing if they had any doubts about the problem, they're not questioning it now. So far I've kept it limited to the outbuildings, though. Don't want them on high alert while you're on the inside."

"Thanks for that," Drake said. "Madeline, you ready?"

"No time like the present," she said, her gun drawn as she waited for him to get into position on the other side of the door.

"Okay, Hannah, we're heading out now."

They moved into the hallway, stopping on the far side of the open doorway. Drake tightened his hold on his gun and then pivoted into the doorway, ready to fire.

"Clear," he said, lowering his weapon as he stepped into the empty room. "I hate to say it but maybe it's a good thing the guard had an itch to scratch." A series of monitors adorned the top of a desk, various angles of the prison's interior shown on each. Beneath the row of screens was a computer, wires extending haphazardly to various peripherals.

"Not exactly a state-of-the-art system," he said to

no one in particular, as Madeline followed him into the room. "Hannah, what do you want me to do next?"

"Find the monitor with a view of the west cell block," she instructed. "Got it?"

He scanned the labels underneath the screens, translating from Spanish to English, stopping when he found the one labeled *oeste*. "Yeah. Now what?"

"Just watch it, while I replace the feed with the loop. Then tell me if you notice anything when I switch it over."

The screen flickered for less than a second and then resumed, the picture seemingly unchanged. "Did you do something?" he asked.

"I did," Hannah replied. "The loop of empty corridor should run until someone discovers it. And if we're lucky that won't happen until we're all miles away from here."

"What about the rest of the cameras?" he asked.

"There aren't any on the exterior except at the front gate. So unless you're planning to tour the rest of the facility you should be good to go."

Madeline moved to stand behind him, her eyes on the monitor. "Looks like the two guards have abandoned their plans." She nodded at the screen, the two men disappearing into an office near the infirmary. "At least for the time being."

"Just as well," he said. "I'm not sure we could have handled two rescues in one night." She smiled at him, her eyes conveying just how much his words had meant. "You find the master key?" he asked.

She held up a key ring. "Right where Hannah said it would be."

"Okay, then, we're ready for the gate." He grinned. "Do we need an incantation or something?"

"You could try 'open sesame,'" Hannah said. "But I suggest using the thumb drive I gave you."

Drake pulled it out of the backpack. "Just put it into the PC?"

"Exactly. The screen should prompt you to execute my program. Just hit enter and the rest should go like clockwork."

Drake plugged the device into the USB port and waited as the computer hummed to life, assessing Hannah's program. A blue box popped onto the screen prompting him for a password, and he typed in the alphanumeric code Hannah had given him and waited while the program went to work.

"I think I heard the click," Madeline said behind him, her eyes on the monitor showing the gate. "Although it's different from before."

"That's because my program's overriding the manual systems. Basically, it's the same as if the door is turned off. Only the security system doesn't recognize the fact."

"Nifty little program," Drake said, removing the thumb disk and pocketing it. "Anything further on Tucker's cell?"

"No. Sorry. I'm having trouble with the administrative files. But I'm certain he's in there."

"We'll find him," Madeline said, tone confident. "We'll start with where I remember him being and work from there. But we'd better hurry. No telling when the guards will be back."

Moving quickly now, they walked through the gate, careful to close it behind them. The cell block was dark, the only light the moonlight streaming through a couple of barred windows in the eastern wall. Cells lined the west wall, their occupants sleeping, for the most part.

Halfway down the block, they started to look more carefully, peering into the shadows, trying to discern what the inmate looked like. It was slow going, and Drake's frustration was just starting to get the better of him when Hannah's triumphant voice crackled in his ear.

"I've got it. He's in cell ninety-two. That's three up from solitary."

"Come on," Madeline said, her hand closing on Drake's arm, her expression determined. "It's just down this way. We're almost there."

As she propelled him forward, his mind tumbled with a million thoughts. Was it really Tucker? Would he be all right? Would he be angry? After all, Tucker could still be working undercover. Although on second thought that idea made no sense at all. Madeline had mentioned how sick his brother had been. And how isolated all the prisoners were. If Tucker was here, it wasn't by choice.

Still, he hadn't used his card.

Which meant that there were a lot of unanswered questions, things that could all be answered from the free side of a cell.

"I think this is it," Madeline whispered, counting down three from the last two doors in the row. "Those are both solitary confinement."

Drake hated the idea that she knew which cells were meant for punishment, and he grimaced, chastising himself for dragging her here to relive it all.

"It looks like someone might be asleep on the bed. I can't really make much out in the shadows." She stepped back so that Drake could better see, but she was right, it was almost impossible to make anything out inside the cell.

She handed him the key, her fingers trembling. He inserted it in the lock and turned, the clicking of the release mechanism seeming unusually loud in the stillness of the cell block.

He looked to Madeline for reassurance, his heart going still. She nodded and gave him a little push. He pulled open the door, and still no one inside moved. It looked as if there was someone in the bed—he thought he could make out the shape under the covers. But it was too dark to be certain.

Summoning all his courage, his mind flooded with hope, he reached down to pull back the blanket, heart stopping as he stared down at the crumpled sheets and pillow on the empty bed. "There's no one here," he whispered, as Madeline came up behind him, her hand warm against his shoulder. "We're too late."

"We don't know that," she said, her tone soothing.

But he rounded on her anyway. "He's not here. You can see for yourself. Hell, maybe he never was. Maybe this was just a wild goose chase. A shot at something that was never really possible. Maybe Tucker *is* dead. Just like the government told me."

"Except that you know that was a lie. And you know he was here," she said, eyes flashing with anger. "Look, there are things here. Someone's possessions." She reached over to pick up a book.

"But not Tucker," he insisted, knowing that he was acting like an ass, but disappointment getting the better of him anyway.

"How do you know?" she asked, waving the book under his nose to emphasize her point.

He grabbed her hand, his emotions getting the better of him, then stopped as the title caught in the moonlight. *Kidnapped.* Robert Louis Stevenson. "Oh, my God," he whispered. "This was always Tucker's favorite. I bet he read it a thousand times. Usually under the covers after we were supposed to be asleep." He turned to face the empty cell, his heart sinking. "But I was right. We're too late. He's dead."

"Stop jumping to conclusions. I know this is difficult for you, but all we know for certain is that Tucker isn't here," she said, her voice gone dangerously quiet. "That much is definite. But the rest of what you just said is ridiculous. He's in this prison somewhere. We just have to find him."

"You're right." He shook his head, running a hand through his hair. "It's just that I want so much for him to be alive."

"So do I," she said, her hands reaching for his. "So let's just concentrate on finding him. All right?"

"Okay. So if he's not here at this time of night, where else could he be? The infirmary? You said he had a bad bout with malaria. I know it can recur. Sometimes for the worse."

"Yes." She nodded, the little crease between her eyes indicating her worry. "I'd say it's a definite possibility. But judging from what I know about this place, I'm thinking he might be much closer than that." Her gaze met his, and the answer suddenly presented itself.

"Solitary."

"It seems plausible. I certainly spent enough time there."

"So what are we waiting for?" he asked, his brain clicking into gear, taking control over his harried emotions.

They hurried out of the cell down the corridor to the last two cells at the end of the block. Unlike the others, there were no bars, just cinder-block walls and a heavily studded door with a small sliding slot so that guards could check on the prisoner.

"The key doesn't work," Madeline said, her frustration mirroring Drake's own. He took it from her and tried to jam it in, but it simply didn't fit. "Use the peephole," she said. "At least we can see if someone is in there."

He nodded, wrenching the little piece of metal aside. It was pitch-black inside, the only light a narrow shaft from the open peephole. "Is anyone in there?" he called, careful to keep his voice low enough to keep from alerting the guards. "Hello?" Silence stretched back.

"Is anyone there?" Madeline asked, leaning close beside him as he peered into the darkness.

"No one." He frowned. "At least I don't think so."

"Hello?" Madeline repeated. They both listened, and then something scraped against the wall.

"Did you hear that?" he asked, pressing his eye back to the open panel.

"Yes," she said, stepping back. The scraping sound came again. "But I don't think it's coming from this cell. It's coming from the next one over."

She rushed forward, but Drake was faster, pulling back the sliding panel. "Tucker? Are you in there?" The cell was quiet, the darkness swallowing any chance of seeing inside.

"I know I heard it," Madeline insisted. "There's got to be someone in there." She bit her bottom lip, the furrow between her brows growing deeper. And then she smiled, and, for all the seriousness of the moment, Drake felt as if the fucking sun had come out.

Edging him aside with her hip, she stood on tiptoe to reach the little opening. "Andrés? Can you hear me? It's Madeline. I've come to get you out of here."

CHAPTER 27

"Madeline?" Andrés's careful whisper came from the back corner of the cell. "Is it really you?"

"Yes," she replied, her heart beating faster. "I'm here."

"This isn't a trick?" Even though his voice sounded cautious, she could hear a note of hope.

"No. I swear. It's really me. I've come to get you out."

Andrés moved forward, the scant light highlighting his gauntness. He seemed to have aged ten years since she'd seen him last. His beard was even more matted than before, a streak of silver running through it. Beside her, she felt Drake's muscles tense, and without thinking she reached over to take his hand.

"I've brought help," she whispered as Andrés moved closer, his eyes the same clear blue as his brother's. "Drake is here."

"Drake?" he queried, his eyes narrowing as he frowned.

"Yes. He's really here," she said, careful to keep her voice gentle. She had personal experience with the disorienting effects of San Mateo's solitary. It wasn't easy to regain equilibrium, especially if they'd been holding him here a while. "See for yourself." She moved back, pulling Drake forward.

"Tucker?" he said, his voice laced with emotion. "Is it really you?"

There was a pause, and then Andrés—Tucker—raised his hand, his fingers pressed against Drake's face. "Holy shit," he breathed, his English suddenly flawless. "I never figured on seeing you again."

Tears pricked Madeline's eyes as she watched the two of them. So alike. So different.

"They told us you were dead," Drake said. "If it hadn't been for Madeline we'd never have known any different. Why didn't you use the card?"

"Complicated situation," Tucker said. "But I figured if Madeline used it, sooner or later someone would trace it back to me. Just never occurred to me it would be you."

"Well, turns out the acorn doesn't fall far from the tree. Looks like we're in the same business, more or less."

"So your coming here was sanctioned?" Tucker asked.

"Hardly," Madeline said, unable to keep the anger from her voice. "Your people are still in Washington sitting on their asses."

"My people are dead," Tucker said, a dark shadow passing over his face.

"Oh, God," she whispered, her heart twisting at her own insensitivity, "I'm sorry, I wasn't thinking...I..."

"It's okay," he assured her, the ghost of a smile crossing his face. "Good to see you're still a fighter."

"Look," Drake interrupted, his tone unusually abrupt, "we can continue old home week when we're safe. Right now we need to concentrate on getting you out of here."

"The key we have doesn't work," Madeline said, her worried gaze still fixed on her friend. "They must have changed it."

"They did." Tucker nodded. "It's electronic now. They're switching the whole prison over. And, of course, they started with solitary."

"Hannah," Drake whispered into his com. "Are you getting this?"

"Yeah," she replied. "I'm trying to find the file that triggers it now, but the computer's turned sluggish. Which could mean someone's on to us. Keep your eyes open."

Madeline nodded and Tucker tilted his head inquisitively. "Ear bud?"

"Yeah. We've got a computer expert on the other end. She's the one who got us in here."

"How many are there?" he asked.

"Five," Drake replied, "including Hannah. Plan is to get you out the way we came in. Only we've got to get this damn door open first."

"Got it," Hannah said, satisfaction coloring her voice. "Should be opening now."

As if on cue, there was a mechanical clink and the door unlocked.

Madeline yanked it open, throwing herself into Tucker's arms. "I was so afraid that something might have happened to you." She pulled back, looking into his eyes. "But you're all right. You're really all right."

"Couldn't let those bastards win, could I?"

He turned to his brother, the two of them standing for

a moment in silence, and then they embraced, Madeline's tears coming in earnest now. She'd imagined the moment many times over the last few days, but nothing she'd pictured could possibly have equaled the sheer joy she felt seeing the two of them together.

Drake was the first to pull away, his smile worth every single moment of doubt and worry. No matter what it cost her, she'd done the right thing.

"Guys," Hannah's voice broke into her thoughts, "I hate to break up the reunion, but there's a guard on the block."

"Hannah says someone's coming," Drake relayed to his brother.

"It's just rounds," Tucker said, sloughing off the ragged prisoner for the steely calm of a warrior. "Tell her to relock the door. The two of you get over there against the wall."

Drake relayed the message and grabbed Madeline's hand, pulling her with him to the right side of the door. Pressing their backs against the cinder blocks, they were swallowed by the shadows, as the peephole slid open, the sharp beam of a flashlight cutting through the shadows.

The light caught Tucker, who made a play of blinking sleepily as he held a hand up to shade his eyes.

Madeline's heart pounded as she pressed closer to the wall, the silence heavy as they waited. Then, after what seemed an eternity, metal scraped against masonry as the guard closed the opening, and the three of them dared to breathe again. The man's footsteps echoed as he made his way back down the corridor, the distant clanking of the gate verifying that he'd left the cell block.

"That was close," Drake said, releasing Madeline's

hand as he stepped back out into the room. "Hannah, I'm assuming you can still let us out of here?"

"I can," she said, static rippling across her voice, "but when I do, the guy in the guards' station may be able to see it."

"How long do you think he'll stay in there?" Drake asked, turning to his brother.

"Probably the rest of the night," Tucker said. "I'm surprised you didn't run into him when you got here."

"We did," Madeline said, shuddering at the memory. "Two of them. But they had other things on their minds."

"We're going to have to risk opening the door," Drake said. "But we need a plan of action first, in case Hannah's right and they figure out we're here."

"I'm thinking there's a pretty good chance they already have," Hannah interjected. "The security tape just switched back to real time, which means they found the loop."

"Damn." Drake moved to the doorway, gun drawn, listening for footsteps. Fortunately there were none.

"Look," Hannah said, a touch of agitation in her voice. "I'm opening the door now, while I still can. I don't want to risk your being trapped in there."

"Roger that." Drake nodded, his mind clearly already searching for alternatives. "Any way we can still make it back to the crawl space?"

"Not without sounding the alarm. At least for now you've got the advantage. They don't know where you are. Or even if you're still there."

"Is there any other way out of this section?" Drake asked, as the door clicked open. "Without accessing the gate, I mean?"

"The exercise yard," Tucker said, moving to stand on the other side of the door. "From there we can access the other cell block. But I'm not sure exactly what that buys us."

"Time," Drake said, reaching into his bag to pull out another gun. "Figured this might come in handy." He tossed the weapon to his brother and Tucker checked the magazine and then released the safety. "How far to the door?"

"It's at the end of the corridor," Madeline answered. "There's a little hallway to the right and then the door leading outside."

"It's about ten feet from here," Tucker added.

"They've got people on the move," Hannah broke in. "So far no alarms, but I'd say it's time for you to get the hell out of there."

"Copy that," Drake said, nodding at his brother, who despite his frail appearance was moving with the fluidity of an athlete. Tucker slipped through the door, leading with his gun, Drake following right behind. Madeline waited for Drake's signal and then joined them in the darkened corridor.

At the far end, they could hear the gate opening and suddenly the corridor was flooded with light.

"Go," Drake said, shoving Madeline forward.

Buoyed by adrenaline, she sprinted for the passage leading to the exercise yard, Drake and Tucker on her heels. Rounding the corner, she heard bullets fly, and then the deafening sound of the alarm. Drake stopped to return fire as she pulled open the door and stepped into the yard, only to retreat into the hallway as the guard in the tower peppered the ground with machine-gun fire.

"We're trapped," she said. "The guy in the tower has a machine gun."

Drake nodded to Tucker, who took his place at the corner as Drake stepped back into the shelter of the hall. "Hannah, can you hear me?"

Static filled Madeline's ear and her heart stuttered to a stop, then Hannah's voice broke through. "Yeah, for the time being. Someone's trying to jam me. But I managed to patch Nash and Annie through."

"Great time for the cavalry," Drake said. "They've got us pinned in. Guns in the corridor and the tower in the yard."

"I can take out the tower," Annie said. "But you're going to have to buy me a little time to get in place."

"Will do. But make it as fast as you can. We're going to run out of ammo. And they'll be bringing reinforcements."

"Roger that," she said. "I'm on my way."

"Nash? You there?" Drake asked.

"I'm here, but only with a little fortitude and a lot of luck," he said, his voice fading in and out. "I managed to get out of the cellar before they arrived, so they have no idea I'm out here. But I'm totally cut off from the gate, and there's no way I can access the van."

"Got it," Drake replied. "Just keep your head down and stay out of sight. We'll figure out our next move once Annie gets the guy in the tower."

"Plan B," Madeline said, her gaze moving to meet Drake's.

"Plan B," Nash echoed. "I'll see you on the flip side."

Drake moved back to the corner, joining Tucker to return fire and hold the guards back.

Madeline scrounged through her brain, trying to think of another way out. The yard was totally enclosed, the building on three sides, the wall on the fourth. She closed her eyes, forcing her mind to visualize the layout. She could see the cracked cement, the plaster peeling from the walls. The scent of mangoes mixed with the pervasive smell of unwashed bodies, the sound of birds filling the air as they flitted from their nests in the eaves over the fence to the trees beyond. She'd loved watching the birds.

She stopped, eyes widening as the memory clarified.

"I think I know how to get us out of here," she said. "Hannah, check the blueprint. On the west side of the yard. Northwest corner. I think there's access to the roof. A ladder built into the wall. I've seen birds roosting there."

"I've got it," Hannah said. "And you're right. It leads to the roof."

"And the building is higher than the wall, right?" Madeline queried, her mind still trotting out images.

"Yes, by like six feet."

"So, theoretically at least, we should be able to get over the wall. Assuming Annie manages to take out the tower," she added.

"It's done," Annie's voice interjected. "But they'll send reinforcements, so you'd better move now."

Madeline pushed the door open, stepping out into the yard, Drake and Tucker right behind her. This time the yard was quiet, but lights across the way in the east cell block meant that they didn't have a lot of time.

"It's over here," Madeline said, already heading to the west juncture between the prison and the wall. The ladder was just as she remembered. Built like a fire escape, it dangled above the ground a good eight feet and was separated from the yard by a chain-link fence.

During the day, between the armed guards and the tower, the ladder wasn't much of a temptation, but now, with the way cleared, it offered salvation. Or at least a Plan B.

"You two go first," Drake said. "I'll stay here and keep you covered."

Madeline shook her head, her mouth already opening to reject the idea, but Tucker grabbed her elbow, propelling her forward instead.

"He knows what he's doing," he said. "You've got to trust him."

"I do. It's just that if anything happens to him—" she broke off.

Tucker's eyes narrowed as her words sank home, and then surprisingly he smiled. "I see."

"You don't see anything," she snapped, shaking her head, angry at herself for revealing too much.

"He's going to be fine, *chica*. This is his kind of party. Besides, he's got something to fight for, no?" The hint of Spanish in his voice was meant to soothe. And she nodded, knowing that this wasn't the time to debate her feelings for Drake.

"Give me a boost," she said, turning her back to the yard.

He offered his cupped hands, and in seconds she was up and over the fence. He followed just as the doors on the east side of the yard burst open, staccato gunfire erupting from the steps.

Tucker spun around, firing over the fence, giving

Drake cover. "Get going, Madeline," he called over his shoulder. "We'll be right behind you."

Scrambling up on a garbage can for added height, she tensed her muscles, channeling her inner gymnast, and jumped for the bottom rung of the ladder, her hands closing on the painted metal, the ladder groaning as it slid downward. As soon as it was within range, she started to climb, risking a second halfway up to ascertain that Drake and Tucker were behind her.

Both men had made it over the fence, but only Tucker had reached the ladder. Drake was still at the fence, holding off the guards spilling into the yard. Scurrying upward again, she reached the top and swung herself over the ledge. Pushing to her feet, she moved to the yard side of the roof, dropping to her knees, pulling the gun from the small of her back, and firing down into the yard.

"Come on, Drake," she yelled into her mic. "Move it. *Now*. It's my turn to provide cover."

Still firing, she heard Tucker moving across the roof, his gunfire joining hers as Drake worked his way up the ladder.

"I'm here," he said. And with a last shot, she and Tucker retreated across the roof to the ladder and Drake. They moved to the far northwest corner, where the building was closest to the wall.

Beneath them, the barbed wire glistened lethally in the light from the tower. And below that Madeline could just make out the rocky drop off the edge of the mountain.

"Not exactly jumpable," Tucker observed, keeping his gun trained on the edge of the roof closest to the ladder. "What do you propose?"

"Wings would be nice," Drake observed dryly, "but since we're not birds, I'm thinking we need a rope."

"My sentiments exactly," Nash said, appearing from around the far side of a chimney stack. "Preferably one with a grappling hook." He held out said item, a knowing grin on his face. "Never leave home without it."

"Impeccable timing, as always," Drake said, turning to scope out the area beyond the fence. "How did you get up here?"

"Hannah found another ladder. I figured you might need some help."

"Anyone on your tail?"

"No. I'm in the clear."

"Well, then we'll concentrate on the yard," Drake said, taking the poly-coated rope and hook from Nash. "Any chance that magic bag of yours runs to grenades?"

"I might have a couple I can spare." He reached into his bag again, already moving in Tucker's direction. "Let's see if we can take these fuckers' minds off the ladder."

Madeline fought a wave of annoyance, thinking that the two of them were just like little boys playing a game of war. But then again maybe that's exactly what they were up to, and she could hardly fault their ability to keep cool in the face of what seemed like extraordinary odds. Straining into the dark, she searched for a suitable tree.

"How about over there?" she suggested finally, pointing to a large black oak just visible in the distance over the top of the wall.

"Perfect." Drake nodded, already swirling the rope above his head. The hook flew across the wall and unerringly twined itself around the tree, the rope pulling tight.

Then, using the chimney stack, he secured the rope from their side, the result a taut stretch of cord angling downward over the wall from the roof to the tree.

Beside them, below the roof, the exercise yard erupted with the sound of an explosion and flames shooting up into the sky.

"Hell of a grenade," Drake observed.

"Had a little help from a propane tank," Nash said, as he and Tucker returned to their side of the roof. "Should keep them busy for a while. You got our ride ready?"

"Taxi's waiting." Drake motioned to the rope. "Actually it's more of an improvised zip line."

"So where's the zip?" Tucker asked.

"That's where the improvisation comes in." Drake produced two large D-rings and a couple of short segments of rope. "We can use these to rig up a pulley of sorts. But I can only manage two. Which means we're going to have to travel in pairs."

"Always more fun with friends," Nash said, taking one of the rope segments and a D-ring from Drake. "I'll take Tucker. You can take Madeline."

Drake nodded as he worked to fashion the rope into a handle attached to the D-ring.

"You really think this is going to work?" Madeline asked, as he clipped the ring into place on the rope.

"It's our best chance," he said. "But we've got to go now. I can hear our friends on the ladder."

A shot rang out and there was a yelp of pain followed by something crashing into the garbage can at the bottom of the ladder.

"Annie." Nash nodded, peering over the edge at a fallen guard. "At least we've got cover. You ready, Tucker?"

"Yeah, just a minute," he said, stopping beside Madeline, his voice full of concern. "You going to be all right?"

"She's going to be fine," Drake answered for her, his eyes meeting hers as he held out the improvised harness, his lips turning up in a grin. "Compared to the waterfall, this'll be a piece of cake."

CHAPTER **28**

Drake was right. Except for the bullets, flying through the trees beat the hell out of jumping over the waterfall. They slowed as they neared the oak, and Drake used his feet against the trunk to stop their forward motion.

"I'm going to hand you my knife," he said. "I want you to cut the rope and then just let go," he said. "Nash will catch you."

"What about you?" she asked. "How will you get down?"

"I can jump. It's not that far. And we need to be certain the rope is severed so that no one can use it to follow us. You've got the better angle."

"Okay," she said, reaching up for the switchblade. "Nash, you ready?"

Below, Nash gave her a thumbs-up.

"You're sure you'll be okay?" she asked Drake, her gaze connecting with his.

"I'll be fine. I'm coming right after you."

She nodded and with a deep breath, cut through the rope. Talk about leaps of faith. She'd taken more in the last few days than she had in her entire life. And surprisingly, each one actually seemed a little easier.

In less than a second, she landed in Nash's arms, and then slid to her feet, stumbling a little as she struggled to regain her balance.

"Careful," Tucker said, sliding a hand under her elbow. "It's a little disorienting."

"It was amazing," she said, stepping away from the severed rope. "Although I'd like to try it again without people shooting at me. Are we safe now?"

"For the moment," Nash said. "But they won't have given up. Which means the sooner we get out of here the better."

Above them, Drake untied the remaining rope from the tree, then dropped to the ground. "Nash is right. We need to get a move on. Our little maneuver bought us some time, but the advantage won't last." He reached to his ear to activate his com link. "Hannah, can you hear me?"

"I'm here." Her voice crackled with static. "You guys okay?"

"Everyone's fine," Nash said. "We had quite a ride. But for the moment at least it's quiet here. I figure our best option is to make our way to Magdalena and try to secure transport there."

"Not a good idea," Hannah replied. "There are people from the prison all over town. Gotta figure they're searching for you."

"All right, then we're going to need a new rendezvous point," Drake said. "Preferably with alternative transportation."

"Already on it," Hannah interjected. "I've been in contact with Avery and he's arranged for a helicopter. I'm en route to pick it up now. There's a cleared field about half a mile due west from the prison. I've sent a map to your PDA. I'll meet you there."

"Roger that." Drake reached into his bag for his BlackBerry. "I'm assuming if we move fast, we won't run into too much resistance."

"I'll keep a good thought," Hannah said.

"What about Annie?" Nash asked. "She okay?"

"Last I heard she was outside the back prison wall, providing covering fire for you guys."

"Did a damn good job, too," Drake acknowledged. "We couldn't have made it without her. Does she know about the rendezvous?"

"Not yet. I haven't been able to raise her. Figure she's gone dark until she's farther away from the prison."

"Probably," Nash said with a frown. "Keep trying. And, in the meantime, I'll see if I can't double back and intercept her."

"Will do."

"Are our transmissions still secure?" Drake asked.

"Should be," Hannah said. "It was a secure channel to begin with and I scrambled it just to be safe, so they shouldn't be able to locate us by signal. But I'd still be careful. We should probably keep chatter to a minimum."

"Okay, then," Drake said, "we'll see you at the field."

"Good luck." Her voice faded as she signed off, and Madeline looked around the jungle, her exhilaration evaporating with the enormity of what they still faced.

"I'm off to find my wife," Nash said, with a quick salute. "We'll catch up with you guys at the field."

"You've got the coordinates?" Drake asked.

"Yes. On my phone. Hannah sent them. I checked."

"All right then. We'll see you when we see you."

Nash nodded and then he was gone, the undergrowth swallowing him before he'd managed more than a couple of steps.

"He'll be all right, won't he?" Madeline asked, still staring at the spot where he'd disappeared.

"Absolutely. We do this kind of thing all the time. Besides, we're better off moving in smaller groups."

She nodded, following Tucker and Drake as they worked their way through the jungle, using the satellite phone's GPS to keep them on track.

The canopy here was thinner than it had been coming down out of the ruins, but the trees were still thick and movement was difficult. Several times they had to make detours around outcroppings of rocks or rushing streams. Twice she thought she'd heard something in the brush, but both times it had turned out to be nothing more than an animal foraging. First a monkey and then a bird.

Finally, she convinced herself to stop worrying. Drake and Tucker were professionals. They knew what to listen for. She just needed to keep putting one foot in front of the other and sooner or later they'd make the clearing and then Hannah and the helicopter would take them away.

The hard part was over. They'd escaped from the prison. Everything else was a walk in the park—or the jungle, as the case might be. She smothered a laugh, realizing suddenly just how close she was to hysteria. She stopped, leaning over, hands on thighs, gulping in air as if it were ambrosia. Maybe there was a limit to her ability to cope after all.

If she got out of this in one piece, she was going to take a long vacation—as far away from the tropics as possible. Maybe the Alps. Or London or Paris. Urban was good.

Again she felt the bubble of laughter. Who was she kidding? She wasn't going anywhere. Except to D.C. And then, if she was lucky, the government would provide protection. Because Ortiz was never going to stop looking for her. Of that much she was certain.

So, in truth, she was walking from one nightmare into another.

Some things never changed.

She sucked in a last long breath, calming her rioting thoughts. Better to stay in the now, if for no other reason than to keep from falling apart. She straightened, focusing on the trail ahead, surprised to find that she was alone.

Fear blossomed full grown, and she forced herself to stay logical. They couldn't have gotten that far. And sooner or later they were bound to notice that she was gone. All she had to do was follow their trail of broken leaves and branches and she'd be fine.

She stopped again, searching the ground for some sign of Drake and Tucker passing this way. How the hell could she have been so stupid? And how in the world had they gotten so far ahead? She hadn't been distracted that long. At least she didn't think so.

Fighting against rising panic, she started forward again, confident when she saw a broken branch that she was heading the right way. What had Hannah said? West of the prison? She glanced up at the canopy, trying to gauge the right direction, but the trees had grown heavier and there was no sign of the sky.

Moss was supposed to grow on the north side of trees. But this was South America and so wouldn't that make it the south? Besides, there was moss everywhere, growing indiscriminately. She forged forward, still looking for signs that Drake and Tucker had passed the same way. And then suddenly she stopped, instinct screaming that something was wrong. The jungle had gone quiet, nothing moving. Not a tree, not a bird, nothing.

She waited, holding her breath, grabbing the gun, trying to tell herself that it was just her imagination. Then the undergrowth in front of her shimmied as something moved closer, a tree gyrating as the brush parted and Drake stepped out of the jungle.

"Thank God," she whispered, her gun falling from suddenly lifeless fingers. And then she saw the regret on his face—and the second man.

"Hello, *querida*," Ortiz said, his handsome face breaking into an ugly smile, the gun to Drake's head explaining everything.

"I'm so glad you decided to join our little party," Ortiz said. "Considering you're the reason we're all here." He nodded over to Drake, who was sitting at the base of a tree, just out of earshot, his hands tied behind his back. There was no sign of Tucker, and Madeline prayed that he wasn't dead.

Three of di Silva's men stood watch. A half dozen more lounged by the creek, their idle chatter carrying across the stillness, their guns relaxed but still at the ready.

Two more men flanked Ortiz as he sat on a rock in the

clearing. "Do you have any idea how many of my men are dead because of you?" he asked, peeling an orange as he watched her.

"Not enough," she said. "But if you'd just let me go, most of them would still be alive."

"They can be replaced," he said, waving a hand. "You, on the other hand, are one of a kind." Something in the way he said it made her blood run cold. There was no question that he'd make sure she paid for her betrayal. "I couldn't possibly let you slip away. You know too much."

"So why didn't you kill me when you had the chance?" she asked, indignation supplanting fear.

"Because I foolishly believed I could keep you under control," he said, running his thumb over the sharp edge of the knife. "Clearly I should have known better."

"So what are you going to do now?" she asked, shooting a glance in Drake's direction, her heart twisting. Ortiz had kept them separated on the journey back to the clearing, so there hadn't been a chance to talk. But she knew that given the opportunity, Drake would make a break for it. She just had to figure out if there was a way she could facilitate his move.

"With Flynn? I haven't decided. I've got friends who might find his particular knowledge quite useful. For the right price."

"And if your friends don't want to deal?"

"Then I shall take great pleasure in watching your lover die." He bit into the orange, the juice running down his chin before he wiped it away.

"He's not—"

"Save it. I've got sources. And they're very accurate. How do you think I found you?"

"Señor Ortiz," a guard called as he broke through the underbrush outside the line of trees, "I've found the other one." Using his rifle, the man shoved Tucker into the clearing. Drake tried to rise, but one of the guards hit him hard, and he slumped back against the tree, eyes blazing.

Ortiz rose, his gaze locked on the other man, and Madeline could hear Tucker's exhalation from where she sat.

"Son of a bitch," Tucker said, eyes narrowed as he watched Ortiz.

"You know him?" Madeline asked, surprise lifting her voice.

"Yeah." Tucker nodded, anger flaring. "Hector was part of D-5. Our munitions expert. And, until now, the man I believed was my friend." A shadow passed across his face as he turned his attention back to Ortiz. "I thought you were dead."

"Thought the same about you," Ortiz said, his Spanish dropping away to reveal a decidedly American accent. "Until I saw that Madeline had your card."

"You knew?" she asked, still confused by the latest turn of events.

"Not in the beginning." He shrugged, his gaze still on Tucker. "If I had, all of this would have been much easier. But after your trip to the Embassy, I needed to be certain that killing Richardson was the end of it."

"You're the reason we were found out," Tucker said, revulsion washing across his face. "You betrayed your own unit. You betrayed D-5."

"Yes," Ortiz said, still fingering the knife. "I did. And I thought I fixed it so that everyone was dead."

"Yeah, well you fucked up. Because it wasn't just me who made it out alive."

"If you're talking about Lena, then you should be speaking in past tense. It took me five months to run her to ground," Ortiz said, dropping back down on the rock, his gaze never leaving Tucker. "She was good at evasion. But I've always been a hell of a hunter."

"You killed her." Tucker's hand clenched, his jaw tightening, his eyes filled with grief, and Madeline knew suddenly that this woman was the reason that Tucker hadn't used his card. *"Why?"*

"Same reason I betrayed the rest of you. You were all getting too close to the truth."

"That you'd been playing both sides of the equation," Tucker said.

"I only ever played one side, actually. Mine. And it was becoming increasingly clear that certain members of D-5 were going to uncover that fact."

"So you tipped off the Colombian military. Told them who we were."

"Actually it went higher than that. I told a new acquaintance of mine. A very powerful man who wasn't at all pleased to find the CIA working within FARC."

"Our mission was much bigger than that."

"Bullshit. It wasn't anything more than two nations posturing, sacrificing people like us to make their respective points. The world isn't about making things right, Tucker. It's about getting ahead. And I grabbed the chance while I had it."

"Never mind the consequences," Tucker spat out. "So what happens now?" He shot a look over at his brother, who was still struggling against his bonds.

"I was just telling Madeline. I'm thinking of selling your brother. But it might be more fun to just hand the two of you over to one of your enemies. I know a couple of junta leaders that would love to get their hands on the CIA. Of course, I might just kill you both myself."

"And what about Madeline?" Behind Tucker, Drake stilled, his gaze turning murderous.

"She's a different story altogether." Ortiz shrugged. "She owes me. And before she dies, I intend to collect. But enough talking." He signaled the guards flanking Tucker and they dragged him over near Drake, tying his hands.

Drake half rose, trying to protect his brother, but one of the guards jammed the butt of his rifle into his ribs, knocking him back to the ground.

"Stop it," Madeline screamed. "Leave him alone. Leave them both alone."

"Two lovers?" Ortiz smiled. "I wouldn't have thought you had it in you. Brothers, no less."

Rage swelled, and she swung at him, but he caught her hand and pulled her hard against his chest, the knife against her throat. "Poor Madeline. You're always such an easy target."

"Let me go." She stared up at him defiantly. If he was taking her down, she was damn well going to go fighting.

"Fine." He released her so suddenly, she stumbled. "But don't think I'm going to let you off that easily. There's still a reckoning to be paid. None of this would have happened if you'd simply kept your mouth shut."

"You murdered my sister. What the hell did you expect me to do?"

"I told you I didn't kill her," he said, wiping the knife blade against his chinos. "If anyone was responsible, it was you. Always trying to make her believe she could be something better. We are what we are, Madeline. No one gets a second chance. Haven't you learned that yet?"

"You're wrong," she whispered, her gaze locking on Drake and Tucker. Drake was her second chance. And she was going to fight for it with everything she had.

"Believe what you want. The truth is still the truth," Ortiz said, dismissing her as he pushed up off the rock, motioning to his men. "Let's go. We've got ground to cover, and I don't want to be late."

"Where are you taking us?" she asked.

"To a plane. And from there...well, it'll just be my little surprise." He turned away from her then, one of his men forcing her to her feet with the barrel of his gun.

"Move." Ortiz's man shoved her forward, his fingers digging into her arm so tightly she cried out.

Drake, who was standing now, just off to her left, lunged toward the guard, his eyes still glittering with anger, but the man knocked him back, slamming Drake with his fist. Tears welled as she met Drake's eyes, remorse making her knees weak, but he shook his head, his lips tipping in a tiny smile. *"Plan B,"* he mouthed.

And despite the gravity of the situation, she smiled back. Even if there wasn't a plan, she loved him for trying to give her hope. And that was it really. The good and the bad of it. She loved him. Completely and absolutely. And she'd be damned if she'd let Ortiz hurt him or Tucker.

All that remained was figuring out what to do.

They moved forward in silence, the clearing narrowing as they headed back into the jungle, forcing them to

move in single file, Drake and Tucker toward the front,
she and her guard bringing up the rear. The sun, just cresting the horizon, had turned the sky a rosy shade of pink.
Insects buzzed around her head, and she wondered idly if
gnats could carry malaria.

Then suddenly the reverberation of a gunshot rang
through the clearing, the man at her side grabbing his
chest as he fell forward. Another shot sounded as guards
from the prison swarmed into the clearing.

Madeline rolled to the ground as bullets hailed from
everywhere. Ortiz's men returned fire, using boulders and
trees to give them cover. Her only thought was to get to
Drake. He and Tucker were sitting ducks with their hands
bound behind their backs.

Grabbing the dead man's gun, she ran forward,
crouching as low as possible, trying to avoid the worst
of the melee. Everywhere there were people fighting, at
least two dozen or more. It was impossible to distinguish
Ortiz's men from the guards. Not that it mattered, since
neither side offered salvation.

Ahead of her she could see Drake. He'd managed
to free his hands somehow, but he still didn't have a
weapon. He was trying to free Tucker, who'd been pinned
underneath a body.

Shots whizzed past them, and Madeline broke into a
full-out run, desperate now to reach them. Ahead she saw
Ortiz rise from behind a tree, his eyes moving to Drake
as he struggled with Tucker. She saw Ortiz sneer and
swivel, pointing his gun at Drake, his finger moving on
the trigger.

She screamed Drake's name, anger and adrenaline
coming together, and she fired the gun. For a moment

everything seemed to move in slow motion: Drake finally pulling his brother free. The two of them coming to their feet. The sound of her voice making him turn. The surprise on Ortiz's face as her bullet ripped through his chest.

Then suddenly everything sped up again and she was moving, running past Ortiz's body, Drake cutting the distance between them. She threw herself into his arms, mindless of the fight still going on around them.

"You're okay. You're okay," she repeated, one hand cupping his face, the other still gripping the gun.

"I'm good," he said. "Tucker, too. Thanks to you. But we've got to get out of here." He took the gun and grabbed her hand, the three of them running for the safety of the trees just as the air above them exploded, the thrum of helicopter blades filling the clearing.

Reversing direction, Drake yelled to Tucker and they headed for the chopper, Madeline struggling to keep up with Drake's long strides. Then suddenly fire seared through her leg, blood spouting like a crimson chrysanthemum on her jeans. She fell to her knees, the fire intensifying.

One of the prison guards rounded on her, leveling his gun, but Drake was faster, his shot hitting the man right between the eyes. And then he was there, scooping her up into his arms, while the ground around them exploded with bullets.

"You're going to be all right," he said, his words almost an order.

She felt his muscles tense as he launched forward, holding her close as he ran for the chopper. The wind sang against her skin, and she could hear the syncopated

beat of the helicopter blades forming a counterrhythm to
the sound of gunfire, a gray haze forming at the edges of
her vision, the jarring pain in her leg coming in blinding
waves.

She could see the chopper but it seemed so far away.
And then it was lifting off, the gunfire coming too close,
the threat of crashing more than they could risk. She
could see Tucker, too. Leaning out of the back of the
helicopter, throwing something to the ground.

"Hold on tight," Drake said, one hand underneath her
as her arms tightened around his neck, the other reaching
for whatever it was that Tucker had thrown.

And then she felt a jerk and the world seemed to wob-
ble, the two of them rising straight up into the sky. Her
pain-racked brain tried to make sense of the sensation, the
air rushing fast now, whipping against her cheeks.

She squeezed her eyes shut, holding on for dear life as
her brain finally crawled through the pain to present the
answer. They were on a ladder, hanging from the helicopter, and people were still shooting at them.

Above her the helicopter screeched in protest. She
thought they were falling, but then she felt the ladder
moving upward, the open hatch coming closer, Nash and
Tucker's worried faces coming into focus as they reached
out to pull first her and then Drake into the helicopter.

Inside, the world was wonderfully quiet and warm.
Annie tied a tourniquet around Madeline's leg and covered her with a blanket, and she tried to stay awake,
the gray moving to black as her body fought for rest.
"Drake," she called, the words hardly more than a whisper. "I need Drake."

"I'm here, love," he said, his big hand closing over

hers. "I'm right here. You're going to be all right." He leaned down, his bright blue eyes staring into hers, willing her to hold on. "The helicopter's going to get us to a hospital. Just hang on."

She nodded, her vision growing even more fuzzy as she reached up to pull him close. "It's a...good... thing...that I...love you," she whispered, the words coming out thick like molasses. "Because...that was definitely...worse...than the waterfall."

EPILOGUE

U.S. Military Hospital, Eloy Afaro Air Base, Marto, Ecuador

Madeline fought against the urge to wake. She'd been having a wonderful dream, although for the life of her she couldn't remember what it was. Still, she sighed, sorry for it to go, certain that it had been lovely.

Her eyes flickered open and she stared at the acoustic tiles above her head, trying to remember where she was. Her last memory was sort of vague, the wind, a ladder, a helicopter.

Drake.

"Hey, there, sweetheart." His voice filled her ears and she turned her head, his face swimming into focus. "I was wondering when you were going to come back to me." He was sitting beside her hospital bed, holding her hand, his eyes narrowed with concern.

"Where am I?" she asked, her voice cracking, her throat dry.

"In Ecuador. In the hospital. You lost a lot of blood. But the doctors say you're going to be just fine."

"Ortiz?" she asked, the name hanging in the air between them.

"He can't hurt you anymore. He's dead." He squeezed her hand, his fingers warm against her skin.

"I killed him," she sighed, the memory returning.

"And you saved me," he said, his eyes full of tenderness. "And Tucker."

"Where is he?" she frowned. "Is he all right?"

"He's fine. Doctors said with a couple weeks' rest and some sound nutrition he'll be good as new. Me, I figure some beer, hot dogs, and baseball ought to fix him right up."

"Not to mention give him some serious indigestion. But really," she said, her mind still a little groggy, "he's okay?"

"Yeah. He'd be in here himself if the doctors would let him, but they're still running tests."

"What about the rest of the team?" she asked. "Did everyone get out okay? Nash and Annie?" She had a vague memory of Annie helping her in the helicopter, but it could have just been part of her dream.

"Everyone's great. Hannah's helicopter saved the day. So there'll be no living with her for a good long while. And Nash and Annie made it to the original rendezvous without any trouble. So everything turned out fine."

"What about me? Does Langley still want me in protective custody?" She shook her head, wincing as she shifted her leg.

"No. Avery had some serious one-on-one time with the people behind the original D-5 operation. Considering the fact that they left people on the ground, and then tried to cover it up, they're more interested in saving their asses than frying yours. They'll still want the information you collected about di Silva's operations, and of course about Ortiz. But Tucker's really the expert when it comes to Ortiz and what happened to D-5."

"Well, I'll be glad to help any way that I can," she said, surprised to find that she really meant it. "But what about the Colombians? Ortiz told me that they believed I was still incarcerated in San Mateo. Now that they know I'm not, they're sure to want me back there. Because of the man I shot. Not to mention my part in the prison break."

"Actually, that's where the CIA coverup works to our advantage. They're obviously not interested in the Colombian government finding out who Tucker really was. So they're arranging for the whole thing to be laid at di Silva's feet. And as part of that package, they've produced evidence that clears you of the shooting as well."

"But there were witnesses," she protested, overwhelmed by how quickly things had turned around.

"Who saw the man attacking your sister. Believe me, no one wants to pursue the issue. You're safe now. It's over. All of it. I swear."

"Another debt I owe Avery," she said. "But what about the leak? Ortiz said he had a source."

"We're still working on that one. The men behind D-5, the ones Avery talked to, are claiming innocence, but there's no guarantee that they're not lying. Which means it'll take time to dig out the truth. But don't worry, we'll figure it out."

"Even if it's one of the team?"

"As much as I hate the idea," he said, a shadow passing

across his face, "if someone from inside A-Tac is behind any of this, he or she has got to be stopped. But not today. Today, I just want to concentrate on you."

"And Tucker." She nodded. "How's he taking all of this? I can't imagine any of it's sitting very well with him. I got the feeling that this Lena woman was someone important to him. Ortiz killed her. Not to mention betraying the rest of their unit. If Tucker feels anything like you do about his colleagues, he's going to have a difficult road ahead of him."

"Yeah," he said, his voice grim. "But we'll be there to help him."

"It's all so sad," she whispered, "but at least he's out of San Mateo."

"Thanks to you." Drake reached over to smooth back her hair. "You saved my brother."

"You did most of the heavy lifting." She smiled. "So when do I get out of here?"

"Another day or so. The doctors want to keep an eye on you. But your leg will be fine."

"And you?" she asked, a little tremor of fear washing through her. "When do you have to be back at Sunderland?"

"I don't," he said. "Avery gave me a leave of absence. I'm going to California. We still own the house where we grew up. I figured it'd be a good place for Tucker and me to reconnect. You know?"

She nodded, her eyes welling with unwanted tears. "That'll be great," she said, her voice taking on the perky falsetto of a college cheerleader. "I'm glad you're going to be together."

"Well, we could kind of use the feminine touch," he

said, his eyes crinkling as he smiled. "Someone to keep us away from the bratwurst and beer."

"Someone to take care of you?" she asked, hardly daring to hope.

"Someone to love us," he said, framing her face with his hands. "Did you mean what you said up there?"

She struggled to remember, her mind still full of drug-induced cotton wool. And then she smiled. "Well, it *was* worse than the waterfall."

"Not that part, Madeline," he said, his icy gaze going meltingly warm. "The part about you loving me. Did you mean it?"

"Yes," she whispered, her chest tightening. "I did—*I do*. Although I'm not sure that's any great thing. I mean, I'm not exactly the girl next door. I—"

He covered her lips with a finger. "I've never been much on sweet and simple. I prefer a woman who isn't afraid to get her hands dirty."

She nodded, waiting, afraid that he wouldn't say the words, that somehow she was reading the moment all wrong.

"What I'm trying to say," he continued, "is that you mean more than anything to me. I almost lost you out there. And I realized that if I had, my world would have ended."

"But you didn't lose me," she said, tears springing to her eyes. "I'm right here."

"And if I have my way, you're going to stay here—with me. Forever." Her heart stuttered as he caught and held her gaze. "I want to spend the rest of my life showing you just how much I love you."

"I think that can be arranged," she said, smiling up at

him though her tears. "What do you say we get a jump on that? No time like the present, right?"

"Your wish is my command," he murmured with a slow, sexy grin. And then he closed the distance between them, his mouth taking possession of hers, his kiss a covenant. She twined her hands in the soft silk of his hair, her heart beating in tandem with his, and sighed, realizing that after a lifetime of searching, she'd finally found her way home.

Tyler Hanson lives by the motto "duty first" and doesn't have time for personal attachments—until she meets British agent Owen Wakefield...

Please turn this page
for a preview of

DESPERATE DEEDS

Available now.

Ambassador Hotel, Colorado Springs

'm okay, Avery. I've got bruises on my bruises but nothing seriously wrong. I swear." Tyler sank down on the bed in her hotel room, cradling her cell phone while she tried to make herself more comfortable. Avery Solomon was A-Tac's commander and one of Tyler's oldest friends. The two had met when she was in the army. It was Avery who'd recruited her to the CIA.

"I'm sorry I couldn't be there." Even with the distance she could hear Avery's regret. "You shouldn't have had to go through that alone."

"It's part of the job." She shrugged, the gesture hurting more than she was willing to admit. "Missions go bad."

"I'm not buying any of this, Tyler. I saw you, remember?" Avery had insisted on being present for her debriefing, and since there was no way for him to be there physically, he'd settled for videoconferencing. "I know how much this cost you."

"I shouldn't have lost them. I should have seen the signs and gotten us the hell out of there."

"But you didn't," Avery said, his tone probing. "Which tells me that something else happened. Something you omitted from the debrief."

Tyler sighed. Avery knew her too damn well. "There *was* something. But I don't want to talk about it over the phone. Not even a secure one."

"That sounds ominous."

"Maybe. I don't know. Maybe I'm overreacting. But it seemed like someone was playing us—or more specifically, playing *me*. Anyway, I'll tell you everything when I get there. Thanks for clearing me to come home."

"There wasn't anything more you could tell them. I can understand Fisher's need to probe. I'd feel the same if it was my people that had been lost. But he was pushing too hard. Barking up the wrong damn tree."

Tyler smiled. "Thanks for that. It's nice to know someone has my back. Have you got any leads on who might have stolen the detonators?"

"Nothing concrete. It's too early. Hannah is working on it as we speak." Hannah Marshall handled intel for A-Tac. If there was anything to provide insight into who'd stolen the detonators, she'd find it.

"So does everyone know what happened?" It's not like she wanted to keep it a secret, but there was part of her that hated having her failure paraded about, even among her friends.

"As you know, word travels fast in our circles," Avery said. "So the whole team knows that the detonators were stolen and that you almost died in the process. But beyond that I figured it was best to keep the details need-to-know.

So Hannah's up to speed. And Nash, of course. He threatened to fly to Colorado if I didn't tell him everything." Nash Brennon was the unit's second in command.

"And if he knows, then Annie knows," Tyler said. Annie was Nash's wife, and there were no secrets between them.

Avery laughed. "Sometimes I wonder how they made it all those years apart. It's like they're two halves of a whole. Anyway, I knew you wouldn't mind if I filled them in."

"Of course not." Nash and Tyler were close. And she and Annie had hit it off almost from the beginning— except for the part where Tyler had thought Annie was a traitor. But that was water long under the bridge.

"So you're sure you don't want one of us to fly up there?" Avery asked.

"No. Honestly. I've got a flight out first thing in the morning. So I'll be home for dinner. And we'll talk then. Right now I just want a stiff drink." She sighed, realizing that it was going to take more than one.

"It wasn't your fault, Tyler."

"Intellectually, I know you're right"—she closed her eyes, seeing Gerardi's body on the roadside—"but emotionally I just keep replaying it, trying to figure out what I could have done differently."

"Hindsight and all that," Avery said, his pragmatism calming her in a way nothing else could have. "And you can rest assured that we're going to hunt down the bastards that did this."

"I'm counting on it. And when we find them, I want first crack. But right now, I just need to decompress. You know?"

"I do. So I'll let you go. But I'll be here if you need me. Nash and Annie, too. In fact, I'm sure they'll be calling."

"Thanks. But I'll be fine." She sucked in a calming breath, ignoring the resulting pain that laced through her chest. "I'll call you when I get to New York." She terminated the call and then turned off the phone. Avery was right. Nash would call. And tomorrow she'd be glad to hear his voice. But for now, she was tired of talking. She needed quiet. And she needed that drink.

Pushing off the bed, she walked over to the minibar and pulled open the little refrigerator door. Inside, lined up as neatly as soldiers, were a platoon of tiny liquor bottles.

She pulled out two bottles of Wild Turkey and poured them into a glass. When she'd turned eighteen her father had taken her to her first grown-up dinner party. The host, a longtime family friend, had asked her what she wanted to drink. She hadn't actually had much experience with cocktails, so she'd asked for a strawberry daiquiri, and she'd thought herself very sophisticated drinking the icy pink beverage.

It was only after she got home that she learned that the host had actually left the party to go to a nearby market to get the supplies needed to make the drink. Her father had been furious, and he'd informed her that she was never to ask for something so complicated again.

He'd taken a bottle of scotch and a bottle of bourbon from his liquor cabinet and poured a stiff tot of each. And then he'd told her to pick one. Scotch or bourbon. The scotch had tasted bitter, with a hell of a bite, and the bourbon, by contrast, had been smooth, almost sweet.

She'd drunk bourbon ever since.

She downed the glass in a single swallow, closing her eyes as the heat slid down her throat, expanding through her chest. She could almost feel the tension coiled inside her loosen as the warmth filtered through her body.

But it wasn't nearly enough.

She opened the refrigerator door again, sorting through the little bottles, but to her dismay, there was no more Wild Turkey. And somehow, in light of the events of the last twelve hours, she didn't think that a thimbleful of Bailey's Irish Cream was going to suffice.

She turned to the telephone, searching for the room service number, and then abruptly replaced the receiver, deciding instead to head downstairs for the bar off the lobby. She'd find a dark corner and nurse a couple of really good drinks. Better to be in a crowd. Less likely that she'd let her emotions take over. And besides, misery was supposed to love company.

She grabbed her keycard and headed downstairs via the elevator. The bar was small. Like a thousand other hotel bars. Nondescript in a high-concept, designer kind of way. Huge vases of flowers had been placed strategically throughout, dividing the space into even smaller alcoves. The perfect place to unwind, or to hide.

Ignoring curious stares from a couple of businessmen sitting at the bar, she made her way to the far corner and a table with two large wing chairs. An electric fire flickered behind a glass screen, the lack of warmth and sound only adding to the sterile feeling of the place. After ordering a Maker's Mark, she settled into the chair facing the room. It would be more peaceful to stare into the pretend fire, but old habits died hard. Better to keep watch.

She had a feeling the theft of the detonators was a first move. And though there was every possibility her part in this affair was over, there was also a chance that she was still very much in the game. Which meant that it wouldn't pay to turn her back.

One of the men at the bar smiled and lifted his glass. Tyler shifted the chair so that she could more easily avoid his gaze. The waitress brought the bourbon and retreated, leaving Tyler to her thoughts as soft music swelled in the background. Just what she needed—a soundtrack.

Gerardi and Mather weren't the first people she'd lost during a mission, but that didn't change the depth of her regret. And even though Avery was right, and it wasn't her fault, she still felt as if she should have done something differently. Something that would have kept both men alive.

She blew out a breath and took a sip of bourbon. Usually, when an operation went south she had backup. People to decompress with. This was the first time in years she'd handled an op on her own. But like she'd told Gerardi and Mather, she was the expert in munitions. So the assignment had fallen to her. Deemed a routine operation, there'd been no need to involve more personnel.

But the mission had turned out to be anything but routine, and now, because of her mistakes, two good men were dead.

She tipped the glass and finished the contents.

"Way I've always heard it, Maker's Mark is a sipping bourbon."

"Didn't know you Brits ran toward bourbon at all," Tyler said, looking up into the dark blue eyes of her MI-5 agent, although for the life of her, she couldn't think why she'd think of him as "hers."

"We do get shipments from across the pond." He shrugged, signaling the waitress for more drinks as he slid into the chair next to hers. "I didn't get the chance to introduce myself before. Owen Wakefield."

He held out his hand, and Tyler sucked in a breath, not certain that she wanted to touch him. Another irrational thought. Maybe he was right and she should have been sipping. With a tight smile she reached across to take his hand in hers. "Tyler Hanson. But considering the circumstances, I suspect you already know that. You're MI-5, right?"

His hand tightened for a moment, his grip strong, his fingers engulfing hers. Then he sat back with a crooked smile. "How did you know?"

"The medic at the scene. He told me. And if he hadn't, the accent would have given you away. I guess I was supposed to be bringing the detonators to you."

"Well, I was just a courier. Same as you. But, yes, I was at the base when we heard about the ambush."

"Yeah, well, sorry I couldn't have done more about that." She sat back, waiting as the waitress brought their drinks. "If it matters at all, I was just sitting here replaying the whole thing."

"Haven't you already done enough of that? Looked to me like you were getting a pretty thorough debrief."

"You were there?" she asked with a frown.

"Yes." He nodded. "At least in spirit. I was listening in via computer. At the base. Reciprocal courtesy and all that. After all, technically, the stolen detonators belonged to us. My government put a lot of money into their development. They're not going to be happy about losing them."

She tilted her head, studying him. He was just this

side of devastating, his dark eyes framed by lashes that would have made Revlon cry. His hair was perfectly cut, and she'd wager a month's salary that his suit was hand-tailored. He carried himself with the assurance of an aristocrat and the stealth of an operative. James fucking Bond with a five o'clock shadow.

"I suppose that's understandable," she said, nodding, feeling somehow violated just the same. "How did you know I'd be here?"

"I didn't. We just happen to be staying at the same hotel."

"Government rates." She lifted her glass in a mock salute. "So I guess I've made a real mess of things for you. I'm sorry."

"Why?" He frowned. "It's not as if you knew what was going to happen."

"Yes, but it was my job to see the signs. Recognize the threat. And instead, I fell for their ruse lock, stock, and barrel."

"Which only means that they were good."

"Or I was bad." She took a long sip, letting the burning liquid soothe her jangled nerves and guilty conscience. "Bottom line, your detonators, and those men, were my responsibility. Which means that everything that happened is, at least in part, on my head."

"You're letting Fisher get to you."

"No. I'm not. I'm just calling it the way it is. I realize that I had no way of anticipating what would happen. But the signs were there, and instead of seeing them for what they were, I let my judgment get clouded." By memories of her mother, but she wasn't ready to share that part of the story. "And because of that two men are dead."

"And the detonators are missing."

"Tell me something I don't know." She frowned at him over the rim of her glass. "Like who the hell you think might have walked away with them."

"I've got nothing," he said, spreading his hands wide. "It's still too early. No one is taking credit, if that's what you're asking. And any number of parties would be interested in the detonators for any number of reasons. They're state-of-the-art. So if nothing else they'll fetch top dollar on the black market."

"That's exactly what worries me. If those detonators fall into the wrong hands..." she trailed off.

"It could go very badly," he finished for her.

"Exactly. And it's not just that they're state-of-the-art. It's that they're designed for nuclear weaponry. We have treaties that guarantee our countries are not engaged in increasing our nuclear stockpiles, particularly new technology. If word gets out that we've been secretly pursuing advances—well, I don't have to tell you what the political ramifications will be. Not to mention the possibility of someone actually using the devices."

"Spoken like someone who knows their way around ordnance," he said, his eyes probing.

"What can I say?" She shrugged. "I've always liked things that go 'boom.' I studied engineering in college and then joined the army, where I spent five years defusing everything our enemies deployed. And another ten working for the Company."

"Still dismantling?" The question was casual, but his stillness signaled his interest in her answer.

"Let's just say I can handle both sides of the equation. Whatever's called for. My unit isn't the kind they trot out when they want to look PC. What about you? Ordnance turn you on?" She hadn't meant to use those exact words, but the bourbon was doing its job.

"Not bloody likely."

The retort was unexpectedly sharp, and she frowned. "I'm sorry, did I say something wrong?"

"It's me that should apologize." He shook his head. "It's just that I've seen too damn many people hurt by little boys playing war. Anyway, once upon a time, the answer would have been 'yes.' I studied nuclear physics at university. Graduate work at Oxford. And then Number Ten Downing came calling. Patriotic duty and all that. I worked counterterrorism for longer than I should have."

"And now?" she asked, instinct telling her there was more to the story.

"Like I said, I'm a courier."

"Well, I suspect you're more than that. But since we've only just met, and since my follies are bound to have caused you one hell of a political headache, I won't probe. And besides, I came down here to try to forget about it all for a little while."

"Except that there really is no way out, is there?"

She stared over at him for a moment, trying to judge his tone. But there was no condemnation. Just a world-weariness that she was more than familiar with herself. "Not really. At least not without a lot of this." She raised the glass and took another long sip. "So where in England are you from?"

"The western coast of Cornwall," he said, accepting her change of topic without comment. "Small village called St. Ives. My father was a fisherman."

"I thought that usually ran to families."

"It did—for something like five centuries. Until the waters were fished out and there was no way to make a living. Anyway, it was never my cup of tea. I've always been more interested in the intricacies of fission than in trawling for fish. Although I suppose I did inherit a bit of the sailor's need for adventure."

"An adrenaline junkie."

Again his expression tightened. "Maybe once upon a time. Not so much now."

"And your father?" she asked, again moving purposely away from probing too deeply.

"Still in St. Ives. Although these days he spends more time in the pub than he does in a boat. He likes talking about the old days."

"Sounds like my dad. Only he's retired military. And not one to take to it easily."

"Rather be out there on the front line."

"Exactly. He's not the rocking-chair type. With him action has always been more relevant than reflection." A trait they shared. That's exactly why she'd joined A-Tac. Maybe if she was a little less of an adrenaline junkie, she'd have made different choices. Maybe she'd never have been called on to guard the shipment.

But then she'd never have been in a hotel bar drinking with a real-life James Bond.

Hell, maybe there was a silver lining to this nightmare after all.

"So which state do you come from?" he asked.

"Technically none. My dad was stationed in Germany when I was born. But I've lived in quite a few of them. We moved around a lot."

"Army brat."

"You're the second person to call me that today," she said, sobering as Lieutenant Mather's words echoed in her ears. "Anyway, it's an apt description."

"Sounds like a colorful life." He lifted his glass to his lips, then swallowed, the muscles in his throat contracting with the motion, and she found herself wondering what his skin would feel like.

"I suppose, looking at it with hindsight, it was," she said. "Although at the time I hated it. Every time I'd get myself settled enough to have some sort of a life, my dad would come home from wherever and announce that we were moving again."

"Hometowns aren't all they're cracked up to be. I promise," he said, thankfully unaware of the shifting direction of her thoughts. "What about your mum? How's she handling the nonretirement?"

"She's dead." Tyler tried to keep her tone casual, to keep the memories from surfacing. She'd already been down that road, and once in twelve hours was more than enough.

"I'm sorry." The regret that flashed across his face was real.

"It's nothing really. She's been gone since I was a kid. My dad remarried, a couple of times actually. An active career in the military doesn't really promote happily ever after. Or maybe it was just my father. Anyway, suffice it to say I've had a parade of stepmothers. All of which went to making my life—what did you call it—colorful?"

"Well, I suppose we should drink to it." He lifted his glass. "I mean, after all, if your father had settled down, you might not have chosen the path you did. Which means that I'd be sitting here drinking on my own."

"Or you'd be back at that pub in St. Ives, lifting a pint and celebrating the successful delivery of the detonators."

"The obvious negatives aside, I think I much prefer being here with you."

His flattery was probably meant to disarm her. And the truth was—it did. She hadn't been with a man in longer than she cared to admit. It was just too damn complicated, considering her occupation. And she'd never shared a drink with someone as alluring as Owen Wakefield. Maybe it was the accent. Or the cleft chin. Or the way his hair brushed back from his forehead.

Or maybe it was because he was part of her world—albeit halfway across the ocean. Hell, maybe *that* was the appeal. A chance for a brief encounter with no worries about future entanglements. MI-5 worked within the United Kingdom, for the most part. Chances of her ever crossing paths with him again were slim to none.

"How about another drink?" he asked, hand already half raised to signal the waitress.

"Maybe we should have it upstairs," she suggested, her gaze colliding with his, the suggestion surprising her almost as much as it did him. She finished her bourbon with a gulp, not sure where exactly she was headed, but certain, in the moment, that it was the right direction. "I've got glasses in my room."

THE DISH

Where authors give you the inside scoop!

♥ ♥ ♥ ♥ ♥ ♥ ♥ ♥ ♥ ♥ ♥ ♥ ♥ ♥ ♥

From the desk of Eileen Dryer

Dear Reader,

Blame it on Sean Bean. Well, no, to be fair, we should blame it on Richard Sharpe, whose exploits I followed long before I picked up my first romance. If you've had the privilege to enjoy the Sharpe series, about a soldier who fights his way through the Napoleonic Wars, you'll understand my attraction. Rugged? Check. Heroic? Check. Wounded? Usually.

There's just something about a hero who risks everything in a great endeavor that speaks to me. And when you add the happy bonuses of chiseled features, sharp wit, and convenient title, I'm hooked. (For me, one of the only problems with SEAL heroes—no country estates).

So when I conceived my DRAKE'S RAKES series, I knew that soldiers would definitely be involved: guards, hussars, grenadiers, riflemen. The very words conjure images of romance, danger, bravery, and great posture. They speak of legendary friendships and tragic pasts and another convenient favorite concept of mine—the fact that relationships are just more intense during war.

So, soldiers? I was there. I just had to give them heroines.

That was when it really got fun.

My first book is BARELY A LADY, in which a companion named Olivia Grace recognizes the gravely

injured soldier she stumbles over on the battlefield of
Waterloo. The problem is that this soldier is actually her
ex-husband, Jack Wyndham, Earl of Gracechurch (You
expected a blacksmith?). Worse, Jack, whom Olivia
hasn't seen in four years, is dressed in an enemy uniform.

Jack and Olivia must find out why before Jack's enemies kill them both. Did I mention that Jack also can't
remember that he divorced Olivia? Or that in order to
protect him until they unearth his secrets, she has to
pretend they're still married?

I didn't say it would be easy. But I do say that there
will be soldiers and country estates and lots of danger,
bravery, chiseled features, and romance.

It certainly works for me. I hope it does for you. Stop
by my website and let me know at www.eileendreyer.com.
And then we can address the role of soldiers in the
follow-up book, NEVER A GENTLEMAN, not to mention my other favorite thing—marriage of convenience.

Happy reading!

Eileen Dreyer

♥ ♥ ♥ ♥ ♥ ♥ ♥ ♥ ♥ ♥ ♥ ♥ ♥ ♥ ♥

From the desk of Dee Davis

Dear Reader,

I have always loved run-for-your-life romantic adventures: *King Solomon's Mines, The African Queen, Logan's*

Run, *Romancing the Stone*, and *The Island*,to name a few. So when I began to conceptualize a story for Drake Flynn, it seemed natural that he'd find himself in the middle of the jungles of Colombia. After all, he's an archeologist when not out fighting bad guys, and some of the most amazing antiquities in the world are hidden deep in the rainforests of South America. And since Madeline Reynard was involved with a drug dealer turned arms trader, it was also easy to see her living amidst the rugged beauty of the high Andes.

There's just something primal about man against nature, and when you throw two people together in that kind of situation, it seems pretty certain that sparks will fly. Especially when they start out on opposite sides of a fence. It's interesting, I think, how we all try to categorize people, put them into pre-defined boxes so that we have an easy frame of reference. But in truth, people aren't that easy to classify, and even opposites have things in common.

Both Drake and Madeline have had powerful relationships with their siblings, and it is this common bond that pulls them together and eventually forces Madeline to choose between saving herself or helping Drake. The fact that she chooses him contradicts everything Drake thought he knew about her, and the two of them begin a tumultuous journey that ultimately breaks down their respective barriers and leaves them open to the possibility of love.

So maybe a little adventure is good for the soul—and the heart.

For a little more insight into Madeline and Drake,

check out the following songs I listened to while writing:

"Bring Me to Life"—Evanescence

"Lithium Flower"—Scott Matthew

"Penitent"—Suzanne Vega

And, by all means, if you haven't seen *King Solomon's Mines* (with Stewart Granger and Deborah Kerr), Netflix it! As always, check out www.deedavis.com for more inside info about my writing and my books.

Happy Reading!

Dee Davis

♥ ♥ ♥ ♥ ♥ ♥ ♥ ♥ ♥ ♥ ♥ ♥ ♥ ♥ ♥ ♥ ♥ ♥

From the desk of Amanda Scott

Dear Reader,

Lady Fiona Dunwythie, the heroine of my latest book, TEMPTED BY A WARRIOR, was a real person, the younger daughter of fourteenth-century Lord Dunwythie of Annandale, Scotland. She is also the sister of Lady Mairi Dunwythie, the heroine of SEDUCED BY A ROGUE [Forever, January 2010] and cousin to Bonnie Jenny Easdale, the heroine of the first book in this trilogy, TAMED BY A LAIRD [Forever, July 2009].

Writing a trilogy based on anecdotal "facts" from an unpublished sixteenth-century manuscript about events that took place two hundred years earlier has been fascinating. From the manuscript, we know that Fiona eloped with a man from the enemy Jardine clan, and as I learned from my own research, the Jardine lands bordered Dunwythie's.

We also know that Fiona's sister inherited their father's title and estates, and that Lord Dunwythie died the day Fiona eloped, while he was angrily gathering men to go after her. Since we know little more about her, I decided that Fiona had fallen for her husband Will's handsome face and false charm, and had ignored her father's many warnings of the Jardines' ferocity, lawlessness, and long habit of choosing expediency over loyalty.

To be sure, she soon recognized her error in marrying Will. However, when she meets Sir Richard Seyton, Laird of Kirkhill, she is not interested in romance and is anything *but* eligible to wed. Not only is she married to Will and very pregnant with his child but her father-in-law is dying, her husband (the sole heir to the Jardine estates) is missing, and his father believes that Will must be dead. Worse, Old Jardine believes that Will was murdered and is aware that Fiona was the last person known to have seen him.

Old Jardine has summoned his nephew, Kirkhill, because if Will *is* dead and Fiona's child likewise dies, Kirkhill stands next in line to inherit the Jardine estates. Old Jardine has therefore arranged for him to take them over when Jardine dies and run them until the child comes of age. Jardine also informs Kirkhill that he has named him trustee for Fiona's widow's portion and guardian of her child. Jardine dies soon afterward.

Kirkhill is a decisive man accustomed to being in charge and being obeyed, and Fiona is tired of men always telling her what to do, so she and he frequently disagree. In my humble opinion, any two people thrust into such a situation *would* disagree.

The reactions of a woman who unexpectedly finds herself legally under the control of a man she does not know seems consistently to intrigue writers and readers alike. But in a time when young women in particular were considered incapable of managing their own money, and men with land or money were expected to assign guardians to their underage heirs and trustees for their wives and daughters, it was something that happened with regularity. I suspect, however, that in many if not most cases, the women and children did know the guardians and trustees assigned to them.

In any event, I definitely enjoyed pitting Kirkhill and Fiona against each other. The two characters seemed naturally to emit sparks. I hope you enjoy the results. I love to hear from readers, so don't hesitate to fire off a comment or two if the mood strikes you.

In the meantime, *Suas Alba!*

Sincerely,

Amanda Scott

http://home.att.net/~amandascott
amandascott@worldnet.att.net